FAERIES NEVER LIE

TALES TO REVEL IN

EDITED BY
ZORAIDA CÓRDOVA
AND NATALIE C. PARKER

Feiwel and Friends • New York

For Lara and Suzie, our very own faerie godmothers

A Feiwel and Friends Book
An imprint of Macmillan Publishing Group, LLC
120 Broadway, New York, NY 10271 • fiercereads.com

Our books may be purchased in bulk for promotional, educational, or business use. Please contact your local bookseller or the Macmillan Corporate and Premium Sales Department at (800) 221-7945 ext. 5442 or by email at MacmillanSpecialMarkets@macmillan.com.

Library of Congress Cataloging-in-Publication Data is available.

First edition, 2024
Book design by Julia Bianchi
Feiwel and Friends logo designed by Filomena Tuosto
Printed in the United States of America

ISBN 978-1-250-82384-7
1 3 5 7 9 10 8 6 4 2

TABLE OF CONTENTS

INTRODUCTION

A Note from your Editors:

This is the third installment of the Untold Legends Anthology Series and we have arrived at what might be the most famous of mythological creatures: the faerie.

If we asked you to name one faerie, we feel confident that you could. In fact, we think you could name two, three, maybe even four or five faeries that you've heard stories of over your lifetime. Whether it's Tinker Bell or Queen Titania, Oberon or the Blue Fairy, Cinderella's Fairy Godmother or our beloved Tooth Fairy, their stories flit through our cultural narratives, ubiquitous and (usually) delightful. But faeries also have a dark side. There's Queen Mab, Morgan le Fay, Maleficent, and the macabre creatures from Guillermo del Toro's mind, who tempt and torment in equal measure.

While these are examples most common in Western cultures, faerie lore exists globally—taking the shape of nature spirits or tricksters from other realms. Stepping into the world of faerie is an invitation to dream and imagine. A metaphor for experiences that defy all reason, and leave us feeling outside the norm.

In this collection, you will find stories that peer into the darkness because they carry within them such sparks of light. Each one will take you on a different, fantastical journey toward what it means to be human. The tropes you know are all here: wild hunts and faerie revels, sumptuous treats and dangerous deals, mistaken identities, and most important—the absolute power of words.

Step into our faerie revel, and stay a while.

Cheers,
Zoraida & Natalie

AN ETERNAL FIRE

Chloe Gong

Tang Dynasty, 750 CE

My grandfather says that I was bestowed "Mimi" for my small name because I've been a chattering menace since birth. Most Mimis are named after the character for rice, mǐ mǐ, because they're so adorable that they could just be eaten up. I was named after the sound that incessant birds make when they're perched over the city walls of Chang'an in the morning: *mimimimimimi*—

"Mimi, stand up straight."

I adjust in an instant. I've learned to behave when I'm working the shop, at least. Grandfather wouldn't boot me out, but Mother comes around often to remind him that he really ought to, so I'm on my best behavior. *Sixteen-year-old girls should be sitting nicely at home sewing something beautiful*, Mother says. Instead of greeting customers by flashing all my teeth and trying to sell every product on the shelves in one breath. It's not that I don't like sewing too. I do. I just have a lot of hours in the day and a lot of teeth when I smile. The customers deserve to see my teeth.

Grandfather glances over again. He's in his chair by the entrance, watching the street. Every morning the main thoroughfare goes through the same routine: The sun rises over Chang'an's walls, the birds flock onto the roof tiles to join the early bustle, the carts selling flat cakes and egg bǐng push out to greet the shopkeepers opening their doors. Today, the city is even more raucous than usual, abuzz while it begins setting up for the annual Lantern Festival. Some years it's a longer affair; this year, it's a one-day extravaganza. Although we're not participating as vendors, I've been bouncing on my toes since I woke up, thinking about the candy I'm going to buy.

Maybe I can't stand still, but at least my spine is straight now. Grandfather nods in approval. "Isn't that so much better?"

"I suppose," I allow. "But it seems horribly arbitrary that we've decided spines should be straight. If humans were built to feel more relaxed while slouched, then we should change the custom."

A small bird lands at the shop entrance. It hops right up to Grandfather, sniffing at his feet.

"No need to change humanity before noon, Mimi."

"I didn't ask to change *humanity*, I asked to change *society*."

The bird chirps. Slowly, Grandfather runs his fingers through his long beard, considering my correction. He's done this since I was a baby: I would hand him a shaker filled with uncooked rice insisting that he needed the entertainment too, and he would examine it sagely, giving it two shakes with utmost gravity. I feel like the smartest person in the world with my grandfather. No one else takes me seriously like he does.

"Fair," he concedes. "Are you ready for your task today?"

"Yes!"

The bird flies off in fright over my loud volume. Grandfather gives me a chiding glance; I pay no mind. Grandfather never misses a day in the shop, but he's getting old and he needs people around to help out. Xiao Bao is the actual hired assistant, except Xiao Bao isn't as good as I am at dusting the top shelves or explaining to customers why our tricolored glazed pottery is better than every other store's in Chang'an.

"Take this." Grandfather leans over the side of his chair, reaching for a case on the floor. His chair creaks and groans in protest, the wooden hinges older than he is. Just as he's lifting the case, Grandfather winces, and I hurry forward in a rush. He doesn't make any audible protest, letting his chair complain for him, but I know what's wrong.

"Are you—"

"All is well, Mimi," Grandfather assures before I can finish my question. Nonetheless, he makes a slow exhale, smoothing his palm over his chest.

Grandfather doesn't like to talk about it, but he's having heart problems. Healer Pei is in and out of the house often, giving Grandfather herbs and cleansing his internal system from blockages. While the problems persist, Grandfather can't go anywhere other than home and the shop, and even when he's manning the shop, he needs to be sitting down.

"Here," he says, passing me the case.

I suspect he is distracting me from asking further, but it works. I open the case, finding only red lining inside, and immediately shake it around as though that might summon an item I can't see.

"There's nothing here."

"Yes, Mimi. Mrs. Wu borrowed an heirloom for her son's wedding last month—I'd like you to fetch it back for me." He still sounds a little pained. I know if I ask, though, he'll deny it. "Do not tuck it under your arm willy-nilly. The glass horse is very fragile."

I go still. "The glass horse? *That's* the heirloom on loan?"

Grandfather pats my elbow. "Yes, yes. Off you go now."

The glass horse is usually on display with our ancestral shrines, in a part of the house where I don't often go . . . which is probably why I haven't noticed it hasn't been there lately. I'm hardly to blame. The shrine room is dark and damp, infused with the smell of burning smoke even when the rest of our house is aired out with the nearby market's fresh bāo, even when light spills through the thin walls to turn the air fiery. I used to cry that there were ghosts in the shrine room, and that's why it smelled so funny. Then Grandfather would always say: *Silly child—there are ghosts everywhere. Why would the shrine room be special?*

"Mimi," he prompts now.

I snap to attention. Right, right—I have a task to do. I bellow, "On it!" and then I'm prancing out from the shop, kicking a cloud of dust under my feet.

A frantic energy has been building and building in Chang'an since the New Year. Once night falls and the lanterns come to life, we'll have marked the final celebration: two weeks of festivities from new moon to full moon. Errand boys have been yelling at the top of their lungs since predawn, pulling stalls into their places and hanging lights off the brown buildings just right.

I turn the corner, skirting around a half-built stall. Chang'an is easy to navigate, even for visitors who haven't been here their whole lives. The buildings rarely move around, and the grid system has everything we need in our ward. I *have* been here my whole life, so I know all the wards surrounding us too, from one side of the city wall to the other, across each of the gates that provide entry and exit to the province outside. In our ward, Mrs. Wu is the nearest fish seller, located two streets away.

"My goodness."

I skip up to Mrs. Wu's shop. It's busier here than I've ever seen. Everyone wants a centerpiece for their table before the festival, I suppose, and a steamed fish surrounded by ginseng and scallion is a top choice. I just barely move around two people waiting by the corner, separate from the fish line—*Is the man in the middle of a marriage proposal?* What *is going on here?*—before lodging myself in front of Mrs. Wu.

"Oh, Mimi, it's you."

I hardly need to say anything before Mrs. Wu wipes her hands on her fading apron. Her daughter continues taking orders while she steps back, waving me to follow her into the shop, past the tanks.

"This was such a lovely decoration," she calls over her shoulder. "You thank your grandfather for me, would you?"

"Of course, Mrs. Wu."

"You're being good lately?"

"Yes, Mrs. Wu."

"Ah, excellent."

Mrs. Wu reaches onto the top shelf. There, I see the glass horse, and with the way I'm suddenly clamping my breath in my lungs, you'd think I've encountered a demonic entity in the flesh.

The thing is, I broke that glass horse once upon a time. Or I thought I did. I had been sent into the shrine room to leave some fresh oranges across the ancestral displays and I wasn't watching where I was walking because I was too busy daydreaming about trying on my new red ruqun when it arrived from the tailor and how nice it would look. Then all of a sudden, my elbow was knocking into the horse, the horse was smashing to the ground, a horrifying sound was echoing through the room, and instead of checking on the horse first I had rushed to the entryway, peering out to see if anyone had witnessed my mistake. Scene was clear. I had time to cover my behind.

Yet when I picked up the horse, it was perfectly fine. No crack. No scuff mark on the glass. It didn't make any sense. I had *heard* it shatter.

"Grandfather invites you for tea soon," I say as Mrs. Wu sets the heirloom into the case. The clear glass catches light, refracting back a dozen rainbows against the red lining before I snap the lid closed. My arms feel ten times heavier immediately.

"I'd like that very much," Mrs. Wu replies, leading the way back out. "Do you need any help carrying the case?"

"No! Not at all!" I heft the case higher as I walk, just to prove my strength. While Mrs. Wu returns to the counter, I turn backward, still yapping as I exit the shop. "We have a new set of porcelain teacups with golden decorative edges. Grandfather is very proud of them. You'll love—*oof*."

In my defense, I thought my path was clear. Who stands at the door, anyway? The fish line was curving to the left. It's not my fault if I slam into idlers hovering beyond the line.

"How much for that?"

He's speaking before I've had a chance to get my bearings, and I'm retorting, "I *beg* your pardon," before I've finished turning around.

"The horse inside that case," the boy in front of me says, as though this is a matter of me misunderstanding him. His eyes are ginormous, blinking down innocently. "How much?"

Huh? What a snoop. How does he know what's contained inside the case?

"This is *not* for sale," I say firmly. "Good day."

When I shove back onto the street, the couple I'd almost collided with earlier are still hovering there. I swerve before either of them can break apart to move for me, though they seem to be in the middle of their conversation anyway—"Miss Qiu, please, I cannot bear another day without you—" "Mr. Zhou, you are the single most dramatic person I have met in a hundred lifetimes, I am not *declining*"—but I'm hurrying through the bustle and before long their voices fade into the rest of the morning busyness.

They call Chang'an the million-man city. All of China wants to be here, and it means some of these new merchant trainees like the one in Mrs. Wu's shop have absolutely no tact. His mentor needs to have a stern talk with him about not soliciting the wrong people, *truly*—

The faint mumblings of a crowd reach my ear before I see it. I turn the corner, and I don't immediately register what might have gathered the other shoppers on the street like this, nor why it's our shop that all the onlookers have flocked around.

Then I see Xiao Bao tugging Healer Pei through the crowd and into the shop. A faint ringing sound begins in my ears.

Grandfather.

"Hey! Hey!"

The crowd shifts for me, making way while I push to the front frantically. My arms tighten on the case, afraid that a stray elbow might send the heirloom flying. The second I break through the crowd, though, Xiao Bao rushes before me and blocks my path. I lunge to the side. Xiao Bao, despite his name, is large enough that he easily steps to counter me.

"Mimi, you should watch the shop," he says. "I will help Healer Pei take your grandfather back to your house."

"What happened?" It comes out hesitant. I get on the tips of my toes to peek over his shoulder, and I only catch the brief glimpse of a stretcher being moved out the back door. The ringing in my ear gets louder. "I can help. Right? I'm sure I can help somehow."

"You're not strong enough to help lift him," Xiao Bao says bluntly. "He's going to be fine. Mind the shop."

Xiao Bao pivots and hurries through the entryway, then out the back exit with Grandfather and Healer Pei. I take another second to blink at the scene. A pit gnaws at my stomach, aching inside out.

"Show's over!" I bellow. I'm full of authority I don't actually feel when I stomp my way to the shop front, waving my arms at the gawkers. "Come on. Go away. Unless you want to buy glazed pottery—then you can come right on in."

I set the case down on the counter. A flash of movement plays in my periphery. The hint of a long sleeve, moving closer. In an instant, I lash out, catching someone's wrist before they can lift the lid on the case.

"*Excuse* me. Were you raised in a pigsty?"

"I could ask you the very same," the boy replies gleefully. It's him again, the one who had tried to buy the glass horse in Mrs. Wu's shop. "Fast reflexes."

"No manners," I shoot back.

This time, I take him in properly. He had looked young on first glance—enough that I would have guessed him to be my age—but on closer examination . . . there's something hard to pin about his features. For a moment, I'm sure I'm only tired. That his eyes don't change with the light. That there's no ethereal sheen to his skin. Then his sleeve flutters at the edges, like it's trying to dart off on its own despite there being no breeze blowing. My grip tightens on his wrist, feeling his temperature to be neither hot nor particularly cold, and I know exactly what has found its way into our shop.

"Absolutely not," I declare. Grandfather has entrusted me with an heirloom, and of course it's today that an immortal faerie creature comes after it.

He slips out of my grip anyway and snatches the case.

"No! *Hey!*"

By now the crowd has cleared out, and there aren't many witnesses when I make chase. If this boy looks so human, he must be a xian. He's too powerful to be a mere huli jing or some other animal spirit. The xian, according to our stories, are morally neutral by nature—neither good nor bad, neither serving yin nor yang. They aren't bound by mortal confines either; the xian could take flight and phase into the air if he wanted. Nevertheless, I pounce off the shop entryway, landing on his back and clinging tight. Morally neutral, my ass—this one is a complete kleptomaniac.

"This is unexpected," the xian says. He's amused. There's a lilt to his words, as though we're struggling over a toy in the neighborhood yard and he knows he's stronger.

"Unexpected?" I screech. Grandfather has enough to deal with, like healing his *heart*. I can't let his beloved heirloom be stolen too. "Release it immediately. Before I make you regret it!"

The xian almost seems like he's considering my threat. I feel the vibrations along his back while he hums. Then he says, "I admire your ambition. Let's play a game."

"What?" I shake his shoulders, trying to force a release. The xian only giggles in return. "No! This is my heirloom."

"Be more fun. Don't you know what I am? If you play and win, you will be granted a wish."

I stop shaking his shoulders suddenly. A wish. *Any* wish?

"How do I win?" I ask, and the xian knows he's got my interest, because the humming in his shoulders grows stronger.

"Find me in the city before nightfall. Then you may get your heirloom back and your wish. If you fail, I will keep it."

Logic catches up. This is ridiculous. There's one wish I want to make, but a xian could not possibly fulfill it. I would need a god. I would need the entire pantheon of Chinese immortals, and then some. "No," I say firmly. "How is that fair when you're stealing it to begin wi—"

The xian disappears. One moment he's beneath me, the next there's only a poof of air. I'm free-falling for half a second before my feet find the ground, arms flailing to regain my balance. A single feather remains in the space where the xian was standing. He's gone, along with the case and Grandfather's heirloom.

"Ugh!"

Obviously, I know where to go first as soon as I close up shop, deciding that we're done for the day. If this is the first clue in the xian's silly little game, the feather comes from a common bird, and at this hour, the favorite perching place for birds in the southeast sector of Chang'an is the Large Tame Fox Pagoda. This xian thinks himself so intelligent, and I'll likely find him before noon.

The sun climbs higher in the silver-washed sky. Mornings during the first month of the year are cold, brittle with the crunch of ice underfoot. The temperature isn't as biting in the main streets, especially not in the wards that are populous and filled with activity, but when I venture beyond those limits to where the temples are, I have to rub my arms through my sleeves to ease down the prickles.

The Large Tame Fox Pagoda stands at fifteen tiers, its exterior built with bricks and curving in a circular manner. Inside, the temperature plummets further, but I barely notice when my gaze lands in the corner, upon a nook smothered by incense and deity statuettes. The xian lounges atop a cluster of pillows, and I march over.

"I found you!" I exclaim.

"Did you?" he returns.

I don't even care if he's a creature of the heavens. I start whacking him with my hand, mimicking Mother when she gets her soft slipper out. "I want"—*thud!*—"my heirloom"—*thud!*—"back."

The xian poofs away again. This time, though, he's only traveled a few feet to the side, out of range from my pummeling. Xiao Bao was right: it's not like I'm very strong, so it hardly resembled a true attack.

"You are supposed to find me in the city. This is an arena of the heavens."

"What?"

Most people who live in the southeast sector know that Large Tame Fox Pagoda is named such because it's host to huli jing. The sneaky fox spirits show themselves among mortals more commonly than the xian, perhaps because they're greater in number and less powerful.

By virtue of the pagoda's function, I suppose he's right. This isn't the mortal realm, technically speaking. It's home to huli jing before it's home to humans, so the space exists within and without Chang'an, located inside the city's walls but beyond its spiritual ground.

"Mimi, was it?" the xian asks, leaning against one of the central pillars. "Like the rice?"

"No." I'm practically frothing at the mouth. "Like the buzzing bee that's going to sting you until you swell up and die and I get my heirloom back."

"Aiya, so rude. Anyway, my name is Tian'er."

At once, I forget to gnash my teeth. Blistering annoyance transforms to disbelief. "Surely it is not."

". . . Are you trying to tell me what *my* name is?"

"That sounds like a fake name. Did you just make it up?"

The xian—Tian'er, *allegedly*—almost looks upset. "Not all of us are granted names at birth, okay? Some of us have to choose them ourselves!"

And with another *poof*, he's gone.

The pagoda settles into silence, leaving only the telltale rustle of ash flaking off the incense sticks. I pinch the bridge of my nose, taking a deep breath. Perhaps I'm going about this the wrong way. Perhaps Tian'er can be talked out of this ridiculous game. There's very little in this world I can't chatter a path through.

I look closer to where he was standing. The pagoda floor is constructed with clay tiles, dry and clean geometric patterns pieced together in perfect form. He's left behind a circular mark on one of them. If someone were to set down a teacup after a spill, it would resemble the imprint on the table made by the bottom rim. In fact, I suspect that's exactly what it's supposed to represent, until I practically fold myself over putting my nose close to the mark and I smell the whiff of alcohol.

Ah, I see.

Grandfather says we're lucky to be living in the time we are now because there have been centuries previous filled with strife and unending war, fathers torn away from their homes to fight and mothers worn into wisps by labor. I don't doubt it; I see how tall the walls of Chang'an are. Some mornings, when my chores are finished and I'm too early for the shop, I'll stand by one of the north gates and stare up at the spikes. I'll imagine what the city looked like during another reign. I'll feel the centuries bend and stretch around me, bringing a feeling in my ribs that I can only register as akin to nostalgia, a fondness for events I have never witnessed. I might like to witness them, if asked. Time is so long; life is so short. Pain passes quickly; memories drift around forever.

Then I'll shake myself back to normal and face the city again, the present returning before my eyes. The first building that every new entrant sees from this north gate is Beautiful Eternal Place Under the Sky. It's a very old entertainment house, sitting upon the end of the street at five stories tall and dangling with strings of red lanterns. Swaths of fabric in every color drape around its side, unfurled from the top floor, where, if the day is nice, the ladies inside will wave out to entice customers who might spend an hour or two drinking tea and singing on the stage.

I barge up the steps into Sky, flailing when I walk into a group of elderly men trying to exit. They all give me funny looks while they circle around and make way, perhaps wondering what a girl my age is doing out unsupervised, and I frown at them in return. What are *they* doing out? Don't they have naps to take?

There's another group directly after them—young men in work clothes—carrying bundles of lanterns. Decorations for the festival, no doubt. The usual lanterns out front hang there year-round, and are hardly enough for tonight.

I step aside, keeping close to the green walls while they pass. The entertainment house rumbles with the low din of its noon patrons, new servings of tea making their way out from the kitchens. In the advertisements around the city, they claim Sky has been established since the Han dynasty, standing through every vanquished throne and every fall of the capital. True or not, the venue's decorating choices have a story to sell: transparent gossamer curtains sectioning off the tables at the corners, gold-trimmed satin splayed over the tables, statues of Buddha smack-bang in the center.

"Are you supposed to be in disguise?"

Tian'er yelps on the other side of the gossamer curtain. I've taken him by surprise, mostly because I haven't stepped past the curtain.

I'm looming right against the fabric, a ghoul with blurry features and my hands pressed forward like two claws.

"I have no need for disguise," he retorts, recovering. His new robes flutter with his every movement: a pale blue bodice and shimmering white sleeves, made hazy by the curtain. It's the usual getup for the ladies working up on the fifth floor, the ones whose jobs are to sit with patrons and look pretty and giggle into a handkerchief.

"Really?" I say. "It seemed like you weren't expecting me to find you."

Tian'er frowns. It finally feels like I'm turning the game around and I'll be able to save Grandfather's heirloom. I knew I could talk my way out of anything.

"Untrue. How did you find me so fast, anyway?"

"You got huffy about your name being the equivalent of Sky Baby and then you left behind this place's signature scent." *Jasmine-infused wine*, the menu boards read in extravagant handwriting. "It really was not a mystery." I shove the curtain aside. "So you're dressed like this for fun, are you?"

"Yes." Tian'er sulks. "And I look very nice too. Humans are so stringent with their little rules about what one should wear."

I look down at my own sleeves. Plain in comparison, I suppose, but it's not as though I brought out my best for the occasion. "Don't even get me started—I've been trying to change human society since six in the morning. They ought to let immortal xian wear pretty clothes and let serving girls onto the battlefields."

The xian tilts his head. "Would you?"

I've lost track of what we're talking about. "Would I what?"

"Join the battlefields."

My snort comes instantly. It summons the attention of the patrons one table over, who cut off their conversations and glance at us. Before I can apologize, Tian'er is frowning, asking, "Why is that funny?"

When I was younger, when Grandfather had a lot more energy, he would take me walking around the city, passing rebellion sites and streets that once burned to the ground. Grandfather has always known so much: he has always made sure I realize how exceptional it is to live during this time.

"Because it's a silly question," I say. "I have this one life and it is nowhere near the battlefields. We're living in peace, anyway."

"But I am speaking in the hypothetical," Tian'er insists.

"And even in the hypothetical, if war came tomorrow, I am a human girl. I would be relegated to the household."

"Homemaking is as important as battle. What is there to fight for if there is nothing to return to?"

Do you know what this city has seen? Grandfather says in my mind's eye. Three years ago, when the spring was extraordinarily warm and the sky was ever blue. *There are no soldiers on the horizon. What a beautiful sight.*

I don't know, I think, then and now. Perhaps I never would have seen them, even if they marched in. Perhaps I would have liked to, if only to know what fighting for something feels like.

"Homemaking has plenty of value," I agree plainly, ignoring the pang in my stomach. "But not in this kingdom." Suddenly I shake my head, realizing I'm getting distracted. I stretch out my palms, clutching them open and closed to gesture my impatience for the heirloom. "Can I have the horse now? I found you."

"All right, all right," the xian says. "Let me go fetch it. Do you have your wish? I have limits on changing human society, you understand."

"I won't ask you to change human society."

"Very well. Find me where I've hidden the heirloom, then."

"But I *already* found y—"

Poof.

I hate immortal creatures.

Tian'er finally has me scratching my head.

He didn't leave a clue behind this time, which leads me to believe that the location must be obvious. But he's nowhere to be found in all the places I've checked thus far. It can't possibly be that he's playing dirty and has disappeared with my heirloom. The xian aren't sore losers—they're known to be quite righteous, in fact. Surely he wouldn't propose a game and then go against his terms. How utterly boring.

I hurry down a familiar main street, huffing and puffing in exertion. The afternoon draws the clouds low, daylight hanging heavier and heavier. An uncomfortable pressure nudges between my ears, whispers that I really ought to go home, make sure Grandfather is okay . . . but each time that thought grows too loud, I brush it away. What good would I be doing? I should help by getting this affair into order.

At this point, I've spent hours going in circles, from the temples that worship the xian to the shops selling precious artifacts related to the xian to the West Market, where they trade heavenly tokens and knickknacks that have come from other parts of the kingdom. I've visited artists' quarters and gone knocking around gardens of sculptors who are famous within Chang'an for inviting xian into their revelries so that they can create art of the creatures' immortal forms. Yet nothing. Maybe Tian'er is *really* in disguise this time.

"Mimi?"

For a second, I consider not stopping. I hadn't stuck around to chat with the neighboring shops after I closed up. If Mother dropped by, I didn't want them telling her that I was on a wild chase somewhere around the city.

But then Aunty Su—who occasionally mans the counter at the restaurant across the street—calls out again, so I halt and pivot on my heel, making a polite greeting. She walks closer, a shopping basket swinging on her arm.

I clear my throat. If I don't get the heirloom back, I'm letting Grandfather down. And if I can't even try to see if the xian will keep his word about the wish . . .

"Aunty Su, I unfortunately have somewhere to be . . ."

"Oh, Mimi, it's so terrible, isn't it?" Aunty Su says, as though she didn't hear me. "Have you been home yet? They've been looking for you."

For me? "My parents?"

"Yes, dear girl. They want you around in case your grandfather—"

I don't hear the rest of what Aunty Su says. I've already bolted away.

In truth, I should have hurried home the moment I found the opportunity to close shop. Or, rather, I should have stayed put and never closed shop, because Grandfather would be so upset to know that customers who wanted to acquire a nice plate had been left abandoned right before the Lantern Festival.

In truth, maybe I've been running around all day on purpose. Because if I'm worried about getting Grandfather's heirloom back,

I've less time to be worried about Grandfather. Because I know that I would have every right to be worried when the Arbiter of Fate only needs one more push to pluck him away from me forever.

It's not fair. I haven't had enough time.

I'm deathly quiet when I enter our neighborhood. There's a market operating between the sectors, packing up for the day so that vendors can go home to prepare for the Lantern Festival. Though familiar faces call greetings and offer treats, I keep shaking my head, and soon I'm on a dusty road, passing quaint houses with low, sloping roofs and thin walls soaking in the setting sun. Dust slathers onto the sides of my shoes. When I turn the corner for our house, I expect to see the usual sight: the one tree to the left and the tall wall that rises directly behind the house, cutting between the sectors. I expect the front door open to let in air, perhaps some sacks of rice left out on the steps if we haven't reorganized the pantries yet to make space.

Instead, my eyes swing right to Tian'er, sitting in the tree.

"What!" I bellow. I hurry to the base of the tree. Then I shake the tree trunk vigorously, like he's a piece of dangling fruit I can loosen. "What are you doing *here*? I've been looking for you *forever*."

Tian'er makes a noise that can only be described as *hehehehehe*.

"You found me too quickly earlier," he says. "I thought this was only fair."

I feel a surge of something hot crawling up my throat. It reminds me of syrup I once burned over the fire, pricking with the sickening revulsion of something gone past its fun. "Do you know how much time I've spent running around looking for you?" I ask, and I fling my arm toward the house. "I could have been here. I could have been at my ailing grandfather's side with his precious heirloom."

Tian'er hops off the branch. He comes to the ground not by the pull of natural weight but by slow flotation, his robes swirling around him like wings. His expression remains curious—he takes no offense by my tone.

"Yes, I suppose you could have," he says. "Why weren't you?"

"*Because*"—I lose some of my fervor—"because . . . you have the heirloom."

Out of nowhere, Tian'er summons the case into his hands. He passes it back, and the matter is so simple that I'm left staring for a few seconds before reaching to take it. I lift the lid, and inside, there sits the glass horse, looking exactly the same as I last saw it.

"Humans always seem to say things one way and mean something entirely different," Tian'er says. "You went everywhere except home first. You continued running yourself in circles. At any point you could have returned to your grandfather's side."

"Fine," I snap. The burn in my throat gets hotter. "It's because I wanted the wish, okay? Will you grant it?"

Tian'er straightens his shoulders. "I keep my word. Of course."

I think about how to phrase my wish. I consider the details, the particulars, but I have only one ask, and there's only one way to ask it:

"I wish for my grandfather to be immortal. Turn him into a heavenly being so that I don't have to lose him."

There's a beat of silence. My burning indignation turns cold. *He's going to go back on his promise.* I feel it in the air, in the way he hesitates.

"I'm sorry," Tian'er says, and suddenly he doesn't sound much like a xian. He sounds my age, someone I might have met in the neighborhood and invited to dinner at the house when we have too much fish to finish.

"Fine, fine," I hurry to interrupt. "If it's too big a wish—"

"I have a feeling you don't know."

The glass horse gleams in my arms, picking up the final rays of the late afternoon. "What are you talking about?"

"That relic you're holding . . ." Tian'er grimaces. "Mimi, it's a relic of the immortals. I'm sorry. I can't grant your wish, but not for a lack of trying. Your grandfather is human now, yes, but he isn't who you think he is."

I step into the house.

At first, I'm terrified by the absolute silence. The hallway echoes when I exchange my shoes for slippers, each sound reverberating tenfold. The daily calendar—turned to today's date with a small etching of a full moon—flaps quietly with the breeze that blows in from the open front door.

"Hello, Mimi." My mother, though, looks perfectly calm when I poke my head into the sitting room. She has a piece of cross-stitch in her lap. In fact, she's definitely more concerned about the needle in her hand than my sudden appearance. "We've been looking for you."

"Why is it so quiet?" I ask in return. "Is Grandfather okay?"

"He's resting." Mother squints at me properly, narrowing her eyes to see. When she spots the case in my hands, she gets up. "Is that the horse from the shrine room? I was wondering where that got to. Here, I'll put it back. Go see your grandfather."

She plucks the case away. It leaves my hands feeling strangely empty, though I didn't know what I had been planning—whether I was going to march before Grandfather and show him this evidence to demand what the xian was talking about. While Mother goes to put the glass horse where it belongs, I drift around the house like a ghost. I walk until I am in front of Grandfather's room. Before I've scarcely nudged the door to see whether he's awake, I hear:

"Mimi, come in."

I shuffle through the door. Grandfather's propped up on his pillow, but it doesn't look very comfortable. I hate that he looks sickly, and I hate that it's an expected sight these days. I hate that he's only getting worse.

"I made a new friend today," I start. "Well, first I made an enemy. He tried to steal the heirloom."

Grandfather adjusts himself. Though he says nothing, I know he's listening very carefully.

"You'll be proud that I put up a grand fight, though," I continue. "And by fight, I mean that it was a trickster xian who took it, and he was willing to give it back if I found him in the city before nightfall. I actually found him sometime around noon. He wasn't very good at the game."

At this, Grandfather snorts. "The xian all overestimate themselves."

I make a noise to agree. Then I plonk myself at the foot of his bed, hugging my knees to my chest. "This one also promised a wish."

"Did he?" Grandfather asks gently. "And what did you wish for, Mimi?"

My arms tighten. I feel the fabric of my sleeves press lines into my chin. "I asked for you never to die. For you to be around forever and ever, and the xian said he couldn't do it, because you had already once asked for the opposite."

Your grandfather is human now, yes, but he isn't who you think he is. I will tell you if you wish to know . . .

A part of me still thinks that it could be another trick that Tian'er is playing. Perhaps to test the limits of what I am willing to believe, who the creatures of the heavens are willing to grant wishes for.

But Grandfather does not deny it. He says: "Can I share a secret with you, Mimi?"

I glance over at the door. No one is walking the hallway outside. "I am a terrible secret keeper."

"I am willing to trust you nonetheless." Grandfather moves to sit up. "Many, many moons ago, there was a time where I had been young for a long, long time. And it turned me very cruel. When there is no sense of the years passing, there is only the present, and there is only nothingness. It is like an unlit firepit. Nothing but wooden logs—no ash, no flames."

"An unlit firepit," I echo slowly. "Sturdy, though. You won't ever run out of logs."

"And what good is that?" Grandfather asks. He reaches to pat my elbow. He always used to do that when I was at the dining table trying to cross-stitch, failing again and again, but it didn't matter because he was sitting with me. "It keeps no one warm. Offers no light. But humanity is an eternal fire only because it has sacrifices to burn. It would splutter to a stop without logs to scorch through. Death keeps it bright."

Without realizing, I have started to sniffle. "I don't like this chéngyǔ."

Grandfather smiles. "You don't have to like it. It's better you don't. It is because you are human that you are afraid of losing me and you're willing to chase after a silly xian all day to ask for a wish. And it is only because I am human too that I can feel it means you must love me very much. I wouldn't give that up for any amount of immortality. I am content with my remaining life if it means enjoying what time I have with you, Mimi."

"But," I say, and my lip wobbles, "what am I supposed to do when time runs out?"

"I'll still be here." He taps my head next. "Just because the log burns into ash doesn't mean you forget what fire looks like."

"I will be so cold."

"Thankfully, there are other logs who love you very much that are nestled close by too." Grandfather leans back again. "Don't worry, Mimi. I'm not leaving anytime soon. The netherworld will have to try a bit harder to claim me when I still have stock in the shop to sell."

There's a moment when I can barely swallow past the lump in my throat. Then a knock comes on the door, and Mother pokes her head in. She doesn't notice the face I'm making.

"Mimi, you must let your grandfather rest. Don't you want to attend the festival?"

I do. I love the festival. But when I think about how few days, hours, minutes might remain for Grandfather, I get this empty feeling in my chest, carving and carving in preemptive mourning even though he's right in front of me. Grandfather must read my mind, because he closes his eyes firmly, nestling deeper on his pillow to shoo me away.

"I have much sleep to catch up on," he declares. "Big day in the shop tomorrow. And then next week we're taking a little trip to the countryside, aren't we, Mimi? I'll have to find a gift for your birthday in two months."

I am unmoving for a beat, tucking a breath into that cavernous opening in my chest. Then I nod. I hop to my feet, and I let Mother wave me out into the night.

Tian'er finds me chomping on an ice stick, standing at the corner of two main roads and staring up at a tiger-shaped lantern.

"Seems a little cold for that," he remarks, coming to a stop in front of me. I watched him approach, so it's not as though I'm surprised, but still I blink at his change of robes. He looks like a merchant trainee again, someone who might have strolled in through the city gates with a cart full of wares.

"That's exactly why I bought it." I take another bite, getting a mouthful of frozen sugar. It's a delicacy more common in the summer. "Poor man was standing there with no sales."

The xian makes a noise of understanding. He shifts to hover at my side, craning his neck up at the tiger too. There are smaller lanterns embedded into the greater lantern shape, making the tiger's teeth. Each year's Lantern Festival aims to outdo the last, and as long as we're in an era where there's little to worry about—except, perhaps, whether the lantern animals have enough variety—the city will continue making a grander and grander effort.

"Your grandfather is well?" Tian'er asks, breaking the silence. The quiet is contained only to the corner we occupy. Elsewhere, the night sings with franticness: rendezvous and secret meetings, parents and children.

"He is mortal," I reply. "So as well as a mortal life can be."

I wonder if Tian'er will apologize, or make an awkward speech about the fragility of life. But those are mortal gestures after all. In a move entirely characteristic of xian instead, Tian'er continues gazing at the tiger lantern calmly, and the tension in my shoulders eases away.

"I *am* impressed you found me quickly," Tian'er says. "I know you think it was some easy task but I do this all the time. Challenge a hunt, keep the treat at the end. I almost never give anything back."

"So you brazenly admit that you're a thief."

"Ah, but not to you. To you I'm a friend."

I gasp. "You were *listening*?"

Tian'er scoffs, as if that should be obvious. "How could I not? Your grandfather was one of us. Not that I remember. I didn't come around until recently."

"That's so . . ." The rest of my grumbling gets swallowed inaudibly. Someone's delighted scream echoes down the street, and alongside it, the rumble of firecrackers. It's almost too loud to hear myself think, and I let that be the case—I let the ringing in my ears drown out the incessant voices, swallow up the worries that have no value except weight.

"You know . . .," the xian says now. He hesitates a second. Very un-xian-like. "You have a birthright to the heavens. Your grandfather was a divine immortal—not just a xian. One day or another, if you were ever to claim that lineage, the Arbiter of Fate would likely not deny it."

It takes me a long moment to understand what Tian'er is saying. The firecrackers finish burning, and in the aftermath, smoke drifts through the streets, coloring the lanterns with a gray haze. Festival drums start from another corner.

"I never used that wish, did I?"

"I didn't fulfill it, so no. You still have it."

I wonder how much longer this city will stand. Whether this is the eternal peace that the kingdom promises. Whether we have reached the best of times, the worst of times. I hear Grandfather's voice, pushing past the new wave of firecrackers elsewhere: *Humanity is an eternal fire only because it has sacrifices to burn.*

"All right." I finish the last bite of ice stick. "Maybe one day I'll use it."

Tian'er frowns. He chews through my word choice. "*One day?*"

"How else am I going to rope you into sticking around as my friend?" I start walking forward. "Let's light a lantern. Unless you're too heavenly for such mortal activities."

In a blink, Tian'er has transported himself a few steps ahead, holding a lantern. "No such thing as too heavenly. How's this one?" He shakes it around, its red surface glinting with a telltale golden coating.

"Perfect," I say.

I wonder where he stole it from.

FOOL

Rory Power

Content warnings: fire, implied threat of sexual assault

I never cared before the girls. They'd always been there on stage, of course, feet pointed and arms held just so, but nobody went to the ballet to see them. People went for the men, to see them leap and turn and try their best to fly. The most incredible music, painted cheeks, flowers in bloom—none of it tempted me until a girl stepped out from the corps de ballet and stood on her toes, the stitching in her shoes going red with blood. The men *tried* to fly; she did.

Marie was her name, and I saw her for a second time when Mab brought her to dance for us. Stars cast in her eyes, cotton stuffed in her ears so she couldn't hear our violins. *Why not*, I wondered, watching her curtsy when she was done. *Why not let her hear the music?* Let it bind her here forever. They don't deserve her in Paris.

Because she has so much to learn, Mab told me later. So much to teach the others, too. When she's done with all that, we will call her back. Decades for her; the blink of an eye for us, time whiled away in idleness, coaxed into a wondrous knot. We wouldn't have to wait long, Mab said, and I could even be the one to go and fetch her.

I dreamed of that for I don't know how long.

I could not cross on my own yet, so when the day came, I was summoned to court. It is a riotous place. The Court of Joy, to some. The Court of Fools, to others. Bells hang from the trees, jewel lanterns and streamers cut from the fine clothes of every visitor. From her throne, Mab watched her nobles waltz and scurry, a jester queen in a harlequin crown.

I found her waiting for me when I arrived. As soon as I stepped onto the floor of the court, marble patterned in black and white diamonds beneath my feet, she lifted her hand and called out.

"Glass," she said. "You're late."

Laughter came from all around me, heady as a cup of wine to drown in. Time was Mab's best joke of all.

I was not often at court, mine too quiet a joy to be at home there, so I hardly recognized anyone as I passed through the crowd toward the throne. I could tell, though, that they knew me: Mab's young favorite, pulled out of some hidden little nowhere and given the name of her most cherished pleasure—something beautiful and easy to break. How could I deserve it? Who could be sure that I'd been born under Joy?

Not even Mab, but she didn't seem to mind. "What is more joyful," she'd said when I asked, "than deciding something will be as I want it to?"

I knelt in front of her throne, that question ringing again in my head. I'd had no answer for it then, but I thought now that watching Marie dance had come close.

"Oh, stand up," Mab said. "Let me look at you."

And me at her. She dressed differently every day, wearing whatever face suited her—or sometimes no face at all—and for this occasion she'd chosen Marie's. The eyes, though, were still hers, alight with the blue-flower madness that shines so brightly in the Court of Fools.

"I'm ready," I told her.

"You are, aren't you? You've put your wings away."

Maybe that was why the courtiers had stared at me so sharply. Wings were newly back in fashion after an age of being cast aside. Mab's were mounted on her throne, still beating now and then as though she'd never cut them from her back.

"They wouldn't do me any good there," I said, a defense more for the crowd than for her. Most of them hadn't left Faerie before. Only a very few of them ever would. Other courts made their bargains and set their traps, opened doors in the attic and lit fires in the mist. Mab kept Joy her own.

She waved a hand and her musicians played louder. The court returned to its dancing, unable to resist. *I won't let Marie join them*, I thought. I would find her someplace to dance alone.

"Come," Mab said, standing from her throne. "I want this over with."

She'd have preferred to send someone else—she hated for me to leave court—but I had asked very nicely, and she owed me after so many refusals. "At least," she'd said, "I will have the joy of seeing you come home."

I followed her away from the revelry into the forest. The trees leaned eagerly over us, even the tall birches bending low to see the scattered pearls left behind where the hem of Mab's gown brushed along the velvet-moss path. We were going, I knew, to her cottage, a stone house in a clearing that hid itself from everyone but her.

"The door will take you to the theater," she said over her shoulder as we approached the bank of a clear, narrow brook. "It will only allow you and your magic through, but you must still promise to close it behind you on your return. You'll let the cold in if you leave it open."

"I understand," I said. "And we'll come right to court so you can present her." I'd endured the same thing when I was very young. Days and days of other faeries fawning over Mab's latest prize, hoping their flattery would win them her favor. The fuss would keep Marie too busy to dance, at first, but that was all right—she'd be useless anyway until Mab's trick-magic settled into her blood and muscle.

The stone house shimmered into view, this time perched near the edge of a small waterfall where the brook turned downhill. We sidled in, and as I crossed the threshold, my dress fell away to reveal another underneath. I recognized its kind—an outfit like the ones the ballet girls wore to dance in. White bodice pulled in tight. White skirt in layers of tulle, reaching just past my knees. And the shoes, the shoes, ribbons around my ankles, leather and stitching along the soles as thick and strong as bones.

"What is it they call them?" Mab asked, looking me over.

"Ballerinas." I had practiced saying it in the silence of my own room, but still it fit oddly in my mouth. I had heard it only once before, that night at the theater when Mab took me across for the first time. That was how they'd introduced Marie when it came time for the audience to clap for her. *Ballerina*, and other things too, but I hadn't learned, then, Mab's trick with language, so I hadn't understood.

"That's right," Mab said. "I'd forgotten. But you didn't, did you?"

She turned away from me, her disdain lingering as she moved toward the uneven counter that ran along the opposite wall. I shut my eyes for a moment, summoned the stillness of a well beneath the earth. My admiration for Marie could dig too deeply into Mab's heart, or into her pride, which was often the same thing. I needed to be more careful with it.

I averted my eyes as she began to work. She would have let me see the ingredients, I think—they would have been good for nothing in my own hands, so what risk was there—but I preferred to watch the door take shape without knowing what had gone into it. So much easier to cross when I couldn't see the writhe of a freshly cut rat's tail in my mind's eye.

"There," Mab said some minutes later. I looked back at the stone house's doorway just in time to see it fill with lilac smoke. "Well? What are you waiting for?"

Marie would be there on the other side. She would know what it meant when she saw me in the corps de ballet watching her rehearse, and she'd take my hand as I held it out to her. The rest of the company would whisper about it across Paris, how she wandered into the red velvet curtains and disappeared forever. A faerie tale all my own.

I stepped into the smoke; I stepped through, across the threshold of emptiness, and into the wings at the Salle Le Peletier.

"Watch yourself," a girl in a rehearsal dress like mine said, Mab's magic spinning her French into a song I knew the words to. "You're standing on my toes."

"I'm sorry," I said. Around us, the rest of the corps were preening, stretching, pinning up loose pieces of their hair. I could not see past the girls at the front, but I could hear the cries of the ballet master, the crack of his hands as he clapped in time with imagined music. Someone was dancing. Marie—it had to be.

"Excuse me," I said to the girl ahead of me, and slipped past her. No step lighter than a faerie's, no pinch of space I could not fit into, and soon enough I had found the front of the corps, the white froth of our skirts lining the edge of the wings like a wave breaking along the shore.

Only it wasn't Marie dancing. It was someone else, her hair darker, her body taller. She turned more quickly and when she stood en pointe—that was what they called it now—she held herself as though it did not hurt her at all.

"Emma!" the ballet master shouted. "You are not counting!"

Emma stopped dancing. She bent to adjust the ribbons wrapped high around her calves, and I saw her face for the first time. She was young, about as young compared with her companions as I was with the other fools at court.

Behind me, one of the corps girls whispered something cruel, and though I heard only part of it, it told me enough. I had arrived during Emma's first rehearsal as the ballet's new soloist, a role she had gotten only because Marie Taglioni had seen her dance.

Marie, who was far too old now to perform.

I had missed her. Time tied in that wondrous knot, unraveling twenty years too late. Was it an accident? No, more likely it was a lesson from Mab, one I'd earned by loving something that was not her.

But I didn't care, because Emma had begun again, and she was better than Marie, so much better that none of Mab's magic would ever astound me again. I could not bring her back to court in Marie's place; she was too beautiful. Too obviously made for this very stage, as impossible to remove as the polished floorboards, the golden chandeliers overhead.

I'd simply have to go home with nothing. At least Mab likely wouldn't mind.

I would, though. I'd mind so much I'd never think of anything else.

I was meant to close the door behind me when I came back to Faerie. But I couldn't bring myself to do it. And despite what came to pass, I cannot make myself wish that I had.

The first time I went back, I told myself I would say nothing. It was betrayal enough to be there without Mab's permission—how much worse it would be if I did anything but watch, and dream.

The company had not begun yet when I came through from Faerie, so I snuck past the boy sweeping the stage and found my way up to one of the boxes. It was home to four chairs, each one as luxurious and broad as Mab's own throne. I sat in the one nearest to the stage, even propped my feet up on the railing for a moment. Was this how she felt when she looked out over the court? Did she love me the way I already loved Emma? Somehow, I could not imagine she did; her smile at my empty-handed return to her court had been so triumphant, so sour.

Below me in the theater, a door opened. I began to hear voices. I did not hide; instead I waited until I caught sight of the girl in the corps who had whispered about Emma.

"Hello," I said into the palm of my hand. The word fluttered. I blew it toward her as though it were a kiss, watched it slither into the shell of her ear. She looked in my direction and her eyes went wide, glittering in the glow off the gas lamps. Carefully, I plucked the shine out of them.

She began to scream, but I paid her no mind. With that shine wrapped around my shoulders, anybody looking up into my box would see only the ripple of firelight.

The girl had gone quiet by the time Emma arrived. She was accompanied by two men, one of whom I recognized, from my previous visit, as the ballet master. The other I did not know, but his hand was on Emma's shoulder and he was speaking with the ballet master with the familiarity of an old friend.

A husband? A father? Whoever he was, I did not like the way Emma's expression seemed to relax only once he had let her go.

He took a seat in the first row while the ballet master helped Emma onto the stage. I leaned forward, eager for her to begin. There had not been a pianist at the last rehearsal I'd been to, but there was this time, sitting ready at an upright in the orchestra pit. It would be almost like a real performance, but even better because I did not have to wonder who else might be watching her with the same admiration I was. I could pretend she was dancing just for me.

"Do we have the costume ready?" the ballet master called from the stage's edge.

"They're bringing it," answered one of the girls waiting behind the curtains. "Just a minute."

"A minute," the ballet master scoffed. "We'll be here an hour yet." He turned away, going to join his companion. I could not hear their conversation, and I would have liked to—I wanted a name to stitch into the hem of Emma's discomfort—but there was a flurry of movement onstage that drew my attention. Attendants moving the dozen or so gas lamps into new positions and lighting them. Girls darting from one side to the other, their shoes dangling from long white ribbons knotted over their shoulders. Two men, dancers both, had approached Emma and were standing over her as she stretched. I watched them help her to her feet as the last of the gas lamps flickered to life, the stage awash in orange and gold.

"Some room, please," came a voice from somewhere behind the curtain. The men backed away from Emma, but she did not move. She stood there alone at the lip of the stage, staring out into the darkness, and I thought, for a moment, that she looked frightened.

Two women emerged from backstage, something white and strangely shaped carried between them—the costume, I realized—and a gasp went up in the company. "How beautiful," I heard a dancer exclaim. Even the ballet master smiled. Emma, though, never so much as looked behind her. I tried to follow her gaze, to see what might have captured her attention, but there was nothing in the audience save empty seats.

I turned back to the costume. It seemed too delicate to be just a dress, and the care with which the women were carrying it was far too deliberate for simple cotton and thread. I rose from my chair in the box and craned my neck, searching for a better angle, but it was only as the garment was slipped onto Emma's body, looped around her shoulders, that I understood.

Wings—it was a pair of white gauze wings.

The spread of them rose above the crown of her head, swept down to the backs of her knees, and they moved almost on their own, almost as Mab's wings did on her throne. A slight lifting, beating as Emma stood there hewn from stone. Had some other faerie snuck through the door before me? Or was there one hiding in the sewing rooms beneath the theater, unfolding a little bit of magic when no one was looking?

No, of course not. It was built from fabric; I saw that now. The wings' supports were built into a harness for Emma to wear, and in the shifting flutter of the gas lamps I could see the gleam of the metal wire that gave the cloth its shape. The effect was as perfect as anything I'd ever seen outside of Faerie.

"We don't have time for a fitting," the ballet master called as the seamstresses continued adjusting the harness.

"Either you wait now," one answered, not looking up from her work, "or you stop your rehearsal in twenty minutes when it falls off her."

"I'm sorry, Louis," Emma said to the ballet master. "Do you know if Marie is coming?"

For so long that name had meant everything to me. Marie, Marie, Marie. Now I hoped against hope that Louis would say no. If Marie arrived, Emma would be dancing for her, not for me, and I didn't think I could bear that.

"Not today," Louis said. "But Ferdinand is staying to watch."

Emma nodded and smiled. "How kind of you, sir."

The man in the front row waved in answer. So that was his name. Ferdinand. He looked older than Emma by many years and he was dressed in clothes that everyone in Paris would have considered fine. Nobility, probably, although I was often left confused by that on this side of the door—Mab's nobility was a different sort.

But faerie or not, I could recognize in Emma a certain unease stirred by the weight of Ferdinand's gaze. It was one I knew myself, one that prickled the back of my neck whenever I stood in front of Mab's throne and left myself open for judgment.

It was then that the seamstresses stepped back, their work finished. Emma began to move, slowly, slowly, limb by limb. One arm extending, the other curving high above her head. The harness moved with her, the wings flexing and quavering. It seemed as though the very theater itself held its breath and waited to see if they would break.

They didn't. Not as the music started and Emma rose en pointe. Not as she turned, leapt, flew. She had left her hair loose, with only the front pinned back, and it moved with her, swinging, shining, hiding the harness and the laces—hiding everything that kept her bound to earth. *Changeling girl*, I thought, though I knew it wasn't true. Still, she was more faerie queen than Mab herself.

If leaving the door open was my first transgression, this was my second: following Emma home. I had not meant to, but when the rehearsal finished and she stripped the wings from her body, it came as close to breaking my heart as anything ever had. They should have been hers to keep. I had to tell her that. Just a moment alone with her and then I would go home, but she had ridden back to the apartments she shared with the other girls in the corps, all of them piled into the same carriage, so here I was perched on her windowsill waiting for her to finish washing up.

It would have been easy to guess which room was hers even without the labels fixed to every door. This one was neat and clean, with no letters from home tacked to the wall and no clothes in the little wardrobe other than rehearsal dresses and a single nightgown. A chair stood apart from the wall in the center of the floor, a pair of ballet slippers on its seat—a makeshift barre, I assumed, so Emma could practice when she was meant to be asleep.

At last the door opened and I straightened, ready to shake the magic off me and appear before her, but it was Louis, instead, who stepped through. I recoiled as he approached the window. Had I chosen the wrong room? Followed the wrong carriage? No, there in the doorway—that was Emma's silhouette.

"Nobody is watching," Louis said quietly. "It's all right." I didn't think it was, not when the look on his face was all sorrow and weariness. He wasn't meant to be here. Neither was Ferdinand, who answered, "Thank you, Louis," and ushered Emma inside.

The two men passed each other, changing places as smoothly as if it had been choreographed. A moment later the door was closed, Louis on the other side. His shadow lingered by the threshold, and I understood. He was standing guard so that nobody would disturb Ferdinand, who had guided Emma to sit on the edge of her bed.

"Your mother sends her best," he said.

Emma was wrapped in shadow, but the tremble in her voice told me enough. "Is she well?"

"Of course. You know I look after her just as I do you."

"Yes. Yes, I'm very grateful for everything."

Ferdinand took off his jacket and hung it on the chair, covering Emma's ballet slippers, before stepping closer to her. "Imagine where you would be," he said, "if I hadn't introduced you to Marie. To Louis."

"I imagine that all the time." Emma leaned back. A thread of moonlight found her eyes, caught on the tears she had not yet shed. Ferdinand reached for her.

What I wanted was to pull all the sharpest thoughts from his head—every snatch of ill will, every speck of pride—and beat them to a point, to a blade so well honed that he wouldn't even feel it as it slit his throat. But there was no time. All I could do was raise my fist, swing it the way humans did.

The window shattered. My knuckles began to bleed, and the trick-magic keeping me hidden burned up to ashes.

"Who's there?" Ferdinand said, lurching away from Emma. "Hello?"

I paid him no mind. Men like him lived easy lives. They were not cut from half-light and secrets; he would never see anything of Faerie, not even if Mab arrived in front of him, wings and all. Emma, though—I could feel the instant she noticed me like the prick of a needle. I held one finger to my lips and hoped she would understand.

"I'll check," she said, before rising and approaching the window. Behind her, Ferdinand was already putting his jacket back on. I felt satisfaction's flush. Whether Emma let me stay or not, I had at least done something useful.

A knock at the door, and then, very softly, from Louis: "Is everything all right?"

Most of the window's fragments had fallen out, down the side of the building, but there were still enough scattered across the floor that I held my breath as Emma neared, her feet bare. Glass on the floor ready to cut, to bleed. Had Mab known that when she'd named me? That it could be dangerous? I had never considered it before that moment.

"I don't see anyone," Emma said. She was looking right at me, her body so close I could see the last smudges of kohl she hadn't managed to scrub from her eyelids. "But I think you'd better go, just in case."

Ferdinand threw the door open and nearly collided with Louis, whose fist was raised to knock again. "Let's be off," he told the other man. "And have someone come and check these windows. Emma?"

She turned to face him. I could not see Ferdinand or Louis, could see nothing but the fall of her nightgown and the stitchwork where the seams had been reinforced, as though Emma had practiced the darning for her pointe shoes on every piece of fabric she owned.

"Yes?" she said.

"I'm sorry to leave you. We'll arrange another time."

"Of course."

"Dance well tomorrow night, my dear. I'll be watching."

There were footsteps, heavy enough that I thought they must be his and not the ballet master's. After they had receded, I expected Emma to go shut the door, but she remained where she was, her shoulders still proud and tense.

"I . . ." Louis cleared his throat. "You needn't attend our rehearsal in the morning."

"But the premiere—"

"Rest is the best preparation."

"Yes. All right."

Was this punishment, or an apology? Perhaps both.

"Good night," Louis said, and at last, I heard him depart. A quiet settled over us, filling the room as though it were smoke. I drew a deep breath, watched the lift of Emma's ribs as she did the same.

"Thank you," she said. "If you're there."

Ah—she had seen me, yes, but she did not know how far to trust herself. I slipped out from behind her, the chill through the broken window brushing across her back without me there to shield her.

"I am," I said. Emma's head turned, and as I passed her, only for a moment, a strand of her hair caught on my lips. She smelled of greasepaint and mint; I swore I tasted dandelion petals.

There is a way in which some things are beautiful, a way that hardly fits inside the word itself. It's what I got my name from—beauty on the edge of disaster, reckless and begging, a ship about to wreck. I saw it rarely in Faerie, where ruin can be flipped like an hourglass and left to run backward.

It was in every bit of Emma. Raging in her eyes, quivering under her skin, all of it bright enough to steal the breath from me.

"He did not see you," she said. "But you're real."

It was not a question; still, I bent and picked up a shard of glass from the floor. Carefully, I pricked my fingertip on its sharpest edge, hard enough to bring blood welling to the surface.

"Yes," I said. "I'm real."

"What are you, then?"

Oh, I thought, *I could ask you the same thing.*

Instead, I told her everything. My name, where I'd come from. How I'd seen Marie dance and come back to collect her, only to arrive too late for her and just in time for someone far better.

"And that's what you want me for?" she asked when I had finished. "To go back with you?"

I was pleased that she'd wasted no time with the unnecessary—with things like doubt and proof. She had seen what she needed to, or perhaps she hadn't and she simply trusted me already.

"Yes," I said. "I think you would like it, really. There is always so much music."

"I hardly need more music," she answered. She was, I noticed, gazing at the broken window, at the gray smear of Paris beyond. "What about quiet? What is there of that?"

"Certainly there is quiet," I said, all too aware of the edge I was treading. "There is whatever joy may be found in." Not a lie, as long as I did not promise she would be the one to find it. Quiet lived in the brambles around my house, in the stillness between spring breezes. If Emma came to court, it was not likely she would be free to revel in it as I was. But that wouldn't matter. She wouldn't miss it once she started to dance.

"Please come," I went on. "Wouldn't it be lovely? You could have a pair of wings of your own. Real ones this time."

That would have swayed me, but I could not tell if Emma cared. She said nothing for a moment, one that seemed to go on and on as though it were one of Mab's jokes, and then sighed.

"Ferdinand. Louis. They would never let me stay."

My heart leapt at the sound of her sorrow. It meant, surely, that she wanted to come with me. "You do not need them to," I reassured her. "There is a door in the theater, one only we two can cross through. They'll never be able to follow."

But she shook her head. "Even the crossing is impossible. I'm never alone at the theater. Someone will see."

"Then," I said, smiling, "we will have to make sure it is not you they are watching."

It is sometimes this way in Faerie—a name giving its own gifts to its bearer. Glass, Mab called me, and glass-magic followed. Sharp edges, shine, and, most important of all, reflection, the talent that permitted me to walk into the Salle Le Peletier the following night wearing Emma's face over my own.

We agreed that she would arrive at the theater just before the premiere began and buy a seat at the very back. Once the overture had started, when nobody was paying any attention to anything but the music, she would sneak backstage and through the door to Faerie. I would follow as soon as I could manage.

"Sit still," the woman curling my hair scolded me.

"I'm sorry," I said. "I'm only staying warm."

I, as Emma, had been escorted to the dressing room as soon as I'd arrived, where my body had been moved this way and that, my face painted and my clothes changed. Only my shoes had been left alone. They were hanging from the back of the dressing room door, waiting for me. Emma had shown me just how she liked to tie the ribbons.

For my part, I had told her how to find the right fold in the theater's heavy red curtains—how to slip into the dark to the other side, to Faerie. And to be certain that the door would let her through, I had turned again to my particular talent. I had arrived at the Salle Le Peletier looking like Emma; soon, Emma would arrive here looking like me.

There was, I supposed, still a chance that the door might recognize her for what she was and lock her out. But even if the glamour failed to fool Mab's magic, it would at least fool Ferdinand and Louis, along with anybody else looking for a familiar face in the shadows offstage.

"There," my hairdresser said, laying the last curl just so over my shoulder. It was too hot, still, and I flinched. "Don't touch it until it sets. With a bit of luck it'll last through intermission."

I did not say, of course, that it would last as long as I wanted it to. My hair would stay set in its curls; my stage makeup would not run or crease; best of all, I would dance almost as well as Emma herself, guided by the magic we had, together, stitched into her pointe shoes.

The hairdresser left me, then, and in the moments before two more assistants took her place to help me climb into my costume, I let myself consider what waited for me back at court. I had done my best not to think of it as I'd waited through the night at the foot of Emma's bed, and when she'd woken there had been so much to do. So many preparations to make. Now I had to reckon with the knowledge that once Mab found out what had happened, she would feel quite betrayed. Perhaps she did already, and I would step through the door only to find a band of courtiers waiting for me, ready to rip the joy from my heart.

I could not regret it. Emma's eyes were wide and dark as they stared back at me in the mirror. I lifted one hand, touched my own cheek, my own lips with its graceful fingers. Which did I prefer? Watching her skin flush and fade, or wearing it myself?

No, I thought, running Emma's palms over the spread of Emma's ribs. I shouldn't have to choose, and I wouldn't. She was already there, through the door waiting for me. Emma in Faerie, dancing in the green clutch of my little house, the doors bolted and the windows shuttered. Emma in Faerie, so prettily and deeply asleep in my bed while I reveled at court, dressed in her body and my wings.

If nothing else, I was sure Mab would understand that.

Emma's role was the most important of the ballet—the sylph, the trickster bride for which the ballet was named—but it wasn't until the first act was well underway that a girl from the corps came to escort me to my place. I had been listening to the muffled swell of the orchestra, trying to match it up with the choreography I had seen during company rehearsal. Still, none of that prepared me for the spectacle of it. The glitter and sigh of the corps as it turned, spun, knit and unknit itself, a living creature as strange and sly as anything in Faerie.

Behind stood slats of painted scenery: an idyllic wooden cabin, gently wizened trees all around. The angles were pulled long by my view from side-stage, details blurred by the shadows the corps cast as they whirled past the gas lamps. I felt hands graze across my back, begin to settle the wings and their harness over my shoulders, but I could not look away. I was sure that as soon as I did, Mab would appear, summoned by the magic of the ballet, and drag me home before I had a chance to feel it for myself.

"Tighter," whispered the woman adjusting the laces on the harness. "Emma? How is that?"

I did not answer. To speak, to think of anything but the music and the dance, would break something precious. And what did I care for any of it? The harness, the laces, the sheer ordinariness of it all was beneath me. I was a faerie. I was born for wings.

The corps finished their part; they bowed as the audience applauded. I heard all of it as if through a fog. Instead, Emma's voice, my own voice, slipped quietly into my ear.

Extend through your fingertips. Come farther downstage on your entrance than you have been in rehearsal. Remember, you cannot leave when you have finished. They will want to clap for you.

I looked down at Emma's pointe shoes, at the spot near the toe where her stitches doubled back. *I know*, I told them. *I'm ready.*

Then put on a smile, Emma's voice whispered, *and ignore how it hurts.*

The orchestra began to play once more. Across the stage, a man made his entrance, gesturing to the cabin behind him, and for a moment his face was not his own but Ferdinand's. Had I imagined it that way, or had Emma, whose eyes I was looking through? *Never mind*, I thought. The man had taken his place on the cabin's prop steps and the orchestra's tenor had changed. It was my music they were playing now, my spirit they were conjuring. With a deep breath, I rose en pointe, gave myself over, and drifted into the light.

How easy it was. To dance, to capture, to glow. The ribbons around my ankles cut into my skin, through flesh and through bone. I bled down the back of my own throat, clawed the starlight from the sky. So many people, all looking at me, and I'd thought it would be as it was at court, the press of their stares like stones in my pockets. But this? To be adored, admired—the joy of it was more than I could hold. I danced and the gas lamps flared high; I danced and fresh flowers spilled down from the painted scenery, their scent dizzying and purple-sweet. Even my crafted wings glimmered as if they were more than fabric, as if they were the pair I'd left in Faerie.

Perfect, I thought, and it sang through my body, rolled over me like summer heat. Perfect, everything perfect, except the rub of the harness along my shoulders—

Except the man onstage with me, except the horror breaking over him as he stood up—

He wasn't meant to move yet. The Emma I lived in knew that but I did too. I had seen her rehearse this, could feel the rest of the solo just ahead of me. I leaned into my arabesque, hoping he would remember himself. Let everything be perfect again, perfect despite the hang of the harness, the tug of my wings. The costumer had asked me if I wanted it tighter, and maybe I should've said yes, but—

"Emma!"

No, no, not yet. Not her. I have so much more to go.

"Emma, your wings!"

I felt it, then, for what it was. Not a sweeping fever, exultation and wide sky, but pain. It was crawling up my neck, along my arms. Wrapping its own around my waist and holding me as a mother holds a child. I opened my mouth to cry out; ash landed on my tongue, bitter and crisp.

"Something's burning," I gasped, steps faltering at last. "Something's—"

"Bring water!" a voice yelled from backstage. "Bring blankets!" I turned my head—was that Emma? Had she come back through to see me dance?—and there, in the corner of my eye: fire. Climbing along my wings like ivy, snapping at my hair with the jaws of a wolf.

The lamps. I must have passed too close. I must have forgotten that the wings were fabric and not real, not—

But my dress caught, the skin beneath beginning to bubble, to melt, and there was nothing more. All I could see was the fire. All I could think of was the sweet, green shade at Mab's stone house.

Get home, said something behind my ribs, another voice added to the screams rising around me. *Get home to Faerie and she will save you.*

I would have given anything, then, to fly. Instead I lurched toward the curtain where Emma would have left the door open. Agony burst behind my eyes with every step, so fierce it had stopped hurting and become something else, something beyond, something wrenching to the very core of me. Was I breathing? I do not think I was. It may be that I took my last right there on that stage, died even as I collapsed to my knees and started to crawl.

It must have looked as though I wanted to wrap the curtain around my body, use it to smother the flames. Surely that was what the corps girls waiting there should have done if they'd had any intention of helping me survive. They did not—what is a dead ballerina but an open position as a principal?—or perhaps they did—there is no competition that burns as brightly as I did that day—but whatever the truth, it made no difference.

My fingertips grazed the curtain's edge. I strained forward, into the gap I could feel there, the sliver of darkness, the threshold between one world and the next. The door was still open. Mab would be waiting with Emma and together they would wash me down, stitch me up, and carve me new.

"Fools," I said, though I could not speak, "fools and—"

I vanished from the stagelight of the Salle Le Peletier. Blinked into the threshold, into the absence of anything, even pain. I knew if I looked over my shoulder I would see a wisp of Paris just as I could see, ahead of me, the court like a firefly, darting and quick.

Almost, I thought, and reached to catch it in my hands. But before I could, it had winked out, leaving me in nothingness, utterly alone.

The door to Faerie had closed, and I was on the wrong side.

I can't tell how long it's been.

The window back to Paris lasted some time, and though I never went back through—it would have been only seconds there before my injuries took too deep a hold—I certainly watched. And I mourned when it closed, wept as it crumbled to ash before disappearing in a weave of smoke and spark. The Salle Le Peletier, destroyed. Would you believe that it burned?

Since then I have been alone. At first I wondered why Mab had not simply opened her side of the door again and come looking for me. I even called for her. For Emma, too, until I remembered, and despair broke over me. When I took Emma's face, I gave her mine. It's very likely she wears it still. Nobody in Faerie will care if she seems to have forgotten things she's meant to have known all her life, or if she cannot dream up even the simplest magic. *What a good joke she's playing*, the courtiers must all say to each other. Glass, finally earning her place in Mab's court.

They do not know I've built a court of my own. One queen, one subject. A perfect fool in the dark.

Well. Dark. I suppose that is not strictly true. There is nothing to see, but I have plenty of light to see it by. My skin, my eyes, my wings—the smell of flowers and oil and a struck match as I dance. I have yet to stop burning.

I don't think I ever will.

THE SENESCENCE

Dhonielle Clayton

from the world of *The House of Black Sapphires*

The perfect faerie kiss tasted like honey. Thick and dulcet.

Ambrosia knew her lips would soften and her mouth would secrete subtle traces of her nectar. She knew the human's blood would sweeten, their pupils blooming and their body turning as weightless as a baccara rose petal. She knew whomever she'd kiss would think of the first sweet they'd ever loved and become consumed with the desire to devour.

The best part of all . . . she knew they'd be ready to bargain their life away for another taste of her. No mortal could ever resist one of the summer-born, the mighty people of the sun.

Ambrosia tried not to anxiously fuss with her ears and mess up the charms her sisters had affixed to their pointy slopes, but her entire body hummed with anticipation as she stood before the royal streetcar and prepared to say goodbye to her family. She couldn't believe she was headed out of the faerie Court Ward of New Orleans and into the mortal one for the very first time. She was ready for her Senescence, her blooming. Her thoughts swirled with possibilities as she readied herself to embark on their divine rite of passage. Every one of her ten siblings had gone off on their own to test their beloved gifts by sending back human conquests to keep their kingdom robust. They'd returned full-fledged members of society.

But she knew as the last child of the king and queen of the Summer Court that all eyes were on her.

The expectation: She'd send back the best of the best, the most worthy.

Ambrosia stood at the edge of the Summer Square. Her parents' devoted courtiers watched her every move. She looked around to avoid their curious gaze and took in her last view of the Court: their white palace and its three steeples boasting the black velvety petals of the baccara roses; the courtier mansions flanking the plaza and park; the misbelief trees stretching high and perfuming the air with their sweet nectar; and a living gold statue of her father on a horse. She wouldn't lay eyes on this Ward again for a year.

A prickle of fear raced across Ambrosia's skin. She'd been told so many things about what to expect on her first season away from home and out in one of the five versions of New Orleans . . . But she still felt like she didn't *really* know what to expect in the Marrow, the Mortal Ward. What would it look like? How different could it be?

"It is time," her father proclaimed.

Her siblings lined up to wish her well.

"Don't forget what we told you," her eldest sister, Mielle, whispered in her ear, then adjusted one of the ribbons laced through Ambrosia's coily hair. "Ensure every bargain you make is sealed of a human's own volition. They must choose. Or you'll let the rot in." That warning sent a shiver down Ambrosia's spine despite the heat;

she tried to straighten up and hide her nerves. The idea of making a mistake had kept her awake for days. Their family couldn't afford that.

"I know." Ambrosia tried to tuck confidence into her voice. "I promise."

"Don't get curious about the other Immortal Wards. They're full of the unworthy. Stay in the Marrow," her brother Benoît added.

"And never reveal who or what you are. Most won't believe, but on the off chance they do, you don't want to deal with human curiosity. They harm those they take interest in," her other sister, Rosamel, warned.

"I understand," she whispered, trying not to let her fear show.

"Don't be like Maël," her brother André whispered. "Rosamel packed you enough misbeliefs to grow your own supply." He tapped the satchel in her hands, exciting the fruit floating inside it like tiny setting suns. "Always use them first. Mortals can never resist the taste. They have weak constitutions. Your kiss is the last resort. Never forget that."

But Ambrosia had never kissed anyone. Not even another faerie-born child of the sun. She was curious about her nectar and its power. She wanted to test it. She wanted to see exactly what it could do. She wanted to experience how it felt and if it changed her. But part of her was terrified about what might come.

Her other siblings planted kisses on her forehead one by one, and she waited for her last brother, her favorite one, if she told the truth. Maël grinned at her, mischief flickering in his dark eyes. The baby's breath laced into his locs caught the wind coming off the Great River. He twirled the stem of a bourbon cherry in his mouth and instead of following procedure and bestowing a divine kiss of luck upon her forehead, he wrapped her up in his arms, letting his massive, beautiful wings envelop her. They always reminded her of a bouquet of black calla lilies.

He spun her around and she couldn't help but giggle.

Their father cleared his throat and Maël released her, but not without whispering in her ear. "If you need me, just say my name."

Ambrosia nodded. He'd always been there, their special bond forged when she'd been born. All she needed to do was whisper his name and he'd rescue her. But she wanted to make him proud and stand on her own two feet this time. Prove to him that she could do this on her own. Prove to him that she wasn't too afraid to do this. He finally kissed her forehead, then met angry scowls with a wide grin before rejoining the crowd.

Ambrosia's parents peered down at her and her heart fluttered. She tried to avoid their impossible expressions; their desperation tucked inside, radiating with their hopes and desires to maintain power, all directed at her.

Her father put a hand on her shoulder. "You leave our warmth today, our last mighty child of the sun headed out into the wide world." His locs swept below his waist and bloomed with dark roses and thorny stems. "You will see what needs to be seen, experience what needs to be experienced, and come into wisdom. We have profound wishes for you, hoping your gifts will sharpen and your ability to exist well in our eternal time will settle. And that no question will linger in your heart after this sacred exploration outside our Ward."

The Court clapped and tossed more flowers at Ambrosia's feet.

"It takes courage and bravery to leave your known world for another." The words boomed inside Ambrosia. She squeezed her hands together to keep them from trembling. "But it is our tradition, and we place our trust and faith in you to be safe, to follow our sacred rules, to practice using your gifts, and, most important, to do what needs to be done."

Ambrosia felt her father's charged gaze fall on her again. The weight of it was crushing.

The queen squeezed Ambrosia's hand, then fluffed Ambrosia's gown, the all-white lace making her look dusted in powdered sugar. Ambrosia glanced up at her mother. She'd always wanted to look just like her; gold dust shimmered over her warm brown skin, catching the sunlight, and her thick coils spilled over with black and red roses. Today they looked like twins. "My precious, my last baby, you will leave us for a season and return changed, settled in divine purpose. Relish this time of firsts, this time away, so that when you return you are renewed and ready to become a full member of the ruling court." She kissed Ambrosia. "Don't forget to plant your misbeliefs and wear your summer cloak to help shield you. I know you know what to do."

And she did . . . Well, at least she thought she knew what to do. She'd been preparing for this her whole life. The lessons, the warnings, the rituals. She felt afraid but wanted her mother to think she was ready.

Ambrosia bowed and turned to board the streetcar. Her father's hand stopped her and he leaned in, away from the listening ears. "One more thing, my youngest love: Your blooming comes at a precarious time for us, as you know. I will not hide the fact that our people's existence, our fate, lies in you right now. The Winter King continues to deplete our Court, taking many of our folk below to his snowy depths, where they perish from lack of sun. You must send us back as many humans as you can. You're never as strong as you are right now. Make the best of it for us. Ensure they're mighty enough."

"Yes, Papa," she replied, trying to shoulder the heaviness of the request and prove she could handle it.

Determination surged through Ambrosia. She would make her first bargain, she would send back as many as she could, she would make her parents and her Court proud . . . But most important, she would have her first kiss.

Ambrosia found a seat near a window and sank down into plush cushions. She clutched her valise to her chest and tried not to stare out at her family and the Court watching her.

A hobgoblin climbed aboard. He bowed at her, then trundled to the driver's seat. "We are ready, Your Majesty."

Ambrosia nodded, fixating on her skirts until the streetcar headed down Decatur for Canal Street. She took a deep breath and prepared to smile and wave as they did a farewell lap through the Vieux Carré. A flight of dragonflies trailed her, buzzing with blessings. The sidewalks and gallery porches spilled over with onlookers who lovingly tossed wish-flowers and blew kisses at the last summer-born princess to head off into the world. Even the streetlamps bowed as she passed.

She looked around the royal streetcar, its grandness feeling too big for just her, and wished she had someone to talk to. She'd never needed friends before because of all of her siblings. True loneliness settled upon her for the first time, the task ahead ballooning in her chest. Her father's words haunted her on repeat: *"Our people's existence, our fate, lies in you right now . . ."*

Ambrosia tried not to even think about the winter-born. She looked at the gallery porches and the wild iron—their protection from the other fae who lurked below them. The wrought-iron railing curled into a rose, acknowledging her presence, as she passed. Her parents' Summer Court had reigned for longer than any of the other courts had held power. But if she was honest, she should worry. The revelers had dwindled little by little. The all-day feasts shrinking, food left to rot; the night parties too quiet, the jazz melodies scant and scarce; the carnival floats thinning to very few parades snaking along the enchanted streets; the shops empty of their beautiful trinkets. Their enemies had been swift and clever at drawing folk to the depths beneath, penetrating their wild iron gates through means that no one had quite figured out yet.

When the streetcar stopped at the Great River, the hobgoblin left and a man dressed in a midnight-black suit that matched his beautiful skin climbed aboard. He bowed his head. "I'm a warden, royal child. Prepare to cross into the Marrow." He sat in the driver's seat and turned a series of cranks and gears. The streetcar swished left and right, shedding its cables.

Ambrosia gripped her seat and took a deep breath. No one ever went into the river; only admired it from afar. They moved forward off the tracks and into the crystal blue waters. The streetcar floated through her mother's legendary river garden—the topiary maze with hedges made of flowers, foliage, and glittering jewels; baccara roses with ruby petals and emerald stems, baby's breath blooming with diamonds and mosaic tiles. She'd never been this close before, and gasped. The hedges spilled over with flesh turned to foliage and faces twisted in agony. The delphinium gowns of the spring-born shredded by thorns. The persimmon crowns of the autumn-born crushed and shattered. Snowy wings of the winter-born blistered by the sun.

"What is this?"

"The queen's garden of punishment, Your Majesty." His voice held a ring of surprise at her ignorance. "Any who disobey our queen or enter our Court without permission end up here."

Ambrosia nodded as guilt washed over her and she came face-to-face with her mother's violent delights and eternal punishments, hidden in plain sight.

"Don't worry. You'd never end up there anyways." The driver's golden eyes found hers in the rearview mirror. "I took each one of your siblings through."

She nodded, not sure of what to say, and tucked herself down into the seat. Summer storm clouds sauntered in, snuffing out the eternal sun. Their daily rainstorm began as they sailed forward. An iron gate rose from the water and foliage ahead. Branches unfurled their grip on the metal as different versions of it appeared one after the other, the iron spindles turning from a buttery gold to emerald green to licorice black to a bloody crimson, then finally settling on a deep plum.

Ambrosia's heart thudded with wonder and fear about all the different Wards of her eternal city. The water darkened and thickened with mud and grime. Its new stench made Ambrosia cover her nose.

The gate opened and the streetcar swept them into the Marrow, the mortal version of New Orleans. It slid out of the river and right behind another streetcar on the line without as much as a notice from passersby trying to escape the rain, before parking at the French Market.

The warden handed her an umbrella and a card with an address printed on it.

3029 ½ St. Charles Avenue
New Orleans, LA 70115

He helped her with the valise onto the sidewalk. "Enjoy your time in the Marrow. May you have fruitful returns for your blooming. I'll be waiting here on the three hundred and sixty-fifth day."

Ambrosia waved goodbye, scooting into the square and tucking herself under an awning in front of an occult shop. She watched all the humans hustling around, trying to escape the rain. She scrunched her nose. This Ward smelled sour. Trash littered the sidewalks and the mortals stank of sweat and liquor. Horses left piles of dung in the streets. Their same Summer Square seemed naked. No flowers. Plain trees without misbeliefs. The Summer Palace gone, replaced with a white building with three steeples. Vendors without proper shops aggressively shouting about their goods. A hideous statue of a man named Jackson perched on a horse. Ambrosia felt it all looked unrefined and uncivilized.

She heard Maël's warning about the Mortal Ward: "The Marrow has changed since my Senescence. Its edges are harder, given what it's gone through—pandemics, flooding, devastating storms, corrupt mortal politicians, an uptick in crime. You need to be prepared."

But how could she have ever prepared for this? The thought of having to stay here for a year made her stomach turn. This wasn't what she'd expected or envisioned all those years waiting for her chance to visit. The beauty of the Court erased. This monstrous version of her beloved New Orleans in its place.

Ambrosia looked down at the card again and plotted how to get to the Garden District, trying to remember what Maël told her about this version of the Vieux Carré. But all those helpful details disappeared from her mind, the chaos of this Ward a perpetual distraction.

A prickle rushed over her skin as she felt eyes on her—ones of recognition. She turned around to face the storefront. Right in the window, a young woman gawked at her. This was the first mortal woman she'd ever seen up close. But this person wasn't exactly a grown woman. Not in how Ambrosia had learned about mortal development. She was between childhood and adulthood, much like herself. No more than eighteen years old, she guessed.

The young woman met Ambrosia's eyes. Her warm brown skin

held the perfect amount of freckles. Her mouth resembled a frayed rosebud, no doubt from her front teeth fussing with her lips. Her eyes were two dollops of honey in chamomile tea.

Ambrosia hadn't expected humans to have this sort of beauty. A strange tingle shot through her, as if someone hummed an unfamiliar song across her skin. She was overwhelmed with the desire to know this gorgeous person.

The window opened and a hand gripped her cloak. "I know what you are. And I want to make a bargain."

Ambrosia panicked and she bolted. She didn't stop running. Not even when she heard the sound of footsteps behind her or the young woman shouting, "Stop!" Instead, she ducked into the crowd of humans trying to find shelter from the downpour and searched for a place to hide. Failure and fear mingled in her stomach. She'd been in the Marrow Ward for only a few moments and had already been spotted. Rosamel's warning about human curiosity with fae folk haunted her as she darted deeper into the Quarter. She thought about whispering Maël's name and admitting defeat, but she finally spotted a taxi.

She raised her hand just like Maël had taught her and it stopped in front of her. A squat gentleman helped put her valise in the trunk while she clutched her satchel of misbeliefs to her chest.

"What do you offer?" she asked.

His brow furrowed with confusion. "A way out of this rain. Now get in, the rates are listed."

She didn't understand but slid into the back seat. Her heart knocked against her chest. She glanced out the window, grateful to have lost the young woman who'd spotted her. Had she done something to accidentally reveal herself? How had she messed up already?

"Where to, baby girl?" he asked.

Ambrosia smiled, letting her heart slow down and find amusement in the rhythm of his accent and his kindness. She handed him the card.

"Garden District. No problem," he replied.

They whizzed along, leaving this version of the Quarter. He introduced himself as Mr. Wayne Broussard and chatted about the weather, where she should eat, how she should navigate the swollen city full of visitors for the Mardi Gras celebrations. Ambrosia was happy for the distraction after what just happened, and she couldn't stop glaring out the window as the tree-lined streets passed her by. This same street looked so different in her version of New Orleans. The trees of the Court always sang softly and swayed. Some held misbeliefs and others everlasting pecans. These trees were mostly boring, some holding multicolored glass bottles, and some covered with twinkly lights.

The cab paused in front of a run-down house, the ugliest on the block. Its windows were boarded up and the mail slot wired shut—all signs that the owner wanted no loiterers and no company. It looked like the sort of place children would dream up in their nightmares, a dark mansion believed to be haunted by ghosts and spirits and any other frightening creature imaginable.

"You sure this is it?" Mr. Wayne glared at it. "Can't believe the fine folks around here would even allow such a thing." He glanced at the card again, scratching his thick hair. "But I don't suppose I know enough."

When Ambrosia glanced out the rainy window, she saw the most beautiful white house, frosted with lacy wrought iron and window boxes, looking like the most decadent wedding cake. She could feel the wild iron, its pull tugging at her. A ring of mushrooms poked out of the beautiful lawn. Trellises of baccara roses climbed along the outside.

A smile tucked itself into the corner of her mouth. "It's okay. My aunt needs to have it worked on." She almost stumbled over the lies she'd been drilled on saying.

"That'll cost you fifteen dollars and thirty-five cents," he said.

She fished out the strange papery mortal money before spotting one of her misbeliefs. She nibbled her bottom lip and watched as he removed her valise from the trunk and ran it up to the porch for her in the pouring rain. Maybe he was worthy? Maybe she could try to make her first bargain with someone so nice? He returned to the cab.

"Everything all right, baby girl?" Mr. Wayne's eyes held concern.

She took a deep breath, preparing to make her first bargain. She pulled her hood back so he could really see her. She knew he would be unable to look away. He turned his head, eyes fixed on her face. Her pulse raced. "Aside from this coin in exchange for this ride, if you could ask for anything, what would you most desire?" She held the misbelief up; its orange glow shined like a tiny sun in her palm.

His eyes ballooned with awe. Sweat raced across his dark brow. The misbelief floated toward him unpeeling itself, the sweet citrusy scent of its flesh a perfume he'd never be able to resist. She steadied her voice as the misbelief hovered right in front of him, ready to be eaten. All the years of lessons on fae-speak being put to the test. "Taste the fruit. Make your wish."

"What will happen to me?" Mr. Wayne watched the fruit spin on its tiny axis.

"You'll receive what you seek." Her heart thudded as she waited for him to taste it, to be her first conquest.

He stretched his hand back and forth toward the fruit, hesitation making his fingers quiver. Her excitement bubbled up and part of her wanted to press a piece of the fruit into Mr. Wayne's mouth, but she'd been warned about what happened to humans if bargains were forced upon them or half made. The bargain would be unsealed, letting the rot enter. They'd be left susceptible to the Winter King's unseelie mischief.

Hail plinked against the windshield, pulling his attention away. Mr. Wayne rubbed his eyes. "What is this witchcraft? Take your cursed fruit and go," he barked.

Ambrosia jumped, crushed by fear. The misbelief disintegrated to ash. She left the money on the back seat and raced out of the car. From the porch, she watched as he drove away, the screech of his tires grating her ears.

This might be harder than she thought.

Ambrosia whispered a word in the old tongue, and the front door opened for her. As she crossed the threshold, her lessons with Maël came to mind. "The old tongue is the language of our blood," he'd said. All the times he'd made her pronounce the words correctly and retell the story about the origin of the Black summer-born—the mighty people of the sun. How the Irish and Scottish immigrants had brought their seelie and unseelie folk in their trunks and trinkets to the New World. How they'd been lured from their new Courts by the plantation work songs of enslaved West Africans. How they'd become enraptured by their melodies, the scent of their food, the beauty of their children, and the ever-plentiful slave burial grounds. She knew they'd been born from a marriage between those bloodlines, but as the Black summer-born grew numerous, their ability to survive iron and their new gifts allowed them to take over the Courts.

A nest of protective thorns retracted in the foyer, making space for her to enter.

A hobgoblin awaited her. "Welcome, Your Majesty." He hunched, his back curved into a question mark. "I am here to make your stay in the Marrow as pleasant as possible."

She nodded. Despite the earlier failure, Ambrosia felt a fleeting sense of pride in this moment as the wild iron spindles plucked her valise from her hands and ushered it upstairs to her new bedroom. A ceiling garden awakened as she passed. Baccara roses waved in her direction and welcomed her inside. The kitchen spilled over with any food she imagined. She peeked into a sitting room; plush tabletops dotted the space, each displaying porcelain game boxes, ornate tea sets, and glass bottles brimming over with faerie fruit suspended in sticky syrup. Chaises and claw-footed sofas circled the room. Warm-weather curtains fluttered along the wall, exposing a gallery balcony. Mirrors gave glimpses back home and she watched as the celebrations of her Senescence continued without her. She tried to push away the pang in her chest, the homesickness. So far she'd found nothing worthy about the Marrow Ward.

Ambrosia planted a misbelief, added one of her tears; the small tree grew with more of the orange fruit. She removed the ones from her satchel and let them attach to the plant to stay fresh and ready. She tried to forget the one that had just turned to ash.

She threw herself on her new bed, gazing at the ceiling and blinking away exhaustion and disappointment. Her body hummed with worry after being recognized and her failure, the twin moments playing over and over again in her head. What if she had messed up? What if she was unable to find anyone worthy to send back home?

She thought about what was at stake: each enemy Court lurking below her version of New Orleans, existing like the sugary layers of a Doberge cake, shifting with the tides of politics and power. The Spring, Autumn, and Winter Courts all wanting to overthrow the

Summer Court and regain their access to the Immortal Wards. If she was unsuccessful in sending worthy humans back to keep their Court teeming with mighty folk, the others could thin them out and challenge her father to put forth a champion and reopen their ultimate bargain.

Twin baccara roses slithered along the floor like a double-headed hydra and crawled onto the bed, a note caught between their petals. Ambrosia plucked the card and flipped it over.

You're doing just fine. You're okay. Meet me in Pirate's Alley just off Jackson Square at midnight.

Maël, your favorite brother

She should be angry with him for watching her and checking up on her, but instead she felt a surge of relief.

"It's fine," she whispered to herself.

She bathed and re-dressed, slipping on gloves to keep her hands from quivering and her summer cloak to help her blend in.

Hours later, the hobgoblin helped Ambrosia successfully navigate the St. Charles streetcar to Carondelet Street and the Quarter. He left her at the mouth of Jackson Square.

She could barely look at the Great River; the ugly muddiness of it upsetting. Humming cicadas and jazz mingled in a late-night melody. She walked through their pitiful excuse for a park and scowled at St. Louis Cathedral. She cut through a passageway, glancing up, and a sign read PIRATE'S ALLEY in English. People darted past, headed for Jackson Square. They wore beaded necklaces, guzzled drinks, and screamed with joy. Food and vomit littered the streets.

"Laissez les bons temps rouler," one shouted in passing.

She sniffed and scowled.

"The scent of mortals and the Mississippi," a voice from behind said. "Not sweet, but you'll get used to it after a few weeks. Don't be a snob."

Ambrosia whipped around to find her favorite brother.

"You called for me," he said with a smile.

"I definitely did not." She tried to pretend to be upset with him but his note felt warm in her pocket.

Maël took her hand. He winked at her and she softened. He wasn't the sort of brother you could stay mad at for very long. "Let's just say I missed you."

Ambrosia rolled her eyes. "How did you get here?"

Maël pursed his lips and pulled her into the darkest part of the alley. He looked left and then right. "Don't tell my secrets, little bee. You promise?" His dark eyes bored into hers, golden suns rimming his pupils.

"I promise."

He held out his forefinger, waiting for her to seal the vow with a faerie promise, forever binding. She kissed her finger and it glowed, then pressed it against his. She'd never be able to speak the words even if she wanted to . . . which she most certainly didn't.

He touched the brick wall. Her eyes bulged at the wild iron revealing itself. The living metal unfurled at his command and revealed a door. Her heart backflipped in her chest.

"This is illegal. You can never tell anyone it exists," he admitted.

"How did you create it?"

He grinned. "I have my ways." He took a bow. He had a reputation in the family for being reckless and troublesome, but she'd always known it masked his brilliance and ingenuity. She jostled his shoulder. "They go to the other Immortal Wards."

She watched as he placed a palm to it and the wrought iron morphed like the gate she'd sailed through earlier today—licorice black, emerald green, bloody crimson, and deep plum.

"So you go to the Wards as you please?" Ambrosia gawked up at him.

"I always do as I please . . . which is why no one in our family loves me, besides you. Though tonight you're acting like you didn't summon me."

She wrapped her arms around her brother's middle and gave it a squeeze.

"Go on and admit it, kid. You did think of me," he teased.

"Not for a rescue. Just the things you told me."

He adjusted his suspenders and wing straps, the pale streetlamp illuminating the thick black sinews of his wingspan and reminding her of a noir plum drenched with candlelight. She didn't want to admit how secretly grateful she was that he sent that note and showed up. She was still troubled about her failed bargain with Mr. Wayne and being spotted by the young woman earlier and . . . and she was incredibly lonely being away from home even if her ten siblings annoyed her with their meddling.

"This place is disgusting. How could anyone here be worthy of the Court?" she asked.

"You must leave your elitism"—he kissed her nose—"back home and take this place for what it is. Debauchery, grit, and honesty. It is alive in a way we could never be for we never know death. Do not let your fear keep you from seeing all this place has to offer. There is beauty here if you look hard enough. Now, this way!" Maël navigated them out of the crowded passageway and back into the square. It swelled with even more revelers waving their hands in the air at people throwing things off balconies.

Ambrosia stepped over cups littering the ground.

"Is this their idea of carnival?"

"Welcome to Mardi Gras in the Marrow."

Maël led her through more crowds. "Their carnival doesn't compare to ours, but it is delightful in its own way." He spun around and pointed up. "But look at their moon. The best part of this Ward. And can you feel the darkness? It's still warm but also cool at the same time. Isn't it grand?"

Ambrosia thought she could get used to gazing up at that silvery disc in the sky. The Court's eternal sunshine felt so different. Maël approached a crowded bench. His presence sent a few humans scurrying. "Did they recognize you?" she asked, not wanting to fully admit to what happened to her earlier with the young woman in the window.

"People in this Ward are scared of people that look like me and even you." He plopped down and patted the space beside him. Ambrosia carefully sat, her nerves on edge at all the unfamiliar things. Her pulse drummed to the beat of the jazz bands snaking down the side streets.

Maël shooed away peddlers selling T-shirts, souvenirs, paintings, and more. Ambrosia couldn't stop sniffing the air and turning this way and that way.

He chuckled. "My plan was a good one, it seems. I can't have you stick out like this, nose wide open, and get spotted."

Ambrosia gulped, preparing to tell him. "Well . . ."

"Did something happen?" She heard the worry tucked into his voice. "What did you do?"

"Nothing, I swear." She recounted the whole story. Her arrival just across the square and the run-in with the strange girl—but made sure to leave out her failure with the taxi driver and the misbelief.

Maël rubbed his beard. "Not good for this to happen so soon."

"But everyone told me mortals are clueless." Ambrosia scoffed.

"Yes, but there's more than one kind of human here. You have to watch out for the Conjure women and Conjure doctors, especially, and the other witch folk in this Ward. They don't take too kindly to our ritual, to us 'siphoning,' as they call it. So you must avoid them at all costs."

Ambrosia gulped. "How can you tell?" She tried to examine a passerby, but they all looked the same to her. She thought of the girl . . . and her eyes. What had she seen?

"Didn't Madame Elise go through all this with you?"

"I didn't really pay attention," she admitted, regret pooling in her chest. She'd spent most of her lessons with her governess daydreaming about her first kiss and her first faerie bargain.

"The Conjure folk have skin marked with roots. Often hidden, so you have to be careful. I broke a Conjure woman's heart once and she hexed my wings. They itched for a year no matter what I did. The other witches wear talismans. These folk have particular talents that can rival even ours at times."

Ambrosia listened intently as he regaled his exploits in the Marrow, and as they "people watched," as he called it. He pointed out easy marks, mortals down on their luck or in need of a change. "Start with them to get your confidence. They'll be easy to test your bargaining power on. Won't require much effort or energy and you'll be saving them."

"I'm scared I can't do it," she finally admitted to him. The story of her terrible first bargain attempt tumbled out.

He squeezed her palm. "Took me a week to get the courage to begin. At least you tried . . . and you'll get other chances. Mistakes will happen."

"And what about . . ." A warm flash of shyness zipped through her. ". . . a kiss?"

He laughed, then stifled it as she shifted, embarrassed. "Your greatest weapon. But don't be like me. Save it. I was too wild during my time away. They were right. I ended up in Bayou St. John, face down and almost dead."

"What happened?"

He looked out into the distance. "I was too hungry. Too eager to test my gifts and answer Papa's wish to fill the Court to its former glory. I didn't pay attention. Sent too many unworthy people back home." His voice lowered. "Many with weak constitutions easily manipulated by our enemies and drawn below to darker Courts. Not mighty enough." He shook his head. "That's why Papa remains angry with me."

Ambrosia's stomach knotted. She pushed away memories of tense dinners, Maël being thrown out of family parties, and the perpetual look of aggravation on her parents' faces whenever he entered the room. She'd never known the true reason until now.

"Be careful like Rosamel."

"But she's scared of everything."

He smiled. "That may be true, but it'll keep you safe while you're out here alone."

Her anxiety sent chills across her skin and her wings tightened against her back as if they could shield her from what was to come, what she had to face when he returned home and left her alone again. The reality that she'd never interacted with anyone outside the summerborn. The reality that she only had stories to go on. The reality that she'd have to rely on herself for the first time. None of her siblings would be here to guide her . . . or rescue her if she got into trouble.

"This wasn't supposed to make you worry." Maël shook her shoulder. "Let's get you another mortal." His eyes sparked, the pupils glowing faintly like two low-flame candles, as he surveyed the square. "Pick someone."

She looked around at all the vendors in the square.

One woman spread a purple drape over her table and placed a crystal ball and fortune cards in the middle. The woman affixed a sign to the front that read FIND YOUR FUTURE, DISCOVER YOUR FORTUNE HERE.

"A fortune teller?" Ambrosia's eyebrow quirked. The cabdriver had felt easy, but this one seemed more difficult somehow; maybe she should pick another. She couldn't put her finger on why.

"It's not real. Humans love to scam people with lies. A promise to be able to see what's to come goes a long way in this Ward. She's not a Conjure woman with actual talent. She has no markings on her skin." Maël handed her more strange papery dollars and gave her a loving push off the bench. "You can do it. I'll be right here. She's supposed to deal in the beyond. See if she will trade herself for a glimpse of the Court. Touch her hands and let her see our Great River with your fae-sight."

Ambrosia steadied herself, prepared to attempt her second bargain and maybe her first-ever kiss.

As Ambrosia slid into the seat, she couldn't stop staring. The woman didn't look up.

"Want to know your future? I'm the most affordable seer in the Quarter, especially tonight." The fortune teller refused to meet Ambrosia's eyes. "It'll be thirty dollars," she said.

Ambrosia handed her all the money Maël had given her, not even counting. The woman pocketed the dollars still without lifting her head. Ambrosia looked back at her brother, who grinned and pointed her back to the fortune teller.

"Remove your gloves and let me see your palms," the woman ordered.

Ambrosia followed instructions, then stretched her bare hands across the table. The softness of the woman's fingers, the way she traced the interior of Ambrosia's palms—she'd never been touched like that before. Ambrosia studied her as she worked, wondering what she would find that lay ahead and suppressing a grin. The mortal would never be able to decipher anything about her future because the summer-born had several eternal lifetimes.

"What do you have to give, and what will you ask?" Ambrosia prepared to lure her in, just as she'd been trained since birth, and prime her for the bargain. She wouldn't follow Maël's advice and offer a glimpse into the Court. She would offer something of more value: the chance to have the actual gift of sight and tell fortunes in perpetuity in her parents' Summer Court. Humans always coveted power. She let her fingers warm to begin inviting the mortal into her fae-sight.

The fortune teller snapped upright, now revealing her face. Her eyes burned into Ambrosia's. She gasped.

It was the young woman from earlier.

"Please don't run this time," she whispered, sweat pouring down her cheeks.

Ambrosia's pulse raced and she tried to calm down to not alarm Maël.

"I'm Lelah. I know you're one of the fae folk and I need your help. I've been tracking you."

"How?"

Lelah pointed at Ambrosia's summery cloak. "See the little bee?"

Ambrosia looked down, noticing a small honey bee no bigger than a drop of honey on the fabric. "How can you see the garment?"

"My mama's a Conjure woman. She taught me how to tell." Lelah also motioned at the slight pointiness of Ambrosia's ears. "You also have a scent. I smell the nectar of the Court on your skin. No one here smells like you."

Ambrosia hadn't been prepared for anything like this. Fear crept up her spine. She'd been told never to make a bargain with a conjuror or a witch because they never held.

"What is your name?" she asked.

"Ambrosia—" She swallowed her title with an awkward gulp.

"I want to make a trade."

Ambrosia had been warned so many times about how to deal with mortals who recognized them, but all her training seemed to evaporate in this moment. She felt too drawn to this person, too enthralled. She didn't understand it. She needed to get back in control. Ambrosia slowed her breathing and heartbeat, trying to coax Lelah's heart into following suit. But Lelah's pulse didn't slow, fighting Ambrosia's compulsions.

Lelah scowled at her and leapt to her feet. "This was a bad idea. Maybe you're not strong enough. Never mind. You can't help me." Lelah packed her things and scurried off into the night before Ambrosia could respond.

Ambrosia looked back at Maël, then took off behind Lelah. The streets swelled with dancing mortals as she navigated her way through the thick crowds. With each step she took closer to the graveyard, Ambrosia's arms and legs trembled with equal parts excitement and fear. What did Lelah want? This was a bad idea. The warnings echoed inside her, but she couldn't stop her feet from moving.

She crossed through the gates of St. Louis Cemetery Number One. The guard didn't even notice her pass. She'd never been this close to death before, those in the Court Ward never experiencing an end or requiring a place for the dead. They'd left that to the Shadow Ward and its Barons of Death.

A sea of crypts and mausoleums spread out before her. Mourners decorated the grave sites with flowers and candles. Some left food. Some arranged portraits. The sight of it all felt both wondrous and terrifying; the ugliness of death mingled with beauty. It made her wonder what it felt like to have only one stretch of time to live. She could get lost in here for hours and forget her task, merely watching people honor those they'd lost. As she snaked through the graveyard looking for Lelah, a pit burned in Ambrosia's stomach. She'd never lost anyone. She never wanted to.

Up ahead, she spotted the young woman kneeling before a crypt and lighting a series of candles. The candlelight warmed her brown skin, and the thick tears skating down her cheeks reminded Ambrosia of nectar. Her sadness radiated, and Ambrosia could feel the intensity of her grief like the heat from the sun.

"You came." Lelah didn't look up as Ambrosia got closer.

"How can you sense me?" Ambrosia crouched beside her.

"Remember, my mama's a Conjure woman, though I didn't get the gift. But I do get to use her tricks." She plucked the tiny sleeping bee from Ambrosia's cloak. "My tracker." She slipped it into a small jar filled with honeycomb.

Maël's warnings about Conjure women drummed inside her, but Ambrosia marveled at her industry and determination. No one had this sense of urgency where she'd come from. Plus she'd said she didn't have her mother's gifts. Maybe she was safe.

"Why did you lure me here?" Ambrosia asked, staring at the portraits. A young woman stared back at her. She and Lelah shared the same warm eyes and pretty freckles.

"I've tried everything. Every ritual. Every spell." Lelah motioned at all the candles and flowers and sachets.

"Who is she?" Ambrosia asked.

"My sister, my twin, Selah." Lelah rubbed her hands over the glass frame.

Ambrosia let herself connect and she now felt the hot shatter of the mortal's pain and grief. Part of her felt compelled to fix it. "What happened to her?"

More tears rushed down Lelah's cheeks. The story poured out: They'd been biking on the Crescent Park Trail along the river and she'd dared her sister to do a dangerous trick, which caused her to fall into the water and get swept away.

"I caused her death," Lelah said. "I always had to win and be better than her. I always had to compete with her. She was born with Mama's Conjure gifts and I wasn't. She was everything I wasn't. Better, smarter, more talented."

Ambrosia thought of that dark river and what had been lost to it, both in her Ward and this one. She and Lelah didn't speak for several long seconds. Ambrosia could hear both their hearts thumping.

"Can you bring her back?" Lelah's watery eyes tugged at her. "I'll trade days off of my life to add to hers. I can live half as long. Or I can fade away, give up my name, let everyone know her and not me. Or I can forgo a true love . . . as she is mine. I'll take care of her forever." The desperation in Lelah's voice made Ambrosia's heart race. She'd never heard someone want to selflessly trade themselves for another. She'd never witnessed this sort of sacrifice.

Ambrosia wanted to lie to her, to tell her that it was possible to bring her sister back from the dead, but she could never say something untrue. The summer-born fae did not deal in the shadows. They did not make alliances with the walkers of the Land of the Dead, the

Shadow Barons. They only dealt in the light. She nibbled her bottom lip, trying to bite back the truth. "I can't."

Lelah grabbed her hand. "What is your price? I'll give you everything I have."

"It is not that. I cannot bring someone back. You'd have to go to the Shadow Ward and consult a Baron."

Lelah's eyes narrow. "I tried that. They don't bargain. That's why I've been waiting for you. One of your kind. It's been three years." Her eyes remained fixed and Ambrosia felt pinned in place. "Can you do anything?"

"I can make the heartbreak go away." Ambrosia let the offer ease between them. "I can make you forget this pain, this suffering."

"And her? Selah?" Lelah bit her bottom lip, making Ambrosia curious about what it might be like to kiss her nervous mouth, to ease her worries, to erase the heartbreak radiating through her like a tiny earthquake.

"I can mend your broken heart." Ambrosia wished she could do more. "I can give you someone new to love."

"What does it cost? This forgetting?"

"Eternity."

Lelah picked up the portrait of her sister and kissed it. "I can't bear it anymore. I accept." She stared up at Ambrosia. "Make it go away."

Ambrosia kneeled. "It will take a kiss to seal this type of bargain."

Lelah perched on her knees to meet Ambrosia's gaze. "I'm ready."

She felt Lelah's pulse, a staccato rhythm, racing and drowning out the midnight Mardi Gras revelers. Ambrosia's mouth watered, her nectar preparing as she leaned forward. Up close, Lelah's mouth still reminded her of a rosebud, the deep red of her lips and the shape of them. She traced her finger along its edge before pulling her chin closer.

Lelah pressed her mouth to Ambrosia's with a surprise force. Ambrosia felt Lelah's tongue finding her nectar and the heaviness inside her dissipating. Ambrosia thought she could feel Lelah's heart being pieced back together like a shattered vase finding a second life. When their lips parted, Ambrosia whispered in the old tongue, sealing the bargain and leaving behind a compulsion mark, an iridescent baccara rose on her cheek. Lelah's feet would know the way to the Court. The warden would recognize Ambrosia's mark and usher her inside.

"You taste like honey," Lelah muttered, out of breath. Ambrosia watched her transform. Golden suns ringed her eyes now, the sadness lifting away, the mortality transforming to immortality. "I could love you."

Ambrosia smiled. Her lips tingled with the memory of that kiss, her very first. "You could."

"Thank you." Lelah stood, took one last glance at the crypt, then scooped up her honeybee jar and started to walk toward the cemetery exit.

"I'll find you this time," Ambrosia said, watching until she couldn't see Lelah anymore. She swelled with pride, after making her first bargain and sending her first mortal back to the Court for eternal life. Lelah was more than worthy.

ROTTEN

Kaitlyn Sage Patterson

Like just about everyone born into circumstances more tired and rusted out than the pickup truck that's been sitting in the yard for more than a decade, I've always wondered if there weren't a way to shimmy into a life that'd be brighter and more interesting than the one I seem to be stuck with. In spite of looking for the last seventeen years, I ain't found it.

After supper Mamaw retreats into the den with her stories. Doesn't even remind me to fill a saucer with milk and set it out for the Folk (or, more likely, the feral cats). She hasn't had much to say to me since Mr. Robinson went and told her I dropped out of orchestra last week at church. She doesn't even have it in her to put me on punishment or whack me with her silver spoon and demand to know if the Folk swapped me out for a faerie child. That's how ready she is to be done raising me. She ain't even waiting for me to turn eighteen. She already threw in the towel. And I don't blame her.

Birdie's late picking me up. I wait out on the porch, and I can't help wanting to dig my thumbnail under the thick layers of paint on the steps and peel up long strips, one satisfying piece at a time. If I were a good granddaughter, I'd lean into the urge, coat the whole thing in Citristrip and peel up a hundred years or more of my ancestors' shoddy work. That and about a thousand other things I could do to keep our house from falling apart. But a part of me would rather just pick it apart, one strip of paint, one loose nail at a time.

Birdie's truck rumbles up the gravel driveway, and I hop up. I should poke my head in, tell Mamaw I'm leaving and give her an idea of when I'll be back. But I don't want to force her to work up something that looks like disappointment, and I know she'll be asleep by the time I come home. Instead, I brush off my jeans like I'm not going to stand around a fire in the middle of a muddy field with a bunch of people I've known my whole life. It doesn't matter how I look—the truth of the matter is that we all stopped really *seeing* each other years ago, and no one's looking at me anyway. But as empty as I feel, I can't help but keep playing my part.

"Did you hear about Tom and Ariana?" Birdie asks as I fasten my seat belt. There's a touch of nasty glee in her voice that shivers over my skin like a cold wind—bracing and refreshing. Birdie has a sinister appetite for gossip that I've always loved. It'd never occur to her to think twice about what someone else was saying about her, so why shouldn't she indulge her own hunger?

"Let me guess," I quip, effortlessly giving in to my sharp tongue and scathing judgment. "Tom cooked up a scheme for them to be declared homecoming king and queen from now until eternity. He can't stand the idea that someone else might come along and take attention from him someday. Even if he's already dead when it happens."

Birdie pulls out onto 321, and the sunset blazes over the foothills.

The Smoky Mountains are coal, and the sky is a wildfire, burning scarlet along the horizon and fading orange into lavender then navy. "He's been cheating on her. With Rachel." She pauses, savoring the drama. "For almost a year."

My stomach clenches with disgust. Tom's rotten, and I've never understood what Ariana saw in him. It's not like she and I are friends, but I feel for her. I can only imagine how much she's hurting right now. Putting myself into the costume of her pain makes a thought skitter through my mind like a frightened deer. *What would happen if you grabbed the wheel, yanked it hard, sent the truck sailing off the road?* I push it away, same as I always do.

"Fuck him," I say, more vitriol escaping on my breath than I'd meant to let out. My daddy was nice, or so Mamaw always says. She talks like he hung the damn moon up in the sky just for her. I might have been nice too, had things turned out different. If I'd been born to another family, somewhere other than Happy Valley. If my mother had stuck around. If. If. If.

But I caught my mean young. And despite Mamaw's prayers and superstitions and my years of trying, I stay meaner and prouder than a snake stealing eggs. Lately I've resolved every morning to be better. And by the time I walk out the front door, I'm slick with sweat and hate in equal measure. I'm like a poison toad evolving to survive in the Amazon. I need my temper to protect me from everyone else who hasn't found a way to escape our home in these hollers.

Birdie flicks the turn signal on and gives me a mischievous smile. "Five bucks says he shows up tonight."

"He wouldn't dare."

"That's why it's a bet," Birdie says, offering me her hand to shake on it.

Reluctantly, I agree. She's probably right, and I don't have five bucks to lose, but that's never the point of these bets. Birdie wants to be right, and I want to let her. Birdie deserves to win.

She pulls her truck in behind Colby's Camry. He hates that he got stuck with his mom's old car instead of a truck and always tries to park it where he thinks people won't see it. He's an ass, so Birdie and I torture him by parking as close to him as we can. Birdie's bright red pickup is hard to miss—especially after she and I plastered it with the most outrageous bumper stickers we could find.

I hop out and take in the scene while she checks her lip gloss in the rearview one last time. The sharp crackle of the bonfire sparks against the music thumping tinnily from someone's truck speakers. There's a crowd around the fire and another around the truck bed that serves as a bar. It's not hard for teenagers to get booze in a town like this. There's always someone in our classes who looks old enough for the kid at the BP to not bother carding him, an older sibling or cousin who shows up to relive their glory days with a case or two in hand, or a liquor cabinet with a handful of dusty bottles we can easily pilfer unnoticed.

I reluctantly follow Birdie as she beelines for the bar truck, ears pricked sharp for gossip. I hate these parties, but I don't have a good excuse to stay home. I wish I could fade into the darkness, escape from the expectations of the people in my life and from their memories. No one really wants me here, after all.

I'm not as hot as Ariana, or even Tom, though most of the time the fact that he's such a nauseating narcissist helps me see past his chiseled jawline and sparkling eyes. I'm not an athlete, not that Coach Brown would know what to do with a sporty girl if he met one. I'm not funny and charming the way Birdie is. I'm a smartass, and turns out, there's not much social capital to be gained by being an asshole.

That's what Mamaw taught me, but the rules she drilled into my bones when I was coming up ain't proved themselves to have much practical use—even the ones that don't contradict each other.

Don't go into the woods at night.

Tell no one your full name, not even the government.

Only eat food you cook for yourself or made by people you trust, but always leave something out for folks who might be passing through.

Mamaw's so exhausted by losing the folks she loved that she doesn't have the energy to pay much attention to me, so these rules was all I got. My dad died before I made a single memory of him, I haven't heard my mama's voice in over a decade. It's the reality of life: People die, people leave, and nobody's guaranteed that there'll be people in this world who've got the energy to care about anyone but themselves. I've been resigned to that for a long, long time. I only recently decided I was gonna try to do something about it.

Mary Greer hands me a spiked seltzer by way of greeting and doesn't miss a beat in her monologue about the Tom and Ariana drama. Mary Greer, apparently, was sitting next to Ariana in the Wednesday night service over at the Baptist church when she found out about Tom and Rachel. Probably the same night Mr. Robinson ratted me out to Mamaw. I take a sip from my can and let my friends' chatter slip around me. I stare past Mary Greer, looking into the dark woods where the field meets the foothills and races up toward the sky like the woods are reaching for the fading remnants of the sun.

Folks get lost in the mountains that butt up to Happy Valley. Tourists die every year from exposure, starvation, bears. Those deaths don't appeal to me—the long ones, I mean. The kind of deaths that drag out like Sunday services. Who would want that? But sometimes people just disappear. *That* has some appeal.

What if I just . . . wasn't . . .

Birdie's fingernails dig into my arm, yanking me out of my dissociative reverie. "Did you hear that?" she hisses.

I nod, even though I wasn't listening. "Wild stuff. But honestly, Tom and Rachel deserve each other. The only thing she cares about is being prom queen, and Tom's attention span is about as long as a tadpole's. I'm surprised he hasn't been caught cheating before."

Birdie gives me a *look*, but thankfully turns her attention back to Mary Greer's story. I let my eyes drift back to the dark woods. I see a flash of silver between the trees, like a firefly, but the season's all wrong for them. I keep watching, and another light brightens and dims in an eyeblink. Then there are dozens of them, turning on and off in sync with each other. It's like the fireflies that lure tourists up to Gatlinburg to pay too much money for a bad hotel and then sit in a traffic jam for hours just so they can look at some bugs. I never understood the urge—until now. There's something captivating about these ones.

I feel the pull of the lights, like a tug on a leash, and I wonder if I should have forced another piece of corn bread down my throat to soak up the booze. But my first drink is less than half-empty, and no one we know has the kind of money that buys drugs just to fuck with other people for a laugh. I touch the chain around my neck and study Birdie, my oldest friend, as she basks in the pleasure that this kind of juicy gossip brings her. I wish I could match her energy or, if I were to stick to my determination to be better, pull her back to something that might be mistaken for concern for the people involved. I don't know why I worry that everyone will see just how delightful she finds—*we find*, I correct myself—Tom's inelegant fall from grace. They're all as bloodthirsty as we are.

Like a girl annoyed that her date is paying more attention to their friends than her, the lights seem to show out more and more the longer I ignore them. The longer I pretend not to know exactly what they are. The Folk are calling for me. But I don't know what mischief they're fixing to pull, and I'm not sure I want to.

I grew up in these mountains. Mamaw made sure I knew the risks. People who follow the lights of the Folk into the woods don't often come back, and if they do, they come back changed. That's what Mamaw said by way of explanation for Aunt Ruthie Mae. She'd been *touched*. Wandered off one day when she was just fifteen, came back a year and a day later, and she ain't been right since. Her mind's always somewhere else, and a person can't ever tell if she's thinking so far ahead that everything's set to go perfect, or if the biscuits are on fire in the oven and she's daydreaming about making butter from milk thistle and pine.

Ruthie Mae doesn't worry about who told who off at the liquor store last Friday night. She's not bothered by the fire and brimstone preachers screaming from the pulpit on Sunday. She leads a quiet, albeit strange, life. I wonder if she regrets walking off all those years ago. I wonder if she was tricked. I wonder if she chose.

"Ben had to know," Birdie says, pulling my attention from the lights, the allure of the unknown lurking in the mountains. "There's no way that Tom could have kept something like this secret from him. Those two spend all their time together."

Mary Greer shakes her head. "He told me that he had no idea."

"And you believe him?" I ask, unable to stop myself. "Ben's lies get more pathetic every day."

Ben's aren't the kind of lies that flirt with entertaining. In the fifth grade he insisted that his parents were in the FBI and were a part of the government's plot to kill JFK, for Christ's sakes. As if none of us could do the math to know that they probably weren't even born when JFK was assassinated.

"Obviously I don't believe him," Mary Greer agrees, "but I don't see what he gets out of protecting Tom."

The lights in the trees begin blinking on and off more quickly, insistently, and I think of Mamaw, always telling me not to go into the woods on my own for fear of the Folk. I want so badly to be free of the never-ending petty drama, the vampiric suck of gossip, the bleak knowledge that this will be the rest of my life. These people. This town. These same conversations. Because when I'm here, I can't help myself. I can't help but be the worst version of me. That's when I decide. If the lights in the tree line are nothing but fireflies, I won't lose a thing. But if they're something more, I might stand to gain a wild, impossible life.

"Hold my drink?" I ask Birdie, leaning in and giving her a kiss on the cheek. Her skin is flushed and warm from the fire, and she smells like the Walmart body spray she swears is a Chanel dupe overlaid with woodsmoke and White Claw.

She scrunches her eyebrows by way of a question. I don't wonder if she'll miss me. She will, in her own way, but I know better than most that grief is like a sunburn. The first few days are full of painful reminders, but after a while, it fades, and you wonder if it really ever hurt in the first place.

"Gotta pee," I lie.

It would be so easy to stay. To squat behind a round bale of hay, wait for a moment, and go back to my friends. I know that my life would be straining against the confinement of expectations and tending to my growing crops of bitterness, resentment, and loathing. I don't want to live like that.

The first steps toward the woods are terrifying. I could veer left, head toward one of the round bales of hay sending long shadows across the shorn field. I could choose to stay. But I don't. I keep walking, letting the lights tug me toward the dark line of the trees. By the time I reach the wood line, I am resolute. Perhaps there's nothing here to be afraid of, perhaps there's nothing here at all. But maybe the Folk are calling to me for a reason.

The branches overwhelm the moonlight, and the woods envelop me in the cool blackness. I should hesitate, should watch where I put my feet for fear of tripping on roots and bone-cracking stones, but I am filled with bright confidence as I follow the dancing lights farther into the trees.

A cool hand slips up my arm and cups my elbow, startling me. A cloud of dizzyingly rich perfume encompasses me in the scent of gardenia.

"You came," a soft voice whispers in my ear. "We didn't know if you would."

I look over my shoulder, and there, impossibly lit in the darkness, is the most beautiful creature I've ever seen. They push their black hair out of their face with one impatient hand, and keep the other on my elbow, reassuring.

"Welcome," they say. "Let me show you the way. The party is just up ahead."

I pause. I could walk away. I know better than messing around with the Folk. But maybe that's just it. I know better. And I chose this.

Their flint-chip eyes flick to mine, questioning my hesitation, and I slip my hand into theirs. Step forward. Choose.

Three steps forward, I hear the bright seesaw of a mandolin. Two more and laughter cuts through the branches. One final step brings us to a clearing swirling with light that seems to come from nowhere and everywhere. Gardenias and rhododendrons erupt in lush, out-of-season blooms, and a thick layer of moss cushions the bare feet of the dancers. A rain-smoothed log is covered in piles of sun-kissed tomatoes, jewel-like persimmons, and heaps of blackberries. A woman the size of my hand lounges on a toadstool, her fat belly and plump legs draped in fabric dew-wet and silky. In the branches of the trees overhead, musicians perch and hang, their notes falling on us like raindrops, playing a tune both familiar and ethereal, like bluegrass burbling up through a spring.

The most gorgeous people I've ever seen dance around us. They are as sumptuous as the surroundings, all shapes and sizes and luscious features as diverse as the pages of the books kept from us in school. A girl with owl eyes and feathered legs peers down at me from her perch, and a pair of tiny men waltz through the air near my head. I suddenly feel that I understand the true meaning of the word "supernatural."

"Where are we?" I ask my guide.

They shrug, smiling, and trail a long finger down my cheek, along my jaw, and across the line of my collarbone. "Does it matter? You're here now."

It does, I think, matter, but I can't quite hold on to the thought. I feel euphoric, almost drunk. Like the buzz of three beers, but without the inevitable melancholy and headache. I had a plan, I remember, but what it is, I can't say.

"Dance with me," they command, guiding my hands.

I don't dance, not ever, but there's something about their hand in mine, the smile in their eyes, the bizarre impossibility of this party that makes me nod before I have time to think of all my normal excuses. They pull me close, and we move together to the tangled, lilting music. I let my hands drift over their body, feeling the swell of their arm muscles, the curve of their hips, the way they tense, ever so slightly, when my fingers graze the soft flesh at the top of their thigh.

"You're greedy," they whisper in my ear. "You don't even know my name, and yet you take such liberties with your hands."

I blush, but I don't stop. They're right. I am greedy. I ache for more of this, this newness, this strangeness, this rich bacchanal. Mine has been a drab life slouching toward a hard, grim future. This is the first time in years that I've felt—anything. I've been empty and aching and cold for so long. I want to feel.

I want to stay.

Recalling Mamaw's rules is effortless, but I don't quite know which apply to the Folk, which to the church, and which are the bastardized results of a generations-long game of etiquette telephone. So I decide to break them all.

When my dance partner's twirling steps bring us close to the log laid with the midsummer feast, I pull away just far enough to pause and scoop a handful of fiddlehead ferns out of a wooden bowl and cram them into my mouth. I chew quickly, and as I swallow, the music comes to a stumbling halt.

"I didn't offer you refreshment," my partner says slowly, picking sharply at their words like the strings of a fiddle.

There is a moment here, a breath when I know that I could apologize and wiggle away from consequences, the same way I've done a thousand times before. But if I were going to take that road, why did I venture into the woods in the first place? I want to change my life, not go back to the same mundane shit day after day.

"My name is Margaret Amaker Fisher," I say, deliberately pronouncing each syllable as I offer them my hand. "My friends call me Maggie."

Whispers rush like wind through the thick leaves of a rhododendron around the clearing. I know what I'm doing, but it sure doesn't seem like these people—these Folk—have the foggiest idea what I'm trying.

"I have not yet *asked*," my host mutters.

I pull a delicate gold ring—my great-grandmother's wedding

band—off my finger and press it into my dance partner's palm. "A gift," I say, smiling up at the blank look of confusion clouding their countenance. "I don't have a firstborn to offer you, and while I'd offer up my cat, I'm fair certain that Ogee would be a menace to your community here."

"What do you think you're doing?" my dance partner asks, glowering.

"Choosing," I tell them.

"This isn't how it's supposed to work," the tiny woman on the toadstool pouts.

"No! The light-snappers bring them, we play with them, and then the moss-rakers push them back where they came from," the owl-girl snaps.

"Did the bear-prodders tell you to do this?" one of the mandolin players demands. "It's the kind of nonsense they'd pull, trying to provoke the rest of us."

"No one put me up to it," I say. "No one told me what to do. I'm choosing. I want to stay here with you."

"You don't know what you're asking," my dance partner grinds out, their voice a low and gritty thing, like the red clay beneath the grass. "You're not entitled to ask anything of us in the first place. We brought you here to amuse us."

In a rush of cold air, the perfume is swept away, the lights dim, and the illusion drops away. Where there was lush greenery, thick moss, and perfect flowers, I see dead vine, rocky soil, and bruised blooms. The cheeks of the Folk, round and flushed just moments ago, are now sallow and sharp. The instruments are out of tune, the produce rotting on the log, and the garments the Folk wear are nothing more than tattered ruins. My guide, however, remains unchanged.

"I didn't ask anything of you," I spit out, using my determination to shove fear out of my way.

"The last one who stayed danced until their feet were broken and bloodied," one of the tiny dancing men says.

"Another lost dozens of years and reentered their world after everyone they loved was gone," his partner adds.

"Your kind can't keep your thoughts ordered with too much time among us," my dance partner warns. "I brought you here for a night, for mischief and play. We chose you for your sharp tongue. To tell the star-singers their trilling falls flat and the light-snappers they've let themselves grow dull. You tell the meanest truths so easily and sharply. But you're not meant to stay."

They want to show me their darkness and have me reflect it back at them meaner and more unflinching. But I know the truth—both are an illusion. The beauty as much a lie as the ruin. Most people, even the ones who ask for it, don't know what to do when faced with their own truths. But these are the Folk. Maybe they'll surprise me.

I can feel the barbs cutting against my tongue, my observations cast like bets against any hint of romance or adventure I'd imagined. All my life, I've watched my tongue. I've apologized and demurred and only in moments of complete inhibition have I let my words free. There's something intoxicating in the promise of simply letting go. What, after all, do I have to lose?

"I've eaten your food," I remind them. "I've given you my name. I belong to this place now."

Laughter, flinty and breakable as fool's gold, spikes across the clearing. They don't know what to do with my willingness.

"What are rules if not things to be twisted and snapped?" my guide asks.

"You don't know what to do if you're not tricking me," I state, careful not to act as if it's a question to be answered. I see it in the tension holding their neck so straight and rigid. In the line of their jaw. In the way they hold their own illusion even when they've stripped the others of theirs.

My dance partner scowls and snaps their fingers once, restoring the artifice of the party. "I'll make you a deal. Your people, when they stumble into our world, sometimes leave things we can't abide. Hoes, shovels, buckles, and picks. Gather them up and take them back to your world, and we'll give you a place in ours."

I look into their eyes, and I can see both sides of their self—the hollow and the healthy, the rich and ravaged—and I find both equally beautiful. I see myself in them. I could wrap myself in and delve into the depths of their polarities, find myself in the spaces between their words. Perhaps I could find some meaning in the picture of myself I see reflected in their eyes.

"I'll pick up your trash," I tell them, letting a smile play across my lips. "But I want two things in return."

"Greedy," they admonish, but the playful tone has returned to their voice. "You want to live in our world. And?"

"You won't do anything to my mind," I say, choosing my words carefully. "I get to stay as sharp and smart as I am today. And I won't forget my world or my life there, or what happens here."

A covetous, scheming expression blends their two selves into one blazingly beautiful and utterly terrifying creature that seems as though it might be as close to their truth as I'll come this night. I am enraptured.

"Done," they agree. But before they lead me out of the clearing, away from the party, and into the swallowing woods, I put a hand on their forearm, stopping them.

"We're not done," I say.

They look down at my hand, but let it stay there, gently resting on their arm. They ask, "What else could you possibly want?"

"I want to know how long." I swallow, forcing myself to be specific. "How long I'll be picking up your trash."

I can see their calculations in the twitching muscles of their jaw. I like this game of looking for the truth hidden among the distractions of their carefully chosen words.

"A piece for every year you hope to stay and one extra to show remorse for your bad manners," they tell me.

"Are you sure I'm the one with bad manners?" I ask. "My mamaw always told me that it's rude to invite someone into your space and not offer them something to eat or drink. You didn't offer me anything."

"You're trying to rile me up," they observe, and cover my hand with theirs as they lead me out of the clearing.

I spot the first piece of refuse before they point it out. An iron buckle surrounded by yellowed, dying moss. I pluck the buckle from the weeds and put it in my pocket. Within moments the moss blooms out around it, surging back to verdant life.

I put a hand to my heart and simper at them, enjoying the feeling of power I get from transforming this world simply by moving a piece of metal.

"Not me," I say, letting my wickedness show through. It doesn't feel bad to me here, I realize. It's like slipping into a hot bath. I can feel the sting of my meanness, but instead of burning, it sends giddy pleasure surging through my skin. "I wouldn't dare."

I've nothing to lose for being myself here. They chose me for moments they saw me at my worst, and all I've done since I arrived was scoff at their rules. I've eaten their food. I offered them my name. I belong to this place as much as I ever belonged to my family's farm, to the foothills of the Smoky Mountains, to the red dirt and fallow fields and the ancient, whispering springs.

My taunting brings a mischievous glimmer to my guide's lovely face. "You lie so easily. How has anyone ever trusted you?"

I pirouette around a sapling, bending to scoop up a trowel, and stick it into the back pocket of my jeans. "Who says anyone ever has?"

Birdie's face shines bright in my memory for a moment. She trusts me. Trusted me. And I left her holding my drink. Thinking I'd reappear at any moment. I shake loose of the thought. She'll get over it. She's resilient.

Our dance continues like this, teasing its way through the strange-familiar woods with me collecting and them questioning, until I've filled my pockets and hands, tucked bits of iron up against my body, rust itching against my skin and bleeding onto my clothes.

"Where do I take these?" I ask, bracing for the turn, the trick I know must be coming.

I follow them, my hands full of iron, and I wish that I could instead lace my fingers between theirs once again. I'm intoxicated by this being, their moods as changeable as the weather in the hollows and their intentions as veiled as the mountaintops. I can't wait for the endless nights I'll spend with them, surrounded by the Folk in their distorted versions of my mountains. They may have brought me here to amuse themselves, but they've freed me in the process. I don't want to be *nice*. I don't know that I ever did. I just wanted permission to be myself.

The air changes. The scent of gardenias fades, and the sounds of pop radio, laughter, and a crackling fire come roaring toward me like I'm speeding through a tunnel with my windows down. I look for my guide, my dance partner, my teasing negotiator, but I don't see them.

I dump the bits of iron on the grass, empty my pockets, and turn in circles, searching.

I feel hot breath on my neck. Their voice whispers in my ear, "You didn't think we would renege on our promises, did you?"

Answering their question won't serve anyone, so I shimmy past it, turning to face my guide. But their black hair, high cheekbones, and wickedly playful eyes are gone. Instead, I see myself. My rosacea-reddened cheeks, my tight knot of a mouth, my wavy brown hair. I thought they might try to trap me here. I had considered ensuring my return with iron, used as a threat. I'd imagined all the ways that the Folk might make mischief with me. But I hadn't considered that they might take my place.

"What are you doing?" I ask, stumbling over my words. "Why do you look like me?"

"I'm about full up with your questions, my girl," they say, their voice becoming more like mine with each word. "First you demand, then you flatter, and now you quibble with how I choose to meet your terms? Learning some manners might serve you well. Back into the woods, now. Follow your nose, and you'll find your way back."

"And what about you?" I ask. "What are you going to do with my life?"

"If you won't entertain me, perhaps *becoming* you will suit me just as well," they say, and give me a gentle shove back toward the tree line. "Follow your nose."

Before I can argue, they strut toward the flickering light of the bonfire—toward Birdie and Mamaw and a life I thought would forget about me, given enough time. I want to warn them, to let them know that this version of me is an impostor. But I can't. I feel the pull of the mountains, hauling me back into the world I chose.

There are things to love in the world of the Folk. I dance with the star-singers. I laugh with the bear-prodders. I tell stories to the moss-rakers. I play my part. But this choice I made hasn't filled the emptiness I brought here with me.

For a time, I thought that it would be different if I'd been more careful with my words, if I'd found a way to make my dance partner stay, but with time—or perhaps not time, but consideration from behind my smiling mask—I've come to realize that I would feel no different were they here beside me.

I cannot, after all, escape myself.

BLUE AMBER

Anna-Marie McLemore

from the world of *Venom & Vow* by Anna-Marie and Elliott McLemore

Valencia has a habit of impersonating faeries, which, if my friend had ever read a single cuento de hadas, she would know is a ruinously bad idea.

When the ring of mushrooms springs up between our beds, I take it as the faeries' last warning. The purple caps have sprouted up through the ground in a near-perfect circle, gills the color of amethysts, and they have a forbidding glow.

"I have a bad feeling about this," I tell Valencia.

"Then don't eat them," Valencia says. She's in our tent for one of her quick changes, and I know from the look on her face that her mind is already elsewhere. Which I try not to hold against her. After all, I've been distracted myself lately. Nessa has kissed my hand once, and the mist around my thoughts still hasn't cleared. Not that I plan to tell Valencia this. I plan to cease being stupid and lovesick before anyone notices.

Officially, Valencia and I are both guests in an enemy kingdom, both of us attendants to our princess. Unofficially, Valencia is here to uncover the secrets of two murderous princes and, if it comes to it, kill them.

She considers this more pressing than any offense she's caused las hadas, and I wouldn't exactly say she's wrong. But when faeries feel spiteful, they lash out. They thwart. They connive. In recent days, Valencia has been caught once, and nearly been made as a royal spy twice. Yet she fails to see any connection.

Valencia ties her hair into a braid that looks loose but that's anchored tight enough to stay in place. And enough to hold the weight of yet another knife she's slipping into her hair. The blade is thin and gleaming, the handle's gold curling into such delicate whirls that when it goes in, it looks like a hair adornment.

Tonight, she's herself, or at least the demure lady she pretends to be, which means she's going to try to charm information out of people.

Just the kind of work a vindictive faerie would love to sabotage.

"They're called faerie rings for a reason," I tell her. "It's the only advance notice they ever give."

"You worry too much." Valencia grabs her cane, and the quartz globe at the top catches the purple of the mushrooms. "Faeries don't exist."

I can't exactly blame her for thinking that.

For years, so did I.

My mother always told me that when I was very small, a faerie came late one night and blessed me with a mysterious gift.

"What was it?" Even as a little girl I asked this with the bored resignation of a skeptic.

"Oh, mija, I wouldn't know," my mother said. "That's for you to find out."

"Then how do you know it happened?" I asked my mother, and she said that in the morning there was a drop of shining blue amber on my forehead.

My mother's benevolent lie was made even more obvious when she whispered, "But don't tell your sisters. They would be very sad that las hadas didn't come to bless them too."

An unverifiable tale that I had to keep to myself. How convenient.

It was the sort of tale kind mothers told to daughters like me. I was less beautiful than my older sister. I was less witty than my younger sister. And my constant nervousness was blood in the water to both of them. They knew they could ask me—tell me—to grind their masa for them—*You don't mind, do you?*—and then be out the door before I'd summoned the will to object.

How could I blame my mother for making up something she thought might make me feel better about myself?

But by the time I became one of the princess's ladies, I knew my mother hadn't made up anything.

The princess, I've learned, always has about twelve things on her mind at once. This goes double during this visit, which is all tense negotiations and tentative agreements. She's always paying rapt attention to everything, except around those she trusts completely.

I am someone she trusts completely. Which is why she doesn't notice that I not only arrange and perfect her gowns, I change them. Subtly, so it won't be obvious. But I can manipulate the fabric as though I'm moving my hands through water. I shape it as though it's earth beneath my palms. This is how I came to be one of la princesa's ladies, with a hearty recommendation from my mother and a chorus of her friends. *Oh, our Ondina, she's just a sorceress with dresses. You think it doesn't fit or that it doesn't flatter, and then, a few pins here, a sash there, and it's the most beautiful gown any girl has ever worn.*

And I've never been more grateful for this gift than I have been since we arrived here.

The princess sighs at tonight's dress. She knows she has to wear it. If I think the offense of faeries is scathing, I should try snubbing an enemy kingdom's gift.

"Do you think you might be able to work your magic?" she asks.

Once, the word "magic" made me wonder if she knew my secret. Now I know it's simply how she asks nicely.

As I fasten her into the gown, I consider our starting point. It's a shade of silvery blue that's almost right on her, but the cut is completely wrong for the length of her torso, and the flourishes are all in the wrong places. Our hosts have been trying to impress us with parties, and prominent families have been sending la princesa gowns. After all, it never hurts to get on a royal's good side. If a treaty goes through, they figure, they have her favor. If it doesn't, they're only out the cost of the dress.

The gowns are, more often than not, awful. Even if the fabric is good quality, the design pretty enough, it's as though rich men think that you can simply buy a pretty dress and it will work on any girl.

Under my hands, the fabric stretches in some places, contracts in others. Seams shift, buckle, or ease depending on the pressure or give of my fingers. This is how I can do the work of two ladies. This is how my two hands can dress a princess as quickly as four. This is how it's believable that Valencia and I constantly attend to la princesa, when, more often than not, it's just me, and Valencia is off sneaking into places she's not even supposed to know about.

The magic streams out of me like unseen threads, reshaping the dress into the picture that forms in my mind. I cinch it over here, give it more ruffle there, all the while wielding a few pins to give the pretext of ordinary methods. I shift the color only as much as I can get away with. Just a little more purple, to a shade of blue that perfectly accentuates the brown of la princesa's skin and the dark red of her hair.

This whole time, she's been reviewing a potential agreement. The enemy princes probably think she won't even read it, but she's already marking stipulations she doesn't care for. So by the time she looks up and sees herself in the glass, she finds the dress utterly transformed.

She gasps in gentle wonder. "I never know how you do it."

I know it's unladylike to take too much pride in one's work. But I can't help being proud of surprising la princesa, every time.

She's beautiful enough that no one suspects how much I've changed a dress; they simply think it's come to life through the act of her wearing it. And she has enough faith in me that she doesn't realize anyone would need magic to pick up the slack for Valencia.

"And what will you wear tonight?" she asks me with all the delight of a girl conferring with a friend about a first ball.

I shrug at the muted purple dress I have on. It's by far my least favorite of the ones Valencia and I have been gifted since arriving, and that's precisely why I chose it.

"No, you're not," la princesa says, "not if that's the face that goes with it. I command you to put on something that makes you feel magnificent. Borrow something you packed for me. Goodness knows when I'll get to wearing them."

"It wouldn't be right," I say.

She grins. "I'm not afraid of being outshone, if that's what you're worried about."

No one could outshine her. Not just because she is lovely, but because she has the regal bearing of someone who's known from girlhood that she would reign.

"I want to see you in something that makes you feel radiant," she says.

I am in no mood to be radiant.

She searches my face. "Is something bothering you?"

What's bothering me is that our princess brought us to an enemy kingdom, and even if both sides hide it under gifts and courteous formalities, we're all one false move away from throwing daggers at one another.

That, and I feel something I do not want to feel for a girl with hair and eyes the color of xocolatl. A girl from this kingdom I have been raised to despise.

I do not want to look radiant, or magnificent. I do not want Nessa to notice me the way I notice her.

I say none of this. When we are at home, la princesa is my friend. When we are at home, I call her by her given name. When we are here, she is simply la princesa. When we are here, it is not my place to bring my princess my problems.

The first thing I see upon entering the tent is that the faerie ring has thickened. The purple mushrooms have grown pink and teal companions, and I wish Valencia were here right now so I could make her look at this increasingly unsubtle warning about her misdeeds.

Then I realize I wouldn't need the mushrooms.

The figure standing in the middle of them would suffice.

Her brown hair flashes dark gold at certain angles. Her wide, dark eyes seem ready to devour something. Her height startles me, and I'm already used to towering over most other girls. Her filmy wings float around her, appearing and reappearing. One second, they look like spun sugar or threads of gold. The next, they're invisible. The next, they're a lattice of darkness scattered through with pinpoints of light.

This is it. Valencia will finally be called to account. And just as it is my job to cover for her in our work as attendants, it is my job to clean up her mess so she can protect la princesa.

I wish I could do this nobly, with the peaceful acceptance of a saint.

Instead, I do it wanting to wring Valencia's neck, because I've told her, I've told her so many times.

"Name your price," I say, shifting my anger the same way I might shift how a panel of fabric lies. I make my anger sound like resolution.

The faerie's face contracts into an expression of confusion.

"My friend has caused offense," I say. "And I will repay it for her."

"Oh, I'm not here about your friend." The faerie's voice is sweet, but with a bite, like spiced honey. "I'm here for you." Her dark gown ripples like smoke. "I need a dress. One which you are uniquely qualified to craft."

I feel the ground drift out from under me. I have to settle myself back into place, and quickly. Too many questions, or a denial, and I might anger the faerie. Too few, or too quick an admission, and I might find myself tricked into a bargain I didn't even realize I was making.

"What makes you think I can help?" I venture.

No offense shows on the faerie's face. Only a strange fondness. "Who do you think bestowed your gift in the first place?" In a gesture clearly meant to look casual, the faerie plays with the jewel on her neck, a teardrop stone the color of a glacier lake. Blue amber.

I've never told anyone the story my mother told me. Not my sisters. Not la princesa. Not Valencia.

The faerie looks my older sister's age, but now I realize she must be my mother's age, at least.

She twirls the cord, and the blue drop flashes as many colors as an opal. "Wouldn't you like to show me your gratitude?"

She is the reason I can do my job.

She is the reason I can do the work of two princess's ladies.

She is the reason Valencia can do her work without anyone realizing.

I know what I owe this faerie.

The faerie comes forward. She takes my hand, and when she does, I feel those threads of magic streaming from my heart like invisible veins. She sets my fingers against the necklace.

I feel the polish of the amber in the same moment that the tent falls out of my field of vision, like a painting washing away to reveal another underneath.

The faerie and I stand in a forest so thickly leafed I can't tell if it's twilight or if the sun simply can't reach the undergrowth. We've gone somewhere else not only in place but in season. The flame colors of autumn coat the trees. Reds and golds stand alongside deep browns. They shine wet, as if covered in rain.

But the branches and trunks don't look wet. And the colors aren't from leaves. Different shades of resin drip from the beeches and laurels. It drapes pine needles like holiday ribbons. Drops as big as sapodilla fruit weigh down maple and oak branches. It trickles from boughs and collects into pools like ponds of honey.

"Beautiful, isn't it?" The faerie dips her hand into a pool. "And I've never seen anyone else wearing it."

I try to stop my expression shifting into disbelief, but I can feel it playing across my face. "What?"

"If I needed something I could get easily, I wouldn't have bothered you with it," she says.

"I've never made a dress out of anything but cloth before," I say.

"Well, you can't know if you can do something until you do it, now can you?" she says.

The faerie sounds so much like my mother whispering that secret story that I can fairly picture it, a gown crafted out of amber. And the moment I can see it, I feel the light stirring in my chest, and my hands moving toward the glowing pond at my feet.

I pull the resin into thin layers, like stretching a sheet over a bed. I keep the bodice simple, using a tree as a makeshift dress form. But the skirt, the skirt is how I am going to dazzle her.

Again and again, I draw a layer out of the resin pools at the base of the trees, and when each one is as thin as soap bubbles, I twirl it into the petal of a skirt. At first, the task fills every bit of my focus. It's stickier than cloth, breaks as easily as pressed masa, and it's far heavier than the finest velvet. But as I fall into the rhythm of the work, space opens in my thoughts. A question echoes through my head so many times I can't keep myself from asking it.

"Why did you give it to me?"

The faerie wanders through the trees, gathering falling orbs of amber as though they're golden apples. "Your mother has always been good-hearted about my kind. Any who denied our existence, she simply let them continue on as the fools they are, but any who ever had a bad word for us, she wouldn't hear it."

I adjust the layer I'm working with. "Then why me? Why not my sisters?"

"I suppose I have a certain fondness for middle children," the faerie says. "I'm one myself. I have six brothers, you know, three younger, three older. Not a one of them, by the way, thought I had anything to contribute to the ruling of our land. They thought they all knew better than I did."

They already sound like the murderous princes Valencia is out to destroy. I fear the end of this story nearly as much as I want to hear it.

"So when they made new friends with powerful men, when they even invited them to our home, my brothers of course would not hear my concerns." The faerie lifts the hem of her dress, and it looks like mist around her ankles. "At least not until it was too late. Not until their supposed new friends acted as though our home was theirs, as though everything they touched was something they invented, as though everything they gazed upon was something they discovered."

The sense I have of the dress sharpens, like light glancing off a knife.

"But while my brothers made concessions," the faerie says, "while they attempted to placate them, I drove those men out, me along with those who'd known I was right from the beginning. We haunted their very dreams until they feared to close their eyes at night. Now they fear the sight of us. They flee from us. And so my own have chosen me to rule, not any of my brothers." She looks at me in a way that both unsettles and thrills me. It's a look of unguarded vengeance. "So I need a dress not only fit for a faerie queen, but one that reminds both my brothers and our shared enemies of their place. And you're the one who can make it for me."

"But how can that be?" I ask. "If you gave me the magic in the first place, how can you need me for it?"

"The gift I gave you needed you," she says. "Magic can do little on its own. It must be placed properly. The magic haunting those men's dreams drove them mad because of their own greed. And the magic I gave you would have come to nothing if you didn't have the right heart to receive it."

The light stirring in me flares with the thought of the faerie's victory, as brightly as if it were my own. I let my hands write it into this dress. I make it more spectacular and richer in color with every sheet of resin.

By the time I finish, the gown isn't what I first imagined, a voluminous golden rose. Instead, the skirt is dozens of overlapping panels, each tapering to a point.

It's a dress of amber knives.

"Oh," the faerie says when she tries it on. She sounds pleased, delighted even, yet unsurprised. "Yes, this, exactly." She looks like the forest itself, veiled in sheer resin. The pale and deep, dark and bright, yellow and white alongside blue-green and deep brown look like a stained glass window.

She nods at me. "Well, go on. There's plenty."

I look at her, uncomprehending.

She laughs. "Make one for yourself. Don't you have a ball tonight?"

Now it's my turn to laugh. I'm having enough trouble pretending not to notice Nessa, and if I swan into the castle in an amber gown, I'll be spending the whole night noticing whether she's noticing me. That I'm even thinking of her name is proof that I haven't put her where she belongs, among countless other enemies.

"No," I say. "Thank you, though."

The faerie sighs. "As you choose." She takes my hand and puts it back on the amber necklace. The forest around us drips away like resin off the trees, and we're back where we began.

Or at least, I am. The faerie has vanished. I'm alone in the meadow just beyond our tents.

The last of the falling sun glances off the river. The water looks like crystals and candlelight. It looks like amber. The magic in me stirs again, and for an awful, anxious few seconds I wonder if I've forgotten some detail on the faerie's dress. But it's a new image forming at the back of my mind, a dress that looks made of water.

If that faerie hadn't done what seemed impossible, everything she loved would have been lost.

If she can do that, I can kneel by the river and dip my hands into the water. I can feel layers of a dress emerging from the current. I can do something that just yesterday I thought impossible.

For once, I don't worry if anyone wonders how I've done it. I simply walk into the hall and let them marvel at the work of my hands. My skirt flows around me in greens and blues and grays, as though I've spun it from the sea.

La princesa catches my eye with a nod of *That's more like it*, and I give her a little curtsy of gratitude. I let the enemy princes wonder if la princesa has a sorceress for an attendant. I let Valencia wonder what I've been doing instead of the other way around.

I look for the girl in the earth-dark trousers and the pressed green shirt. Nessa stares at me like I'm a mermaid and she's a lovesick sailor, and for once, when she looks at me, I don't look away.

Whatever the murderous princes of this kingdom have done, I cannot hold an entire kingdom to account for it. I cannot count Nessa as my enemy when I barely know her. And I can handle my enemies, including her, if she turns out to be one. A flash of amber in the corner of my vision confirms it, as though the faerie is laughing and it's fluttering the amber knives of her skirt.

I go up to Nessa. I ask her to dance without saying a word. I simply hold out my hand to her, como una sirena beckoning a sailor into the sea.

REVELRY

Kwame Mbalia

No one stopped Sei and his buddies from dragging me down the beach. I'm not sure anyone could if they wanted to. The crowd of teens were lost in a fury of dance and excitement that bordered on rage. I'd never seen anything like this. In the whirling sand and the spinning shadows, there were no individuals—just a writhing, seething beast with a thousand arms and legs, roaring into the black of night. Even Sei's goons looked at them nervously.

The Hour of Ozu had come.

When I was ten, my grandfather warned my brother and me about the beautiful ones.

I listened. My brother didn't.

At a time when the world was young, my grandfather would say, *two immortals fought over a gift from the gods. The winner renamed himself Ozu,*

Lord of Lords, and his followers the Avakir, the Court of Dreams. The losers he named Jaakir, and cursed them as the Court of Nightmares. And the gift they fought over?

Humans.

Both sides raided our villages, our towns, and our cities, while still fighting among themselves. Finally, the leader of the Avakir, Ozu, defeated and banished the Jaakir. But one of his own sided with the Jaakir. Ozu's sister. She abandoned her family, cast aside her titles, and kept only the blade she forged herself, the flame of truth embedded within.

To this day, my grandfather would whisper, *she and her brother still fight over our blood. Our vitality. It nourished them, and the only thing they valued more was that vitality in their service. In exchange, humans received a boon.*

But after centuries of cursed gifts, misspoken wishes, and lies hidden in truth, we realized that very few boons were worth the cravings of the Avakir. Humans fought back, until attacks by the beautiful ones became rarer and rarer. So much so that, over time, we mostly forgot about them—except for the last hour of the longest day of the year. That hour was called the Hour of Ozu, and a festival was always held then, as much a prayer as it was a celebration. Only teenagers were allowed, the soon-to-be adults, because the vitality of youth was irresistible. Our town still held it, centuries later, even if most didn't remember why. It was an offering. A ritual to ward off the Avakir and beg for protection from Jaakir raids. We islanders danced our way to the coves beneath the lightning cliffs ringing our beaches, playing music and singing loudly to the sea. The story goes that if worthy, instead of feasting on our blood, the beautiful ones would become enamored with our dancing.

But, my grandfather would always say, leaning in and lowering his voice, *never lose yourself. Never eat their offerings. And you always have to wear a mask during the Hour of Ozu.*

The Avakir and Jaakir still craved our vitality. Our blood. If they chanced to look upon our faces, nothing—not war, not death, not the gods themselves—could stop them from claiming one they desired.

I remembered my grandfather's story when my brother went missing during last year's festival. This year's festival was scheduled for tonight. I loved my brother. I hated the Avakir for what they stole from me.

I knew what I had to do to get him back.

"This wasn't mentioned in the instructions," Djari whispered to me as the blindfolds went over our eyes. A hand grasped my wrist and pulled me forward, but I was so preoccupied by what else I was wearing that I didn't pay them any attention.

"Relax," I said, trying to adjust my shorts. They kept rising up as we climbed the rocky path, and I was trying not to fall flat on my face. Djari was one of my two best friends, but the boy could complain like he was getting paid to do it. "I'll go in hog-tied if they want. They'll be talking about tonight for *years*."

"Who's they?" Djari muttered. "The news? After I fall to my death?"

I tugged at my shorts one more time, then sighed. "I'm more worried about why I have to wear these shorts. Are these for toddlers? They're so tiny!"

"Chill," a third voice said, laughing to my left. Kaleb, my other best friend. "No whining. Besides, all the girls love thick thighs, and no disrespect to Djari, but his toothpick legs ain't reeling them in."

"Thick thighs save lives, it's true," Djari said happily.

"For your thighs only," Kaleb added.

"All thighs on me," I said, putting my own pun out there before pausing. "Wait . . ."

"Nope, too late. Bring 'em here, big boy."

I shook my head, then realized they couldn't see me anyway. "Y'all—"

"Before you whine again, look," Djari interrupted, and yanked off my blindfold. True to description, he was rail-thin, practically swimming in his trunks. Kaleb was bigger, his tan skin exposed as he pulled his shorts as high as legally possible. Both were on my high school's wrestling team with me, so we were used to tight uniforms. But they must've switched my trunks with Djari's, because they were by far the shortest, clinging to my legs like I was a chocolate life preserver. We were in said trunks—and I was excited—because the festival we definitely were not supposed to be at was on a hidden beach where the shallows were the dance floor. To keep the location a secret, all attendees had to be blindfolded and led by a guide.

I was also excited because my grandfather's stories echoed in my ears, and I saw hints of this *otherness* layered on top of the real world. Like the tall woman who was our guide. When we took off the blindfolds, she stood on a cliff-top plateau overlooking the sea. A tunnel we must've walked through was behind us and another waited in front of us. The woman wore her own tantalizingly short swimsuit and stood near the second tunnel's entrance, and I couldn't tear my eyes away from her. I mean, she was a vision, seven feet tall at least. Her dark brown legs and stomach were painted in swirls of silver and she wore a mask carved in the shape of a nymph. Her soft eyes narrowed mischievously as I noticed the small horns curling from above the ears. The mask stopped just above her mouth, which quirked expectantly.

Djari nudged me, then handed over a mask.

"Did you see the horns?" I murmured.

"What horns?" he asked. "On your mask? They're cool. Now shut up and let me seduce her."

I slid on the mask I was handed, a stag with majestic antlers carved from some hardwood. The nymph smiled at me as she ignored Djari's advances, as if she had listened to our conversation. In fact, I was sure she had heard it. My grandfather's stories echoed in my ears as the nymph's eyes met my own, but instead of making me nervous, it only made my resolve stronger. There would be a moment tonight, an opportunity, when the chance to break through the veil of otherness would present itself. I would be ready. I *had* to be ready, and when the time came, I would get a boon tonight, and I would find my brother.

The nymph motioned for us to follow, then, with a twirl of her hips, disappeared into the tunnel entrance. We all looked at one another, then scrambled after her.

"This is wild," Djari said, walking with me as Kaleb tried his luck at flirting with the nymph. "I've heard the stories. I mean, everyone's heard the stories, but . . . how did *you* find this?"

A memory of my brother, Jameson, sneaking out of our room last year, making me promise not to tell anyone, flashed in my mind. Another memory followed—my mother, tearful, as she filled out a missing person's report. My grandfather's picture on the mantel, staring at me. Accusing me.

I shrugged away the reminders. "Heard about it from a friend," I said.

"I'm glad your moms let you go out tonight. After . . ." His voice trailed off awkwardly. My friends knew about Jameson and how tight we were. Are. How tight we *are*. What they didn't know is that my mother didn't let me go. She never would've let me, and she was asleep on the couch when I sneaked out. By the time she woke up, I'd be back with my brother.

Hopefully.

"I'm surprised *you* decided to come," I said, switching the subject. "Did you ever talk to Sei like I told you?"

Djari winced. I loved him, but the boy had a weakness for a pretty face. *Especially* pretty faces already in relationships. All week he kept bragging about a new girl who couldn't keep her hands off him, only for us to find out yesterday morning that she was our wrestling captain's girlfriend. I wrestled Sei Lewis once. Only once. I could still feel the sensation of my shoulder nearly popping out of my socket after I pinned him. Sei could be a lot of things, but forgiving wasn't one of them. Word around town was he ripped a locker door off its hinges when he found out about Djari and his girl. I'd been trying to broker peace ever since. Not that lover boy cared.

"No, but I will. On everything." He crossed his heart and pulled on his own mask. "Tomorrow. Tonight, I'm not even worried. No one's going to know who I am, and we're going to have the time of our lives."

He skipped off (yes, skipped) to catch up with Kaleb, who'd reached the tunnel exit. It was a ten-foot drop to the beach below, our guide waving us through. As I passed and her fingers trailed along my back, our eyes met. I wondered if Jameson took this same route. If she touched his shoulders, too. If, as I did, a thought popped into his head. A question.

"How do we get back up when it's time to leave?" I asked.

The nymph smiled. "Why would you want to leave?"

The beach was a beautiful storm. Torches circled the shallows, a submerged sandbar serving as the dance floor, and shadows flickered on the water as everyone splashed about in a frenzy. The air was electric as musicians played drums, shekeres, and wind flutes on an elevated platform. Dancers in half-masks, full masks, and horns of every kind swayed and twirled and pressed against one another to the rhythm. More nymphs slipped through the crowd holding platters of fizzing drinks, berries topped with cream, and frozen ice spheres with pockets of citrus inside that melted into a tantalizing sticky mess when passed between the lips.

And my god, the lips.

Everyone kissed everyone. It was a game, or a competition. In the orange glow of the torches it felt like I'd entered a dream. A dancer in a swan mask climbed onto the stage and kissed a drummer, who laughed as he pushed her back into the crowded shallows. A sea of hands passed her overhead while she screamed with laughter, only to try again a few moments later. The flutist blew a kiss to two bare-chested boys in lion masks. A tiny antlered sprite snagged Djari's lower lip between her own, while Kaleb divided his eager attention between a doe and a stag. And the nymphs . . . the nymphs poured drinks, passed out more citrus spheres, and whispered in the ears of everyone.

Wait.

I squinted at Djari, then swore under my breath. The sprite he was kissing had her mask lifted up on her forehead, revealing her face, and I recognized the girl—Sei's girlfriend. I swore again and stepped forward, only to be yanked back in the nick of time as a giant, bare-chested boy in a stag mask barreled past me, knocking over several dancers as he rushed by with a hand clamped firmly over his mouth.

"Careful!"

I turned to see a silver snake staring at me. It took me a second to shake out of the confusion and realize it was a mask, and a marvelous one at that. It covered the top half of the wearer's face where silver tears were engraved beneath the eyeholes, before slanting to the right of their nose and ending in the shape of a curved dagger, the point on the side of their chin. My gaze continued down until I realized the person was wearing the thinnest of gossamer dresses that clung to all the wrong places . . . places I definitely shouldn't be looking at while I wore these shorts. I jerked my gaze up to find hazel eyes narrowed and gold-dusted lips twisted into a slight smirk.

"Find what you were looking for?"

"Sorry," I said, flustered and backing up. "I didn't mean . . ."

She laughed, clearly delighted by my inability to string words together. "Oh, you meant to look, but it's fine . . . this time."

"Seriously, I'm normally not this . . ." I paused.

"Blatant?" she suggested.

"Disrespectful."

The girl put her hands on her hips. "The kissing really threw you for a loop, huh?" She turned to survey the mob of dancers drunk off mysterious spheres and vibes, then pursed her lips, an act my traitorous body found absolutely fascinating. Ridiculous shorts. Never should have worn them.

"I can't blame you," she continued. "I would be terrified of all those bodies pressing against me, grinding, holding me hostage as the music turned everyone around me into monsters. Beautiful, mesmerizing monsters. That would be terrible."

I clenched a fist and swallowed, hating how her words held more than one meaning, and the way my mind conjured images to accompany them. She was doing it on purpose. I cleared my throat. "I need to find my friends."

"No," she said, turning back to me and pouting. "Stay."

"I can't. One of them can't say no to trouble, and trouble is about to punch him in the face."

"And you're the only one who can help?"

I blew out a puff of frustration. "Sometimes it sure feels like it."

"Here." She stepped past me to take a citrus sphere from a passing nymph, winking at them. "The realms of gods and mortals will not cease to exist just because a single boy took one second to relax. Especially a boy"—she glanced down—"with nice thighs. Would you like to share?"

The realms of gods and mortals?

If I was out of sorts before, I was definitely thrown for a loop when she placed the sphere between her lips and raised an eyebrow. The crowd and the noise faded away as the only thing filling my vision was this mysterious girl in a snake mask. Warning bells went off in my mind as she stepped closer, the ripples of the shallows wrapping my ankles.

"I shouldn't," I said, trying to back up, but she kept pace with me.

"Just a taste," she said.

"I—"

She moved so close to me I could feel the chill of the citrus sphere, and I let her. The cold was immediately followed by the warmth of her lips closing on mine. The sphere melted, sticky and sweet and sour all at once, almost pushing my senses toward a cliff, and the kiss sent me hurtling over the edge.

The world began to disappear. Jameson began to disappear. But no, I was here to get him back.

I groaned and took a step back and tugged at my shorts. I couldn't do this. Couldn't lose focus. And based on how *painfully* obvious it was that I needed to dunk myself in the sea or find a dark corner to count to seven hundred, I'd say I was definitely close to losing focus. I pivoted toward the tunnel in the cliffs, just to clear my head, only to swear under my breath in disbelief.

Sei and three boys from our wrestling team stood outside the tunnel entrance, arms folded and glaring. Of course he'd be here. It looked like the whole town was. Still, it was a shock seeing him. They all wore forest-green wolf masks, though Sei's was atop his forehead as he scanned the crowd. A nymph flitted by, but a comment from Sei sent her scurrying back into the crowd. Not that he noticed—when I followed his gaze, my heart rate shot up. He'd found what he was looking for.

Djari now sat on the shoulders of one of the lion-masked partiers as he flung citrus spheres into the crowd, Sei's girlfriend on someone else's shoulder beside him. His mask was up as he laughed before tossing her a sphere, and I turned back to the cliffs to see Sei pull his wolf mask over his face and stalk into the crowd, his cronies following him.

"Shit," I muttered. "Shit shit shit." But when I started to head to the throng of madness, a hand gripped my wrist.

"Don't go," the girl in the snake mask warned.

"I wish I had a choice," I muttered.

I pulled away and plunged into the crowd. Her reply was nearly lost beneath the music. Later I'd have all the time in the world to think about what she meant, but at the moment, I ignored it and went to help my friend.

She'd said, "I wish you did, too."

I was swamped immediately. Masked dancers shouted in my ear, grabbed my arms and my face and my hips as they threw themselves side to side. The spirit of the celebration coursed through everyone around me, and I could feel the energy rolling off them. It would be so easy to lose myself in the madness. Let the thrill carry me off to places unknown. Is this what Jameson found last year? Did he lose himself? Did the ocean claim him, like some people thought? Did he run away with a nymph who traded him sweet delicacies and kisses? Or did something else happen? Something that reminded me about the danger of the Hour of Ozu, and how time was of the essence.

As I pressed toward Djari, the crowd pulsed, almost as one. It wasn't hard to imagine some powerful being arriving at any second, masked like everyone else, pulling their chosen aside like lovers sneaking into the dark of the tunnels, draining them of will and vitality with a kiss, a bite, a nibble across the soul or however it was done, whispers of how to claim their boon the last thing they heard. The flickers of lightning across the face of the cliffs, the pounding rhythm in the sand, the meeting of eyes tucked behind masks—it all combined to drive out the normal world and welcome in madness.

"Jahai?"

A hand grabbed my shoulder, and Djari peered up at me. I blinked at the waves lapping at my feet. I was on the other side of the crowd. When had I—

"You okay?" Djari asked.

I started to ask him how I got there, then forced the question aside and yanked off my mask. That could wait. "I am, but you won't be. Sei is here, and he brought backup."

My friend's eyes went wide and he started to turn to look, but I gripped him tight and shoved my mask in his hands. "Take this. Put it on and give me yours."

Djari looked at the obsidian face, confused. "But—"

"No time, just grab Kaleb and get out of here. I'll meet you in the Cookout parking lot by the high school once I laugh in Sei's face. Now go!"

I pushed him gently back into the crowd, snatching his mask from his hands as he stumbled back, and after a moment's hesitation he pulled on the one I'd given him. I watched him weave through the dancing masses and toward the cliff tunnels for as long as I could until I lost sight of him, and then a flash of green caught my eye. A wolf mask. I slipped on Djari's bird half-mask and reentered the crowd, arms up as if I was dancing.

"That was nicely done," someone shouted into my ear.

The girl with the snake mask swayed next to me, her lips once more twisted into that knowing smirk. I groaned but kept scanning the crowd for Sei. The sharp, triangular ears of the wolf masks knifed through the crowd like sharks scenting blood.

"You know, if you danced you would be less obvious," the girl said.

"Don't you have someone else to annoy," I shouted back, but there wasn't much heat in the words because hers rang true.

"Nope! You'll do. You'll do nicely."

"Lucky me," I said to myself.

I don't know how she heard but she laughed and grabbed my arms, pulling me closer as she turned around and resumed swaying her hips to the frenetic drumbeat. "Oh, shut up and dance, or do you want them to realize you're not who they're looking for?"

My teeth ground together, not only because her hips were brushing against me—shooting fire through my skin and up along my spine with every glancing touch, rooting me to the spot, breaths coming in short gasps—but also because she was right. Djari needed more time to escape. My hands rose to circle her waist, and she glanced back over her shoulder, smirk still twisting her lips as she grabbed the hem of my shorts and pulled my hips closer to hers.

Everything else faded away. Only the music remained, along with this girl whose name I didn't know and who knew more about me than

I was probably comfortable with. Something nagged at me to remain focused, that I was here for a reason, but the way she moved and how my body responded on its own . . . it was addicting.

She swayed. I swayed.

She dipped and I followed.

Dancing was a game of chase, or tag, two reflections syncing their movements, one we played tentatively at first as we learned each other's rhythm. But as the drums roared and the shekeres beckoned and the flutes laughed, we grew more confident, and what she threw I caught, where she went I followed.

She tossed her hair and twisted in my arms so we were now face-to-face.

I grabbed her hands and lifted them high in the air, then wrapped them around my neck.

Our hips found rhythm.

Behind our masks, my eyes found hers.

She leaned in—rising on her toes so that our cheeks were level, so close I could feel each shape her lips formed, her teeth as they grazed the side of my neck—and whispered:

"This was just getting interesting."

And then a hand gripped my shoulder and yanked me around.

Sei.

There was an outcropping of stone jutting out from the lightning cliffs at the southern end of the cove, and that's where Sei and his henchmen took me. My handlers shoved me forward, and I stumbled to the sand at Sei's feet. He stared up at the cliffs, squeezing and twisting at his mask he was holding.

"You couldn't keep your raggedy hands to yourself," he said.

The two wrestlers on either side of me stepped back, but I remained hunched over on the sand. Djari was nearly a head shorter than me, and as soon as I stood the game was over. But if I could milk this confrontation for as long as possible, it only guaranteed Djari's escape. Finding Jameson would have to wait a little longer. So I wobbled a bit on my knees and grunted, as if I'd taken whatever it was the nymphs were handing out.

Sei made a noise of disgust in his throat. "Look at you. I don't know what Alayna sees in you. Just a stand-in to make me jealous."

He finally dropped into a squat to look at me. He frowned. This was it, then. "Wait . . ."

I feigned a groan again and sat back, pretending to look around in confusion. "This . . . this isn't the party. Where'm I?"

Sei glared, then reached forward and ripped off Djari's mask. "Jahai?"

I pretended to let my head loll forward, then squinted at Sei. "Sei? Issat you? Where's . . . where's Djari? He was gonna get another bead from the nymph. The cute one, did you see her? So cute . . ."

Sei stood and fury twisted his face. "Get him up," he said, his voice shaking with anger. "NOW!"

The two wrestlers leaped into action, yanking me up by my arms and pinning them behind my back. Out of the corner of my eye the third wrestler turned and stared. There was something . . . off in their movement. And in their eyes. I had no time to puzzle it out because Sei grabbed my chin in his hand and leaned in close.

I played for time and continued to squint. "Sei? Where's Djari?"

"I am asking you the same thing. Why are you wearing his mask?"

He stepped back, releasing my chin, and I racked my mind for an excuse.

"He . . . said we were going to find some nymphs and play the kissing game," I said, trying to remember the explanation I came up with on the fly. "Have you tried those ice things the nymphs are passing out? It's like—"

"I know what it's like," he snapped. He frowned again, and I thought about the crowd again, racing to remember how they acted. I sagged in the wrestlers' arms, the shift of weight nearly sending us all to the ground. They jerked me upright and I let my head loll again.

Sei growled in impatience. "You're a slob. I knew you didn't have it in you. No discipline. When Coach hears about this, you know you're off the team, right?"

That struck home. Luckily, my head was lolled to the side, so Sei couldn't see the flash of anger on my face. I'm sure he would've seen through my ruse at that moment. Instead, after a few seconds, he stepped past me to the third wrestler, the lookout. After a whispered conversation, the lookout left, returning a minute later with something clutched in their gloved hands. They passed it to Sei, who walked back to stand in front of me.

"Well, let's make sure you get what you came for. I don't want any doubts when I show pictures to Coach on Monday. Here."

He grabbed my right hand and dropped something into it. I didn't have to look down at it to know what it is. The cold bit into my skin, colder than I even expected, and it felt wrong. All wrong. And yet that was nothing compared with the aroma that suddenly filled my nostrils.

Otherness.

Cinnamon and cloves. Salt and iron.

Blood and bile.

It took everything in me not to immediately hurl the ice sphere across the sand. This was what I was looking for. The otherness. What my grandfather's stories warned me about. It had to be.

But why now? I'd already had one earlier when the girl with the serpent mask kissed me. What was different about this sphere?

"I'm starting to see the real you." Sei's tone was light, but it didn't match the hard, flat gaze he turned on me, eyes flicking from my hand holding the nymph ice sphere, back to my face. "Well? Isn't this what you wanted?"

I hesitated. Jameson's face flashed in my mind and my grandfather's warning whispered in my ears—never lose control . . . never eat their fruit. Is this what happened to my brother? One slipup, one dance and one sphere shared with a stranger in a mask, and he was lost to the world? I could turn back now if I wanted. Pretend to sober up, claim I was misled by Djari. Jameson would have wanted me to be smart.

But Jameson wasn't here. He left for the Hour of Ozu last year and never returned, and I needed to find out why.

"Eat it . . . now," Sei said. His eyes glittered. He wanted me to admit I was lying. I could see it. He was calling my bluff. Little did he know how he was helping me. How badly I'd searched for this opportunity. So I smiled woozily at him and tossed the fragile ice treat into my mouth.

"No need to rush, Sei! We can get you some and—" I paused as the ice didn't melt in my mouth so much as completely disappear, leaving a fragile knotted bead of sweetgrass in my mouth. I looked up, confused. "This isn't—" I began to say, just as the third wrestler, the lookout who'd remained silent to this point, looked over in alarm.

"WAIT," they shouted, startling both me and Sei with the sound of their voice. It was like a boat being dragged across sand. Raspy. Harsh.

And as he pulled up his mask, revealing a hawkish brown face underneath, it occurred to me that his horns had remained in place.

Because they weren't a part of the mask. "HE'S BEEN CLAIMED, DON'T LET HIM—"

Whatever the wrestler was about to say was lost as, in the confusion, the other two dropped me, and I accidentally crushed the bead of sweetgrass between my teeth and pain like I've never felt before ripped across my skull.

My vision was a kaleidoscope.

Faces fragmented between normal and grotesque. Smiles and teeth and horns. Masks morphed into faces and flickered back. Whispers and shouts and screams. Torch flames expanded into bonfires, then infernos, before shrinking into sparks that drifted around me in a whirlwind. Sei and his friends ran away screaming as a wolf and a dragon chased them. No. That had to be the sphere's influence. I couldn't tell what was real and what wasn't.

Meanwhile, the drums and horns and singing increased in tempo until it sounded like boots marching and armies chanting. I grabbed my skull with both hands and shoved my face into the sand at my feet, screaming into the earth for it to stop, for everything to stop, just for a moment so I could breathe free of madness.

A hand gripped my shoulder and pulled me upright, as if I weighed nothing. A horned wolf lifted my chin with a claw. The brown face seemed familiar. The third wrestler? They weren't . . . human? "This one has a touch of silver in the blood."

I moaned. "This isn't real, this isn't real, this isn't real."

A giant nymph walked over to examine me. The guide who led us to the party, only now she was a giantess with arms like boulders and hair that drifted down to her waist. She slapped the wolf's claw aside and lifted me, her face as big as my torso. "Easy," she rumbled. "You don't want to scare it."

"You're both going to send him into a coma if you don't move out of the way. Give him to me." A third voice, a familiar voice, came from behind me, and the giantess turned me around but continued to prop me upright, an act that—somewhere deep inside me where sanity still ruled—I was thankful for. But the sight before me threatened to send me back into mental spasms.

A girl clad in a silver form-fitting tunic and matching pants, carrying a long, narrow dagger with a ruby embedded in the hilt, stood in the shadow of the cliff tunnel entrance. Like the wolf and the giant, she also had horns, tufted antlers no bigger than a fawn's, and I realized I recognized them. When she stepped out onto the cove's shoreline and into the light of the moon, her eyes met mine, and her lips quirked in a familiar half-smile.

"You?" I breathed. "The snake mask?"

It was the girl I'd danced with on the beach, except she was . . . different. Less human. More dangerous. More beautiful.

She smiled. Her twists were gathered behind a silver circlet pushed high on her head, and she twirled one with her free hand as she stepped closer before dropping into a squat so her face was inches from mine.

"I told you not to go," she said, almost apologetically.

"I had to," I said, gasping for air as another wave of pain threatened to split my skull.

She nodded. "You did, didn't you? I don't know if that makes you brave or a fool."

"My grandfather used to say the brave have a touch of the fool in their soul—"

"And the fool a touch of the brave." The nymph grinned. "Yes, I know that quote, too."

The giantess beside me cocked her head as the tempo on the beach increased again. "Nadira, we have to leave soon. Your brother will be here at any minute, and if he sees you the treaty is over."

The girl—Nadira—sighed, then stood. "The treaty was over when Ozu started his little hunts."

"Nadira," the wolf rumbled.

"Fine. Let's go. Find the muscle-heads and drop them in the tunnel. They'll wake up with a headache, but they should be fine."

Somewhere in the fog of my thoughts I realized she must've meant Sei and the other two goons.

"And him?" The giantess tilted her head at me. She easily stood over all of us, but deferred to Nadira, and again something tickled my memory, as if to say I should know who she was.

Nadira studied me, the point of her dagger tapping against her thigh. The ruby winked as it caught the moonlight, a trick of the bezel causing me to imagine a flame burned inside. Almost like it was trapped in the jewel.

And that's when I remembered.

"But one of the Avakir sided with the Jaakir," I said. The words fell out of my lips. "She abandoned her family, cast aside her titles, and kept only the blade she forged herself, the flame of truth embedded within. Soldier. Conqueror. Queen."

With each word Nadira stepped closer, her eyes narrow and the dagger aimed at my heart. The giantess growled and the wolf gnashed her teeth. I snapped my mouth shut, cutting off the rest of the story my grandfather would tell, and his words rattled around my foolish skull.

Don't lose control.

"Choose me," I whispered. "That's why you're here, right? To feed? I volunteer, if you'll take me to my brother, or tell me where he is. Give me a boon, please."

"Who are you to make demands of me? Not everything you hear is the truth, little boy," Nadira finally said, standing in front of me so I had to gaze upward at her. She still wore a smile, but it didn't reach her eyes. "My people are hungry. Who are you to place your burdens at my feet?"

I swallowed. "Then let me just find my brother, and then I'm yours."

She paused. "Excuse me?"

"My brother, Jameson. He disappeared at last year's festival. Help me find him, and I'll . . . serve you. Isn't that an option? Instead of eating me or something?" I was seriously hoping my grandfather hadn't been embellishing the stories he told me.

She rolled her eyes. "Boy, we don't eat you. I don't know why everyone always assumes that."

I offered up my arm, palm outstretched. "Still. Try me. I'll go with you. Serve you. Just . . . help me. Please."

"We're not thieves, stealing boys in the night," Nadira snapped. "I'm not my brother."

Both hands were raised now. "Please."

The drumming was frenetic now as Nadira squatted in front of me again. Near the tunnel her companions pulled their masks back on. Instantly, the giantess shrank several feet until she was just a tall girl with powerful shoulders and a nymph mask, and the wolf was a slender girl with red curls behind a sapphire mask.

Nadira gently lifted my chin with her thumb and forefinger. Her eyes stared into mine and I didn't look away, even as I felt the sharp prick of her dagger on my palm. Even as she brought my finger to her lips and the rest of the world fell away. No drums, no companions, no moon, and no sea. Just her. And me.

"Speak your offer," she commanded.

"Save my brother," I whispered. "Please."

"And in return?"

"I . . ." I licked my lips. "I'll be yours for a month."

"No," Nadira said. "Not good enough."

"Two months?"

"A year and a day."

My entire senior year. My wrestling scholarship opportunity. My friends. Mom. My life on hold, with the possibility that I'd never live long enough to return to see any of them.

Jameson.

I swallowed. "A year and a day."

Nadira stared at me for a moment longer, then stood. She still held my chin, gently, and after a breathless heartbeat, she nodded. She bent at the waist, her twists falling over me like a curtain sheltering this moment from the world, and she touched her lips to mine. The kiss, no more than a glancing touch of her lips, was salty and searing, but the words she whispered branded themselves letter by letter into my memory—a promise and a curse.

"I will help you bring your brother back to your world," she breathed against my cheek, "and you will kill my brother in mine."

LA TIERRA DEL OLVIDO

Zoraida Córdova

Palizada, Ecuador—1953

Every morning, Maria Soledad watched the world stand still.

Out there, banano and cacao exports fueled new wealth into the country. Past fields of tall grass and roads that led to the cities, like a network of muddy arteries, the world was allowed to change. That world was a fairy tale of new cars, new buildings, new fashion.

In the rice paddies tucked deep into the countryside, Maria Soledad didn't know the concept of new in the same way. The youngest of five daughters, everything she owned once belonged to someone else, from her first name to her worn leather sandals to her training brassiere.

Even the shape of her life had already been arranged. Like Maria Rosaria, Maria Carmen, Maria Azulita, and Maria Luisa (God rest her soul), the youngest Morán sister was expected to marry before eighteen, have children by twenty, if not sooner. She would make three meals a day, while still tilling the soil when her hands were free. She'd clean the house, and hang the clothes, though if she were lucky like her sisters, she'd be able to hire a servant girl from the nearby village.

Maria Soledad didn't want the same life as her sisters, but her days were too busy to worry yet. Every morning she woke up, sticky with sweat. She set water to boil for coffee and rice. Collected eggs, still warm and flecked with white droppings. Swept, dusted, laundered. She took care of her poor widowed mother, whose back resembled the rusted sickles they used to cut weeds.

At sixteen, Soledad was taller than her sisters, and broad from hours of laboring over their small plot of land, though every free moment she got, she swam in the muddy stream that ran beside her house.

On this ordinary day, Soledad's world, which normally stood still, shifted, though she wouldn't realize it just yet.

She was busy swimming in the cool stream. There was nothing there but wild grass and wilder insects. Mosquitoes had learned that Soledad was not sweet, so they did not bite her. The stream was the only reprieve from the thick, humid air, and calmer than the Vinces River on the other side of the pond.

Soledad raced the yellow and spotted fishes that hid in the reeds. They were still too small to catch for dinner, but in a few weeks she'd bring out her net. She was about to surface for air when she noticed a strange patch of blue. Turquoise, really. She had no reason to fear what lived in the stream. She knew the green places around her house. She knew the frogs and snakes and spiders, and they knew her. But she did not know this creature, this blue thing snared in a net. Long limbed, pale hair moving like grass in the current. *Human*, she thought, *but more*. She'd watched fishermen bring in large catches, but none as big and strange as this one. Without thinking of the consequences, Soledad knew she could not let anyone else happen upon this creature.

She swam to it. Grabbed the net with both hands and heaved it to the surface like a sack of rice. The creature was larger than she'd anticipated and thrashed against her help.

"Stop it!" Soledad warned. "Before someone less kind tries to claim you!"

It growled in response. It was, of course, a fairy. Though she'd only heard about them from stories, she knew in her racing heart that this was what she'd found. It had to be.

"I know what you are," Soledad said, reaching for the things she'd left in the dry grass. She found the tiny knife she carried everywhere and unsheathed the blade.

The fairy bared his teeth. "You don't know half as much as you think you do."

Soledad's mother called her name from the house.

"Shhh!" Soledad lowered her voice. "Now you've done it."

"Let. Me. Go," he seethed.

"I'm *trying*, but if you don't stop moving, I'm going to accidentally cut off some of your pretty green hair or maybe a finger."

The fairy sat up, as much as the net would allow. He blinked through the hair matted to his face, and seemed to understand she was his only hope. "Very well."

Soledad tried not to stare, in case she *did* cut something off, and she sawed at the tough fisherman's rope until there was a hole big enough for the fairy to break through.

She would have thought it a human boy her age from the local parishes. His bronzed brown skin was dusted with mossy and gold freckles. The turquoise sheets of his hair were already drying pin straight. He had a beautiful nose, curved like a hawk, and full lips that glistened when he licked the stream water off them.

"Get on with it," he practically snarled at her, picking limp blades of grass off his taut naked torso.

Soledad quickly scanned the area. She was in a soaked shift, practically naked herself. If her mother caught her, she'd whip Soledad's backside until she couldn't walk. Fear twisted in her belly, not at the impossible fairy creature, but at what would happen if she was seen.

Only the promise of his words knocked some sense into her. *Get on with it.* In her mind, she scoured everything she knew about faeries. There were the old spirits that were born out of this land. There were also the new spirits that sneaked aboard ships over the centuries. All those stories told her that if she caught a fairy, she could ask it for a wish in exchange for its freedom.

He kicked the net away from his long legs. His shorts had no seams or buttons or zippers. The material hugged his musculature, and reminded Soledad of waxy palm leaves and moss instead of any fabric she'd ever seen.

"Well?" he asked, exasperated.

"Well, I don't know." She tucked her knees against her chest to cover the sheer material and kept her knife in one fist. "I've never met one of you before."

"One of what?"

"The people of the hills. The fields. Wild things."

He grimaced at her. "The only wild things I've ever known are your kind."

"There's no need to be rude."

"Then give me your wish and let me be on my way." His dark eyes took in her tanned cheeks, red from the heat and from seeing a boy so *naked* even if he wasn't a human exactly. "I assume you wish for a rich husband. Or better yet, that your land will always yield plentiful no matter the season."

"What do other people wish for?" Soledad was so overwhelmed with possibility that it was all she could think to ask.

"Others wish for something to possess," he said, less angry and more defeated. "Land. People. They'd possess the wind and clouds themselves if they could be grasped."

"What do I call you?"

He made a sound that resembled a slow breeze through the tall grass. Then he sighed and made a slower effort of overpronouncing the word. "You may call me Tumas."

"Tumas," she repeated. "I'm Maria Soledad Rizzo Morán."

He raised a turquoise eyebrow. She hoped that by giving her Christian name, he would know she meant no harm. "What do you wish, Maria Soledad?"

They both turned at her mother shouting after her again. "¡Niña! Where are you?"

"Coming, Mother!" She stood and gathered her things. "Can I hold my wish for later?"

"That is not how it is done."

"Do wishes rot or expire like milk?"

Tumas crossed his arms over his torso. "No, but I can't sit around waiting for you to make up your mind."

"Tomorrow, then." She walked across the stream. The water almost reached her chin there, so she had to carry her things over her head.

"Tomorrow," he said.

When she looked back, Tumas was gone.

The world stood still once again.

"Get inside, wild thing," Soledad's mother shouted from the window of their stilted house, built with planks of sugarcane. The widow

Rizzo Morán rarely left her perch or let go of her coffee laced with aguardiente. "I need you to go into town."

Soledad climbed out of the stream. She scooped a cup of clean water to wash off the bits of grass that clung to her shift, then hung the wet clothes on the line to dry and skipped up the stairs to their house.

"Don't you bring that water in here," her mother droned on. "And you better not have used the clean water after bathing in the stream."

Soledad was used to her mother's tirades, though over the years her mother's voice had turned into the hum of dragonflies outside the window.

"What do we need from town?" Soledad asked, entering the bedroom she shared with her mother.

She had one dress for church, and one dress to run into town. Both were on the clothesline.

Her mother used her walking stick to point to clothes on the bed. "Rosaria brought those while you were running around in the sun." She sucked her teeth. Before her mother launched into the proper etiquette for nice young girls, Soledad snatched the pretty blue dress from the top of the pile and tugged it on.

She tamed her thick black waves into a low braid and wished for one of those long mirrors Carmen had up in her big house. All they had was the foggy silver thing in the vanity. Soledad admired the way the simple linen dress tapered at her waist and flattered her strong shoulders. She'd never thought of her own shape before. One of her cousins had told her she was destined to look like a sack of rice in a Sunday dress, like her mother. Soledad thought she looked nice. Too nice for town.

Her mother's gray eyes, full of cataracts, roamed her body. She nodded, like she approved. "Take this to the new tailor."

"New tailor?"

"Are you deaf, girl?"

"No, Mother." Soledad took the dress shirt from her mother's lap. It was one of her father's. A question burned on the tip of her tongue—why did the shirt of a dead man need urgent mending? But it wasn't worth the reprimand.

With a couple of sucre jingling in her pocket, Soledad stuffed her dead father's shirt into her purse and made for town.

She picked up an oar and climbed into their narrow canoe like a frog jumping onto a lily pad. For a moment, she thought she caught a flash of turquoise in the deepest part of the pond, where a boy from the village had drowned the year before, but kept paddling.

By the time she reached the other side, she was sweating again. She let her hair down, now away from her mother's critical eyes. *Gorgona, Medusa*, her mother and aunts would call her, on account of her black curls. She was the only one of her sisters to get their Italian grandmother's hair, instead of the smooth, silky strands of their Indigenous grandfathers.

Soledad dragged the canoe onto the shore and skewered the oar into the mud, before walking the mile and a half into the town.

"Town" was a generous word. There was one road that ran parallel to the river Vinces, and that was all of it. Palizada had one of everything—a small general store run by one of the wealthier families, a church, a butcher, a cobbler, a school, which Soledad was not allowed to attend because she needed to stay home and help. Somehow, there were now two tailors, which had caused a whole to-do.

She inhaled the stench of horses, avoiding the heaps of manure they left all around, and wondered if she could get away with just going to the old tailor, who'd known her since she was a little girl. But then, she spotted her sisters sharing a Coca-Cola by the wooden bench across the general store.

Carmen shouted at her kids playing too close to the river, and their nanny chasing after them. Azulita dramatically melted against the tree trunk beside the bench. Rosaria, her light brown skin splotchy from the heat, toyed with a lace fan.

"Is that new?"

Rosaria snapped the fan shut and slapped it at Soledad's wanting fingers with river mud caked under the nails. "Your hands are filthy. You're too old to do nothing but swim in the stream, you know."

"I do stuff!" Soledad said indignantly. She was ready to list all her chores that kept their house clean and running, but then she saw what her eldest sister's fan had been hiding. An ugly bruise, like spoiled fruit, spread across her jaw.

"What—" Soledad started to point, to reach for the painful thing marring her sister's pretty face. But she got whacked on her hand again. "Ouch!"

"Leave it," Carmen, the second-oldest, murmured. She took a sip from the glass bottle and offered it to the youngest.

Soledad didn't have to be told twice to have her favorite drink. The bubbles hurt as the flavor exploded over her parched tongue. She knew she wasn't supposed to comment about Rosaria's bruises. Her husband came from the richer families in town and her father-in-law was a lawyer down in Guayaquil. Their great-grandparents had settled here first. Everyone had wanted to marry Gregorio Morales. Soledad wondered what Rosaria would do with a fairy's wish. Would she make her husband disappear? Would she wish for an entirely new husband like the time she cried and begged for a doll to replace the one that had broken? Perhaps she'd ask for something else completely. What more did a woman, who had achieved all that women were told they should have achieved, want?

Soledad considered telling her sisters about her encounter with Tumas. About her fae wish waiting for her.

But she had nothing, not a thing that was hers and only hers, so she kept quiet.

"Has it always been so hot?" Azulita whispered. She was only two years older than Soledad, and already swollen with a baby. "I begged Alberto to take me up to the mountains but it's always work and more work." She kept one hand on the bump.

Soledad tapped her sister's belly. "It looks like you're hiding a watermelon under there."

Azulita flicked Soledad's forehead. When they were kids, they would have run around screaming, pulling one another's braids and biting anything within reach. *Savage things, wild things*, their mother would call them. Remind them that nice, quiet, polite girls get husbands and nice houses. So, one by one, the youngest Morán sister watched the others become just that. Nice, quiet, polite wives.

Soledad knew it wouldn't be proper to hit her pregnant sister back, like they had once done. Instead, she dreaded her chore.

She wanted to go back to the other side of the pond, where the world stood still. Where neighbors couldn't whisper about the state of her clothes, the shape of her changing body, her untamed hair.

"Why are there so many people here?" she asked, finally noticing the bustling street.

"There hasn't been a newcomer in a while," Rosaria said, fanning her face. "So naturally, everyone is parading their daughters in front of him like cows for sale."

"Watch your mouth," Azulita warned as their gossipy neighbors forced smiles their way.

"You sound like Gregorio," their eldest, bruised sister whispered. Rosaria's sadness spread like the fine cloud of dust kicked up by bikes and horses crossing their path. But it lasted only for a moment before she held her head up high. Her forehead was already full of frown lines that weren't there two years ago when she'd gotten married.

Soledad bit at her bottom lip. "Mother sent me to get something mended." She showed her sisters their dead father's shirt bundled in her bag.

The three of them did not seem surprised. Carmen tugged at her pointy chin. "I heard the new tailor has a wife and kids up north but he came down here to work."

Soledad did not know much about relationships, but she knew there were men who had many families, just not in the same town. How many families did one man need exactly?

"Why can't he bring his wife here?" she asked.

"I heard his wife's people don't like the heat or the coast." Rosaria fanned herself harder.

"You take it." Soledad shoved the white button-down at Carmen. "Please. Please. I'll owe you."

Azulita snatched the shirt. "We can't. Someone will tell Mother that you didn't do as she asked. Besides . . ."

Rosaria pinched Soledad's cheek hard. "There are older, more experienced, prettier women he could choose from. You have nothing to worry about."

"Too bad there's not a spare Morales brother for you, too," Azulita said brightly.

"Yes, too bad," Rosaria added dryly.

Soledad groaned. She knew she sounded like a child, but she still felt like a child sometimes.

"Fine." She wrenched the shirt from her sister and walked right into the tailor's shop.

Three weeks later, he chose her.

The Tailor chose Maria Soledad for his new bride. Her mother accepted the proposal, asking only that they spare a servant a few days a month to care for the old woman, and for plump, happy grandchildren as soon as possible.

Soledad was crossing the pond on her canoe when she felt it drag. Hands surfaced and grabbed her oar, but she was graceful and perfectly balanced. She yanked it back and hit the fairy on his head.

"Ow, you wretched girl," he said, rubbing his forehead. He slunk out of the water, using lily pads as stepping stones. They did not sink beneath his weight.

"How do you do that?" Soledad asked. She should have asked why he was trying to drown her, but her thoughts had been busy since the proposal.

Tumas tucked turquoise strands behind his pointed ear. Gold cuffs rounded the lobe. "Oh, that? The same way you travel on this ancient canoe and never falter."

"That feels a very fairy answer."

Tumas sat on the other end of her canoe, and he was so nimble the vessel did not bobble the way it did when her sisters clumsily climbed aboard. No, instead he let his feet dangle on either side, submerged in the water. He tilted his head back. The sun was hotter than any other day thus far, and she knew she had to get in the shade before her face turned red like radish skin. Tumas didn't seem to worry though. He drank in the light, which deepened his dark bronze complexion, impossibly beautiful.

"Why have you come?" she asked, cutting them across the pond. She shouldn't be looking at anyone like that, let alone a fairy.

"You have still not collected your wish and I do not like owing humans a single thing." He plucked up an empty tin can and grimaced as he tossed it into the canoe. "Well?"

"I haven't been able to make up my mind." Soledad let her oar drag deep. She did not feel in a hurry to get to town.

"There must be something you wish for. I hear you are betrothed." Tumas glanced back at her. His lashes were long, and beads of water clung to the tips. When he blinked, the water would not shed, like even drops of the pond wanted to cling to him. "A bowl of salt that never empties. A machete whose blade never dulls. A door that keeps out visitors with bad intentions. A new bride must be in want of something like these."

Soledad laughed loudly. "And what would you know of new brides?"

"I know enough." He winked at her, then turned his attention to an egret landing between his legs. It dropped a silver fish on his hand and flew away.

Tumas returned the startled fish to the pond. "Tell me about your new husband."

"Why would you want that?"

"You've kept me waiting for weeks, and I require stories in exchange for your rudeness."

"If you must know, my *promised* husband is from the mountains." Something low in Soledad's belly felt sour at the topic of conversation, but she'd have to get used to it. "He is a tailor. He is forty years old and he has a mustache. He left his wife and kids and came looking for work here."

She resumed rowing when she could not think of anything else to add.

"That is all?" Tumas asked, unimpressed.

"What else is there?"

Tumas shrugged. "Does he sing to the stars? Does he hurt the palms when he doesn't have to? Does he sleep through the night?"

"What does sleeping have to do with marriage?"

"Oh, a great deal," Tumas said severely. "Sleeping through the night is a sign of a clear conscience."

"Or someone very tired."

But Soledad thought of her own mother, who rarely slept. Who had to pour the bitter white cane liquor into her teas and coffees to knock herself out, and even then tossed and turned until morning.

"Why did you say yes, then?"

"It is simply the way of things," she explained. "I must marry. Become of a man. Have his children. Keep a clean house."

Tumas nodded along to her hollow words. "What does it mean to 'become of a man'?"

Soledad nearly skipped a row, and the canoe jostled. She'd never lost her balance. Never. But now she did. She could see the water coming at her, when she stopped with her nose an inch from the surface, her reflection in the black mirror. Then she was pulled back by her fairy friend.

Her heart slammed against her ribs as she sat in the muddy middle of the canoe, and Tumas took up the rowing. "You don't want to fall there."

She knew, of course, that the middle of the pond was deep. People had drowned there. Some said that at the very bottom there was a door to the land of faeries—la Tierra del Olvido.

"I don't know what 'become of a man' means, exactly," Soledad mused, drumming her fingers on the side of the canoe where pink moss liked to grow. "But that's what everyone says. I think it means that you stop being only your own and now you have to share yourself. Though I don't know if you could ever become of another woman . . . Or—" She looked at Tumas. His long torso, his strong chest, his webbed toes and fingers. Whatever thought was tickling at her, she scratched it away.

Tumas looked up at the sky. Smoothed the start of a smile into a frown. "What a pity it is to be a girl child thing like you."

At that, Soledad could not argue. "I would be anything else, if I could."

"Why can't you?"

"I could not go to school because Mother needed me here. I have never left these fields, this pond, not farther than three miles. The world out there changes too much and I am so afraid of it. My sisters are great women who married great men, but—" She cut herself off, worrying her bottom lip.

"But . . .," he urged on.

Soledad met Tumas's steady stare and she felt like telling him all her secrets. Things she never let herself say out loud because her family told her they were things that should not be spoken. "But Rosaria is covered in bruises, and Azulita's husband's mistress gave birth the *same day* as her, and Carmen is starting to drink like Mother just to get through the day. And Luisa left for Guayaquil and died from a fever and her body came back so gray and cold." Soledad turned to the great tree in the distance, beside her house. "If only I could be like that tree, with its bright yellow and orange flowers. Or like the stream. Or like you."

"If you wish to be a tree, I could make that happen."

Soledad sighed, but smiled at him. They'd reached the bank, so she got out to drag the canoe into the mud. Her feet sank up to her shins, and the hem of her dress got dirty. "I think I know my wish."

"Go on."

She thought of her sisters, her mother. She thought of the plight of girls like her, and those who had it worse. "I wish for you to change men, and make them kind."

Tumas stood in front of her. Angel rays seemed to find him like headlights through the clouds. A pink grasshopper, which she only saw during the wet season, landed on his shoulder. When he smiled, he was the most beautiful thing Maria Soledad had ever seen. She felt it too, that peace that only came with the sun warming her skin, the stream enveloping her on hot days.

But then he started laughing at her, falling into the mud, rolling around in it like a pig.

Soledad changed her mind. He was ugly and mean and she hated him. She kicked his thigh, but slipped and fell, too. Her clothes were ruined and now she would be in trouble.

"What did I say that was so funny?" She flicked the side of his arm.

He wiped his face as best he could and sat opposite her. His teeth were white against the mud, canines too sharp to be confused for human.

"I cannot change all men. The power required for that . . . well, it is not in the hands of nature spirits."

Soledad felt her eyes sting. What a stupid thing to ask for. What if her family wanted riches and baubles instead? Her mother would want to make everyone rabidly jealous after decades of being looked down upon—that poor widowed mother of five girls living in a cane house on the other side of the pond.

Now that Soledad was engaged, was her wish not partially her husband's? She had a list of very practical possibilities for the Tailor—

never-ending thread, perhaps. Or a needle that never skipped a stitch. She could wish for anything. She could wish for the world itself.

But Maria Soledad was afraid of the world, and perhaps that was why she could not make herself ask for it.

Perhaps she *should* become a tree.

"Forget it. I do not want it anymore."

"Oh, Maria Soledad," he said, his deep voice soothing. "Stop your tears, you curious creature. If this is what you want . . . I cannot change all men, but I can change one."

She glared up at him. "Is this a trick?"

"Which man would you want to change? Your promised husband, I assume."

"No, my sister's husband."

"Be specific, querida. Which man do you want me to change?"

Soledad wanted to frown at the sweet endearment. Querida. *Loved.* Instead, she smiled, just for a second.

"Maria Rosaria's husband, Gregorio Morales."

A warm breeze blew around them, carrying shimmering pollen aloft. She felt it land on her skin, and when she rubbed it away, iridescent freckles remained there. A mark of her bargain. A promise.

"I will need ingredients."

"Why can't you get them?" she asked, indignant. Even in fairy bargains, she had chores.

"You can blend in." Tumas looked at her muddy dress and made a face of doubt. "Sort of."

She rolled her eyes. "What do you need?"

"A new moon." He stood and offered his hand to help her up. Normally she had good footing, but she slipped again. Tumas caught her flush against him. She felt dizzy from the heat, and surely that was why she held on to his lean, strong arms.

"A new moon," she repeated, regaining her land legs. "Clean slate. That's in two nights."

"You retain knowledge from some of your ancestors, at least." Tumas walked with her to the path through the cacao trees that led into town. "Let's see, Gregorio must be present. I will also require a chicken's heart, twelve achiote seeds, heart of banano, a bone from a rotten man, and a bottle of aguardiente."

"Is that all?" She smacked her hands on her hips, where her sucre jingled in her dress pocket. She could make due with all those other things, but how was she to get his bone?

She turned to ask Tumas that very question, but he was already gone.

The next day, hidden between the bedsheets hanging out to dry, Soledad counted the ingredients she'd already collected.

"Chicken heart. Achiote seeds. Heart of banano." The chicken had been easy enough. She'd gone to town to accept the hen her fiancé gifted her family, one for each of her sisters too. On her walk back, with her chicken fluttering in its sack, she'd collected an achiote pod from one of the trees along the river. The easiest was the heart of banano. She found a small one. The oval purple thing reminded her of the extraterrestrials they spoke of on the radio, but when she held it, it was merely a funny-looking fruit.

There was only the question of her brother-in-law's *bone* and some aguardiente.

"How am I to get a bone?" she asked herself.

"You strike me as resourceful." Tumas's voice came from somewhere between the hanging garden of bed linens and undergarments.

Soledad's face flushed. "I wish you'd announce yourself."

"Too bad your wish is already made." He was different. Clean. Dry. *Dressed.* Mostly. He wore white pants as thin as rose petals, and a vest of a thousand gossamer dragonfly wings.

"What do you want? I still have time until tomorrow's new moon." Soledad reached for his collar and rubbed the fabric between her fingers.

"Pardon me," Tumas said in a huff, though he did not stop her from touching his strange clothes.

"Are these real dragonflies?" She marveled, still touching. She noticed the crown of wildflowers and thorns woven into his hair. "Do you have a party?"

"In my realm, they shed their wings and grow back," Tumas explained. "And yes, I do have a revel."

"Where?"

"My world."

"Isn't this your world?" She let him go. She should not be touching him this way. It was rude and inappropriate. So she busied herself taking down some of the linens, and he paced between the rows just as she'd been doing.

"No." He hid behind a white sheet. She hadn't been able to get her monthly bloodstain from it, and was humiliated that he might see it. She snatched the bed linen from the line, but he wasn't there. He was behind her.

Her heart leaped to the base of her throat at his nearness. "What do you mean, 'no'?"

"I mean, land cannot belong to anyone, despite what your kind has done. I mean that before your families arrived here, there were others living in these fields, and before them, and before them."

"Where is this party, then?"

"At the bottom of the pond, of course. But you must never try to go on your own."

"Why not?" She thought of the dark water, of the bodies pulled out over the years. Had they been trying to get to the land of faeries, too?

Tumas did not answer her. Instead, he took the bottom of the sheet and began helping her fold it. "We always have parties, one for every night of the moon's phases."

"Sounds exhausting."

"Oh, it is."

"We have a party tonight, too." She reached for her nice dress, only worn for church. The buttery yellow did not compliment her ruddy face, but it was all she had. "My sister, Maria Azulita, had her baby boy, and her in-laws invited the whole town for the celebration."

They folded the sheet once the long way, then again. With every turn, it brought them closer together. She closed her eyes and listened to the hum of insects in the tall grass, the frantic rhythm of her wild heart. She inhaled his scent of rain and wildflowers, not sour like boys from town.

"Maria Soledad," he whispered. No one ever said her whole name. Maria, like the holy mother, of course. And then, Soledad. She'd often wondered why her mother had given her a second name that meant loneliness. It felt like a self-fulfilling prophecy.

But no, she was engaged. She wouldn't be alone, even if she wondered if she might prefer it as an alternative to the things she was supposed to want.

"Maria Soledad," he said again.

"Yes, Tumas?" Her eyes were shut tightly. She could not look at him, even though he spoke her name softly. She was afraid her heart and skin and mind would react to his otherworldly beauty the way she had moments ago.

She felt something brush along her cheek. A petal? A feather? "Look at me."

She shook her head.

"I will come for you at dawn to prepare the brew. You *must* get the last ingredients tonight or the wish will spoil."

When she opened her eyes, he was gone. Yellow and orange petals were scattered at her feet.

She shook off her meeting with the uncanny. That's what faeries did. They were enchanting and beautiful. They made you want things that were not possible for girls like her. She had to get her wish and never see him again.

When she reached to bring down her dress for the party, it was different. Instead of the pale, faded yellow, there was a brilliant thing the color of pure saffron, with delicate gold embroidery along the short sleeves and rounded collar.

She pressed the dress against her body. She'd never worn anything so fine in her life.

"Thank you," she whispered, hoping the wind would carry her message.

"Look at them," Rosaria said. She hid her distaste and the bruise on her chin behind her lace fan. There was a new red mark on her forearm, but she pulled on her long sleeve to hide it, even though she was sweating. "You give them a little music and they forget all their worries."

In the courtyard of the Morales house, the whole town danced. Plates were heaped with rice, seco made with duck, sweet plantains grilled with fresh white cheese, and juicy ripe fruit.

After greeting her fiancé, Soledad had gone to sit with her sisters. Her fiancé, instead, congregated with the older men from town to smoke cigarettes and drink.

"Music and whisky." Carmen raised her own glass.

"We should *dance*," Azulita said, rocking her baby against her bosom. He was a good sleeper, even at the party. "Soledad has to show off this magnificent dress, after all."

They had assumed the dress was a gift from her future husband, and she'd let them think that. "I'd rather sit here. I wish Mother had come."

"You know she's always too drunk to leave that house." Carmen slurred her words.

Azulita rushed in with a pleasant smile. "I'll have to wait until the baby is bigger before we cross the pond."

"You're next, Maria Soledad." Rosaria did not smile when she said that, but they all pinched Soledad's belly and she was happy enough to be with her sisters, and feel a tiny bit of the way things had been, to be annoyed at their comments. Besides, Carmen had brought her own bottle of aguardiente, and Soledad planned on stealing it by the end of the night.

"Can I visit you tomorrow?" Soledad asked her bruised sister. "Mother says I have to practice my seco and soups for my husband."

"Practice makes poison," Carmen barked.

The others shushed her.

Rosaria squeezed Soledad's shoulder. "It would be nice, thank you. My mother-in-law never uses enough salt, and it would be much easier to blame you than me. Now, go get us some cake."

Soledad didn't like lying to her sister. She was a perfectly good cook, but the wish required Gregorio's presence. All she needed now was one of his bones.

She went to the dessert table, cut a big piece of cake, and added chunks of papaya, banano, and her favorite grosellas. She handed the plate to her sisters, and kept the grosellas for herself, biting on the salty, sour green berries. She spit the hard seeds on the ground. It occurred to her that Tumas never said *the* rotten man. Would any rotten man do? She was half contemplating digging up any man in the cemetery behind the church when a scream cut through the music.

A woman ran out of the house. Soledad recognized her as a third cousin from her father's side. She was married to a cacao farmer's son. Urbano was their surname. Mrs. Urbano clung to her husband's arm like an anchor trying to steady a ship in a storm. Her husband smacked her and she let go.

Everyone looked up from their plates, and slowly gathered to the scene. Mr. Urbano marched across the courtyard, making right for the Tailor, and punched the cigarette out of his lips. Soledad clapped her palm over her own scream as her fiancé hit his assailant back, and the men from the town swarmed around Mr. Urbano, one of their own.

Her sisters dropped their plates on the table and yanked her out of the courtyard.

"What is happening?" Soledad asked, startled.

Azulita susurrated at her crying baby, and Carmen encouraged the brawl with a whistle.

"Stop that!" Rosaria said, fanning herself harder.

"The Tailor should have kept his needle to himself, then," Carmen shouted.

"Oh," Soledad said. She understood little of men and women and relationships, only what she was *not supposed to do* until she was married. And now this. The Tailor and Mrs. Urbano. Together.

"He does work fast," Soledad said, and her sisters delighted in the comment. "I should go home."

"Party's over," Rosaria announced as her husband joined the fight. "Do you want to sleep at mine? You shouldn't cross the pond in the dark."

But Soledad wasn't listening. She was too busy watching Gregorio get punched so hard his head snapped back. A tooth flew out of his mouth onto the ground. *Bone from a rotten man.* After how much he'd hurt Rosaria, Gregorio was certainly a rotten man. Teeth were not exactly *bone* but it came from inside him.

And it just might work.

Maria Soledad ran barefoot through the cacao trees. In one hand, she clutched the bottle of aguardiente and in the other, the cavity-pocked tooth. Her head hurt from the heat, the music that still pounded in her eardrums.

She unlocked the flashlight from the toolbox in her canoe, but it would not work. She knew her field, her pond, better than herself, but crossing was dangerous in the moonless dark.

Soledad didn't know why, but of all the things that had occurred that night, her faulty flashlight was the thing that made her cry. Her tears were silent and angry, and she wiped them away with trembling fists.

She blinked at the sky. There were so very many stars illuminating everything around her. She could see her house on the other side, a single, soft yellow lamp at the window to guide her home.

There was that, at least.

And then there was Tumas, appearing from the ether, with lipstick smeared on grinning lips.

Soledad did not want him to see her in that state, but he simply moved with her every turn.

Tumas's face softened with worry as he took in her dress, stained with frosting. The tears cutting rivers across the dust on her face. "What happened?"

She pressed her lips together and shook her head. She did not want to cry in front of a fairy, as she'd heard they drank tears. That didn't seem so bad considering the cruel things humans did to one another.

Tumas climbed up onto her canoe and took her spot for steering. She sat on the center bench, and sniffled as he took her home.

In the water, fish glowed like stars. Fireflies gathered, replacing the flashlight she would have had to use. With every oar stroke, every splash, every gust of wind, Soledad shed her tears until she felt like herself again.

"Good party?" she asked, her voice scratchy from crying. "I did not expect you until dawn."

"Maybe I missed you. Or maybe it was a boring party. Though I did eat my weight in raspberries." He reached down and cupped some water in his hand. Splashed it on his face.

"Is that what that is?" She asked like she didn't care, because she didn't. She couldn't care about what a nature spirit did. Faeries were wild. They belonged to themselves. To another world that wasn't hers.

Tumas smirked. "What did you think it was?"

"I don't know. Lipstick. Do faeries wear makeup like the ladies in town?" Soledad frowned. Why should she care if he kissed a thousand others?

"In a way. I take it your party was eventful?"

She told him everything. How she was enjoying her time with her sisters when the fight broke out. The Tailor, her promised husband, and the man he made a cuckold.

"We're not even married and he's already unfaithful." Soledad took a steadying breath. "Though I suppose it's the way of things."

"Perhaps in the world you know." Tumas jumped into the shallows of the other side and pulled the canoe in. "It's not too late. You can name a different man you want me to change."

Soledad felt tears sting her eyes again. She thought of the new bruise on her sister's arm. Mrs. Urbano clinging to her husband, asking for forgiveness. How what the Tailor did wouldn't matter, and Soledad would still have to marry him and pretend, like other wives, that her husband was faithful.

She sighed, a resigned sort of sigh. "No. Let's get on with it."

She picked up the bottle of clear liquor she'd stolen from her sister. "Do we mix everything with the alcohol?"

"The alcohol is for us."

Soledad scoffed. "You tricked me."

Tumas chuckled, and she could see the shadows of his smile as the fireflies encircled them. "I did. But I was angry that I let myself get snared in a human's net. Perhaps I was lucky it was you who found me."

They trod through the tall grass until they reached home. She tried to ignore the sweet, warm sensation she felt at his words. Should she say it back? She did feel lucky that she found him. She didn't even want to think what someone else would have asked of him.

She pressed her finger to her lips. Whispered, "My mother will wake."

Tumas understood, and they went around back. She brought out all the ingredients and laid them on the wobbly table. Then offered up her knife and let him work. He picked up a smooth rock, and used it to grind everything together. The chicken heart, a slice of the banano heart. With the edge of her blade, he pried open the achiote bulbs, whispering as he counted each kernel. The twelve powdery seeds turned everything a burnt orange. Last was the tooth.

"Will it do?"

Tumas grimaced at the cavities on the yellowed surface, and said, "I believe it will."

He ground the paste until it started to harden into what looked like a sugar cube, though it was a sickly orange. He offered it to her. "Put this in Gregorio Morales's food tomorrow night. Only *his* food, do you understand?"

"I understand." She pocketed the cube. "What now?"

He unstoppered the aguardiente bottle and took a sip. Grimaced at the stuff. "Now we wait."

They sat side by side, watching the rushing stream.

"Tumas," she whispered.

"Maria Soledad." He handed her the bottle.

She never drank, but she accepted it. She had her fairy wish. She should wash up and go to bed. Mentally prepare for what lay ahead. And yet she felt a yearning for more than she could dream of. A distant land, hidden at the bottom of a pond. An unspoken wish taking the shape of a brown-skinned fairy.

So she stayed.

She put the glass bottle to her lips and drank. It was nasty and tasted like a future headache. But she had a feeling she was never going to see Tumas again, so she made an exception. "Thank you for my dress. Is your world very colorful?"

He drank and passed it back. "Oh, yes. There are colors that do not quite exist here."

"I bet it's better than here."

"We are not so perfect, but I think you might like it."

Take me, she wanted to say. *Take me.*

But she swallowed the words with her next drink. The bottle, which had only been half full when she stole it, was now empty.

"Maria Soledad," he said softly. "I have a gift."

"I should be wary of taking another gift from a nature spirit."

"This is not for you." He held the bottle, and it was full again.

Soledad blinked, fearing she was so inebriated she was seeing things. And she was. The bottle had refilled itself.

"For your mother," Tumas offered.

"My mother does not need any more spirits."

"This one is different. She will think she is drinking her aguardiente but it will help her rest. When she finishes it, she will find enough strength to leave the house again."

Her throat burned with emotion and hope. "I don't know what to say."

"Say nothing." She felt his soft lips on the apple of her cheek. She blinked her tears away, hating that she was a crybaby in front of the fairy. But there was something freeing in crying with a friend. Even if he'd already left.

She slept in the grass that night with the critters and birds keeping guard.

The next day, Soledad went to her sister's house to help with the meals. Gregorio was moody, since he was missing one of his canines. His mother cooed and babied him, while siblings and cousins reenacted the fight. Soledad felt grateful she was busy in the kitchen, cleaving chicken parts and vegetables and grazing her finger over her pocket where the fairy's cube waited.

Soledad ladled soup into a bowl, scolding herself as she spilled. She forced her mind to calm, to think of Tumas and his promise that this would work. That this wish would change Gregorio, and, in turn, Rosario's life for the better.

Fueled by purpose, she wiped down the soup splatters, and carried the first plate to the head of the house. In the small hallway between the kitchen and the dining room, she dropped the fairy cube into the soup. It melted instantly.

She carefully set the bowl in front of her brother-in-law. Gregorio's dark eyebrows were furrowed at her, then he softened a bit. He pinched her cheek hard and told her, "You better toughen up before marrying that old bastard."

Soledad lowered her head and nodded while the others at the table, except her sister, laughed.

She hurried back to the kitchen to bring out more plates now that Gregorio was served. By the time she returned, he was already eating, shoveling white rice into his soup and then into his mouth.

Soledad ate last, but she didn't have much of an appetite. She tapped her foot so fast Rosaria grabbed her by the knee. "What is wrong with you?"

"Nothing." Everything.

She watched the clock. There was still no change in Gregorio. Maybe she had done something wrong. Or Tumas had tricked her. Truly deceived her this whole time. The conversation at the table felt like the hum of bees and dragonflies, and when they cleared the plates and washed up, Gregorio was still himself.

"It didn't work." Soledad felt numb, though the dishwater was scalding.

"What didn't work?" Rosaria asked. "Your soup was incredible. Come, we are taking a stroll along the river."

Soledad followed, holding her sister's hand. Gregorio led the way with his mother.

One moment he was laughing at his own joke, and the next, he was choking. Orange liquid spilled from the corners of his mouth. His mother clapped his shoulders. His father shouted for help. One of his cousins tried to squeeze out the thing choking Gregorio but nothing worked. His face was purple from the effort, and sent the children screaming.

Neighbors and passersby gathered to watch or help. Soledad continued holding her sister's hand tightly as Gregorio made a horrible gurgling cry.

His head was the first thing to change, then his body. Shrinking, twisting, fluttering until, where once stood a man, was now a red and yellow chicken.

Men made the sign of the cross over their torsos. Gregorio's mother fainted, and Rosaria clutched her heart, but she did not cry once during the terrible transformation. She kissed Soledad's forehead, as if *she* needed to shield her baby sister, then gathered her kids to her side.

Soledad, however, ran home. She cut through the trees and pushed her canoe out into the pond. She shouted Tumas's name, but he did not show. She paddled to the other side and swam down the stream, but nothing.

She had an idea. A terrible, dangerous idea. She took her canoe back out to the pond. Stood at the heart of it, the deepest gateway to his world.

Soledad jumped.

She held her breath as the water sucked her down like a stone. She fought her own impulse to swim. But when all she saw was fish in the murk, and her lungs started to burn for air, she kicked toward the surface.

Her feet, however, snagged in curling vines and roots. Tiny thorns dug into her skin and began to pull her down. She kicked, but that made it worse. Her knife! She reached for it in her pocket. But when she tried to unfold it, the blade slipped out of her hand and sank quickly. A scream burned in her chest as something grabbed her by her collar. All her remaining air rushed out in a desperate attempt to breathe. Then she realized she was going up and stopped fighting. Held on for just a bit longer until she broke the surface.

Tumas dragged her out of the water. She sank down to her elbows in the mud and coughed up slippery roots that had made it into her mouth.

"You tricked me!" she shouted. "You said—"

He grabbed her feet to keep her still. How had she gotten so tangled up down there? "I said I could change one man. You never said what I had to change him into."

Soledad stilled. Repeated the words. Then, splashed muddy water at him. "My sister will be thrown out! She—"

"She will be pitied. She might be feared. She has a son to inherit. And if she loses all of it, the hen might provide some food."

Soledad let herself calm down. "Still."

"Still." Tumas flashed something in his hand—her knife. "Still you feel, not because a man is gone, but because you are happy he is gone. Perhaps now others will think twice of their behaviors. Pray to their new god. Humans only fear when something is taken from them."

"Yes, I am happy he is gone." She breathed hard. "I wish I could change them all, but you do not have that power, do you?"

Tumas shook his head and grabbed the gnarly roots and vines winding from her knees to her toes. "Now, I believe I have caught a human attempting to enter my kingdom. In exchange for your freedom, I would claim a wish."

Soledad sat up. Watched his face—the angles of his high cheekbones, his hawk nose, his smirking lips.

"I am not bound by wishes." She looked away, heart thundering.

"You should ask no promise from me, either, because we break them. Every vow, every word. What could *I* possibly give you?"

"I claim your heart, Maria Soledad Rizzo Morán." He sliced through the thorns and vines. "If you will have me, I claim your heart, and if you are not ready, I will wait as long as it takes. I will take you down to the doorway, to the places we have made. I will dance with you under the stars and swim with you in the streams and roll around the muddy banks you love more than I ever thought I could." He brushed away the muck drying on her shins.

"If I will have you," she repeated.

If.

A choice. A real choice that was hers alone to make.

Soledad looked back at her house on the other side of the pond. The cane house on stilts had everything she'd ever needed. Her mother would be okay now, wouldn't she? She looked to the cacao trees. Her rice paddies. They'd have to be harvested without her.

What would happen to the Tailor? He'd surely find someone else, and she'd never think of him after that moment.

There were her sisters. But they would be okay, too.

That's when she knew she'd already made up her mind.

She met the fairy's eyes. She'd seen him angry, cranky, irritated, curious. Now she saw him shy. Waiting patiently.

But what if things weren't different with Tumas?

What if the other side of the pond was a world she could not adapt to?

She might ask herself *what if* for the rest of her life, and she'd never be satisfied.

She simply had to live.

She leaped onto her fairy, wrapping her arms around his neck, and kissed him. They sank into the pond that way, and he only let go to lead her to the doorway, where moss and stones rolled away and opened up, welcoming her to the land of forgetting.

Palizada, Ecuador—2023

There is a girl stepping into a rickety old canoe. She crosses with her cousins, and they tell her of the magic of the fields their family have tended to for a century. Of the pond where people drowned in search of the fabled Tierra del Olvido. Of the man who turned into a hen because he beat his wife. Of an ancestor, a great-grandaunt who ran away before her engagement and was never seen again. Of the wishes people started making at the lip of the pond after that summer of change, and how some came true, but not many people believe anymore.

The stilted house built of cane is long gone. The stream has dried out, mangroves reclaiming its old course. A pink grasshopper lands on the girl's shoulder, and the birds sing, "Welcome home."

She makes a wish on the wind.

ALWAYS THERE AND NEVER SEEN

Natalie C. Parker

I know I'm not supposed to admit things like this, but I'm not sad that my grandfather is dead.

First of all, he was old. Ninety-two according to his government records, but that's just a guess. He ran away from home when he was a boy and started lying about his age to avoid being put into foster care. To hear him tell it, he was born two hundred years ago, sometimes three! By the time he stopped lying, it was too late. His real age was lost along with his original surname. The point is, he was plenty old, he wasn't in pain or wasting away or anything, and that's the sort of thing we're *supposed* to be grateful for.

But I'm also not sad because he didn't want me to be. He told me more than once, always when Mom wasn't around to hear, that death was his next great adventure and he was ready for it. I'm glad he got to meet it on his terms.

That's not the sort of thing I should say out loud, though. It's right up there with, "Mom, I'm bi." Which I also shouldn't have said out loud, but live and learn, I guess.

ALWAYS THERE AND NEVER SEEN

I paste a stoic expression on my face as Mom turns up the long narrow driveway that leads to grandma and grandpa's house and I vow to remain stoic until I'm sure I'm alone. The driveway is bumpy and overgrown, tunneling through oaks and blackberry brambles—the only things that can truly love the heat of a Mississippi summer. The drive from our house in Maryland takes two days, but I've always loved coming here. Even now, with the pallor of death clinging to everything like a layer of humidity, there's a part of me that's looking forward to being inside the house again.

My grandparents named it Second Star because it was their second house, and it's shaped a little like a star with various wings added on by previous owners over dozens of years. Nestled in a gentle valley amid ninety-six acres as sprawling as the night sky, it's just isolated enough to feel like it's in a world of its own. Brimming with magic and adventure. That's definitely what it felt like when I was a kid anyway.

"Oh, Harrison *Ford*!" Mom curses when she nails a pothole. "I can't believe they haven't had someone come out to fill these. What would they—" She pauses, grits her teeth, and swallows hard. "I mean, what would she do if an ambulance or a fire truck needed to get down here?"

"Make s'mores?" I suggest.

Mom shoots me a dark look. "Get it out of your system now, pigeon."

"Sure thing, Michaela," I answer. I'm the daughter of a psychologist. I know how to fight fire with fire.

I know that I've won by the way Mom's mouth pinches shut. She doesn't hate her name as far as I know. She just doesn't like when I use it. As if by doing so, I'm breaking some unwritten law about mother-daughter etiquette. But if she's going to irritate me with that wretched pet name, then I'm going to irritate her right back.

We don't really have time to get into it though because we dive through one last tunnel of viciously green foliage and then the house appears before us. From this angle, it looks small. Just two wings joined at the center by a cottage door complete with a white ruffled curtain in the window. That's the thing about this house. It's really good at convincing you that it's something it most definitely is not.

"Remember," Mom says, putting the car in park without cutting the engine. "Grandma's been dealing with a lot on her own and we're here to help. Not stress her out more."

"I know, Mom." I don't mean to sound recalcitrant. It just comes out that way. Even I hear it. But I'll be damned if I let her know I didn't mean it that way.

Mom sighs through her nose and doesn't say anything. Just stares straight at the door with its frilly white curtain.

Grandpa died three days ago. The funeral is next week, and between now and then we're here to help Grandma get the house in order. Start sorting the things we keep from the things we don't, prune it all down until it looks tidy again.

Finally, Mom says, "I just don't want you to be taken by surprise. It isn't going to feel the same in there. There will be a lot for you to process and I might not be able to help you do that."

"You don't have to worry about me," I say, working overtime to make sure I don't sound sullen or, worse, saccharine.

The muscles in her jaw flash as she grinds her teeth. Bites back some emotion she would never dare to show me. I have the sudden desire to reach out and comfort her in some way. Press a hand to her shoulder or something, but my whole body freezes. Rejects the notion that my mother would ever accept comfort from me.

"Just," she starts, voice softer than usual. And I almost do it. I start to reach for her when she says, "Don't . . . talk about anything she doesn't *need* to know about."

"I—wasn't," I say, stunned and confused by the sudden shift.

"Her generation does things differently and they aren't used to talk about things like . . ." She waves her hands through the air. "Gender or sexuality, and so just leave that alone. Okay?" She turns to me and fixes me with an accusing gaze I don't think I did anything to earn.

Nausea settles in my belly, cold and gross. I know she blames me for everything going on with Dad right now. They've been fighting for years, but it was only after I came out—and he responded by hugging me and telling me he loved me no matter what and my mom responded with questions and I got so incandescently mad that I blew up at her and then he did, too—that they really stopped talking.

I know it's not my fault, but that's hard to remember when every other look from her is an accusation.

I give myself one count of three to make sure my voice doesn't waiver when I answer, "O. K."

"Great." She turns off the car, unbuckles, and gets out first.

The real shit of the thing is that she's not wrong.

The house *is* different. The second we walk into the little entryway, I feel how true that is. I feel it the same way I feel the air-conditioning drag goose bumps out of my skin.

Every other time I've arrived at Second Star, this room was flooded with light and sound. My grandparents issuing joyful whoops and whistles as we passed through the door. The air a tantalizing blend of smells pouring out from the kitchen—everything from salty corn bread to the acrid bite of simmered turnip greens to savory fried fish. Food I only ever got when I was here.

Today, it's dim and quiet; the only sound is the steady tick-tick-tick of the cuckoo clock in the hall. The air smells cold and stale. The contrast is severe enough that I stop right in the entryway, waiting for something that will never come again.

"Shut the door," Mom whispers, even though we're alone. "Grandma's probably in her bedroom resting. Will you bring our bags in while I go talk to her?"

I nod, too weirded out to do anything else, and Mom gives my shoulder a reassuring squeeze before she disappears in the dim haze of the hallways.

It's worse without her around. The silence is creeping and heavy. Everything inside the house looks grayscale compared with the world outside, an old sepia photograph that I somehow fell inside.

It takes actual physical effort to move my body and make even that much noise, but once I get going, it's easy to keep going. By the time I've moved my bags into my usual room—the one with a single twin bed, butter-yellow walls, and tiny fairy statues everywhere—and mom's into the one she usually shares with dad—the one on the other side of the shared bathroom with a queen bed, slate-gray walls, and a vaguely nautical theme—the weight of the moment has landed squarely on my shoulders and I lay back on the bed.

My eyes land on the fairy statue sitting on the bedside table on a cream-colored doily. The fairy sits cross-legged on top of a red-capped mushroom, its smile a little more vicious than friendly.

Probably most people would assume the fairies are my grandma's obsession, but they'd be wrong. Grandpa loved fairies. He used to tell me all kinds of tales about them. He'd come sit in this bed with me and say, "Pick a fairy and I'll tell you a tale."

He told me stories about every single fairy in this room.

"Hello, pigeon." Grandma's voice startles me from my thoughts and I sit up as she steps into the room. "I'm so glad you're here," she says.

I'm not sure what the right response is. *Me too* seems too selfish. *I'm glad to be here*, too morbid. *How are you*, too obtuse. I settle on, "It's good to see you," because that seems to skirt the line between being considerate and being aware that things are bad.

She gathers me into a hug and I lean into her warmth. Smell the powdery scent of her favorite lotion, the hint of must that always lingers in her clothes.

"The purple is new," she murmurs, running a hand down my hair. "It was blue the last time I saw you, I think."

Instantly, I think of the last time I was here. How Grandpa was already slowing down and mostly confined to his bed, which he hated. "Who is this?" he'd asked, his raspy voice sparking with humor. "Is that blue hair I see? Must be a mermaid."

"It's me, Grandpa," I'd said, settling on the side of the bed. "Paige."

He reached out to take my hand, that familiar glint in his eyes as he tugged me closer. "You look like a mermaid to me, and I should know. Some of my best friends were mermaids. In fact, did I ever tell you about the time—"

And then he'd spun me a story for thirty straight minutes. Never once losing the thread of what he was saying, always, always, telling it like it had actually happened.

"Peter would have liked it," Grandma says, gently curling one strand around her finger.

"It was supposed to be pink, purple, and blue," I admit. "But it all kind of ran together."

When she pulls away, I can see the exhaustion carved into her and I understand why Mom has been so focused on getting here. Before

Grandpa died, a nurse came in the mornings and evenings to help, but with all my aunts and uncles flung to the far corners of the world and every single cousin younger than me, Grandma's been mostly alone.

Over her shoulder, Mom leans against the doorjamb, and for just that split second, they look like echoes of each other, the years between them nothing more than the skip of a stone over water. In between one skip and the next is nothing but grief and regret.

"You must be hungry," Grandma says. "Let's go find something to eat."

I follow my mom and grandmother to the kitchen and help cut apples and cheese for a modest charcuterie platter that will tide us over until dinner.

"You should let Paige make us a stir-fry, Mom. It's her specialty and these vegetables need to be used," Mom says, peering into the fridge with a slight frown.

"Is that so?" Grandma asks, turning to me.

"Mmhm," I answer. Because it's true, but so is the fact that I've started cooking because half the time Dad doesn't come home from work until late and Mom stays in her bedroom until the sun sets. So is the fact that if it weren't for grocery delivery, I would probably have spent the past few months sustaining on ramen and Starbucks.

"That sounds divine," Grandma says. "I keep ordering groceries like I'm still cooking for two and I'm afraid I throw out more than I keep."

That, for some reason, is the first thing that's made me want to cry.

Instead, I pull the broccoli, carrots, and onions out of the fridge and get to work.

When I was little, Grandpa used to tell me stories about when *he* was little. They were filled with flying children and fairies and pirates and mermaids. Totally bonkers, but there was one that was a little bit different. One that always felt like, out of all the others, it could be real, even if most people would agree it couldn't possibly be.

When Grandpa was a little boy, maybe ten years old, he ran away from home. This, as far as I know, is totally true, because he has no parents and all of Mom's efforts to map out some sort of family tree have gone nowhere. Grandpa left home with nothing except his favorite teddy bear and a pocket full of candy and he ended up in the woods not far from here. Alone, but not afraid, because where he'd ended up was better than where he'd been. Still, he was very sad. He sat down beneath a big old oak to have a good cry and soon realized he wasn't alone at all. There were the crickets and frogs, singing in the branches above, and through the speckling of oak leaves he could see the stars twinkling in the sky above.

That was when he noticed that one of the stars was winking more than the others. Winking and apparently getting closer. At first, he thought it was falling, and since he'd heard of falling stars, that seemed reasonable, but then he realized it wasn't falling. It was flying. And it wasn't a star at all.

It was a fairy.

Grandpa knew dozens of stories about fairies. He knew that he should never give one his real name, that he should avoid stepping inside a ring of toadstools, and that fairies liked offerings—so he pulled a piece of hard candy out from his pocket and set it on top of a small stone. Then he sat back and waited.

It didn't take long for the fairy to arrive. Whenever he got to that part of the story, I imagined this tiny little creature landing inside a cherry-red Lifesaver or atop a bright yellow lemon drop. Grandpa was never specific about the candy, only that it was bigger than she was and yet she ate the whole thing.

When she was done, she offered him a gift in return and he said, "I want to go somewhere where I'll never be sad again."

She'd dusted him with fairy dust and that was that. Grandpa's first flight and the origin story of every other tall tale in his arsenal. He lived in a faraway land dominated by all the things a ten-year-old would love, where he would never grow old or die.

"I spent so long without sadness that I almost forgot it existed," he'd said. "But it was still here when I returned."

"I wish I could find a place where I never felt sad. Why did you come back?"

At that, Grandpa gave me a knowing smile, placed a hand on my cheek and said, "At a certain point, the best adventures in life are all right here. And sadness, believe it or not, is part of what makes each adventure worth having."

After dinner, the three of us do the dishes together. Grandma starts humming "Summertime" and soon all three of us are reaching for high notes we have no business hitting, harmonizing and laughing together as we wash, dry, and return every dish to its place.

"I'd say we've still got it," my mom says, grinning.

"You can't beat the Pan family pipes." This was one of Grandpa's favorite sayings. And even though it's Grandma who says it now, I'm pretty sure we can all hear his voice and, for just a second, I think the sorrow eases out of my mother's and grandma's eyes.

For just a second, it's nice. But Grandma—maybe swept up in the romance of the song—asks, "Anyone special in your life, pigeon?"

And before I can answer, my mom is glaring daggers over Grandma's shoulder. Promising me nothing but pain and argument if I take this opportunity to tell anything resembling the truth.

I feel numb for an instant. A stone skipping across smooth water. When I land, I sink into a sudden sorrow. A sadness that has been waiting to consume me.

It is like a lake with a great gaping maw that opens beneath me. Inside it is every kind of emotion I've been avoiding. There's the sorrow that sharing my secret with my parents tore them apart. The anger that my mother is so embarrassed of who I am she'd rather I stay silent about it. And there's shame. A twisting, gut-wrenching shame that I'm not brave enough to speak up. Not now. Maybe not ever.

I don't understand why it all hits at once, but I feel like I'm drowning in it. Like I can't take a full breath because sadness has flooded my lungs and I just want it to stop. The same way Grandpa wanted his own sadness to stop so many years ago.

I cling to that thought. Hold on to it for dear life because Grandpa found a way to make these feelings go away. And he told me exactly how he did it.

"No," I say, doing my best not to reveal any of this to Grandma. Then I ask, "Hey, do you have any candy?"

Late that night, I leave the house with a pocket full of Werther's and my phone to use as a flashlight.

I had a lot of time to change my mind about this, but just before bed, my mom popped into the shared bathroom while I was brushing my teeth. She looked soft and tired. Probably exhausted from the drive and from starting to go through Grandpa's closet.

"I'm going to need your help tomorrow," Mom started, waiting for me to spit and rinse before she continued. "With Grandma. She's working too hard and I'd like us to take over most of the housework so she can get a break."

"I know. You already asked me to help and I already said I would." I don't know why it irritated me so much that she felt the need to repeat things like that. As though I would have forgotten or am too immature to get what's going on here.

She'd nodded. "You did. Just, please also remember that she's old and there are things that it's better she doesn't know."

I stared at her, waiting for her to say what she meant. But her specialty has always been making me guess. Making me fill in those gaps and disappointments myself.

"You mean like how you and Dad are probably getting a divorce," I snapped.

"I mean you don't need to talk to her about your—" Her eyes flashed to my hair.

"I'm bi, Mom, not a plague carrier," I'd said, choosing violence so the sadness swelling in my throat couldn't escape.

"Carrie Fisher," she hissed before returning to her room.

And I'd stayed awake until I was sure she and Grandma were asleep, then I snuck out of the house.

There are half a dozen trails cut through the land and I used to know them inside and out, but ever since Grandpa got sick there's been no one to maintain them, and even in the daylight they look like tunnels of poison ivy. I choose the driveway and walk until I come to a familiar break in the trees where I can cut through the tall grass to the hill beyond. When I reach the top, I scan the ground for a flat rock and a good place to sit. Unwrapping a single candy, I set it on the stone, take a seat a few feet away, and then pocket my cell phone and wait for my eyes to adjust to the dark.

I'm not what anyone would call a "country girl." I don't hunt or say "ma'am," I don't know how to ride a horse or sew a dress, and despite my mother's satin drawl, I don't have even the whiff of an accent. But I do love the feeling of being in the middle of nowhere. With no one to judge me by things I haven't done or to wonder if being bisexual is code for anything, or to tell me to grow up one minute then treat me like a child the next. Here, it feels like the waters of sadness are in the distance. I can hear the little waves lapping at the shore, but it can't pull me under.

I lean back and fix my eyes on the clear sky above. It gets darker here than it does at home. The stars seem brighter and closer and there's so many of them. For just a second, I can imagine that I've found another land. A hidden world like Grandpa's.

In the dark, a shooting star streaks across the sky in one long arc. Too long, actually. I blink and sit up, staring as the star continues to move—straight toward me.

I don't even have time to climb to my feet before it lands, alighting on two little feet resting softly on top of the caramel brown candy I unwrapped a few minutes ago. Their body is lean and dressed in paper thin scrolls of tree bark, their skin iridescent like the exoskeleton of a beetle. Wings blur behind them, moving too fast to see. Like those of a bee or hummingbird. They smile and flash their teeth at me.

"Um, hi," I manage.

They open their mouth and a sound like the tinkle of bells tumbles out. Somehow, though, I understand the words tucked inside of them.

They ask, "Is this for me?"

"Yes," I say. "It's a gift."

The little creature grins and crouches low, running a pink tongue along the curve of the candy. They smack their lips and speak again. "Salt and sweet, what a treat."

I watch as they bite into the candy with sharp teeth. The air fills with the sounds of crunching and smacking as the fairy devours the candy with surprising speed. Definitely faster than I can typically eat a Werther's.

When they're finished, they lick their fingers and smile up at me; flash those sharp teeth once more. I can't help but wonder if they could cut through my flesh and bone just as effectively as they cut through that candy.

"I will give you a gift in return," they say, then produce a small pouch from somewhere within their tree bark skirt and hold it out to me. "What is it that you want?"

My grandpa's words are there in an instant: "I want to go somewhere I'll never be sad again."

"An adventure," they say. "Take it and you can come away with me."

"Come away where?"

"To a place far from here. Where there is nothing but endless delights. Where joy is more than a feeling. Where there is no room for sadness and you will never want to leave." They raise one arm and point toward the sky. "To the place that is always there and never seen."

Always there.

My grandpa's words are fresh in my mind. His stories about flying children and mermaids and fairies. And I'm not even all that surprised to discover how true they are. My mother would be. Except my mother would never do anything like this. She's been dismissing Grandpa's stories her whole life. The same way she dismisses me.

Maybe some people wouldn't take an offer like this seriously. But

I do. I try to remember everything Grandpa ever told me about his interactions with fairies. With one fairy in particular. There were always a few rules: never give them your true name, be wary of making deals, and remember that though they cannot lie, truth is elegant and flexible.

I consider all this and remind myself that an invitation to go with them is not a promise to return again one day. I ask, "Can I come back whenever I want?"

The fairy tips their head to one side, blinks seamless amber eyes at me. "Yes," they say. "You can come back whenever you *want*."

The emphasis on the word is playful yet intentional. A promise, and also a threat. One that suggests I may never want to return, and if that happens, then I won't. I will disappear from this world forever.

I imagine how that would make my mother feel, and I know I shouldn't take joy in the thought of her guilt and pain, but I do.

I want her to hurt. I want to do something so extreme that she'll realize all the ways she's hurt me, too. How I was always, always here and she never saw me. How she only ever saw a version of me that was selfish and fickle. How she saw that version so clearly I started to wonder if maybe there was something wrong with me. "Wouldn't you like to dance until your tears turned to laughter? To sing starlight into the world? To fly and fly and never be bound by anything or anyone again?"

I imagine what that would feel like. To dance until the only things I knew were laughter and joy.

I imagine how my mother would weep and wonder. How she would never even consider that I had followed in my grandpa's footsteps, because they existed outside the realm of possibility. How she's so unhappy herself that she assumes being bi is a rebellion and not simply who I am.

"You can leave all this behind," the fairy says. "It will all become like a dream you had once. One that can never hurt you again."

The thought of taking off right now and leaving everything behind sounds great. Swept up in a vision of my mother's tears, I almost say yes.

But then, I remember other things. I remember how my mother helped me clean up the bathroom after I murdered it with the colors of the bi pride flag. How she uses her favorite celebrities' names to curse. How she loves my stir-fry and sings with me while we do dishes.

How I've heard her crying in the bathroom after she and Dad fight.

How I care and can't bring myself to ask if she needs anything.

How if I leave the pain behind, I also leave the joy.

"I don't want to forget her," I say.

"She will not forget you," the fairy answers, bells chiming softly in the warm, summer night. "Her sorrow will only grow. Isn't that what you want?"

I imagine my mother old like Grandpa. Lying in a bed with acres of sadness behind her. Something sharp pinches at my lungs—a feeling I didn't have when I thought of Grandpa dying.

It hits me all of a sudden. If I leave, she will wonder and rage and regret. She will hurt, and while that gives me some degree of selfish satisfaction, it isn't what I want.

What I want, more than anything, really, is for her to see me. Really *see* me. And how can she do that if I'm not here?

Grandpa was right. Sadness and pain and hurt might suck in the moment, but they're a part of life. A part of me.

And I'm not ready to live without them. "No," I say, remembering at the last second not to say "thank you," which was another of Grandpa's rules. "I'm staying."

The fairy smacks their lips one more time and then they're gone. Quick as a flash of light.

I stay there for another minute or so, just staring into the sky, searching for the place that's always there and never seen. As I search for something I know I will never find, I feel an ache cracking open in my sternum. A surge of sorrow climbs up my throat and makes it impossible to breathe for a second. The tears come before I can stop them and I cry for the adventures I'll never know and for the loss of my own happy family; I cry for my mother's pain and for the way she hurt me so badly when I came out to her; I cry for my grandma's loneliness and for my grandpa. Whom I miss so much.

It hurts. It feels endless and awful.

But sometime later, I take a breath and it fills my lungs from top to bottom, and no tears follow. I take another, watch the stars winking overhead, then I pop a Werther's in my mouth and climb down the hill, heading back to Second Star and my grieving grandma and my irritating mother. Ready for the next adventure.

DEAR DIARY

L.L. McKinney

AUGUST 6

DEAR DIARY,

Do people even say "dear diary" anymore? I don't remember what I used to say. Write. It's been months since I ripped everything out, so I can't even check. God, why did I keep this? It doesn't even look right with half the pages missing. But it's the only thing close to a journal I have, and Dr. Morris says I need to try journaling to "excise my stronger emotions" so they don't boil up and lead to me giving people broken noses.

Darren Warnock is a racist piece of shit. End of. I would have broken more than his basic, bitch-ass face if I could, but try saying that out loud to your court-mandated therapist who believes "words are never cause enough for violence." Yeah, well, this word means you get your ass beat, Mathilda. That's my therapist, Dr. Mathilda Morris. Sounds like some boring comic book name.

Anyway, MATHILDA, here's your damn journal. Not like you'll even bother to read it, but my mom asked me to give it a try. She says Darren deserved every bit of what he got, but I could still probably benefit from getting my feelings down on paper, so here we are:

Fuck you, Mathilda. Fuck Darren, too.

AUGUST 12

DEAR DIARY,

I guess that's what we're going with for now.

Started school this week. Kinda sucks being the new face, even at the beginning of the year. I don't know nobody here, and nobody knows me. Could be worse, I guess. Like those movies where the new girl starts fighting with the popular kids over some ridiculous misunderstanding.

A few other kids in my homeroom are new, too. This one girl, Stacy? Expelled from her last school for dealing pills. Not for money; her family rich. She traded for favors and information—who might be pregnant or who was cheating on who or sleeping with a teacher. When her old school found out, she cried and claimed she was trying to help her friends. By handing out narcotics like Halloween candy. They expelled her with the warning that it could have been worse. That's it. Busted "selling" drugs and she just moves on to a new school, no charges. Some serious wipipo shit; you know no one else could get away with that.

This other girl CeCe, she cool. Cute. Got this goth thing going on. Just moved here this summer. No idea why someone would CHOOSE Kansas City over New York, but she said it had something to do with her dad's job. They move a lot, so she's used to it. Her parents try to make up for it by buying her stuff to fill her nerd addictions. She's into anime like me. Wants to learn Japanese so she can watch without the subtitles. And she wants to spend a year in Japan. I like her, real chill.

Kalvin is the last one. He didn't say much. Kept his nose buried in a book about fairies. Apparently, during the orientation tour that I refused to go to, he found out about this girl that supposedly disappeared on school grounds back in the 80s, and has plans to dig up more information about the whole thing.

And that was my day. Met some people, made some friends, didn't punch anybody.

Yay me.

AUGUST 14

DEAR DIARY,

Talking to Mathilda is still a waste of time. I'm not sorry for what I did, never gonna be sorry, and if I ever got the chance to do it all over again? The choice would not be taking the *high* road. Maybe Mathilda should talk to Darren about choosing not to say "nigga." Twice. And I know, I KNOW, there would've been a third if I hadn't fed him my fist. People think because I'm small they won't catch a supersized order of these hands.

Anyway, school is fine, I guess. Kinda boring. Boring enough I actually listened to Kalvin talk about fairies during study hall. My dude is REALLY into them, okay? And I don't mean like Tinker Bell, which is what I thought at first. Apparently, there's like nice fairies and mean fairies that steal babies and eat your dogs and shit. It's wild, a lil creepy, and kinda interesting. Like the part where he says he thinks the school is built over a fairy circle, and that's why kids go missing from time to time.

Then he pulled this old yearbook and showed me a picture of the girl who was supposedly kidnapped by fairies a long time ago. He pointed out her name was too faded to read and said missing names were a sign of fairy activity. I don't know about that, but it didn't really matter because right then one of the library skylights shattered.

Mr. Hensley, the librarian, found a dead raven in the physics section. He said it must have been blinded by the glare off the glass and didn't see to pull up in time. It hit the window hard enough to break the glass *and* its neck, killing it instantly. The library was closed for the rest of the day.

AUGUST 19

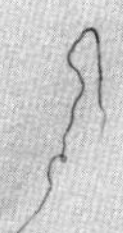

DEAR DIARY,

Another raven broke another window today. It was during chemistry class, and I almost dropped a beaker full of something that smelled like booty juice. I'm glad I didn't—that stink would NEVER come out of my shoes. Miss Arnold tried to keep going with the lesson like there wasn't a dead animal in the middle of the floor. It wasn't until the janitors came and cleaned up the mess that we started paying attention to her, but class was pretty much over by that point.

Lunch was weirder.

Normally I sit with CeCe. Not just because she's adorable and I like complimenting her to see her smile, but her dad is a professional chef. He's been packing us baskets full of amazing food and jars of homemade lemonade to enjoy picnics together while the weather has been nice. I want to think he's secretly trying to help me woo his daughter.

Stacy comes with us sometimes. I say sometimes because half the time she might show up and the other half she's working. Girl's still trading pills! Mostly to kids from her old school. They really drive all the way over here on they lunch break. Wild. She's got a few local customers, though. So she can get a proper lay of the land, she says. Kalvin spends his lunch in the library lately. We told him he could join us, but he says he likes the quiet. I've caught him napping in there more than once. He seems so tired these days.

Anyway, Stacy's the one who spotted the ~~herd~~ flock while we were looking for somewhere to set up the blanket in the courtyard. "What the hell is that?" she asked. Her voice has this Southern twang that makes her sound annoyed whenever she asks a question. She pointed at the trees that line the side of the gym.

There had to be at least a hundred ravens in this tree. So many it made the branches droop, nearly touching the ground. The birds were quiet though. Not a single tweet. Caw. Whatever noise they make. Everyone already sitting in the courtyard acted surprised to see them, like they hadn't noticed until Stacy pointed them out.

Someone threw a football to try and scare them. I jumped when it hit. There was a horrible crunching noise, then a few ravens fell over dead. The rest didn't move. Everyone stared for a second. Then most of us went inside.

AUGUST 20

DEAR DIARY,

Mathilda had some "advice" for me today. She thinks, along with journaling, it would help if I found a creative outlet so I didn't lash out at my peers in frustration. I asked why she thought racists were my peers. Her lips got real tight. I smiled. She said I should smile more in one of our previous sessions. That it would present a less combative air.

I made her mad. I know I did. Whenever I say or do something she doesn't like she writes a lot of notes. I thought her notepad might catch on fire.

I might look into this art thing though. CeCe draws. She's good. Good enough to be a professional. She's got a webcomic and everything, about this Black girl that goes to sleep at night and dreams she's the soul of a mecha suit that protects a distant colony of space explorers from this hive mind army of insects trying to enslave the universe like the Borg. I'll ask if I can watch her draw some of the next issue. No spoilers, of course.

It'll be nice to be able to spend more time with her since we can't do our usual lunches. We still eat together, but no one is allowed to sit in the courtyard anymore. It's been taken over by ravens. More and more show up each day. They filled up the trees and started perching on the tables and benches. And they're all so quiet. It's creepy.

Kalvin says, according to his research, ravens are attracted to evil fairy magic and are messengers of the Un-see-lee court. I'm not sure what that means, but he seems excited about it.

AUGUST 23

DEAR DIARY,

Last night I had a nightmare. I dreamed I was walking. I don't remember where I was, just that I was alone in a forest. I think it was a forest. There were trees and a dirt path that led to a small pool of water. The water was bright blue and glowed a little. The whole thing looked beautiful, until I noticed eyes watching me from the trees. Following my every move.

Small, beady, glassy eyes reflected the light. I could feel their gazes, like burning but from the inside.

The Wind starts blowing and feathers fill the air. The pond ices over. I'm frozen, too. I can't scream, I can't run. I can only stare back. Helpless. Then the eyes vanished, and I woke up.

I could still feel the burning under my skin, but it faded while I sat in the dark of my bedroom shaking, too terrified to move until the sun started to rise and light peeked through my blinds. I'm not sure, but I thought I saw the outline of something perched in the tree by my window. It looked vaguely bird shaped.

I didn't check.

AUGUST 25

DEAR DIARY,

I think I might have a girlfriend. While I was hanging out with CeCe—she was working on her webcomic—we started talking about our first fictional crushes. I asked if she knew about this old cartoon called KIM POSSIBLE? My cousin got me into it. Of course CeCe knew about the show and of course she knew about Shego. That was my crush, I admitted.

Hers was Sailor Uranus. She said I kinda remind her of her. Then she leaned across the table and kissed me. Her lips were soft and tasted like peach-flavored gloss. Damn she can kiss. Made me lightheaded and shit.

We kept kissing until she couldn't breathe, and I couldn't see straight. Then we kissed some more. We finally stopped when her mom came home. She finished her comic. I finished my homework. Then I kissed her good night.

Can't wait to kiss her good morning. That's a thing, right?

AUGUST 28

DEAR DIARY,

This morning at breakfast, Mom asked if I was okay to go to school after what happened to that poor teacher yesterday. Things are kinda getting a little much with the ravens, and Mr. Porter decided to fuck around with Mother Nature and found out. I didn't see it, but I definitely heard about it afterward.

According to the stories, about 15 minutes before he came stumbling down the hall, his exposed skin torn to shreds, Mr. Porter and some other teachers had been gathered to discuss the bird issue. A lot more ravens have been showing up every day. Kal is very . . . excited isn't the right word. More ravens means fairy magic, I guess. Anxious. He's anxious.

Anyway, with half the trees covered in ravens every day, the school got complaints, so animal control was called. They could send someone, but not until after hours. A couple of volunteers would need to stay with Principal Ayers. Apparently, Mr. Porter did not want to miss kick-off of his son's game and said he'd just scare the stupid birds off. Then he took a bullhorn outside, despite the other teachers trying to talk him down, and started hollering and honking at the birds.

Next thing anyone knows, they swarm. And the screaming starts. It was panic, people trying to see what was going on, then trying to get out of the way as he was half dragged to the nurse's office, where he kept screaming "Beware the Raven Queen" until EMTs showed up and sedated him.

At least, that was the story.

AUGUST 29

DEAR DIARY,

Another window broke at school today. This time during precalc. I already knew the cause without looking. Another fucking raven. No one knows where the hell they're coming from.

A few students crowded around the mess of glass shards and still fluttering wings. Guess that one wasn't lucky enough to break its neck on impact.

I stayed in my seat and *tried to focus on my* workbook. I didn't want to see the creature suffer; I don't like seeing animals in pain. But the more I tried to concentrate on my work, the more something kept pulling at me, snatching at the edge of my attention and rising over the teacher's calls for everyone to go back to their seats.

It was a voice. Shrill, rough, like someone who chain-smoked a dozen packs of cigarettes every day for a hundred lifetimes was swallowing sandpaper while trying to yodel. The voice cracked and hissed, repeating a single word over and over. It wasn't until the rest of the room went quiet that I realized three things.

One, everyone was looking at me, staring like I'd grown a second head.

Two, the voice wasn't a voice. Not a person's. It was the raven, squawking as it flopped about in its death throes.

Three, which I still don't want to believe, but I was there. I saw it. I heard it. I sat there, staring at everyone while they stared at me, and a dying animal called my name, over, *and over, and over.*

AUGUST 30

DEAR DIARY,

I dreamt about the eyes again. They stared. I burned. This time it was more than the cold fire. This time it felt like something wrapped around my neck and started squee*zing. The harder it* squeezed, the hotter I burned.

Then the pressure ~~eased, and~~ I sat up in my bed. Only, I wasn't in my bed. I was on the ground. Grass and black material spread around me. A dress maybe? *I tried to get up*, but I couldn't move. I couldn't do anything but sit there and slowly lose myself to panic twisting up in my chest while my body re*fused to listen to me.*

Then SHE was there.

I don't know who she is, but she stood over me, slowly petting my head. I wanted to tell her I wasn't nobody's damn poodle, but I couldn't talk. Just sat there staring up at her.

She wore a black dress, and her skin was pale. I couldn't see her face. I tried to talk to her, ask her what was going on, but the tightness around my throat cut off my words and crushed my windpipe. It felt like drinking razor blades.

Then there were the fingers in my hair. Her fingers. And her nails raked against my scalp, splitting my skin I was sure. She yanked my head back and drove her fist into my neck.

I woke up choking and coughing, fighting my sheets and screaming at the top of my lungs. I don't know when they came in, but suddenly my parents were there, holding me, talking to me in soft, hushed voices, trying to calm me down.

They let me stay home from school.

SEPTEMBER 2

DEAR DIARY,

Against my better judgment, I finally decided to tell my friends about the dying raven calling my name. During lunch, I pulled out my phone and showed the video because of course I recorded it.

We all stared at the screen in shock as the bird flopped around making a ruckus, but it was just random bird noises. It didn't sound like words at all, let alone someone's name! But I know what I heard. Except that's not what's on my phone. And when I ask some of the kids from my class, they either laugh or give me weird looks. Even Mrs. Wemzy denies it happened. I feel like I'm being pranked, but it's not funny. I'm over it! Plus, now I look like a liar who wanted to show something gross to her friends. That . . . bothers me.

To make things worse, Stacy called it an Animal Planet snuff film. CeCe tried to assure me that it almost sounded like the bird said my name. Kal didn't say anything, just picked at his food.

When it was time to go back to class, Kal stopped me in the hall and said he had to tell me something important. He was acting all cagey, glancing around, like he was worried about someone seeing us together or being caught in the hall, but it was between classes. *EVERYONE was in the hall.*

I started to ask what was wrong, but he cut me off saying he couldn't talk here and to meet him at his locker after school. Before he ran off, he warned me not to give *anyone my* name. No idea what he was talking about and didn't get a chance to ask. I went to his locker, but he never showed up. I missed my bus and ended up asking Stacy for a ride. I'm gonna wring his neck tomorrow.

SEPTEMBER 6

DEAR DIARY,

Kalvin hasn't been back to school this week. He won't answer any of our texts or DMs except to say he's fine, then it's silence again. I'm two seconds away from going over to his house and kicking his ass in front of his mom for worrying me like this. Stacy agrees. CeCe thinks we should give him space.

Fine. I'll give him the weekend.

See, Mathilda? I can be patient.

SEPTEMBER 9

DEAR DIARY,

Had *another* nightmare. It started like it always did, the eyes following me, their gazes searing. I thought you weren't supposed to feel pain

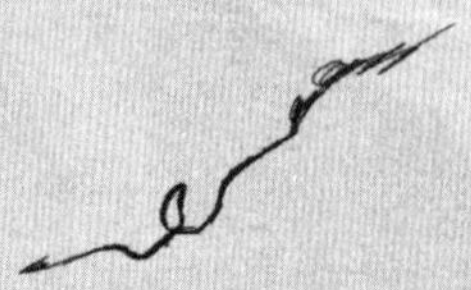

in dreams. My whole body felt like my skin was going to melt off my bones. When the pain finally faded, I sat up in a field of grass wearing the black dress. Just like last time.

And just like last time, a girl wearing the same dress came to me. I still could not see her face, but her eyes shone like stars and her hands burned like ice when she dug her fingers into my hair and yanked. My head snapped back. My scalp was lightning and glass shards. Her fist plunged into the flesh of my throat. There was pain. So much pain. I wanted to scream WAKE UP! Why wouldn't I wake up! I did last time!

But then, on the heels of the pain, there was relief. I coughed and hacked, reaching for my wounded neck. I froze when I realized I could move.

I scrambled to my feet, panting, wheezing, clutching at my throat. It was fine. I was fine. And I was staring at the girl fully now. Her face was still . . . strange. I remember seeing it, thinking she was pretty, but I can't remember what it was I saw. When I try to describe her even to myself, I can't. It's just blank.

I remember hearing myself ask her what she wanted, why she was doing this to me.

She asked if she could have my name. *Without thinking about it I answered.*

The woman smiled, and told me I belonged to her now.

Then I woke up.

SEPTEMBER 13

DEAR DIARY,

Raven eyes followed me everywhere at school today. It didn't matter if I was sitting near a window or not, I swore I could see them glinting in corners or glaring from the shadows of doors and desks. Every sudden movement or sound made me tense. My whole body felt like a bell that's been rung too many times. My bones have anxiety now, okay?

Good news, though. Kalvin was back at school, though he looked worse than I felt. He had rings around his eyes, and he was still wearing the clothes he had on last time I saw him. It had been a while, but I was certain of it. I'd complimented his Demon Slayer T-shirt, the black one with Kyōjurō on it from Hot Topic? I remember because I wanted it, too.

He avoided us most of the day, but I managed to corner him during study hall. I demanded to know why he ghosted on us, and why he left me hanging after telling me he had something important to show me. Get this, he acted like he had no idea what I was talking about! I could have fold him six ways. Fine. Whatever.

That's not even the weird part. He didn't mention fairies, not once. That nigga ALWAYS talking about fairies.

Anyway, Stacy and CeCe were happy to see him, too, of course. Neither of them caught on to the fact that he was still wearing old clothes. Well, maybe CeCe did, but she didn't say anything. She just squeezed my hand every time she looked at him. She was worried.

At lunch, Stacy offered to give me something to help me sleep. I'd finally broken down and told her and CeCe I was having nightmares. Night terrors, really. CeCe kissed my cheeks and poor-babied me. Stacy started digging through her stash, claiming to have something that would knock me *OUT out*. That meant not dreaming. I was tempted to take her up on it, but a look from CeCe made me refuse. Stacy stared for a second, then shrugged and told me to let her know if I changed my mind.

On our way back from lunch Stacy gave me a side hug and said she hoped I feel better. I thanked her. For the kind words and for what I felt her slip into my pocket.

September 16

Dear Diary,

Kal been *acting* real weird. *For Kal.*

I mean, he seems fine. Back to hanging out with us, even eating lunch with us. On the surface it's all good, but something just doesn't feel right.

Did I mention he ain't said boo about fairies for over 48 hours? Went from talking about them damn near all day every day to not saying a thing. Scratch that, not only does he not talk about fairies, but he changes the subject whenever WE talk about them, which is mostly to ask him why he's NOT talking about them. Confusing as hell.

CeCe is worried, because of course she is. My girl has a big heart, s'why I love her. Stacy says he probably outgrew it or just changed his mind. It happens. She emphasizes this by talking about how one day she was happy having long, blond hair, and the next day she cut it all off and dyed what was left crayon red.

I told her that's not exactly the same thing, but I get her point.

Still, though, something's off with Kal.

Now I'm worried, too.

September 18

Dear Diary,

I might be losing my mind.

Or I'm sleepy enough to think I am. The nightmares are worse. The ravens are there, the girl and her black dress, punching me, demanding my name, waking me up, over and over and over. I'm fucking exhausted. Fell asleep in class three times today. But that's not the crazy part.

Now I'm seeing things.

Bird-shaped shadows glide through the halls, along with the flutter of wings that only I can hear. Well, me and Kal. Every time I catch a glimpse of something out of the corner of my eye, or turn after hearing a sudden sound, if Kal is nearby, he's staring straight at me. I don't like it. And I don't like that my nightmares have followed me into the real world. The least they could do is give me some damn peace at night if they're gonna plague me during the day!

Stacy's "gift" is still tucked under a pile of bras in my underwear drawer. After dropping the pills in my pocket, she texted me that they were Ambien and I should only take ONE when I was absolutely ready to sleep because "boy howdy" they worked and they worked fast. She knew from experience. I've been hesitant to take them. Google says they're pretty addictive.

CeCe has started giving me lingering looks, and not the romantic kind. She knows something's up. I don't know what to tell her, because I don't know what the hell is going on, just that I would kill for a good night's sleep.

SEPTEMBER 19

DEAR DIARY,

I took the Ambien. Five minutes ago. I need to sleep. The world is tilting sideways, everything looks like it's being filtered through blue light, the birds won't leave me alone. Stacy said it should kick in pretty fast. Please. That's all I want.

I don't care about the nightmares. I just want to sleep.

Please let me sleep.

I know you're there. Watching me.

You watch me all the time, you see everything I do.

Through the ravens.

So many ravens.

They caw and flap and scratch and peck.

Let me sleep.
Let me SLEEP!

SEPTEMBER 20

DEAR DIARY,

Stayed home from school today. Again.

I'm so tired. Why can't I sleep? The pills didn't work.

Stacy says she's got something stronger. Might take her up on it.

Parents are starting to worry. Don't know what to tell them.

More nightmares. No ravens, just her. She doesn't hurt me anymore. She tells me she can help me. She calls someone's name. My name? She sings a song. I'm hers, she says. She takes care of hers. I just have to come to her.

Friends came to visit. CeCe gave me worried kisses. Stacy gave me another "gift." Stronger she promises. Kal didn't give me anything, just smiled.

Parents didn't let them stay long. I need my rest, Mom says.

What rest.

I don't rest.
I never rest.

Kal came to my window last night. Told me he was here to take me to her.

Or maybe that *was* a dream.

I miss dreams. I miss dreaming. Even night*mares*.

Even her

So tired.

Can't think straight. CAnt see

See her

who is she

she is me who **is** me me is she

am i

her

herrrrrrrrrrrrrrrr

Hers

Don't go

mAb

OCT. 6

Alexis finally came back to school today. I was starting to worry since she wasn't replying to my texts. Or Stacy's. Kalvin doesn't do texts anymore, not since he decided to unplug from technology for a while.

My girl looks so much better than the last time I saw her, which was almost a week ago. The bags under her eyes are gone, she doesn't look like a walking zombie. Seeing her now, so vibrant and practically glowing, I'm relieved. Mostly.

Don't get me wrong, I'm glad she recovered from whatever she had, but some small part of me is still uneasy about it. I can't help but feel like something is wrong . . .

Anyway, last night I had the weirdest dream about ravens.

THE NIGHT AND HER DARKNESS

Nafiza Azad

Trigger warning: Child abuse

The sea is a song in blue,

but I am deaf to its music.

A scream, its edges sharp, is caught inside me, leaving me unable to hear any song except the one it sings.

I stand at the water's edge, gazing out at the blue before me. The waves are tame, behaving for the tourists gathered to see the sun set. The sand is gritty underneath my almost bare feet—almost because my flip-flops are two steps away from death.

A wave, larger than normal, suddenly attacks, wetting my pants. The backs of my legs sting in response to the salt. The welts there are a consequence of last Thursday's sin.

Mr. High School Principal, also known as my father, fashioned a switch out of a branch of a lemon tree, leaving a thorn or two to spice things up. He gave me five lashes and stopped only because he drew blood. Blood scares him—even when he is the cause of its appearance.

Did it hurt? Yes.

Did I cry? Yes.

Will I sin again? Absolutely.

The sin?

Being in the front yard when tourists were walking by.

The house I live in is right beside the beach. Tourists are *always* walking by.

I used to pray for a monster to eat my parents. I waited but God didn't listen to my prayers. So I decided to **become** that monster.

I sin, intentionally, once a day. The sins include:

- *Leaving the bedroom door open at night.*
- *Leaving my homework incomplete.*
- *Listening to the radio.*
- *Not being hungry.*
- *Being hungry.*
- *Sometimes, existing. Though I suppose that's not intentional.*

I collect the consequences of my sins in bruises on my body, days marked by the absence of food, and confinement in my room.

I don't understand why they hit me. Their reasons don't matter to me.

What matters is the way they unravel every time they realize their control over me is fading.

After I turned sixteen, a frothy feeling—the sea during a storm—coalesced within me. The little sins I committed no longer satisfy me. These days I smile at strangers, most of them tourists who crowd the beach. I don't smile at them because I'm feeling friendly. No, I smile at them because I have been expressly forbidden to.

My actions enrage my parents. Mr. Principal, in particular, feels that my smiles advertise my loose virtues. According to him, my smiles are a prologue to an immoral life.

I have snapshots in my mind. My parents' faces, frozen mid-grimace. Their eyes, narrowed in contempt. Lips, peeled back in snarls, spittle flying as they rain down expletives that used to hurt as much as their slaps do. Grotesqueries.

I consume them every time they lose control. Every time they cause me pain. Every time they lose the thin veneer of civilization they put on for the world.

The consequences hurt but *I* choose the pain. You may not believe it, but there *is* a difference.

I became a monster so I could reveal their monstrosity.

My presence on the beach at this moment is the biggest sin I have committed yet.

Mr. and Mrs. Principal have a school event tonight they couldn't get out of. They were obviously not going to take me. I am something of a dirty secret for them (I don't meet the standards they set for a child inheriting their genes). They even homeschool me. Anyway, I was left at home, in my room, with two locked doors between me and freedom.

I waited two minutes after they drove away in their dingy old Mazda. Then, I removed the louvres from the windows in my room, knocked the screen out, and escaped.

The grass was brown under my bare feet but the earth had a pulse to it. Freedom smelled like ripe mangoes and the sea. The coconut trees that make a barrier between the house and the rest of the world looked upon me approvingly as I slipped on a pair of flip-flops and slipped out the front gate and onto the beach.

And so, here I am. Among the tourists spilling over from the resort down the beach, pretending to wait for a sunset I don't care for simply because I can. For once, I can. I raise my face to savor the feel of the sea breeze and notice something glinting in the air.

Immediately after, an apparition, or maybe a phantom, appears before me. I look around to see if anyone else can see it? him? her? them, perhaps, because their form defies gender. But the tourists around me look unaffected.

I reach out a hand to see if I can touch the see-through creature, and electricity bites my fingers.

Physically, they look human, with short hair that springs outward in tight curls, silver in some parts and dark in others. Their eyes are brown like the earth and blue like the sea at noon. Their nose is aquiline and arrogant. No smile dares to move their lips. They have a human form, yes, but somehow, I know, as clearly as I know my name, that they aren't human. They shimmer in the air, barely held together by motes of light. I can't even tell what they are wearing.

My body recognizes them as a threat, a sharp blade at my neck. Being before them feels like being in the shadow of a mountain. When I look at them, I feel an emotion that is not fear, pain, anger, or ennui. I don't know what it is. A spark in my blood. A desire to laugh out loud. Recognition.

I am not the only monster around.

"Will you help me?" The entreaty appears inside my head; the sound is velvet, snug over thorns. I don't know what language the creature spoke in but I understand them.

"With what?" I answer them in a thought.

"Let me shelter within your mind for the night," the creature answers.

It doesn't occur to me to ask how.

"Why me?" Does the creature find me familiar too?

"Of all the humans on this beach at this moment, only you have a scream within you. Your scream will shield me from my enemies."

Oh.

I take a moment to think. It would be safer to refuse. Agreeing with the creature would be agreeing to play with knives. Then again, I have learned to like the feeling of being cut.

Before I can convince myself otherwise, I nod my acquiescence.

The edges of the creature flare when they comprehend my answer. They reach out a hand toward me. At the first touch, their form flickers, and a moment later, they slip under my skin, lodge in my heart, and anchor in my mind. That's all it takes before I am them and they are me.

I become a starburst. A meteor. I burn so brightly it's a wonder no one runs from my inferno. My vision improves to the point of madness. My skin grows so sensitive I can feel each individual grain of sand sticking to my feet. I am strange and glorious.

Maybe this is what taking drugs feels like.

No one around seems to realize the immensity of all that has occurred in the little time it took for the sun to set. The tourists are far too busy moving on to the next item on their itinerary.

"I will stay with you until the first minute of dawn," the creature speaks in my head, more intimate than anyone has a right to be.

"Are you a ghost? Am I possessed right now?"

"No."

"What are you?"

"I am . . ." They pause, hesitating. "You can call me Siga. I am a creature of the Bogi, the night."

"The night is alive?"

"To my kind, she is."

"What is your kind?"

They pause again for such a long time I think they're not going to reply. But finally, they do.

"We are the energy you feel when you stand on the ground on bare feet. The heat that rises like a fever at noon. The whispers the coconut trees use to woo hurricanes. We are the secrets in the cowrie shells on the beach. The sugar in the sugarcane and the glint in the sea. We are in the light but mostly we are of the shadows, moving in the shade of mango trees."

"I get it. You are monsters."

They are silent for a moment before they reply. "*You* are the monster to me."

"Thank you. I try. In case you are curious, my name is Hania." They don't reply but I don't mind. The only people who use my name are my parents, and most often, it functions as an expletive. "By the way, who are you hiding from?" This is important, so perhaps I should have asked sooner. I wait but they don't reply. "Well?"

"Give me a moment. I'm trying to find words that are easy for you to understand," they say.

I wonder if that was a dig at my intelligence. Then again, I did just accept a strange, nonhuman being into my mind.

"I am the future leader of my kind. To truly become the leader, however, I have to survive the horrors, or as we call them, the Gata—a collection of fears who will hunt me through the hours until dawn. I can't fight them, so my greatest chance for survival is to hide within you."

"Because the scream inside me provides a barrier between you and these horrors?" I ask.

"Indeed."

"Am *I* going to be in any danger?"

"If they find me within you, yes. They will take you apart to find me."

"Like I am a gift box?"

They don't reply but the answer is obvious.

"Since I am risking potential annihilation for you, I want a reward if you make it through this night alive." Death doesn't scare me. No, that's a lie, but not really. I fear death less than I fear being robbed of color and life by my parents.

"I give you my word that should I make it to dawn still in possession of my self, I will compensate you for the shelter you've given me." Their words heighten the smell of the salt in the air. I take a deep breath.

"So what do I do now?"

"What were you doing before I came to you?"

"Sinning," I reply promptly.

"According to the god you believe in?" they venture after a moment.

"Oh no." I wave my hand. "According to my parents. For them, a child is nothing more than an opportunity to impose their will upon this world." I turn around and start walking. Nothing like Mr. and Mrs. Principal to trigger my fight-or-flight instinct. "God's rules are easier to follow than theirs."

Walking with a passenger in my mind is easier in theory than in action. I stumble a few times, my perspective skewed by Siga. After I get my bearings, I make my way down the beach, closer to the resort and farther from where my house is. I don't want to return home right now. I might as well see some sights.

The crowds are thicker nearer to the resort. Music filters out from a patio restaurant together with quiet laughs and intimate conversations. The scent of frangipani briefly lights up the night. I stand for a moment, looking at the families in the restaurant. They all seem to like each other. I can't imagine what that must feel like.

Tourists lounge on the beach, waiting for the evening's activities to commence. The only locals present are wearing either uniforms that identify them as staff or costumes that label them entertainers.

I stick out like an elephant at a dinner party with my shabby clothes that cover every inch of my skin (bruises invite questions I don't know how to answer). People look at me; some whisper. I ignore everyone and sit a little distance from a bonfire around which most of the tourists are sitting. A minute later, a man, possibly in his thirties, sidles up to me, holding out a can of chilled beer. "Slake your thirst?"

"I'm sixteen," I tell him without looking away from the undulating flames in the distance. I fancy I can see faces in them.

"I don't mind," the man says, shifting closer.

"I do, and most probably, the authorities will, too," I tell him, and get to my feet.

"Didn't you say you were determined to sin?" the voice in my head says when I've walked to the other side of the bonfire, where the meke dancers are prepping. Beside them, the drummers are tuning their instruments. Vaguely rectangular and hollow drums called laali take up the most space. I read somewhere that these drums were once used to send messages from one village to another.

"Well?" Siga prompts when I don't reply.

"Why didn't I agree to that man?"

"Yes."

"I didn't want to wrong myself," I tell them. "I want to destroy my parents, not myself."

"Are your parents not good to you?" Siga asks.

"Were your parents good to you?"

"We aren't born like humans are. Bogi creates us; she is our mother, our father, our family. She gives us both life and death."

"She also created the horrors that are hunting you?"

Before Siga can reply, the performance begins. When the drummers hit the side of the laali, the creature in my mind flinches, a discordant snap in my synapses.

"They're here!" Siga wails, the cry reverberating in my skull.

Driven by their panic, I jump to my feet even as the sound of the laali creates welts on my skin. The pain is immediate and brutal. The horrors are in the beat of the sticks on the laali. Without needing Siga to urge me, I turn on my heels and run, but the sound follows me. I can feel nails raking down my back as if another monster, one with a desperate need for a manicure, is trying to tackle me. I run until the only sound I can hear is my own gasping breaths. Panting, I stop when I reach a wilder patch of the beach where the roar of the surf drowns out the sound of the laali. My cheeks are wet with salty kisses, and my heart is still convinced it is going to die.

"*That* was the horrors?" I ask as soon as I have enough breath to form sentences. My arms have ugly long scratches down them. My lips are bleeding and my ears feel pummeled. The pain is familiar. It feels real. Somewhat comforting. "*They* are your enemies?"

"I didn't say they were my enemies. The horrors are an obstacle any member of the Bogi wanting to be the leader must successfully overcome. Surviving them is how we prove our worth."

"But you are hiding from them. Don't you have to confront them?"

"No. Didn't you hear me? I said I have to survive them in any way I can. They are not my enemies. They are simply fulfilling the purpose for which they were created. You don't understand, do you? Humans never understand. The world is black and white to you. You keep the things that you can exploit and destroy the things you can't. My people are struggling to survive because you humans are so intent on ruining the land we shelter upon and the air that sustains us."

I am stung by their words. I refuse the responsibility they impose on me. "And yet, here you are, ensconced in the fleshy shell of a human being that will be destroyed in the process of saving your sorry ass." I pause a moment before asking, "Have you considered that you might be a hypocrite?"

"Are you saying humans don't cause destruction?" they challenge.

"No, I'm saying that you cannot judge me for the actions of other people. I don't represent all of humankind. I represent me. That's all. As the future leader, you can perhaps represent your people, but I am no one's leader. I can't even control my own life, let alone anyone else's. I'm helping you as one monster helps another. Not because I am human but because I am me. Don't make me regret it. Please."

I sit down on the rocks, not caring about the sea spray, the pain, and the discomfort. It is difficult to express my anger to a voice in my head but I try.

The silence between Siga and me lengthens. The ocean lies before me, intimidating in its vastness. The sky above me is choked with stars.

The first time I realized that the way my parents treat me isn't normal was the only time I accompanied them to a school event. I was very young, perhaps six or seven. Reasonably cute. Cute enough that the adults who saw me made cooing sounds. Many other families with children attended this event. I saw children running, screaming, being willful without fear of pain. So I asked one of them, a boy with missing teeth, "Did your parents smack your teeth out?"

The question horrified him enough that he told his parents, which made them talk to my parents, who immediately gathered me up and returned home. Three bruises on my hip and a sore back were the consequence of that one question.

I can see a line of houses from where I am sitting with my back to the ocean. A welcoming light spills out from the windows. Could I go to one of those houses instead of my own?

No. I tried once. They sent me back.

When sufficient time has passed and I am reasonably sure the music has ceased, I get to my feet. I look up and down the beach. I can't go back to the resort for obvious reasons. There are no stores nearby and even if there were, they'd be closed at this time. The only place I can go is the house I live in.

"Where are you going?" Siga asks when I start moving.

"You'll see," I reply, wishing they wouldn't.

I've lost my flip-flops somewhere. I use that as an excuse to walk as slowly as I can. My breath grows shorter as the distance between me and the house shortens.

A brief horror curdles my insides when I see the red Mazda standing in its regular spot in the garage beside the house. My parents have returned earlier than I thought they would. I intended them to discover me gone, but I didn't think there'd be a spectator to their madness.

I rub my face, forgetting the scratches on it. The resulting pain reminds me that I was just attacked by drumbeats. That there are things far more dangerous than my parents out there. Besides, I *want* to be caught.

I *want* there to be consequences.

Still, I have to force myself to walk a few steps closer to the house. A bare light bulb glows on the porch; a moth attacks it madly, asking it to reciprocate its obsession. The light bulb remains indifferent.

I was that moth once.

The front door is slightly ajar. The air near the house is heavy with the fragrance of the night jasmine growing wild by the steps leading up to the porch. I take a deep breath, welcoming the night and her darkness into my already crowded body.

"Don't be surprised by anything that happens from now on," I tell

Siga before emptying my expression. I need to prepare myself to face the consequences of this sin. They don't reply, but I can sense their apprehension grow.

I walk up the steps, onto the porch, then across it to the front door. I can see Mr. Principal standing in the middle of the living room, talking on the phone. He is a tall, lean man with little hair and a genial smile when he is in front of other people. In front of me, he is quite different. My heart races. I lick my lips, push the door open, and walk inside.

When he sees me enter the living room, Mr. Principal throws the phone down and stalks over, grabbing me by the shoulders. His fingers press down on my skin as if wanting to break the bones within. "Where have you been?" he screams, his saliva spraying my face. There, the monster peeks out through the cracks created by his shattered composure.

He doesn't seem to notice my bloodied lips . . . or maybe he does and takes the credit for it.

"I went for a walk," I tell him.

As a response, he slaps me. My skin burns, the pain more intense than usual. I wipe the blood from my lips, look up, and give him a smile. I have practiced this smile in the mirror: It's gentle and forgiving. Mr. Principal's eyes widen and a little bit of fear creeps into them. His response pleases me.

"Do you want to hit me some more? Surely one slap isn't enough," I ask him, keeping my voice low, courteous even.

He sputters and backs away, bumping into a chair in the process. He loses his balance and falls to the floor without looking away from me. I've disarmed him.

Whenever they hit me previously, I cried. Once I begged.

Until I realized they relished the control they have over me. That they took pleasure in my pleading.

"What's wrong?" I ask.

Mrs. Principal emerges from the kitchen at this moment. With beautifully coiffed hair and twinkling eyes, she complements Mr. Principal perfectly. Mrs. Principal looks from Mr. Principal on the floor to me standing above him. The twinkle in her eyes dims. Her mouth opens but she doesn't speak. She helps Mr. Principal to his feet and they stand in front of me, united in their disapproval and judgment.

Ever since I can remember, I have known that in this family there are two parties. Party A, my parents, are the superior and Party B—that is me—is inferior. Party A speaks a language designed to exclude Party B. No matter how hard Party B works and no matter what she does, Party B will not receive the affection and approval of Party A.

"Where have you been, Hania?" Mrs. Principal asks sharply.

"As I told Baba, I went out for a walk. This seemed to irritate him, so he slapped me once. I asked him if he wanted to slap me again. Then"—I look at Mr. Principal, who keeps his face turned away—"he seemed to have some sort of reaction, which led him to the position you found him in. Do you want to hit me instead? Maybe a punch to the stomach like you did the last time?"

Mrs. Principal sucks in a breath at my words. Several different expressions flit through her face but none of them reveal the elegance she is known for. I keep my face stoic, prepared for whatever she'll do next.

Suddenly, abruptly, tears fill her eyes. This show of softness is so uncharacteristic that when she walks closer to me and takes my hand, I let her. Mr. Principal snorts his disgust and strides away to their shared study. The tears in Mrs. Principal's eyes spill over, making their journey down her cheeks before meeting at her chin, which they abandon to fall on my hand.

"The horrors are in her tears!" Siga yells in my mind, but it is far too late. The tears fall on the soft skin at the back of my hand, sizzle, and try to sink through it and into my body. Pain, the likes of which I've never felt before, assaults me. I wrench my hand away from Mrs. Principal and sprint into the kitchen to the sink. I turn on the faucet and shove my hand under the water. It takes five minutes before the tears on my hand are overwhelmed by the onslaught of the flowing water. My burnt skin hurts. Cradling my hand, I all but crumple onto the linoleum. The tube light in the kitchen dims and brightens.

"Hania!" Mrs. Principal appears in the doorway of the kitchen, her eyes narrowed. She looks at me a moment too long, as if I'm no longer the girl I was when she left a few hours ago.

I get to my feet and attempt to walk past her. She grabs my burned hand and I flinch, trying to push her away. She doesn't let go. "What is wrong with you?" she demands. "Why don't you obey us? Why don't you listen?" She shakes me.

"I don't want to listen anymore, Mother," I tell her. "You can hit me like you always do. You used to punish me when I didn't do anything. I'm giving you a reason to hit me. Isn't that much better?"

She doesn't speak.

"Will you hit me or shall I go into my room?"

Mrs. Principal staggers as if my question has somehow undone her. I wait, but she doesn't move, so I walk past her and through a long corridor into my room. As soon as I walk in, I see that my windows are back up, screen and all. My parents have priorities.

"Close the windows. Quick!" Siga issues the command and I find myself helpless to disobey. I mutter a few rude words but close them as best as I can. And not a moment too soon because the rain beats the glass through the screen the next second.

The raindrops have a texture distinctly alien to water. They cling to the glass, casting shadows in the shape of monsters. I look a little too long at them.

"Stop," Siga says, and I drag my eyes away.

To distract myself from the horrifying rain, I turn the lights on. When I walk past my dresser, I catch sight of my reflection and freeze. Siga's high cheekbones lift *my* cheeks and their dark gaze shines from my eyes. My lips have an unfamiliar curve and my hair a silken quality that it doesn't deserve.

"Why do you push your parents so much?" Siga asks.

"What's the alternative? Let them hurt me as they wish, when they wish?"

"What if they hurt you too badly?"

"Why, are you concerned for *me*? A *human*?"

"I'm already regretting it."

"If they hurt me, no, if they end up killing me, I will have completed what I seek to accomplish." I look out into the night and I swear she looks back at me. "Dying on my terms will be better than living on theirs."

As I am speaking, lightning flashes and I freeze, not knowing what to do. Anticipation builds, then thunder booms. Something explodes on the inside of my ears. The only thing I'm conscious of at this moment is pain. The horrors are trying to cleave me from the inside! My eyes are wet. Thunder again. The cleaving intensifies. I clutch my head and scream.

"Breathe," Siga yells from within.

"Easy for you to say!" I yell back at them. I look around wildly for something, anything, that will help. I notice a sack of neem leaves sitting in the corner where I left it yesterday. It emits a scent that pulls me closer. I stumble toward it even as lightning flashes for the third time. I sit down on the floor, clutching the neem leaves, rubbing their green off on me.

Thunder shakes the world again, but this time, without the pain. I sag against the wall, not daring to move.

"Why do you have neem leaves in your room?"

"I heard the grandmother down the street say that neem leaves protect you from nightmares," I tell Siga. "So I got them, then realized nightmares aren't my problem. My parents are. Anyway, why do neem leaves keep the horrors away?"

"We are allied with neem trees," Siga says.

"You can ally with trees?" I ask, my voice still shaking from the pain I experienced a few minutes ago.

"The Bogi are part of the natural world. To us, trees are more precious than humans."

I will not respond to that. "What do we do now?"

"Just sit tight and don't move."

"Until dawn?"

"Yes."

"How?"

Siga doesn't reply but I can feel their exasperation.

"Fine. I will try."

I spend the first hour asking Siga all the questions I can think of about the Bogi, their people, their culture, and their magic. They don't answer any of them, telling me I have no need to know. In the second hour, *they* ask me questions I refuse to answer. I must fall asleep somewhere in the middle because I suddenly open my eyes, conscious that time has passed.

"It's dawn." Siga's voice is soft in my head.

"Are they gone?" It has stopped raining and an eerie stillness seems to hold court.

"No, but they will no longer harm me. They can't. I survived the night."

"Thanks to me," I reply, exhausted. "My reward?"

"You have enough courage of your own, so I will leave you with wonder. What you see in things and the world around you and what they will see in you." Siga separates from me and I feel a sudden loss. They shimmer in front of me as they did all those hours ago. They meet my eyes, face solemn. "Thank you for the haven you were for me."

In the next second, without another word, they are gone, leaving me bemused. I would think I dreamed up the entire night but the scratches, welts, and various other hurts on my person remain.

Wonder, huh.

I walk to the mirror again and look at the sculpted planes of my face and the sheen of my skin. My hair grew and my eyes are deeper now than they used to be. Siga left a small sun burning inside me, keeping the darkness at bay, preventing the scream from drowning out all the other songs. Maybe I will be able to hear the blue song of the sea now.

Is this the gift Siga left me? This wonder?

To be honest, I would have preferred money.

When I look outside, I see the grass glistening from the rain, the coconut trees even more graceful than before, and the bougainvillea's majesty. The dark is pliant now, devoid of hostility. All these are invitations to live. Loudly and in full color. Should I accept this invitation?

Can I accept this invitation? Dare I?

Maybe after I have pushed my parents all the way off the edge. Maybe then. If I am still alive.

Maybe then I will.

THE NEW GIRL AT AUTUMN PREP

Christine Day

It was welcome week at the prestigious Autumn Court Preparatory Academy, and Meadow Cloudbank was late for orientation.

Whorls of amber leaves swept across the school grounds as sunlight spilled over the gorgeous stone buildings, the pointed steeples, the winged marble statues, the verdant lawns. Stained glass windows dappled the grand halls in vivid rainbow hues. In the library, the tomes upon the wide shelves—bound in leather, embossed with gold leaf—shone bright in the slanting light.

For the past two days, faeries from all across the realm had been arriving on campus, filling the student dormitories, the cafeteria, the benches around the fountain in the quad. Autumn Prep was a renowned boarding school. Students from the four Courts of Faerie—Summer, Autumn, Winter, and Spring—could apply, but its admissions process was highly competitive and selective. Its acceptance rate was less than 6 percent.

And Spring faeries accounted for less than 1 percent of the entire school's enrollment.

Meadow was the first in her family to pursue a higher education. She was also the first faerie from her hometown in Spring to attend Autumn Prep. Before she left for the academy, dozens of her friends and neighbors had gathered at her childhood home to wish her well. They all danced and laughed and sang deep into the night. And Meadow had been relaxed and happy, seated by the warmth of the bonfire in her backyard, surrounded by her loved ones. By the faeries who believed in her.

Her heart drummed anxiously now as she sprinted up the stairs in the Hall of Riddles and Treaties. Her patchy, embroidered book bag swung awkwardly at her side, and she emerged on the main floor with her floral crown askew on her head.

She was keenly aware of the passing stares from other students, the open curiosity, judgment, even resentment in their gazes. She was also aware of how brightly colored she was, in contrast to her peers; she wore a sundress with frilly lavender ruffles, paired with glossy, lemon-yellow rain boots while they all wore sleek, monochromatic clothes of gray, beige, or cream. Their faces were glamoured to seem humanlike, yet they were impossibly beautiful, their lips like rose petals, their eyes and skin luminous. This was a popular trend among the faeries of Meadow's generation: They detested mortals, but they borrowed their likeness—the skin and hair and eye colors that were commonly seen in the human lands. They hid their wings, hid their tails, hid their horns. They assimilated themselves, opting for sameness, disguising the unique traits of their own homelands.

Meadow, however, was a proud Spring faerie, with fern-green skin and pale golden hair that cascaded gracefully to her waist. She tailored slits into the back of everything she owned to accommodate her iridescent green butterfly wings. And she never erected glamours, humanlike or otherwise. To all who looked upon her, it was clear she came from the eastern borderlands of the Spring continent, and the Court loyalists were often prejudiced against the folk of her region. After all, Meadow's ancestors were among the last to join the Courts of Faerie. The last to sign the Treaty of Everlasting Peace.

By all appearances, their rebellion was crushed a long time ago. Yet faeries rarely forgot these things. And they seldom forgave those perceived as traitors.

As the stares and sneers continued, Meadow reminded herself that she wasn't here to make friends. She was here to pursue her academic ambitions, and to bring more Spring representation into the Court system. Her goal was to eventually become a legislator. Meadow wanted to work within the Courts of Faerie to create a better justice system for faeries of all backgrounds—for those from Spring, for those who were Courtless, for the entire realm.

Meadow reached the classroom door, and paused to compose herself. She brought her fingertips to the circlet on her head and called upon her magic: Her palms tingled as it gathered, cool and smooth and rippling, like a brush of silk against her skin. There were tulips, peonies, forget-me-nots, and daffodils woven into her crown, and they all responded to her magic. Their petals brightened and blossomed; their stems and leaves curled and grew. The fragrance of the flowers intensified, paired with the clean scent of rain.

It was a simple spell, but it grounded her. After months of hard work and giddy anticipation, she was determined to do well at Autumn Prep. To make her ancestors and relatives proud.

But truthfully, she was already homesick for Spring. Everything was so different here in Autumn—even the smell and feel of the rain.

"Well. That was beautiful."

Meadow spun toward the smooth voice. A Winter faerie leaned against the square-paneled wall opposite her, his arms crossed casually over his chest, crisp white shirtsleeves pushed up to his elbows. He was tall and lean and immaculate, from his gleaming black shoes to his blue-black hair. His skin was pale, and his eyes were blue, *luminescent* blue, like the shocking cool glow at the center of an iceberg.

Meadow's wings fluttered—girlishly and involuntarily—in response to him. He was the first glamourless student she'd seen on campus. Judging by his appearance, he probably came from the southwestern region of Winter. This meant that his ancestors, too, might have resisted the Everlasting Peace, out of loyalty to the monarchs that once ruled their lands.

He started to grin, and Meadow became abruptly aware of the fact that she was staring.

"It was nothing," she muttered before ducking into the classroom and away from his gaze.

The lecture hall was an immense auditorium. Chairs with swiveling armrests were arranged in sweeping, crescent-shaped rows. The space echoed with the low murmur of voices, as the other students settled in.

Meadow hurried to find an open seat while a professor furiously scribbled on a blackboard with a tiny fragment of chalk.

He was also a Winter faerie; his skin was the palest shade of blue, his white hair was slicked straight back, and his black robes hung heavily around his frame. He dropped his chalk and straightened his spine, and suddenly, everything dimmed—the lights, the voices, even the rhythm of Meadow's boots on the steps was muffled by a surge of magic. And this magic was cold. Unsettlingly so. It smelled of fresh-fallen snow and pine. It carried the brisk chill of a winter wind, despite the stillness of the air.

The sensation made Meadow shudder.

"Tardiness will not be tolerated in the Autumn Court Preparatory Academy." The professor's words were crisply enunciated; his magic continued to hang in the air, and Meadow felt as if her face and fingers were going numb with the cold. "Nor will we accept laziness, arrogance, ignorance, lack of preparation, or lack of commitment. Attendance at this school is a privilege. And privileges can be easily revoked."

Finally, he released his spell and turned to face the students. His face was severe. His pale gray eyes flicked pointedly in Meadow's direction as she dropped into her seat.

"Furthermore"—the professor sneered—"we abide by a strict dress code in this school. Leniency will be granted for now, since it is orientation day, but make no mistake: Once classes are in session, you are all expected to be presentable."

Meadow tensed. She was the only faerie in the entire auditorium with fern-green skin and butterfly wings protruding from her clothes.

"Rise," the professor commanded. "We will begin with the Pledge of Allegiance."

The students stood eagerly, confidently. Meadow followed suit with some reluctance, though she recited the words on the chalkboard along with everyone else:

I pledge allegiance to the rightful Courts of Faerie
Winter, Summer, Autumn, Spring
Wherein all are treated justly and fairly

THE NEW GIRL AT AUTUMN PREP

Furthermore, I pledge to study and to live
In perpetual service of the Everlasting Peace

After orientation, Meadow went to a café on campus, hoping to find a new haunt for her future study sessions.

And this one happened to be called the New Haunt Café.

It was an opulent yet disquieting space. Couches upholstered in rich, velvety shades of plum and burgundy were arranged around the room. Ornate candelabras stood on the tabletops; each held taper candles with flickering black flames. There were paintings of ravens and skulls and dark farmhouses along the walls. A small stage consumed the far corner of the room; upon it, a lone bewitched cello strummed a trepidatious tune.

Meadow hovered uneasily near the entrance. The New Haunt was packed. Students were crowded around the tables and clustered by the pickup counter, talking animatedly, indulging in deep gulps from steaming mugs. Many of them were dressed in blazers with the Autumn Prep crest on their chest pockets: a black dragonfly poised over a crimson shield and encircled in golden maple leaves.

Meadow's presence drew their attention. Conversations dropped. Narrowed eyes flicked in her direction. She could feel the heat of their glares on her precious wings, her floral crown, her green skin.

She joined the line for the cash register, and distracted herself by watching as the baristas worked—dispensing coffee grounds, frothing small pitchers of milk. The baristas were Autumn faeries, and unlike the students they served, none of them wore glamours. One had a sleek curtain of black hair, wide dark eyes, and stud piercings through his pale cheeks. Goat horns protruded from his forehead.

Another had vibrant orange eyes, long chestnut hair, and bronze skin smattered with brown freckles. She wore an apron with enchanted embroidery. An autumnal forest scene had been sewn into its fabric, but the stitches pulled apart and came together in an easy, slow rhythm, to create the illusion of a breeze moving through the trees.

Meadow pressed a hand to the top of her book bag. She wondered if the enchantment was easy to learn. Her main focus would be legal studies, but she was also interested in tricks to enhance her clothing.

Perhaps this fascination came from the stories she'd heard about her Spring ancestors, who used their textile skills to survive after their lands were invaded.

When foreign representatives from the Courts of Faerie tried to claim their lands, the Spring faeries resisted. Under banners of peace, Meadow's ancestors negotiated for their sovereign rights. And despite those banners, the armed forces of the Courts of Faerie descended upon their villages, razing fields and scorching cottages, spilling Spring blood with gluttonous abandon.

The Spring faeries fought back. These skirmishes were hard-fought and heartbreaking. Entire families were lost. Refugees scattered across the realm. Sumptuously green lands were blackened and hollowed. Rare plants in sensitive ecosystems were exterminated. Serpentine rivers were rerouted with explosives. Forests were annihilated.

The destruction was inconceivable.

After they surrendered and signed the Treaty of Everlasting Peace, the Spring faeries were banished to the eastern borderlands—a territory that was not quite Spring, nor Winter. The region was deemed to be barren. Magicless. The land was flat and brown and marshy, home to scraggly grasses and a few gaunt, crooked trees. The invaders from the Courts didn't expect the Spring faeries to survive there for long.

But Meadow's ancestors were clever. They might have been forced from their homes with nothing but the clothes on their backs, but the women in their community had a secret: Before the battles were lost, and before the treaty was signed, they'd begun sewing seeds into the linings of their dresses. Seeds for a variety of life-sustaining foods and flowers. Together, they carried these seeds as they traversed the continent. They weren't sure if anything they planted would thrive in their new home, but they kept the seeds safe until the end of their arduous journey.

Only then were they rewarded for their tenacity.

The soil wasn't sterile—its magic was merely dormant. With their songs and their skills, the Spring faeries managed to awaken the land. They called its stubborn magic to the surface, and the seeds were then able to take root and thrive. They kept the community alive.

Generations later, the eastern borderlands were gorgeous and abundant, filled with dazzling wildflower fields, rolling green farms, and thriving ecosystems. These lands were a testament to the power of Spring magic. To the enduring spirit of their resilience.

This was the legacy of her ancestors, of the folk who dwelled in the eastern borderlands: the Courts of Faerie had the most powerful army in the history of the realm, and they had tried to destroy the independent clans of Spring, to steal their lands and end their ways of life.

But they couldn't. Not completely. And Meadow stood here as proof, in all her green-skinned and butterfly-winged glory.

Meadow inched forward in the line. Whispers hissed at her back. A susurration of giggles and insults ebbed around her. She bristled but tried to ignore them, casting her gaze around the coffee shop's walls.

Her attention landed on a filigreed mirror and Meadow glimpsed herself as she was: her tall, willowy frame; her crown of Spring blossoms;

her lavender dress; her iridescent wings; her green skin, golden hair, and bright silver eyes; the slender, pointed tips of her ears.

Then her reflection winked of its own volition.

Sudden, silent dread rooted Meadow to the floor.

Conformity is easy, a sinister voice whispered within Meadow's mind. *Watch and see how simple it could be.*

With those foreboding words, the reflection transformed. Meadow watched as her likeness appeared to cast a humanlike glamour: Her green skin turned peachy; her silver eyes turned hazel; her ears became gently rounded; her frilly dress changed into a school-issued uniform; her floral crown and butterfly wings vanished altogether.

"Be careful of the trickster mirror."

Meadow shuddered hard, her wings snapping wildly. One of them clipped the girl behind her, sending the textbooks in her arms to the floor.

"S-sorry, I'm so sorry," Meadow said as she bent to gather the girl's books.

"It's okay," she replied softly. "I'm sorry for startling you."

The girl was dressed in her school uniform, and she wore a humanlike glamour over her features—with the exception of her violet eyes. Purple irises were common among faeries of both Spring and Summer, but she spoke with a slight drawl, which led Meadow to believe she came from Summer.

The girl thanked Meadow for returning the textbooks to her arms, then nodded at the mirror. "It's an Autumn spell," she explained. "The enchantment is impressive, but definitely creepy. I'll never forget that voice in my head, the one time I looked at my reflection." She whistled. "Nightmare fuel."

Meadow realized, belatedly, that her hands were trembling. She knotted them together, trying and failing to steady herself. "Why would they hang a trickster mirror in a student café?"

The violet-eyed girl shrugged. "They play all kinds of mind games here."

The line inched forward again, but Meadow decided she no longer wanted to be a part of it. She turned her back to the mirror and excused herself, brushing past the violet-eyed girl. Her legs were wobbly; her skin felt clammy and cold.

As Meadow left the coffee shop, snippets of chiding remarks and cruel snickers trailed in her wake.

Meadow returned to her dorm, which was a narrow, beige room with a yellowish laminated floor. It contained a small bed, a walnut desk, a matching set of drawers, a microwave, and a cramped closet. It also had a window with white shutters; soft light glowed through its slats from outside.

Meadow removed her yellow rain boots by the door. She had arrived on campus two days ago, and was still in the process of unpacking and organizing. A stack of secondhand textbooks claimed her desk. Posters of famous figures from Spring hung along her walls. A full-length mirror was propped in the corner of the room. And she'd draped enchanted vine garlands and twinkling string lights around the ceiling.

Through the walls, Meadow could hear all kinds of commotion as students raced up and down the corridors, slamming doors, playing jaunty music, chattering excitedly. There were countless back-to-school revels scheduled throughout the night, parties big and small happening all across campus. A few had open invitations. Others were more exclusive. Autumn Prep was famous for its party scene, for mischief and mayhem and debauchery. And there were plenty of students who attended this school for its "social networking" benefits, as well as its stellar academic record.

But Meadow wasn't interested in partying.

She crossed the room and placed her floral crown on the desk. It had wilted over the course of the day, so she called upon her magic again, tracing her fingertips across its waxy leaves and soft petals. The fresh scent of rain filled the air around her. The colorful blossoms leaned into her touch, as if seeking warmth from the sun.

In Spring culture, floral crowns were significant. Treasured. These circlets were created through a complex process of spells and artistry. And this particular crown had been a gift from Meadow's mother, who had spent hours singing incantations, weaving green stems, summoning bees and other pollinators, and spelling rain clouds into existence. It was time-intensive, intricate work.

With the crown restored, Meadow sat on her bed and plopped against the pillows, her wings folding delicately behind her. Then she lifted her hands. She drew rotating circles in the air, flexing her fingertips, flicking her wrists with each dip and rise. Her magic gathered in the space between her palms—cool rivulets that seemed to braid around her fingers. She grasped these invisible tendrils of magic, weaving them into a new spell. This one required a song, which she gave voice to in low, melodic tones, matching the rhythm she'd learned from her mother.

The pressure of the magic built between Meadow's hands. It started to feel as if she were pushing and pulling underwater, her biceps working harder with each movement. As she reached the final verse of the song, she formed a circle with her arms and pulled the magic in close to her chest. Then she threw her arms out in a broad, sweeping motion—and her ceiling was shrouded in a fine, gray mist. Little pools of light glowed in Meadow's upturned palms, and she watched as the mist drifted down, casting rainbows in the air above her hands.

In Spring, this spell was often sung as a lullaby. Meadow remembered snuggling against her mother's side when she was small, begging her to repeat this spell over and over. Meadow loved everything about it: the warmth and safety of her mother's body, the reassuring cadence of her voice, the sheer joy and wonder of the rainbow-casting magic.

Within moments, the spell's effects began to fade. The mist cleared overhead. The light dimmed from Meadow's hands. The room came back into clearer focus: its beige walls, its worn walnut furniture.

This dorm didn't feel like home yet. Meadow wasn't sure if it ever would.

On the morning of Meadow's first day of class, it rained heavily, furiously.

Dark clouds loomed overhead. The air smelled of dank soil and decaying leaves. Wind thrashed through the trees, causing spindly branches to scratch against classroom windows. Splatters of rain struck the winged statues, dripping from their stone limbs, trailing tears down their mournful faces. The fountain in the quad had been shut off; its black pool was on the cusp of overflowing, like a cold and bubbling cauldron.

Meadow hurried along the slick cobblestone path. She had left her dorm with a black umbrella angled defensively behind her, but it hadn't helped. Her first class was in the Hall of Riddles and Treaties, and by the time she found shelter inside the building, she was completely drenched.

Meadow folded the umbrella and glanced down, assessing herself. Now that the semester had begun, the students were required to wear school uniforms. And so, like every other female student on campus that day, Meadow was dressed in a white polo with a crimson-and-gold-striped necktie, layered with a crimson sweater vest that bore the dragonfly-shield logo on its chest pocket, plus a gold-and-black plaid skirt, knee-length white socks, and shiny black loafers.

This wasn't an outfit Meadow would ever choose for herself. The colors were stark and dour, and they contrasted oddly against her green skin. The materials were also stiff and slightly scratchy; the seams of the polo drew taut ridges down the length of her torso. Plus, the student handbook expressly forbade alterations, so Meadow's wings were uncomfortably folded beneath her top layers.

And the loafers, Meadow noted, were completely impractical in this weather. Her toes were wet. Her feet squished and the shoes squeaked as she trudged across the polished marble floors, heading toward her first-period class.

She knew exactly where she was going. She had already memorized her class schedule:

Period 1—RIDDLES 101: An Introduction to Riddles and Bargains
Period 2—FOREIGN REALMS 102: Mortal Relations and Foreign Realm Affairs
Period 3—FAERIE HISTORY 101: The Founding of the Seasonal Courts

Period 4—FAERIE JUSTICE 102: Introductory Interpretations of Law and Justice
Period 5—MAGICAL CRAFTS 104: Textile Arts and Enhancement Spells

Meadow arrived at Riddles 101. Her classmates leered in her direction as Meadow sat at a desk near the front of the room. The professor was an Autumn faerie with long brown hair, honey-colored eyes, and creamy vitiligo patches across her bronze skin. Unlike the students, she met Meadow's gaze with a kind smile. Meadow smiled in return, grateful to see a friendly face. She unpacked her supplies from her school-issued black backpack, her fingers fumbling as the first-day jitters set in.

The bell rang. Class began. The professor passed around copies of the syllabus—and a crumpled paper ball struck Meadow's shoulder, landing on the edge of her desk. Someone behind her giggled. Another student coughed forcefully.

Meadow hesitated, her wings twitching uneasily beneath the polo.

Then she grabbed the rolled-up paper, stuffing it inside her backpack.

From there, she tried to focus on her professor, on the course description outlined in the syllabus. But she spent the rest of the hour distracted and agitated.

After class ended, Meadow hurried from the room and ducked inside a lavatory down the hall. With her back turned to the stall door, she dug into her backpack and opened the crumpled paper ball.

Her blood ran cold.

It was an illustration, drawn in colored pencil. Someone had depicted a green butterfly and a black dragonfly. And once the paper was unraveled in her hands, an enchantment played out, animating the two figures: the green butterfly started to flap its wings, fluttering aimlessly about the page; the dragonfly buzzed toward it in a direct line.

Meadow watched in silent horror as the dragonfly attacked. As it descended and tore the butterfly's wings from its back.

The weeks wore on and Meadow remained unsure of who had drawn the illustration. The message seemed clear: Someone was trying to bully Meadow into believing she couldn't survive here at Autumn Prep. That, or someone in her class meant to harm her.

She was in her dorm now, preparing to leave for her first-period class, getting dressed in her dragonfly-marked school uniform. As she gathered her homework from her desk and loaded it into her backpack, Meadow glimpsed her reflection in her full-length mirror.

Sometimes, in her loneliest moments, Meadow remembered her encounter with the trickster mirror and considered its advice: *Conformity is easy.* Yes, she imagined, it would be. She could cast a humanlike glamour over herself. She could try to blend in with and befriend her cruel classmates. In her lessons, she could stop arguing against the "truths" described in the standardized textbooks. She could accept history, as it had been written by the conquerors. She could submit to the way things were.

It would be so easy to go along with the status quo.

But she couldn't. She wouldn't.

Months ago, when Meadow's acceptance letter from Autumn Prep had first arrived, her mother had warned her about this: *You've chosen a difficult path*, she cautioned. *The Courts were never designed for us, from their schools to their judicial system. This will be an uphill battle, every step of the way. From your student days to your career as a legislator and policymaker.*

As usual, her mother had been right.

Meadow sighed and drew herself to her full height. She turned to the floral crown on her desk. It was shriveled and brown; the life-giving magic that had sustained its blooms was almost completely depleted. But Meadow replenished it every morning before she left for her classes, and every evening when she returned to her dorm. Because despite how much Autumn Prep tested her, she remained committed to her community. And she continued to find power and purpose in the beauty of Spring magic.

She cast the spell, and her dorm filled with the fresh scent of rain. The flowers flushed with color. Their petals opened wide, and Meadow sensed something like relief radiating from them.

With the crown restored again, Meadow hoisted her backpack over her shoulder.

Generations ago, her ancestors had crossed a continent with seeds sewn into their dresses. Throughout the long walk, they had remained steadfast in their hope that their actions would make a difference. That they were setting a foundation for future generations.

Meadow felt the same way about her education.

Fortified by this belief, she left her dorm and resumed her daily uphill battle.

The days turned to weeks. Weeks turned to months. Then months became semesters, which eventually turned into whole academic years.

Four years later, Meadow graduated from the Autumn Court Preparatory Academy with honors.

There was no strict dress code for the graduating class; each participant was given black robes, as well as a black mortarboard with a crimson-gold tassel. But they could choose which clothes to wear beneath their robes, and they were allowed to personalize their commencement attire.

By all appearances, Meadow's customizations seemed minimal. She had cut slits into her robes to free her wings; she had also attached a charm to her tassel with the crest of the Winter Court Law School. Winter Law was the most respected legal program in Faerie, and Meadow's journey toward becoming a legislator would continue there.

As Meadow was called forward, she stood tall and started to recite a spell—one she had learned through independent study. An ancient and powerful incantation that could only be cast by a faerie from Spring.

Before the commencement ceremony, Meadow had sewn seeds into the lining of her robes. Seeds that typically required soil and sunlight and water to sprout. But as Meadow spoke her spell into existence, she could feel them awaken. The life in them responded to the magic in her. It began as a tingling sensation along her arms that crept inward, toward the center of her torso. And as it reached her core, the magic intensified; it gained a sudden density that nearly brought Meadow to her knees. It knocked the air from her lungs, made her wings tilt and spread.

She gasped between verses, but her voice was resonant with a strength summoned from deep within. The spell demanded a specific timing and rhythm, and Meadow maintained its cadence, despite how unwieldy the magic felt. How it rose and crested like a great wave, threatening to crash over her.

This was the most difficult casting she had ever attempted.

But she would survive it. After these four long years, she knew she could.

As she crossed the commencement stage, the hundreds of seeds she'd sewn all burst into bloom. And Meadow's supporters in the audience—her family and closest friends, all of whom had traveled to Autumn from Spring to witness this moment—ululated joyfully, raucously. Their applause was thunderous, in contrast to the stony silence of Meadow's peers and *their* families.

Fragile green shoots erupted and twined together, forming new threads as the traditional black robes fell away from Meadow's body in tatters. Petals unfurled all around her. The scent was heady and fresh and floral, and her new flowered robes were heavy around her shoulders, but the weight of them felt *good*. Everything about this moment felt right.

Meadow accepted her diploma with an unabashed smile.

THE HONEST FOLK

Holly Black

Once upon a time, there was a girl. She was just twenty and there was a hole in her memory.

When Heather tells her mother she can't recall the whole last week, they get an appointment at a doctor's office that same day.

A white nurse practitioner with hair the color of sand holds his finger in front of her face, moving it back and forth. He shines a light into her eyes and frowns a lot. Checks her reflexes. Asks her questions about the color of the wall, the year they're in, the name of the president.

"Have you been under a lot of stress?" he asks, finally.

I can't remember, she thinks but doesn't say. She doesn't want to scare her mother. "My girlfriend ghosted me, I guess."

Heather does remember her girlfriend and she does remember that she and the girl—well, that part's fuzzy. What she doesn't understand is why, if they were only together for a week, she feels so devastated by her loss. The nurse practitioner and her mother share a glance over her head the way they did when she was a kid and she would lie about strawberries making her mouth itch because she didn't want them to be taken away. *It's not like that*, she wants to say, except maybe it is and maybe it isn't.

"I'd like to get some blood work done and an MRI just to be sure," he tells her. "But the mind can do funny things sometimes."

"But how can I not remember—" Heather starts and then bites off the end of her own question. It feels like something from a soap opera, except if it was, there would have been a hot-air balloon crash, a flower vase to the head, a fall off the balcony of some enormous staircase.

"Our minds protect us in different ways," the nurse practitioner says, attempting to seem wise, despite not looking all that much older than Heather, and apparently having just as few answers. "Get some rest, okay? We'll know more soon."

Heather looks down at her brown toes, the polish on them a chipped, glittering aqua. She forgot to moisturize past her ankles and her feet look as tired as she feels.

Next, they go to the clinic, where Heather lets the phlebotomist, an Asian woman with truly excellent winged eyeliner, draw three vials of her blood. Her mother makes light conversation on the drive home, but the edge of worry never leaves her voice.

Heather stares out the window at the familiar landscape, her mind poking at the holes in her memory, the way you run your tongue over the sore, bloody hollow of a missing tooth. But the more she tries to concentrate, the more it's like when she's trying to fall asleep and pictures a peaceful seashore, only to have her mind unhelpfully supply her with images of zombies walking out of it or sharks chewing on her arm. Every time she tries to remember the past week, there's some distracting thought to yank her attention away.

For three days, Heather stays home from community college, even though it's her last year and she needs to keep her grades up if she wants to transfer to the art college that finally, grudgingly has accepted drawing comics as a major. Her father brings her buttered toast like she has the flu. Her mother stays home from the office and comes into Heather's room at odd intervals, with laundry or complaints about the trash in the back seat of her car or more questions about how she's feeling.

Heather doesn't lose any new memories. Her MRI comes back normal and her blood work reveals that she needs to take more vitamin D, but is otherwise healthy. Maybe it really was just stress.

And if she'd spent any of that missing week getting over being dumped, she's lost that along with her memories. It feels as fresh as if it happened the day before. Fresh enough that she's cried into her pillow about it. And even though it's ridiculous to be this upset when she can't even remember exactly how things ended, knowing that doesn't make the upset go away.

She can't *keep* crying about it, though. She sits cross-legged on her bed, writing out advice for getting over a breakup in her bullet journal, along with silly illustrations. She has the idea that she might post them on her Instagram, one per day.

Eat a lot of chocolate.
Cry over sad songs.
Get revenge hairdo.

The thought of a revenge hairdo distracts her enough to get her to pick up her phone and thumb through TikTok, looking for a style. Heather has had pink hair sewn in for the last three years, but she wonders if maybe she needs a change. Twists? Locs? Microbraids past her butt? Microbraids so long that she could push them over her face and hide behind them like Cousin Itt from the Addams Family.

Maybe Heather should add *feel extremely sorry for self* to the list.

When her phone rings, she's so startled that she drops it on her comforter.

"Carl," she says when she retrieves it.

"You missed Printmaking," he says. "You coming to Commercial A&D tomorrow?"

At school, Heather has a crew of friends. Most of them Black kids like her who grew up in white places. Most of them queer and artists. All of them in one another's business. "I'll be there."

"Come for coffee after," he tells her. "Brew-ha-ha Café. As per usual."

Heather isn't sure she wants to go anywhere except back to bed.

Maybe it will be good to go out. Maybe she'll feel better. Maybe someone will remind her that she was in a hot-air balloon crash after all.

"Fine," she says, and hangs up before he can talk her into anything else.

When Carl broke up with his last boyfriend, he had to be physically restrained from texting him at all hours of the night. She and Rose alternated keeping his phone in their bras to keep him from reaching for it, which only mostly worked. Given all that, Heather feels he should be more sympathetic.

Of course, it's possible this is what that kind of sympathy looks like from the other side. Still, Heather looks at her phone and begins scrolling through it, looking for old texts. Looking for *something*. But as far as she can tell, if there were any messages between her and this girl, she's deleted them.

It's strange, though, that she didn't think to look before.

That night Heather dreams of being at a wedding, but there's no bride or groom and no aisle. She's in a hedge maze, lost, able to hear a reception but not get to it. She can discern music and laughter, but when she calls out, her throat doesn't work right.

Is it her wedding? Rose petals are blowing through the air, but she has a sense of foreboding, as though something awful is about to happen.

The bushes around Heather start to grow, looming over her. A moment later, she realizes they're not growing; she's shrinking. She looks at her hand and watches it curl, fur sprouting from her knuckles. Her mouth opens, but instead of a scream, what comes out is a long and terrible hiss. She feels someone reach for her and lashes out, fighting her way loose from their grip.

When she wakes, she has blood under her nails, but it doesn't take long for her to realize that's because she's been scratching her own arms.

Heather decides that what she really needs is a shower. And clean clothes that are not just sweatpants. And coffee. And to swear off girls forever. Maybe swear off sleep too.

She makes herself a peanut butter sandwich with some mango-guava jam her mother gets from a Jamaican lady at the farmers market. The lady also does braids, Heather remembers, and goes back to imagining her revenge hairdo. Imagining her ex seeing her and—

Her head starts to hurt again. Maybe she should go back to bed.

Two cups of coffee and a sandwich later, her headache goes away. *It must have been caffeine withdrawal*, she decides. She's sure of it when the pain doesn't come back even after she turns up the music in her car as loud as it can go.

"What is that saying? Best way to get over someone is to get under somebody else." Carl is drinking a mocha and holding forth from the head of their table at Brew-ha-ha. The room is full of students cracking jokes, doing homework, in study groups. Laptops are open on tables. In the corner, someone is sleeping, a textbook covering their face to shield them from sunlight.

Heather's cousin Mikey is there too. Heather and her friends have been looking out for Mikey since she's sixteen and was homeschooled before starting college this past semester. She's not used to being around tons of people, much less people a lot older than her. Also, she might be a genius.

"That's Dorothy Parker you're quoting, right?" says Rose, an art major who does tattooing as a side hustle. Both her arms are covered in sleeves of images, bright colors etched in her skin. Her twists are pulled up into a topknot, a few of them flecked with blue paint. "The one who didn't like glasses, but did like martinis? Bequeathed her estate to the movement?"

"*Yes*," Carl says, with the air of someone who feels his wisdom is not being appreciated properly. "But the important thing is to remember there are lots of hot bitches waiting for you to swipe their way."

Rose gives him a repressive look and turns to Heather. "You've got that comic project. I've got to do four more big-ass oil paintings for the end-of-year show. Let's go to the studio and make stuff. We'll drink all the coffee and Red Bull. And when you're a lion announcing your TV deal in Hall H of Comic Con, you can talk about how you used the power of heartbreak to make the greatest animated series of all time. Or you can forget her, which is way more devastating."

"I don't know if she's the kind of girl who would even go to Comic Con," Heather says, the words "forget her" clanging alarmingly in her head.

In a horrible flash, she realizes she doesn't know her ex-girlfriend's name. She can't remember what her ex even looks like. It feels like being in the nightmare again, the hedges looming around her.

How can Heather be sad about someone whose *name* she doesn't remember?

"What did I tell you about my ex?" she asks Carl, hoping he will say the girl's name. Maybe if he does, she'll recall something more.

For a moment, he frowns. Rose frowns too. As though they're concentrating. As though their heads hurt. As though maybe there are holes in their memories too.

Heather feels a sharp jolt of panic.

"What about *her*?" Mikey says, nodding toward a blond white girl with her hair pulled back in a ponytail. She has pointy features—a sharp chin, and the kind of cheekbones that make her face seem slightly triangular, but in a pretty way. She's wearing a loose white shirt, tight pants, and high boots.

Heather hadn't noticed the girl when they came in, and now that she's looking, her fingers itch to draw her. But there was something on Heather's mind a moment before . . . something important . . . It feels as though it is on the very tip of her tongue.

"That's the kind of girl that goes to Comic Con?" Rose says, frowning in confusion.

"No, a hot bitch," Mikey says. "She was staring."

Heather gives Carl an accusatory look for corrupting her cousin. He shrugs, unfazed.

At that moment, perhaps feeling the weight of their stares, the girl glances up.

"Oh shit," Heather says, turning her face toward the table.

"She's heading this way," Mikey says, sounding entirely too pleased about it.

Heather turns, knowing she shouldn't. Her arm knocks against her latte. The paper cup hits the ground, splashing Heather's leg with lavender-scented milk.

And spattering the top of the girl's green leather boots.

"Shit," Heather says, standing. "Sorry."

Carl hands over a big wad of napkins. Mikey snickers.

"Hi," the girl says.

"Hi," says Heather, feeling the skin of her neck go hot, feeling her cheeks burn.

"Can I buy you a latte?" the girl asks with a lopsided smile. She has the oddest color eyes, a brown so light it looks yellow.

"I should buy you one since I spilled mine *on* you," Heather says. Her palms are sweating and she has no idea why.

"We can buy one for each other," the girl says. "I'm Vivienne."

"*Vivienne.*" Heather echoes, follows her into the coffee shop line. A mom in front of them is trying to persuade her son to choose between several flavors of cake pop. "Does anyone ever call you Vee?"

"Just you. But people sometimes call me Vivi."

Heather has the strangest feeling. It's the spark of desire, sure, but also the excitement of being near someone you're interested in, a kind of fizziness like someone carbonated your blood. But it ought to be too soon to feel this. Especially so much *this*.

"Lavender, right?" Vivi asks.

Heather nods. Brew-ha-ha makes all kinds of flowery coffees—rose and lavender and hibiscus. Carl says they all taste like soap. "What about you?"

"An espresso, I think." Vivi gives her a dazzling smile. A flash of white teeth.

Heather shivers.

After they order their coffees, they stand together at the end of the counter, talking as they wait for the drinks to be made. Vivi has watched all of Heather's favorite animated shows and read all of her favorite comics. She has funny opinions about them, too, and gestures with her hands when she talks. Heather's gaze drifts to her mouth several times.

"Want to get dinner tomorrow?" Vivi asks, and Heather realizes suddenly how long they've been standing there. She's finished her latte without noticing. Vivienne took her espresso shot ages ago.

"Sure," Heather says, fishing for her phone.

"Meet me at the corner of Craggmere and Cottage?" Vivi says. "At seven?"

"Okay," Heather agrees.

Vivi chucks away her tiny cup, then heads for the door. "Perfect," she calls back, not asking for a number and not giving one.

The next day, Heather goes to class. Her professor gives her back a folder of sketches she turned in for her upcoming project. It's supposed to be a comic, set in a Faerieland that was hidden in the middle of Portland, Maine.

Vivid backgrounds, he wrote at the top. *Looking forward to seeing more!*

She flips through the art, feeling pleased with herself, until she stops, fingers bending the edge of one page as they tighten.

She drew a girl standing beside a hedge maze—a girl with cat eyes and pointed ears, but in every other way a mirror image of the girl from the coffee shop.

Freaked out by the drawing, she thinks about canceling the date with Vivienne. Then she remembers that she doesn't have her phone number. And imagining Vivi standing on that corner, waiting for her in the cold, makes Heather go out despite herself.

Vivi is at the crossroads, just where she said she would be, wearing an enormous black coat and enormous black boots and an enormous grin. She has a basket draped over one arm, as though she's cosplaying a modern Little Red Riding Hood.

"I wanted to take you someplace weird," the girl says. "But weird good."

"I like weird," Heather says.

They walk together until they come to a park. Heather has that strange lightheaded feeling of excitement again, the one it ought to be too soon to feel.

"We're going to eat up there," Vivi says, pointing to a tree, a little shyness in her voice. She seems as though she isn't sure if Heather will be game. "Of course, we don't have to. We could get pizza instead if you want."

Heather laughs. It all feels like it's from a story. A fairy tale, a romantic manga. "Up in a tree? Sure. No reason for us to pretend to be normal people."

This has been one of the best things about spending so much time in the art department, the feeling of being with people who welcome strangeness, who see the world as beautifully off-kilter.

Vivi laughs and scrambles up onto a branch, giving Heather a hand when her foot slips on the bark. Soon they are sitting together on the swaying bough of a tree.

In the basket, Vivi has brought little cardboard boxes full of appetizers from a noodle shop in town—lemongrass ribs, vegetable dumplings, scallion pancakes. Stowed beside them are a bottle of fizzy elderflower soda, a pair of wineglasses, restaurant chopsticks in their paper sleeves, and cloth napkins.

Vivi doesn't ask her the regular questions about music and hobbies and past relationships. She asks Heather what games she used to play as a child and whether she would be willing to trade her sense of taste for a new sense, even if she wasn't sure what it did. It's a strange, magical conversation and Heather doesn't want it to end, even though her butt gets cold and hurts a little from the branch.

"How about you?" Heather asks. "What games did you play as a child? And who did you play with?"

"I have two younger sisters," Vivi tells her, seeming to choose her words carefully. "And a little brother. We used to play with weapons mostly. Archery contests. My sisters had a lot of sword fights."

Heather has the strangest feeling of déjà vu, but she forces out a laugh. "Were your parents actors or something? Survivalists?"

"My father is high up in the military," Vivi says after a long, strangled pause.

Heather tries to think of something to say to shift the mood. "You must have moved around a lot."

"Just one big, permanent move." Vivi looks so sad that Heather leans forward, putting her hand on Vivi's shoulder, trying to give her some kind of comfort.

Vivi looks at her in a stunned kind of way. Goes very still.

Before Heather can decide if she's brave enough to go for the kiss she's thinking about, a drop of rain strikes her cheek, another hits her hand.

"We should—" Heather starts, planning on suggesting they run for a café.

"There's something I have to give you," Vivi says, cutting her off. But instead of speaking, she takes a deep, ragged breath.

For a moment, they just stare at each other. Heather looks into the unusual yellow-brown of Vivi's eyes and chews on her own lip. Thinks about her drawing, in which Vivi's pupils are like those of a cat. Feels as though she's impossibly become part of her own comic in that moment. Rain patters the leaves all around them.

From the bottom of the basket, Vivi draws out a line of beads. They look like rose quartz, soft in the moonlight. "Can I see your wrist?"

Heather feels flattered and also a little confused. Vivi didn't need to give her a present. But she lets her tie the bracelet on.

"Keep this on, okay?" Vivi says. "Even if you're mad at me. At least until tomorrow, at dawn."

"Why would I be mad at you?"

Without answering, Vivi jumps out of the tree, landing soundlessly on the grass. Then the girl walks off, head bent. Hands fisted.

The rain comes down harder.

Heather jumps down out of the tree, basket in hand. "Wait!" she calls. "Your stuff."

It's a stupid excuse, and ridiculous to chase after someone she just met, but she doesn't understand what happened. She races after Vivi. As her footfalls get close, the other girl turns around. Hair is plastered to her face, stuck to her cheeks.

Heather holds out the basket wordlessly, but Vivi ignores it. She takes Heather's face between her hands and kisses her. Kisses her with a drowning desperation. This doesn't feel like the first kiss that it is. It feels like the kiss someone gives their beloved before they are dragged away to their death.

Then Vivi steps away, breathing hard.

"I'm not like you," she says. "I'm not human. And I don't want to scare you . . ."

Heather can feel the incredulousness writ on her face. This is the wrong side of strange. Bad weird. For a moment, she wonders if this could be a joke, a prank. But Vivi's face is too serious, too sad.

"I don't think I can do this," Vivi says, her voice breaking.

This time when she walks off, Heather is too stunned to do anything but watch her go.

Heather walks through the streets, soaking wet, basket hanging from her arm. She thinks of her umbrella, lying useless in the back seat of her car. Three streets later, she ducks under an overhang to wait for the rain to slow.

Her eyes sting with tears, even though she just met Vivienne and the girl clearly has problems. Maybe she thinks she's some kind of alien, or maybe she's one of those people who believe they're vampires because they have an iron deficiency and treat it by drinking their friend's blood. Any which way, it was better that Heather found out early. Better that she knew to steer clear.

A pair of rats are sitting near the opening to an alley. A gray one is chewing on a beetle. A brown one is sitting up on his back haunches, surveying the street. A few cars go by, their beams lighting up the sidewalk.

"Hiding out from the rain too?" Heather asks them conversationally.

"Don't like the feeling of it on my whiskers," squeaks the gray one.

Heather gives a little squeak herself and takes a step back in surprise.

"What a polite girl," squeaks the brown. "Asking after us. But then, you'd better be."

Heather feels a little lightheaded. "What do you mean?"

"You're on a quest, aren't you?" The brown rat looks at the other one. "Trying to save the sister to the Queen of Faerie. Got to be nice to any potential animal helpers."

Heather seems to have stepped into the pages of a fairy tale. But she's read a lot of them and at least she knows some of the rules. Animal helpers are important.

Reaching into the basket, she sets down some of the remains of the meal. A half-eaten scallion pancake. A single vegetable dumpling, some of its insides coming out of its torn wrapper. "In case you're hungry."

The rats scuttle back in alarm, then come forward to sniff at her offerings.

"She's not on a quest." The gray rat sniffs the edge of the pancake and takes an experimental bite. "She's the prize. The sister to the Queen of Faerie is trying to steal her away from the mortal world."

"Then she definitely needs our help," says the brown rat, turning toward the dumpling and nibbling at the edge.

"How is it that I can understand you?" Heather asks, thinking back on the surrealness of the night. Maybe there was something hallucinogenic in the fizzy elderflower soda, some fungus growing inside an improperly sealed cap. *The sister to the Queen of Faerie.* Was that what Vivi meant when she said she wasn't human?

"You're under a spell."

"A spell?" Heather echoes.

The gray rat gazes up at her. Sniffs the air. "Maybe more than one."

Heather thinks of her lost week of memories and then looks down at the pink crystal beads circling her wrist. If Vivienne isn't human, isn't lying, then she's part of the mystery. Part of the memories that are gone. And after that kiss, Heather can easily believe they kissed before. But was Vivi on her side? Was she really the sister of the Queen of Faerie, trying to steal Heather away?

"How can I remove these, uh, spells?" she asks.

"There's one on your wrist. I could chew it off," says the brown rat.

Even though they seem friendly, she's not willing to let those rodent teeth that close to her skin. She pulls at the string of the bracelet, but it is tied fast, the knot so tight that she'd probably need to cut it to remove it.

Keep this on, okay? Even if you're mad at me. At least until tomorrow, at dawn.

"And you could give it to us," says the gray one. "In payment. But whatever you do, you need to throw it away."

"What about the other spell?" she asks.

"Bryern could help," says the brown rat.

"Could he? Should she go to him?" says the gray.

"No," said the brown. "Bargains with the Folk are always full of tricks. They can't lie, so they never say what they mean."

"Okay," says Heather slowly. Despite the warning, this is her only clue. "Where should I avoid, since I don't want to find him?"

"That's easy," says the brown one. "Especially on full moon nights like tonight."

"Don't go to Fort Williams Park," says the gray one.

"Definitely not inside the walls of the old Goddard Mansion."

Heather knows exactly where that is. Not an actual mansion, but the stone walls of an old estate. You could see through it, to the grass inside. There was fencing up, so you couldn't actually go in there. But maybe this Bryern guy could.

"There's a stone," the gray rat continues. "Whatever you do, you must not go up to it and say: *Stone of old, heavy and cold, move aside from the way foretold.* If you do, you'll find a great hall underground where the solitary Folk gather to make merry when the moon is high in the night sky. Mortals aren't allowed."

Heather doesn't like the word "mortal." It feels like being in a fairy tale again, but in a not-so-good way. As if she's Little Red Riding Hood, hearing the pad of the wolf behind her, waiting for her to take a step off the path.

"You've got to be joking," Heather says.

"That's rats for you," says the brown one, taking a huge bite of the insides of the dumpling. A piece of carrot sticks to its nose. "Huge jokers."

On the drive over to Fort Williams Park, with her heater turned all the way up, Heather tells herself all the reasons why she shouldn't do this, from the fact that cops might draw on her if they spot her trying to break into an old fort to the worry that hearing rats talk was a sign she might be having a break with reality.

"Hey, Siri," she says.

"Hmmmm," says her phone in an alarmingly real pantomime of a human.

"Are faeries real?"

"Faeries are paranormal creatures that exist or existed in nature," her phone says, as though that's supposed to help.

"Siri, are fairies dangerous?"

The pleasant voice in her phone speaks again. "Yes. Shakespeare wrote, 'There are fairies; he that speaks to them shall die: I'll wink and couch: no man their works must eye.'"

"Well, that does sound bad." And yet, she can't talk herself out of taking a look, at least.

Bargains with the Folk are always full of tricks. They can't lie, so they never say what they mean.

Once she's pulled over, she gets to work on the bracelet. It isn't long before she has it off. But that's just the beginning of what she's got to do.

The park is quiet and dark as she approaches. When she was younger, she went here with her mother and danced around the wildflowers in the children's area, splashing in the pond and trying to catch frogs.

Now she walks through the rain, head down, soaked to the bone.

The closer she gets to the remains of the Goddard Mansion, though, the more she feels as though the wind is bringing her faint strains of music. A few more steps and she is sure she can hear it, coming from everywhere and nowhere at once, as though it emanates from the earth itself. Occasionally the sound is smothered by the crash of waves on the rocks of Casco Bay, but then she hears it again, louder than ever.

She wonders if kids have broken into the mansion already and have set up a speaker. It doesn't sound digital, but who would play live in the rain?

Of course, it could be the faeries partying underground, like the rats told her.

As she steps onto the paved driveway, now spiderwebbed with cracks and weeds sticking up through them, she sees lights beyond the chain-link fences, in the roofless rooms with their empty windows.

There's no movement other than the lights, which seem to dance around, almost like fireflies if they burned brighter. Almost like falling stars.

Heather's heart hammers as she paces around the outside. She half expects something to jump out at her, hidden by the dark. She tries to pay attention to what she's there for and notes that despite rocks resting all along the perimeter of the old mansion, there's only one that could be considered a boulder.

She places her hand on its rain-slicked surface.

"Stone of old, heavy and cold," Heather says, feeling as though she's reading lines from a play. "Move aside from the way foretold."

The earth beneath her feet begins to shake and Heather takes two steps back, stumbling over uneven earth, sliding in mud. The boulder rolls over. In the space it once occupied, she can see a passageway. A tunnel, hung with roots and lit with glowing bits of some kind of blue, phosphorescent mushroom. For a moment, it seems to be a gaping mouth, beckoning her to its gullet.

The sound of the music is much louder.

Forget this, she thinks. *Go home.* But she's forgotten so much already.

Gingerly, she gets down on her hands and knees and lowers herself into the hole. Scrabbles downward, her path lit only by moonlight.

A few feet into the passageway, she hears the terrible sound of the rock sliding firmly into place behind her. Panic catches her by the throat. The darkness is absolute, unending. She feels as though she's been buried alive.

She tries to force herself to stillness. To breathe. The scent of soil is all around her, but when she breathes, the air doesn't taste stale. And the music is coming from somewhere nearby.

She thinks about Vivienne and plans what she will say when she sees her again. *Tell me*, she will demand. *Tell me who you are to me. Tell me what you did to me.*

Heather feels the tunnel widen and hears the sounds of people nearby. Laughter along with the music, the rustling of fabric, footfalls. And then, after a curve in the path, she sees a golden glow ahead.

She emerges, hands and knees covered in dirt, in an enormous hall. The walls are packed earth, but the floor is a dizzying pattern of stones laid out in connected circles. And everywhere there's shifting light. Candles sit in nooks in the walls, spilling wax. Glowing creatures dart above her head.

And in that light, she sees all the monsters.

Winged and fanged, some with tails and a few with what appear like leaves or bark growing over their bodies, they gather in knots. Some dance in circles that seem to follow the pattern of the floor. An enormous creature, large enough that he must have had to stoop to enter the room, sits against one wall. He has what appears to be the body of a deer spread out over his lap and is sawing off a leg. When she passes, he looks up and she realizes he has only a single eye, centered above his nose.

Heather shudders.

Three tables rest along one wall, all of them made from doors set on sawhorses. And atop are bowls of fruit—apples, beach plums, blueberries, chokeberries. Small cubes of gleaming stewed meat on orache leaves. A chipped porcelain bowl holding dandelion greens covered in dried berries and nuts. A plank of cedar with purslane, a soft white cheese, and honey.

A small band of musicians are gathered in one corner—a fiddler who looks almost human, except for the points of his ears and the sharpness of his features; a shaggy, spindly creature drumming on a bodhrán with a knot of cloth wrapped around the end of a stick; and three tiny winged creatures plucking at the strands of an enormous harp.

It seems as though Heather is walking through a terrifying dream, but not a totally unfamiliar one. She's drawn beings like this, impossible creatures for which she no long can congratulate her imagination. Had she been afraid like this before? Had she forgotten more than a week? A few of the winged, fanged partiers glance in her direction, suggesting that she's been noticed.

Mortals aren't allowed.

"I'm looking for Bryern." Her voice shakes a little as she speaks to a woman with skin as brown as hers and the wings of a dragonfly.

The woman makes a buzzing sound when she speaks. "There," she says, pointing to a man with the head and hooves of a black goat, clad in a waistcoat, a cloak, and a bowler hat.

"Oh," Heather says, blinking twice. "Thank you."

The woman scowls at her, as though insulted, and moves away.

Heather approaches the goat-guy, not sure what she did wrong in the last interaction and not sure how she's going to avoid insulting Bryern too. "Um, excuse me."

Bryern looks down at her with his long-lashed, horizontal-pupiled goat eyes. Then, holding his hat by the brim, he makes an extravagant bow. "You've come a long way if you're looking for me."

"Is this your party?" she asks.

"Mine? Oh, no. It belongs entirely to itself," he says with what might be a smile, but she finds expressions hard to read on a goat head.

"Okaaaay," she says, feeling entirely unprepared for this level of whimsy.

At that moment, Heather spots Vivienne across the room, except that this Vivi looks *exactly* like the drawing in her comic book, with cat eyes and sharper features. Ears that rise to points on either side of hair the color of wheat. Terrifying and yet Heather also has the entirely unwise desire to cross the room and take the monstrous girl in her arms.

Instead, she turns abruptly, so that her back is toward Vivi. But goose bumps bloom all along her arms.

Her heart thuds. Fear makes her palms sweat.

"Someone you know . . .," Bryern begins, but then trails off. "Ahhhh, yes. I used to employ her sister, although that's a touchy subject now."

The sister to the Queen of Faerie. It didn't seem likely that this guy had employed a queen. But maybe the rats were wrong? What did rats know anyway?

"Can you remove the spell on me?" she asks. "The one that's taken my memory?"

He peers at her for a long moment, his gaze falling to her wrist where the bracelet used to be, as though he can see its residue. "Is that what you want?"

He doesn't contradict her by saying no such spell is on her. And in this hall with the scents of melting candle wax and mead and spilled beer eddying through the air, she wonders if any of her reasons for coming here were good ones.

Maybe she doesn't want to remember. She's already scared—who's she kidding?—she's *terrified*. And now that she knows about this world, she will never be able to *not* know there are all these creatures with power over her.

Maybe she shouldn't ask the goat-guy to remove the spell. Maybe she should ask him to extend it so that she forgets Vivienne. Forgets about tonight.

"I'm sure," Heather says, although she isn't.

He points a finger in the direction of Vivi. "You'll have to talk to the woman there—the one leaning on the cane. That's Mother Marrow—a hag, which is something like a witch, but worse and more powerful. She set the spell and she will have to remove it."

The woman he points to appears elderly, with hair the color of smoke, a sharply curved nose, and bird feet. Around her neck she has a strand of river rocks. A cloak rests on her shoulders, but where Bryern's is lined and elegant, hers is worn and tattered.

"Is it bad manners to thank you?" Heather asks him, thinking of the dragonfly woman.

"It would be better to give me something in return for the service I've rendered you. A lock of hair, perhaps?"

Heather thinks about every fairy story she's ever read, about the rules she knows and the ones she's still trying to puzzle out. And she asks herself what she's willing to give up to know the truth.

Maybe she could still walk away.

"Sure," Heather says, reaching up for a pink curl. He produces a small brass pair of scissors from within his waistcoat and snips. Then he bows again.

Taking a deep breath, Heather crosses the room to Mother Marrow. Vivienne spots her. She's too close to the hag not to.

"Hello," Heather says. "I understand you put a spell on me."

Mother Marrow's smile ought to belong to a cat.

Vivi's gaze goes to Heather's wrist and she seems to brace, as though for a blow. "What have you done?"

"Oh, no," Mother Marrow tells her. "We're all bound to our bargains. And it seems I have you now."

"Bargain?" asks Heather.

Vivi flinches.

The hag puts a hand on Vivienne's arm. "This one made a foolish promise that was beyond her skill. And so, she came to Mother Marrow. But I bet you know exactly what she asked for, don't you?"

"To erase my memories," Heather says, remembering how unsure she'd been about wanting them back. Suddenly she has a very good guess what happened.

Mother Marrow's smile widens. "Clever girl. But you see, she offered to serve me for ten years if you rejected her token. She had three days to convince you. And our Vivienne thought she was clever. She waited until the last day to approach you and gave you the gift on the final night. Gave me so little time to persuade you to throw it away."

"Those were your rats," Heather says.

"They were in my employ, yes," says Mother Marrow, turning to Vivi. "And now you've lost her forever. That should teach you not to dally with mortals. A lesson we all must learn."

Vivi's expression is so filled with longing and loss that Heather feels as though she can hardly breathe.

"As for you," Mother Marrow goes on, her attention returning to Heather. "I saw that you gave away a lock of your hair. And when I get it, I will use it in a spell."

"Leave her alone," Vivi says. "She's not part of this."

"And you'll help me, Vivienne," Mother Marrow says, looking delighted with herself. "After all, you will be my servant."

"Jude and Cardan are going to—" Vivi starts.

But Mother Marrow only laughs. "Pay handsomely for your release? Make a bargain of their own? Let them. In fact, I am counting on it."

"You must think I wasn't paying attention," says Heather.

Mother Marrow frowns at her. "Is that so?"

"Rats told me that your people can't lie," Heather says. "That instead they had to trick and deceive. I know they were acting like they were warning me about Vivi, but they were warning me about you too."

Vivi's gaze on Heather is hard to interpret, with her strange cat eyes.

"They told me to take off the bracelet and throw it away. But I wasn't sure that was good advice." Heather pulls up the cuff of her jeans to reveal the beads threaded around her ankle.

"What is that?" Mother Marrow demands.

"I decided to take a chance," Heather says. "I took the bracelet off and then put the beads back on. Tied new thread to the old. I assume there's nothing in your bargain about whether or not I added some length. My ankles are thicker than my wrists."

Vivi's smile is wide and wonderful. She looks as though she wants to throw her arms around Heather, but something is holding her back. "But why? Why trust me?"

"You tried to tell me the truth," says Heather. "I wouldn't listen. If you were trying to trick me, why tell me all that? Besides, I think I just figured out the rest. When you asked Mother Marrow to take my memories, it was at the request of someone else, wasn't it?"

Vivi nods, her eyes shining.

"Me," Heather says. "I asked you to take those memories, didn't I?"

Vivi nods again. "You did, but then you regretted it—at least kind of. And you told me to find you again. I didn't do things the right way the first time and I don't know that I'm doing much better now."

"This is all very touching, but I believe you've forgotten that Bryern over there still has a strand of your hair," Mother Marrow says. "One way or another, I will have control of Vivienne through you."

Heather grins, really feeling herself right at this moment. "Oh, no," she says. "That *is* a strand from my hair, but not the hair growing from my scalp. Not the kind you can use to control me. I have a sew-in."

Mother Marrow gnashes her teeth and stomps her bird feet. "You're going to regret crossing me," she says.

But Vivi only laughs and loops her arm around Heather's waist. "No one crossed you. My clever, beautiful girlfriend won the day."

"Your clever, beautiful girlfriend needs to get out of here before she passes out," Heather whispers into her ear.

Vivi grins. "So long as—no, I won't make conditions. You won the day and won me too. I just hope you'll agree to see me again, knowing what you know."

Heather pauses. The idea that there is a world of creatures out there with fangs and tails and magic frightens her, just as it must have before, but part of her is thrilled to be part of something that feels like a story. And she managed this, didn't she? Won the game, won the girl.

A girl who isn't human, but who loves Heather enough to risk years of her own life for a chance to be together again. A girl who fascinates her. A girl who she must have loved too and who she can imagine loving again.

"We can go on another date," Heather says. "And you can meet my friends. I think you'd like them."

Vivi nods. "I already do."

Right, because she met them before, even if she doesn't remember it. Heather rolls her eyes as they head toward the tunnel, Vivi stopping to grab a bottle of mead. "Is this going to be annoying? You know me so much better than I know you."

"*Very* annoying," Vivi promises with a heavy-lidded look. It's clear she's imagining all the ways she will be able to use that knowledge to her advantage.

Heather's cheeks heat. "But no more hiding things from me, right? This time around."

"And no more running?" Vivi asks.

"No more running," Heather agrees.

"So perhaps we could finish our picnic under the stars?" Vivi asks, holding up the mead. "And you could ask me all your questions and I could answer them in full—for a price."

"It's raining and I am tired of riddles." Heather groans, but she still can't stop smiling. Can't stop feeling a thrill when her body brushes against Vivienne's.

"What if the price was a kiss?" Vivi says. "One per answer."

Heather laces her fingers through Vivi's with a laugh, pulling her close. "Now there's a price I would gladly pay."

ASK TWICE

Ryan La Sala

I

The first time I asked my mother if she believed what our small suburb was saying about me—that I was different, that I was strange, that I could not be hers, that I could not be *human*—she smiled big and said, "Don't be ridiculous, sweetie."

The second time I asked her, she was forced to tell the truth.

Leaving would have been easier if my mother kicked me out, but the reality is that after I ripped the truth out of her, she begged me to stay. There was even a moment when I thought she would chase me into the night. But she didn't.

When I ran away from home, all that followed me was my shadow.

And then I ran from that, too, to the brightest place I could think of: the stage of the Ballet Maléfique.

I stand on that stage now, eyes adamantly opened against the spotlights, posing and pretending that the empty theater before me is packed with a rapt audience. I stand still—*so* still—as Riggs makes the final adjustments to the lights for the performance I've been rehearsing for all week. It's the stillness that allows these old, familiar thoughts to finally catch up to me. Thoughts of home and shadows and running.

"One step to your left, Saturn," Riggs instructs me, and I oblige. The lights shift imperceptibly. "Okaaaay, hold that position. The spotlight will be set ahead of time, so if you miss your mark, no one will see your final pose."

I check the corners in my periphery and memorize where I'm standing. Riggs continues to make adjustments. *Hurry up, Riggs*, I pray, *so I can get back to dancing for my life.* If I'm still for much longer, it might find me.

My shadow.

I still see my shadow sometimes, crawling toward me across the great distances I'm always careful to keep between me and it ever since I cut it from my heels. Without my body to give it form, it's disfigured into something monstrous. It has many more legs now, spread down a body that has unraveled into an undulating ribbon of night. My hands now wave at me from the ends of arms with six elbows. They swish toward me from the dark, but tentatively, as though eager to hold me but embarrassed to be seen.

I think I understand. Sometimes, I wonder what shape I would become if I wasn't always holding myself together in the shape of a person.

My shadow scares me, but I don't resent it. Maybe it's monstrous, but it's the only thing that has ever chased me. My parents never even bothered to call the police when I vanished. I know because after I'd been on my own for a few days, I decided I'd made a mistake, and I walked into the nearest police station to introduce myself as missing.

They told me I didn't match any of the profiles of people reported missing by loved ones. *Ah*, I thought. *That's the problem right there. You've got to be loved to be missed.*

That's when I found the Ballet Maléfique, and now, months later, my thoughts rarely turn back the way I came. I wonder why now, a week before I'm set to debut as Saturn, my brand-new stage persona, my thoughts return to the house.

Suddenly, the spotlight pinning me to center stage drops out and I'm swallowed in darkness. A screech echoes in the emptiness and somewhere high up Riggs swears. My heart clenches. Is he falling? Did he catch himself? All I can make out above me are the pulsing afterimages from the lights, but then I see it . . . not Riggs, but *it*. A writhing darkness nestled into the curve of the proscenium. It slithers upward, and I only catch a glimpse of it—arms, dozens and dozens of arms, a snaking body that curls with boneless fluidity, pitch-velvet skin—before Riggs adjusts the spotlight and I'm blinded once more.

"Sorry to scare you!" he calls.

I breathe and regain my composure. My shadow isn't actually here. *It can't be.* It's never followed me inside the theater, which is one of the many reasons I need to earn my spot here. It is the only place I feel safe, from both my past and myself.

Still, I drop into a crouch, hands twisted over the knot of my racing heart.

"Saturn? You good?"

I have to calm down before saying anything.

"Saturn?"

I give a rigid thumbs-up.

"Overheating is no joke." Riggs's voice bounces around the stage as he climbs down to me. He's like a spider, always jumping between cables and catwalks up there. That's how he got the name Riggs. I'm quiet as death. That's how I earned Saturn, short for saturnine.

Back on earth, Riggs's footsteps are heavy and sure. He strides toward me. I stare at his boots.

"You know," he says, as he ducks down to my level, "you don't need to wear your costume if we're just doing lighting cues. Titania doesn't even get into drag until the bar serves fifty-seven vodka sodas."

I am calm now. I accept his hand and stand. He is the opposite of my shadow; solid, stocky, observant of gravity. Nothing drifty in his shape, nothing mutilated by multiplication. He is always warm, always in a black sleeveless band shirt, always absently clipping his keys into the plentiful holes in the shirt's hem instead of his belt loop. He smells like sawdust and cinnamon gum. I don't fear the dark of backstage, because I always know I'll find him within it.

I am, of course, in love with him. I've never asked him how he feels about me because I am very, very careful about the questions I ask people. I limit myself to just transactional questions, never digging below the surface of what I know someone will readily share. I learned from my mom the hard way that I should never ask twice.

Right now I ask: "Can we practice the descent again? Just one last time before we add the dancers?"

Riggs rolls his eyes, but he's smiling, so it's a yes. He kicks off his favorite safety lecture as we climb up to the catwalk and he resets the trapeze.

"Two hands at all times, no sudden movements," he says as he clips me into the safety belt. "And lastly—"

"Don't look down, I know, I know."

"Nope." He grins. "I was gonna say: *Sing*."

"Oh."

I actually do look down. The stage is very, very far away, but the idea of singing scares me even more.

While Riggs tests the harness, making sure it's tight but not too tight, he says, "It's the one thing you haven't actually rehearsed to death, Saturn, and it's the whole point of this, right?"

"It's harder than it looks," I shoot back. "Once I feel safe, I'll sing."

Riggs looks a little hurt. "I won't drop you. I promise. Do you want to just try? It's just you and me here. I can do the music cue on my phone. Okay? Just try?"

"We'll see."

Riggs lets me go, and I swing a little before catching the catwalk with my toes. He spiders off to the flies, leaving me to take breaths that are so heavy I'm surprised the whole trapeze doesn't come down.

He's right. The song is the whole point. It's my chance to make my claim on the stage that has saved me. If I do well, I'll have earned a spot among Titania's ballet. I'll get to stay up here. But if I fail, I know what awaits me: the dark beyond the doors, and my hungry shadow crawling within it.

Breathe, Saturn. For some reason, when I encourage myself, the voice in my head is never mine. It's either Riggs's warm bass or Titania's tough-love tenor.

Breathe. I let my new family hold me up.

I nod. The signal. The ropes creak as the safety is released, and sudden heaviness seizes the contraption. I grit my teeth so I don't scream when I fall, but then Riggs's muscles take over and I'm caught. He lowers me to just above where the audience can see me. I fight to keep breathing while the music starts. I try to open my mouth to take my first breath, but my teeth have fused together. It's like my body knows that my voice is something dangerous and should be smothered. Locked away. I'm the cage, I'm the creature, I'm the thing my mother couldn't love enough.

I miss my entrance because I am thinking about my mother's bloody teeth. The way her gums bled with the force of her jaw trying to stay shut, as the truth slid up her throat and filled her mouth. The truth she didn't want to give me. The truth she herself didn't want to acknowledge, until I wrenched it out of her.

I look at you, and I wonder where my child has gone.

When it finally broke out of her, it was a scream. Hours later, in the mirror of a gas station bathroom, I finally wiped away the smattering of blood from where the words slapped me across my face.

I miss my cue and my music plays on without me. Riggs doesn't pull me up to try again. It's clear I'm choking. Like always. Instead, he lowers me gently back to the stage.

Someone who has been watching from the back of the house steps into the light.

"If you can't sing for yourself, how do you expect to sing for everyone?" Titania chides. "It's getting late, bunnies. Rehearsal is over. It's time to turn the stage over to the night." She speaks with an authority I have never seen matched outside of a drag queen. She is right. Rehearsal *is* over. And it's as if the sun itself has just set on her orders. We begin resetting the stage without a word.

Titania circles over to the light board, clicking off Riggs's arrangement with her sharp nails and dousing the entire theater into club mode. The space goes from antique cabaret to Victorian disco in a blink. In a few hours the dance floor will be packed with men, women, and everyone between, all dancing as they await the famed Fairy Queen Titania to take the stage. I know that the outside of the theater has also just lit up in the same neon, blazing the words:

Like a promise against the night. Against the people who have tried to pry the theater out of Titania's claws for years so they can bulldoze downtown and build condos. Against the shadowy creatures that chase kids like Riggs and me out of our homes and into sanctuaries like this.

"You both can't be out here once the bar is open. You're underage. We could get shut down for that," Titania says. A favorite line of hers. "The girls are arriving soon, and what do I always say?"

"The only drag queen who is on time is the girl with six hands," we recite.

"Good. Go make yourselves useful in the back of the house. And Saturn?"

"Yes, ma'am?"

"Riggs is right. A showy entrance is not enough. Once you're on that stage, you've got to be able to show the world why you deserve to be there. We know you can do it. *You* need to know it, though. Got it?"

"Yes, ma'am."

Titania's eyes soften, though in the flashing lights it's hard to tell. She switches so fast among mother, crone, damsel, and dame. She changes so often and so easily, I wonder if she's like me.

"And never call me ma'am again. Now, go."

We do as she says.

II

The same night, the backstage becomes its own kind of show as the boys arrive and begin their transformation into queens. They talk incessantly as they apply makeup and shimmy their way into padded hips and butts. Riggs is out front, running cues for Titania, leaving me to manage all the small, last-minute requests that come up right before a big night. And when you've got this many drag queens wearing this many costumes, there are a lot of requests. Right now, as I listen to them chatter, I'm gluing rhinestones into a wig curled like the gigantic ear of a seashell.

The current debate: What's up with that car that's been circling the theater all week?

"It's a real estate agent. Or more developers. Or the FBI. Or a Republican. No matter what, we're doomed," moans Chassy, a queen not much older than me, who is exceptionally talented at finding the drama in anything. She sits with her back to her mirror so that the vanity lights ring her like a dotted halo.

"Shut up, Chassy. You're being naive. What's doomed is your number if you don't glue that wig down this time. Last week I saw so much hair fly I thought I was watching the scene where Edward Scissorhands makes a housewife orgasm with a shag cut."

"*You* shut up, La'Dynasty. I'm not being naive. *You* are."

La'Dynasty, pronounced "Lady Nasty," has been at the ballet since it opened. According to her, she's been here even longer, having danced in the actual ballet that called this theater home when it was known as the Magnifique, before it closed and Titania reopened it as Maléfique, the club. I believe her. She is tall and willowy, and because of her deep skin tone her makeup spread is a mosaic of warm brown powders and liquid neons. The contrast between the room full of girls, with half their faces still missing, and her, face perfectly painted like a bioluminescent siren, gives an extra weight to her words as she turns in her chair—turns very, very slowly—and serves Chassy with a look.

"Little girl," she starts, and the room goes so quiet you can hear the ice in Chassy's drink clink as she clutches it for support. "We queens spend too much time reveling in transformation to begrudge anything else its turn at evolution. This theater has lived many lives, and it will live many more. But it's *not* naive to believe that, for a little while longer, we can call this home. Titania has held the ballet together with eyelash glue and determination for over a decade, and so far as I've been here, which has been—"

"Since the Cretaceous Period," cuts in Babs, who rotates before the big mirror in the corner, gauging if her padding is just right. The shelf of her immense, fake ass will soon be balanced out by breasts so big they require their own suitcase. Babs is very mean, very funny, and beloved by all.

"Who the fuck taught you a word like 'Cretaceous'?" La'Dy asks.

"Your birth certificate."

They bicker and banter until La'Dy's patience runs out and she picks her point back up.

"I know doom." La'Dy resumes applying glitter to her collarbone. "I see it all the time, but I've never seen it step foot in here. Places like this are made from hope. They're special. The doom can't survive so long as we keep giving that stage everything we got. That's the same as giving each other everything we got. It's how we've always kept on going. So maybe the theater closes, but the ballet always dances on."

The room is quiet. I'm amazed Babs resisted softening the moment with a joke. Chassy kicks out her heeled feet, pouting. "But I don't want the theater to close."

"Then glue that wig down and dance for your life," La'Dy snaps. "Trust me. Trust Titania. This place has been a home to too many for her to let it go without a fight. Right, Saturn?"

The room turns toward me. I have been pretending to glue the same rhinestone onto this wig for the entire conversation.

"Right," I say.

"Always a lot to say, that one," Babs groans.

"Hey, Saturn." Chassy sounds like she just noticed me. "When are you debuting? Is that tonight?"

"Next Saturday."

"Nervous?"

"Yeah, definitely."

"Why? Does the song have words?" Babs jokes. I crack a smile. She winks at me.

The queens are off in another match of wits, forgetting me. Thank god. I know about the debut tradition, of course. Before I knew what this place was, I'd heard it mentioned with marked reverence by drag queens and performers trading stories about the different venues in the city. Whenever Maléfique came up, it was with a note of nostalgic love, but also a groan of embarrassment. Everyone has an origin story here. I desperately want to have my own.

As I place each rhinestone, I listen to the queens, and pray: *Keep me, keep me, keep me.*

III

Saturday. The day of my debut.

And I have yet to sing a single note on the stage I'm allegedly about to make my own. I know the song—every phrase, every breath—and I even sing through it a dozen times with Titania giving notes at her piano in the greenroom. But, as she reminds me with a gentleness threaded with steel, everything is harder on a trapeze.

At this point, I'm about to just ask Riggs if he'll consider dropping me.

Despite my nerves, I do what Titania has taught me to do. I put on a cute outfit. I do my hair. I dot sparkles into the corners of my eyes.

I paint my nails. I dress myself as strong, and by the time I'm walking into the empty theater at midday, I *feel* strong. Riggs is there already, crouching onstage beside a set piece we'll be using. Seeing him in his messy overalls, with paint smeared up his arms, I suddenly feel silly and overdressed.

"Satty, look!" Riggs hops up excitedly and pulls me over to look at what he's done. Spread on the floor are large, flat trees, expertly painted so that they look almost real from afar. "I used a base of cardboard and then papier-mâché to give them the bumpy, flaky texture of birch bark. What do you think? Is it what you envisioned?"

It's perhaps a little *too* close to what I envisioned. The storybook quality of Riggs's painting is exactly like the trees in the literal storybook I showed him when we first got the idea to work together on my debut. In the book, a forest of moonlit birch trees spreads beneath a deep and starry sky, and from above descends a crescent moon strung with pearls. Cradled in the moon is a beautiful woman, or something that looks like a woman. Her skin is an otherworldly azure, her ears point to the stars, and wings of shimmering cellophane flow from her shoulders. She is leaning forward, dangling something toward earth. It's a woven basket hanging on a single, starlit strand. In the basket is a baby, its skin a lightening blue like the night is letting it go, its ears only a little pointed, and its eyes . . . they shine black.

I'd never shown anyone else at the ballet the storybook before. It was the only thing I'd taken with me when I left home. Riggs seemed to know better than to ask why, and instead he simply began to plan *how* we would bring this to life. The trapeze, the backdrop . . . all of it. How he created so much in only a few weeks amazes me, and I find myself watching his hands as he talks. What magic do they hold?

Riggs's demonstration is suddenly cut short when the theater doors slam open, and in walks Titania. Seeing us, her face flashes with momentary vexation. She wears a long, flowing robe, and it whips around her ankles as she paces.

"I need . . ." She purses her lips. I've seen her do this in drag when she's trying to find a way to delicately break bad news. Finally, she says, "I have an errand for you both. We need . . . light bulbs. From the hardware store."

"Light bulbs?"

"Yes. For the greenroom. The girls won't stop complaining about the vanities."

She's right. Half the vanities are missing bulbs because the girls keep stealing them from one another's stations. One time, just to make a point, Babs did her makeup in complete darkness, and she came out looking like my drunk aunt.

"Oh, we need some paint, too!" Riggs says. "Not a ton, we can get the cheap kind, but we need—"

"Here." Titania thrusts a wad of cash at Riggs and sweeps us toward the back doors where she parks her truck. The keys are, per usual, in the wheel well of the passenger's side, and even though I'm curious about Titania's agitated mood I just let Riggs talk through the show tonight.

He's still talking when we enter the store. We find what we need quickly but when it's time to go home, we both slow down. I have been pretending we are on a date and I wonder: Has Riggs finally felt the irradiated intensity of my delusion?

"Saturn," he states. "Titania gave you that name?"

"Yup."

"After the planet?"

I shake my head. "Kinda. The word 'saturnine' means gloomy. Quiet. Steady."

After a pause, Riggs says, "I don't think you're gloomy. Quiet for sure. I know you don't like to talk."

"I don't mind talking."

"But you don't like to ask questions." Riggs says it so quickly I know it's something he's been meaning to poke at for a while. That he's paid this kind of close attention to me is thrilling. It makes my neck prickle with heat. "Why not?" he prompts.

"Because. You ask enough questions for the both of us."

"Fair," Riggs says, looking up at the towering shelves of supplies. "You know, I actually came here for the first time with Titania. I'd been hanging out at Maléfique for a while. After I ran away, I didn't know where else to go. When Titania found me, I was terrified, but she just asked me if I was good at anything. Somehow, we ended up here. For paints and building supplies. She showed me the ropes. Literally, showed me the ropes for the fly system. And I became Riggs."

"She's amazing," I offer. It's so much less than what I actually feel for Titania, but I'm self-conscious when it comes to saying too much. I keep it short and sweet. Riggs, however, waits for me to go on.

"I used to come here with my parents," I offer. "When I was little. We even went to Maléfique, back when it was the Magnifique."

"Wait, you're from here?"

"From the city, yeah."

"You didn't run very far." This is said without judgment. If anything, Riggs sounds wistful. "Aren't you afraid that you'll run into your family? That they'll figure out where you are?"

"I think they know," I confess. "But to be honest, no one is looking that hard for me."

This is a lie. It's true that my I've spotted my parents now and then since leaving home—they look happy. Unburdened. The lie I'm telling is that no one is looking for me. Even though it's easy to forget when I'm in the theater, out in the world I can feel the thing that searches for me always: my shadow. I glance up, like I might catch it now, but the store is a vast, brightly lit warehouse. If my shadow is here, it's hiding very well.

"Do you ever think about going back?" Riggs asks. "Home, I mean."

We turn down another aisle, walking by walls scaled with paint cards.

"I am home," I assure him, bumping his shoulder. "Home isn't where you are but who you're with. All the people I want to be with are at the Maléfique."

"That's poetic, Satty. Are you excited for your debut?" Riggs asks.

"I'm getting there. To be honest, it all felt like a dream until I saw the set. It's truly amazing, what you can do. It feels . . . magical."

"Ha. I wish. Your storybook just has me inspired. All those faeries, all those queens and princes and monsters. I've always wished that stuff was real. I think that's why I love working in the theater. When those queens hit the stage, it's almost like for a moment we're looking through to another world. And then when the queen struts onto the dance floor? It's like that world invades ours. Sometimes when I'm on lights, I'll steal a look at the audience during the big moments of the show. If you saw what I saw, you'd never know magic wasn't real."

"That's a beautiful thought."

"Thought, or theory?" He bumps me back. "What do you think about magic? Real or no?"

He says the last part in a low voice, his head turned so the words catch me in the curve of my neck. Chills rush down my exposed arms. I step away from Riggs. Does he know about me? I wonder if it was a mistake showing him my book. It would be a mistake I've already made once before, when I sat at the kitchen table in my old home and slid the book to my mom. She'd barely read a word before closing it, but I found it open the next day. The corners of the pages were bent, as though hastily read and reread. Just the one story, though. The tale in which a faerie queen descends upon the moon, and into the life of one lonesome family drops a child of loathsome nature.

A changeling.

My parents looked at me differently after that. Or really, it was a familiar expression of doubt that had been coalescing in their eyes for a long time. Like when my baby teeth fell out, and my adult teeth came in pointed, and the dentist had to cap each one individually. Or when I got sent home from school because something I said had made my teacher cry, even though I hadn't said anything at all and had only asked too many questions. Doubt here, fear there, flashing darkly in the eyes of my family as they backed away from me.

And then when I found the story of the changeling, something clicked. Something about that story gathered together every shred of fear they had long suppressed, and pulled it into something dangerous. A theory. A belief.

That story ruined everything.

Or, I guess, *I* ruined everything. Me, and one simple question aimed at my mother when she caught me running away.

Do you believe I am your child, or do you think I am something else?

The first time I asked it, my mother gave me a rush of reassurance. Of course she believed I was her child.

But then I asked again, because in the story, the changeling always asks twice.

And what had remained adamantly, lovingly, desperately unsaid was said.

"Saturn?"

Riggs shakes my shoulder, and I realize I've just been standing there, staring at him. Did he ask me something? I almost ask him what he said, but my usual hesitance around questions cuts me off.

"Sorry. I forgot what I was going to say," I say.

"It's cool. I asked if you believe in magic?"

I get ready to lie, but as soon as I open my mouth the lights in the warehouse go out. They buzz back on a second later, but from the flickering I know they're about to go black. Questioning shouts go up all around the massive store, and the speakers cut their music so someone can make an announcement, but then it all goes dark again. As though also on a switch, the screams cut off, too.

No, I think. *Not here. Not now.*

The lights give one final surge and I force my eyes wide so that I don't miss it. And there! At the end of the aisle: a twisting mass winds up the scaffolding, slithering between stacks of drywall. The last thing I see is the shimmer of too many insect legs before false night swallows everything.

"Riggs, take my hand," I command. My voice sounds so big in the dark. It's awfully quiet. It's like I'm the only person in the store.

"Riggs?"

I reach out but he's gone. How did he move so quickly? Where did he go? The lights flicker. I backpedal out of the aisle, into the open part of the store, but when it goes dark again I slam into what I think must be a washing machine. A row of them. I follow their path, listening for anything behind me even though I know my shadow barely makes a sound.

"Saturn?"

Riggs's voice calls out, impossibly far way, and I see a weak beam of light cut the dark. A flashlight! Smart boy, running for the flashlights in a hardware store. I stumble toward the light but when I reach it, the aisle is empty. A lone flashlight rolls toward me, bumping my toe, its battery already faltering.

"Riggs, are you there?" My hands shake as I reach down to grab the flashlight. I slowly turn the beam left, then right. I'm in an aisle of power tools. High up on the walls shine blades in every shape.

"Riggs, show me where you are," I plead.

"Got you!"

A hand lands on my shoulder and I jump, but the sound of Riggs's voice instantly drops my guard. A prank. I huff, relieved. Then I turn to face him and my relief vanishes.

It is not Riggs's hand on my shoulder. Because Riggs stands at the end of the aisle, several strides away. His shape smudges as a shadowy mass curls around him. In the beam of light, the thing glints like the chitinous armor of a bug, and its coiled body is fringed with a hundred bristling legs. They undulate as the shadow tightens, hugging to Riggs, but he wears an expression of serene curiosity. He can't see it, or feel it.

"Riggs, come here. But do it slowly."

"Hmm?"

Riggs only blinks. His glassy eyes look on the verge of sleep. There's a twitch in his arm, like he might move, but the shadow tightens. I gradually drag the flashlight up the long, jointed body, up, up, up, until I'm aiming the beam directly above myself, into a face that has been unrecognizably mutated. Like the rest of my shadow, it now resembles a nightmarish centipede. Wide-set black eyes, shivering mandibles, and two curling antennae that arch through the air between us, ending in hands as delicate as my own. One rests on my shoulder. It gives a little squeeze, like *hello*. I slide out from under it with a shiver.

Then my shadow speaks.

You-u-u can c—c—c—commmme h—hom——home n-n-now.

The voice is my own. Perhaps that's why I know right away that it does not mean the Maléfique, nor my house with my parents, but another home. I think of the book, and the drawing of the women cradled by the moon.

"Who sent you?"

C—com—c—comme hhome.

I take a deep breath. Will my power work on this thing that was once my shadow? I feel close to a truth that risks everything I have built for myself in the Ballet Maléfique. All I have ever needed to do to get to the truth was to ask twice, but is a truth that ruins everything really worth knowing?

I look at Riggs. I told him home is not where you are, but who you're with. Did I mean it, or did I *want* to mean it? Both feel true, but which truth matters most?

I start to ask again.

"Who—"

The centipede tears backward, fleeing the question, but in doing so it drags Riggs into a violent tumble locked in its skittering legs. I try to cut myself off, to stop, but the question builds in my throat with blistering determination.

"Who sent—" I say, out of my own control.

The centipede writhes, and Riggs is twisted into a contortion I am sure will rip apart in another second if I don't stop. I bite my words in half, forcing them back down into me, releasing the beast from the vice of my interrogation. Tension shivers through the massive insect's body, but it gradually slackens. It's letting Riggs go, because I'm letting *it* go. It's not easy, not at all. The question blazes in my chest, ravenous with curiosity, but I smother it for his sake. It's like swallowing a star.

Somehow, I do it.

In the same moment I realize I'm going to survive this agony, my monstrous shadow flees up the shelves and into the deep-space of the warehouse. I'm at Riggs's side in a heartbeat, dragging him toward a seam of daylight in the distance that I am praying is an exit. I can hear my shadow clicking above us, but I don't look. I slam through the door, and sunlight punches into the dark warehouse, breaking the shadow's spell. The overhead lights buzz back on, and the music resumes cheerfully as shoppers—all standing like slumped mannequins—straighten, put their hands back on their carts, and push onward like nothing happened.

"Did we already get everything?" Beside me, Riggs squints against the sunlight as he tries to read the shopping list he wrote himself.

I look back into the warehouse and, like Riggs, it's all just as it was. Whatever happened happened only to me. But it got close to hurting Riggs, too. I can see scratches on his arms and legs from where my shadow held him.

"We need to get you back to the theater," I say.

"Lead the way, Saturn," he says cheerfully.

IV

By the time we make it back, I've made up my mind.

Riggs can tell I'm caught in some sort of spiral, and he gives me space all afternoon even though we're supposed to do our final dress rehearsal with the dancers before the club opens. He probably thinks that when I finally close the distance between us, it'll be because I'm ready to sing for him.

That's never going to happen. The attack at the hardware store showed me just how delusional I really was, thinking all it would take to reinvent myself was a song, a dance, and a costume I could keep on forever.

As the sun sets, the girls arrive through the back door, and I hear their cackles shaking the old bricks of the dressing room I've been calling a bedroom. I set the bed and fold all the hand-me-downs from Titania's closet. I line up the shoes she got me, and the sketchbooks, and the cracked cell phone, and anything else she provided. I even lay out the beautiful costume I was supposed to wear tonight: an ivory leotard tufted with blushing starbursts of crinoline that Chassy helped me dip-dye, that La'Dy helped me pattern and sew, that Babs made sure fit like a dream. I made it, but everyone helped. It belongs here. It's the version of me they loved, and it's the part of me I'm leaving behind. Saturn, shed like a skin.

All I take are the clothes I arrived with and my storybook. Then I rush down the back stairs and out into the alley just as the sky finally softens into a perfect, deep periwinkle, and the neon signs of the Ballet Maléfique buzz to life.

Every step I take is a fight against the urge to turn around, to run back home to Riggs, to Titania and the girls. While I walk, I imagine Riggs racing after me, worried and angry and hurt, and in my imagining he is asking, *Why are you running away, Saturn, why?* I imagine what it would be like if his questions grew sharp with magic and cut the truth out of me. What would I say? That I am a monster? That I'm neither Saturn nor my shadow, but something hopelessly unresolved, and therefore entirely unplaceable? That I am undeserving of a home like this; a love like theirs?

I laugh at myself. I thought I was scared to sing, but I think now that I was scared to be heard. It's like my body knew all of this before I did. It's like La'Dy has said: *The doom can't survive so long as we keep giving that stage everything we got*. My shadow knew better. Now, I do, too.

I keep walking. Traffic slows as I leave downtown. The show is probably starting soon. Once it does, they'll have no choice but to go on without me. Good. At a deserted intersection where a green light shines for only me, I promise myself I will learn to go on without them, too. I promise myself the answers I am owed about who, or *what*, I am will make leaving the ballet worth it. It's time to be brave.

By the time I walk to the home improvement store parking lot, it's empty and glowing a bloody red cast from the large, ever-lit sign mounted atop the building's entrance. It's misty now, like the melancholy gray sky of the day isn't sure if it's ready to fall into rain, so it just hangs in the air, holding everything in a state of in-between.

I stand in the light from one of the lampposts, drop my bag, and shout up at the glowing red sign, "Come out!"

I take a breath to repeat myself, but hold it. What eventually moves me forward is not bravery, but the relief of yet more self-destruction. The truth, I am sure, will prove that I never deserved Riggs and Titania's sanctuary anyway.

"Come out. Now!"

It's not a question, but for some reason the repetition itself still buzzes with authority. I feel the night paying sudden attention. Perhaps my power is changing, now that I've started to embrace it. The red sign flickers, blinking like the question in my mind: *What am I? What am I? What am I?*

Finally, the answer flows toward me in the dark, on a river of clicking legs. It weaves between the lamplight and I catch its silhouette. It's bigger. More solid. I whip around, trying to never give it my back. I need to be ready.

"Come fucking get me," I whisper over and over. Finally, I hear it shift, close now, and I catch a flash of red light carving down a plated back. It's about to strike. I spit out my question as fast as I can: "What are you?" The question thickens the air, and the monster coils back, but it's close enough now that I've got it. No escape. I snap out the repeat: "*WHAT ARE YOU?*"

The monster's hundred legs curl inward like ribs over its underbelly as a lump works up its body. The truth. *My* truth. My questions dragging it out of the monster's clicking jaws in a spray of plasmatic membrane.

I am . . . your shadow, it screams. *I wa-s-s sent to watch over you. Follow and . . . protect you.*

"By who?" I stop at the very edge of the spotlight. The first time I ask this question, the monster pulls toward me, like my voice is a lasso. The second time I ask it—"*BY WHO?*"—the monster is crushed to the pavement at my feet.

Your . . . mother. No-t-t Titania. Nor the human. Your fae mother.

Fae.

I think of my storybook and all the other books I hoarded over the years, full of beautiful drawings and cruel stories about faeries. I read those books like they were confirmation of a world more magical than my difficult, mundane reality. What they were, instead, was confirmation that some part of me always knew I was wrong for this world, that everyone else was right about me. That I was different. "I'm a . . ."

Changeling, whispers my shadow.

My control over my power falters. I expect the monster to lunge, but now it cowers from me. It shivers, like I'm the nightmare, and its legs slip on themselves as I step toward it, out of the light and fully into the night.

"In the stories," I start, "the worst thing that could happen was that you woke up one day and found that your baby had been replaced with a changeling by the fae. Changelings look just like children, at first, but as they grow they become horrific. They rot. Turn hideous and insatiable. A burden and a monster, a thing that can be simply hated because it's replaced the child you actually wanted." I don't realize

I'm crying until my words have to be pushed out through gritted teeth. "Like even though it had no choice, and knows no other home and no other mother, it deserves to be hated simply for existing."

When I ran away from home, all that followed was my shadow. But I remember now that my mother stood in the door to stop me. She did that, even though I had just hurt her with my questions. Made her hurt me to prove my point to both of us that I was a monster, after all.

But she is not the only mother who has let me go. In the stories, I never found out why the changeling was left behind. It was a punishment sometimes, but it must have been someone's child first, right? Are the fae cruel enough to simply create children for the sake of hurt, or could there be a good reason why my first mother parted with me?

I have to know because maybe, if she wanted me at all, she could want me again.

"Why did she abandon me?" I ask. "And would she take me back?"

The double questions open like huge hands, gathering up the creature into a knot in the air. Suddenly, my power feels wild. Unfocused. Is it because I asked two questions at once? Or is it because as I asked, the mother in my mind splinters in half, then in thirds? The fae queen layers over the human woman who raised me; layers over Titania watching me from behind her piano. They kaleidoscope in their own ballet of grief, rejection, and love. But only one among them has chosen me as I am.

And that's the answer, isn't it? I am searching for a reason one mother let me go and another won't take me back, when a third—Titania—has given me a world meant for me. For Saturn. The changeling.

Pain lances through my entire body as the questions twist in my throat. I can feel the wrongness of asking too much, too quickly. The violence of the revelations will rip the shadow apart. It screams like it knows I could kill it.

Kill it with words alone. The realization horrifies me. I finally understand that my curiosity is a weapon I am now wielding against only myself. It will destroy me, too.

"SATURN!"

A truck screeches to a stop behind me, half in a spotlight. A head pops out of the sunroof and there's Riggs, waving me down.

"We found you! Get in!"

The driver's window is already down and a huge head of hair ducks out. Titania, all in drag! Relief blazes in my heart. They're here. They came for me.

"Well?" She flaps a hand of glittering nails. "Are you coming home or not? We've got a show to do, bunny."

Behind me I can hear the scraping armor of the centipede as it's dropped to the pavement. When I look back, it's retreated into the pitch black beneath the red sign. I let it go, binding down my curiosity. Joy and an uplifting wonder sweep me into a run toward the truck, and soon I'm tucked with Riggs in the cab as Titania spins us toward *home*.

"We're just gonna make it," she says. "The show's already started. You won't get another chance to warm up, so let's save the reunion speech for later and jump some lip trills to loosen up those articulation muscles."

Titania rockets through a red light as she trills through a vocal scale, indicating for me to echo her. Her sudden laser focus on my debut, which feels so childish now, makes my heart break in two. Half love, and half despair. How did they know where to look for me?

Riggs must see me trying to work through it. "When we got back,

I sensed something was off. Trust me, I know the look of a runaway. But it was just a lucky guess that we looked here first. I guess it's because this was the place I first felt you leaving me behind, this afternoon."

I want to ask why. Titania seems to know. She cuts off her vocal trills and serves me with a look in the rearview mirror.

"I don't know how they do ballet wherever you're from, darling, but we—the queens and I, and Riggs, and the rest of the Maléfique—we work through the bad stuff together."

"But . . ." My throat is still tender from beating up my own shadow. "I can't stay at the Maléfique unless I'm officially on the books. We could get shut down."

Titania grins, hearing her own line tossed back at her. Riggs nudges her. "Titania, do you want to tell him what went down after he left?"

Titania squeezes my hand. "You're right. Being underaged, you can't work at the Maléfique unless you are officially on the books as a performer, and even then you need the permission of a parent or guardian. And babe, I wanted to wait to tell you until after the show—god knows you didn't need to be *more* nervous—but you have both. The permission of your parents, *and* the permission of your guardian. Me. You're officially in the ballet. You are no threat whatsoever to the Maléfique. You can stay as long as you'd like."

"I don't understand," I say.

"Please don't get mad at me, but I spoke to your mom," Titania says, eyes fixed on the highway as the glittering downtown comes into view. One of those bits of glitter is the Maléfique. "Finding her wasn't hard. I've done it before with the kids that come to me. Riggs, Chassy, some girls that have moved on. I find their homes, and I see what I can do to make it right. Sometimes, I can help, and the child returns. Sometimes, there's nothing to return to, so I offer to take the child and give them at least a chance at a different life. And the parents, with so much hate and fear of our world, seem to realize that no matter what world their kid is in, it's better if they get to live. Some parents even send me money or birthday gifts. Usually it's the moms, if I'm honest."

I listen to all this while watching Titania's hand around my own. I admire the way her nails form an armor around me, a stylish warning to anything that might try to take me away that she is willing to fight to hold me here.

"Your parents know where you are, Saturn. At least your mom does. She knows you're safe, and she's already signed the paperwork I need to keep your employment aboveboard. I walked her through it all this afternoon when I sent you both on that fool's errand. More light bulbs? Ha! As if. But anyways, when your mom saw you would be a performer, I think she was excited. She got quiet on the phone, and she said: *That was always his dream.* We didn't say much more after that, but Saturn, I think she wants this for you."

"Is she coming? Did she say—"

I stop myself from asking two questions in a row, but the air is already harsh with static. Titania winces, but she doesn't let go of my hand.

"No, sweetie, she's not coming. I'm sorry."

"That's okay," I say quickly. "Tonight is for us, anyways."

The final few blocks to the theater are locked in traffic, so Titania sends us ahead. Riggs and I rush through the back, and we can barely hear each other over the roar of people and music bleeding into the backstage. The girls, however, are ready, and they throw me in front of one of the vanities. It's like being put into drag by a hurricane.

Somehow, when they're done a few songs later, I've been reborn. All the pieces I'd felt breaking from me while I spoke to my shadow have been painted, polished, and reassembled into a new me, a grander me, a me as luminous as the woman held by the moon in my storybook. I go to touch my cheek but pause, noticing that somehow I'm dressed, too. The queens give me space, and a moment to admire myself as I turn in the vanity.

"There she is," La'Dy admires.

"But," Babs cuts in, "will she sing?"

"Oh, like her life depends on it." Chassy grabs my hand and leads me through the backstage and up the stairs to the fly system. Riggs is already there, lit from below by a grid of neon shining up through the grates.

"Ready?" He shouts over the music.

"She's ready," Chassy shouts back.

"She can answer for herself, Chassy." Riggs laughs. "We just have to avoid making her *ask* questions, like Titania instructed. Is that right, Saturn? Is that how we can help you talk more?"

I feel, for the first time, this burden lifting. I never thought there would be such a simple solution. I never even considered that my monstrosity might have a solution at all.

"Yes!" I shout, and Chassy claps with encouragement.

"So we just gotta make sure none of the songs you perform have questions in them. That rules out 'Will You Still Love Me Tomorrow,' which is a drag standard. Oh, shit, and I guess you can't do 'What Is Love.' Or 'What Now?' by Rihanna. Or—"

"Chassy, we're good," Riggs says quickly. "Can you let Titania know we're ready?"

Chassy's hair rocks with a curt nod. She descends, giving us a few more minutes to prepare. Riggs checks all the straps and does a quick confirmation that my microphone is working.

Then he does it all again while reminding me about the order of operations: "Titania starts the track and I release the safety. I lower you and stop two measures before verse one. I lower you again during the first chorus, until you're all the way down. The dancers unclip you. I lift up the trapeze right away!" He points a finger sternly up, because that's the part he kept forgetting in our run-throughs. "Then I open the middle curtain, revealing the forest set. On the final refrain, you find the secondary trapeze, which is already down—I checked while you were getting ready—and leading into the final refrains, I lift you up, pausing for your big note. And then I lift you all the way up and away. And your star is born. Right?"

I shake my head, no.

"What? I forgot something?"

"Yeah," I say. "The part where I motherfucking sing my ass off."

Riggs takes a huge, relieved breath, his face opening into a delighted smile. Then he's hugging me. It's awkward because of the moon-shaped adornment around the trapeze. It all wobbles, but the safety holds, and his hug tightens. He lingers, and there's a moment when I think we're about to kiss, but even as I lean into it, he stops me.

"If I mess up your makeup, La'Dy is going to gut me."

I grin. "Mess it up after?" I offer.

"Don't have to ask me twice," Riggs growls, giving me a gentle push as he settles back onto the catwalk. He blows a kiss and heads to the fly system, and I'm alone. I hover over the light, but for now I remain in the dark. I can feel my shadow still, wounded and scared of me, but attached to me all the same. It feels close, but I don't feel frightened.

The dance song playing ends and Titania's voice booms over the speakers as she introduces me as the next, final act of the night. A debut act that, in the moment, she dubs as:

"SATURN, THE FALLING STAR OF THE BALLET MALÉFIQUE! CATCH HER NOW, CATCH HER FOREVER!"

The song begins and I feel all safety release as the vision I have danced through one thousand times begins to come true. A new vision takes its place now, as the crowd comes into view. I pretend I'm looking down at the rows and rows of velvet seats in the original Magnifique, all of them filled with shadowed faces, but one face I know. My own, as a kid, watching the ballet with ferocious hope. It could be any kid, really, who needs the chance to look up and see someone like them on a stage like this. I think if I can just show one of the kids that I'm here, that they can find their own home, too, this fear of living brightly will always be worth it.

It's just a vision, though, a dream. In reality, I'm gazing down at a crowd of every kind of face. They look up at me with love and expectation. They see me. *Me*. I finally begin to sing.

I thought I would be scared in this moment, and I am. But I feel powerful, too. Adored. My voice grows stronger. I never knew I could be so loud! The crowd screams with excitement as my moon falls to earth, and the dancers are there to catch me. I don't notice until the second chorus, but in the balconies, I can see La'Dy, Babs, and Chassy clutching each other like stage moms, pride written all over their expressions as they sing along.

"That's our baby!" Babs is screaming.

I miss a word because I'm laughing, but I get back on track, finding my way through the rest of the choreo I'm sure I practiced to death yet can't remember a step of now. Somehow, we make it to the end of the dance break, and the crowd is even more rapturous as I nail every note in the final verse. All that's left are the refrains. I twirl back to the trapeze, just like Riggs instructed. I'm standing in it as the dancers clip my belt in, and then I'm rising. My body and my voice. The big moment is coming up and I need all the air I can get.

The lights in the theater flicker. All of them—in a rolling blackness that causes something nestled around the chandeliers to glitter. My voice chokes off.

Oh no, I think. *Not now. Not here.*

Just like in the store, the people muffle and their expressions turn dreamy. It's like time is slowing down. The last refrain stretches out into a warped roar as the shadow spools down from the ceiling and unveils something hanging in the needles of its legs.

My shadow holds a woman who looks like me. She is luminous and lit from within, like a storm cloud. Her skin is an otherworldly blue, and her ears would point to the stars if she had come to find me one of the many nights I stood outside and begged for the faeries to come back for me. She never came. Why is she here now?

Come home, she offers.

My shadow begged when it said this. She commands it. Everything about her—from her smooth, rich voice, to her twilight skin, to the way her silvery hair swirls over her lithe form—feels strange yet familiar. Enchanting. I have to force myself to see the shadow cradling her, the slick, mutilated version of me she now strokes like a pet; with love, but also with possession. I could ask her why she left me, I could maybe use the answer to rationalize a way back. But back to what?

A world I have only ever imagined. A world I know was once cruel enough to let me go.

Come home, my child, she repeats. The repetition fills the air with an electric tang. Even as she calls me her child, her face flashes with steely annoyance. She is not someone who tolerates having to repeat herself.

All of me shakes as I try to stand tall on the swinging trapeze. My voice feels like it's broken in my throat, but I force myself to find the words to my song, to sing as if this performance can still be saved.

Because I want to stay *here*.

I want to do *this*.

I want to be *Saturn*.

I am home, I think. I focus on finding my way through the warped music, and I nail my entrance to the final refrain. It's like I've popped a needle back on track in an old record player, and the song sews itself back together. I can hear the crowd coming back to life below us, too. The cheers fight upward, joining with my own voice. I steady my voice even as the trapeze rocks with the force of the faerie's magic.

Her words cut through the rising cacophony.

You will always be their monster, she says with regal indignation, but I sing on. Finally, I sense her go, taking my shadow with her.

I belt out the final, staggering notes of the song, with so much power in my voice that I feel the trapeze pulling after me as I float forward. The restraints catch as if I've fallen, but I'm flying. For just a moment, I swear I fly. Then my breath is gone, my voice reverberating around the theater as the trapeze surrenders to gravity and swings backward, causing the crowd to gasp. Did they see what happened just now? If they couldn't, they for sure just saw me float. Was the faerie right, that to them I will always be a monster? I have learned that I cannot hide who I am, so the real question has become: Knowing what I am, will they love me or fear me?

The cheers come all at once, overwhelming me as I rock on the trapeze. Instead of lifting me up and away, Riggs makes me hang there and absorb it all. I blow kiss after kiss. Then I'm being dropped again. My feet meet the stage, and I notice a new shadow slide beneath my heels. It's shaped just like me, dancing under my feet playfully as I try to see it. Titania joins me on stage and takes my hand, lifting it like I've won some major Olympic victory.

"SATURN, THE FALLING STAR OF THE BALLET MALÉFIQUE!" she repeats into her mic, and the crowd erupts in more applause. Titania hugs me, and even though it's deafening on the stage, I can hear her whisper right in my ear.

"I am so proud of you, bunny. But there's just one more thing to do before I let you run backstage with Riggs."

For the first time since lowering from the catwalk, I feel fear. What now?

Titania smiles bright as she takes my hand again. Her eyes glitter as she cocks her head at the crowd, and I finally listen to what they're chanting.

Encore! Encore! Encore!

I look back at Titania. There's a challenge in her expression. Am I ready? Is this what I want? Is this who I am?

I step forward, into the spotlight, and from somewhere in the darkness, my music begins.

BIRCH KISS

Tessa Gratton

You said the Prince of Birch fell in love with you, and that's why you had to go.

I said love doesn't work that way. You looked between me and West and pursed your lips like *What do you two know about love*, but West and I aren't like that. (Not really, not yet, not every day.)

We dropped it, kept trying to make plans with you, for prom, for summer, for which play West should petition the rest of drama club to pick for next spring so we could land meaty roles our senior year. For the rest of our lives. You hummed, listened, and pretended to agree.

Today West and I head through the sticky woods to the fairy pool. You've been gone a month. After your mom reported you missing they took statements from everybody, and the last time you were seen was on the sidewalk at the edge of these woods, near the start of the path out here.

The kid who saw you remembered because you were wearing a

long, ruffled white dress and no shoes. You had lace gloves on—white, too—and the kid said you looked like you were getting married.

Remember what you said when you bought that dress?

West and I had dragged you with us to the mall in Kansas City because it still has three dress stores and when we asked you to be our date for prom you hummed and stared into the middle distance and that's always counted as a yes when you were in those moods before. I'd been planning to wear a suit, but West talked me into letting them build me a vest-bodice-binder thing out of duck canvas and vivid blue jacquard they found in their mom's stash. They'd brought a swatch of it, and the pattern was blue on blue in a way that caught the light. I loved it, and could imagine a gorgeous binder shaping me right, flashing under a black bolero jacket or something short and cute. I'd wear a thin bow tie and high-waisted slacks and my favorite polished Oxfords. West wanted their gown to compliment the jacquard. They were inspired by the end of *Sleeping Beauty* when the princess's dress switches between blue and pink because the fairies are fighting. Instead of a color mash, West planned a mash of princess and prince costume: a high-collared vest with puffy-sleeved chemise and faux chain mail for their top half; for their bottom half, blue and fuchsia skirts as voluminous as possible. Tulle would definitely be involved. Hoop skirts potentially.

On the way to the mall you lounged in the back seat changing the music with your phone while West and I discussed it. West asked if I thought their hair would be long enough yet to braid around a tiara, and you answered, "You could do horns instead, like that evil fairy."

"Maleficent," I murmured, eyeing West's tan temples and dark hair. I could imagine it.

West kept their eyes on the highway and said with every prissy ounce in them, "But I *want* a tiara."

"Horns are sexy," you answered blandly.

"I could give East horns," West suggested.

I touched my forehead.

"Not like Maleficent," you said. "East would need horns like a stag. A king of the forest."

Under my fingers the skin of my forehead seemed to tremble, and I imagined horns bursting out, growing a crown. I felt warm all over, pleased.

West said, "Stags have antlers."

"The Prince of Birch has golden leaves in her hair, as if it's always autumn," you said.

My hand fell back into my own lap. "Why don't you bring your prince to prom?" I twisted in the passenger seat to look at you.

A tiny smile graced your lips and you ducked your head bashfully. "She's older than the cutoff."

I laughed, but it wasn't a joke, was it?

You drifted behind us from store to store, trying on nothing. You held the jacquard swatch up to this dress and that dress, commented on which colors brought out our eyes or made our complexions sallow. Nothing caught your attention until we were lost in a pastel wasteland of off-the-rack bridesmaids dresses that would only look pretty if West Frankensteined them into much gayer rainbow monsters. You fell behind while we bickered about baby blue verses baby violet. We noticed, and you pulled the white ruffles out, fanning the wide skirts. It had to be a wedding dress draped against the weeds.

That's when you said it: "The Prince of Birch will like this one."

Prom was five days ago. West and I skipped.

In the woods it's hot and humid, even under the lusciously draped summer trees. West has their hand on my shoulder because the path is too narrow to walk side by side but they don't want to let go. I get it. We always touched a lot but since you've been gone it's more constant.

We're both wearing long sleeves and jeans for this hike because it's tick season, so we're sweltering, backpacks trapping sweat against our spines. The creek we follow cuts a little two-foot canyon through the trees, a pretty babbling guide.

Birds sing, too, and squirrels chitter, and the wind blows sometimes, thank god. If you were with us, you'd be naming the chickadees and finches and cardinals by their voices alone, and telling us this is an old beech tree, that's an oak, here are the junipers, which are also called red cedars. You downloaded an app on my phone that identifies flowers but I can't use it without you or the tears start trembling in my guts. All I know is there are some white flowers, and these look like trumpets, and probably those over there are various kinds of sunflowers. I've heard you say morning glories and mallow and maybe a name that sounded like ditch parsley or hedge parsley but is related to something poisonous. (You said once that everything in a garden is related to something poisonous.)

It's the wrong time of year for your favorites anyway: pear blossoms in the spring, and the American persimmons giving fruit in the fall.

The moment we emerge from the trees into the meadow with the fairy pool, both West and I are dropping our backpacks and stripping down. West has on a strappy bikini top and speedos for their junk. I've got a tight sport bra and my usual briefs. We dig into one of the bags and West puts on a floral peasant skirt and I have high-waisted cotton shorts and a white tank with a John Deere logo because symbolism I guess. It made West smile and they haven't been doing that much lately.

Then we lay out our blanket on the sloping bank of the creek and sit with our knees knocking together. The opposite bank is a wall of limestone and shale that catches the creek, curving it into a whirlpool. It spins, churns, slow as a witch's cauldron.

The fairy pool.

It looks like a spring, but it's backward. Here the water sucks underground. *A sinkhole made it*, some people in town say. It's an underground waterfall into a cavern carved through the soft sedimentary bedrock. Drop something into the fairy pool—a wish, a sacrifice, trash, bones—it won't come out.

When people die here, their bodies are never found. You used to talk about it, obsessed. You're the one who told us it's sometimes called the Devil's Bath and you liked to bring gifts like paper stars and Fireball.

It's where you met the Prince of Birch.

I look to the south end of the pool where three river birches bend over the water, as if looking for their reflections. They're slender and stately, white bark peeling only a little around vivid black eyes. Oval leaves, a pretty silver-green, shiver in the wind.

The sun glares directly down on us, but soon it will be sinking behind the trees. Dusk is when *she* comes, you said. Your fairy prince. You said she likes fruit and alcohol, so we have raspberries and strawberries in a refrigerated bag and honey and some gin from West's mom. You always gave them whiskey or elderberry wine, but gin is what we have and it's *botanical*, so maybe it will please her.

We're early, but we didn't want to get lost in the dark or be late because we couldn't find it. I've only been here twice before and West once, and you always led the way. My first time was last spring when the mimosa trees were blooming along the edge of the forest, which I only remember because I thought mimosas were orange juice and Prosecco and you pulled one of the branches down so I could stick my face in the spindly pink blossoms. We came back with West in the summer and then it was honeysuckle because you taught us to pinch the flowers and taste their kiss. That's how you said it. *Taste their kiss.* Little honeybees buzzed around and the air was hazy with allergens.

(I kissed you later that night, and West, too. On the roof of your garage when West told us they weren't a boy, so shy like I'd be upset, as if they were rejecting what I wanted to have. You said, "We should call you West!" And I smacked you, said, "West is so far from East." But West understood and took my hand. "A western wind blows toward the east," they said, smile blossoming from the uncertainty. I kissed their mouth for the first time.)

You never brought us here after you met the Prince of Birch. But you told us all about her.

"She comes just past dusk when the moon is in the sky, and there's nothing in the world as beautiful," you said. "She holds my hand like I'm precious, as if her weird long fingers could break the skin too easily. She has little talons on her wrist bones, like the dewclaws on your dog. She likes fruit and whiskey and kissing."

Your blush when you said it turned your cheeks into fruit, I told you, and mimicked trying to bite them until you laughed and shoved me away.

On our blanket now, under the setting sun, West slumps into me. Melts until I wrap my arm around them despite the humidity and our tacky skin. "She was such a bitch," they say about you.

I stiffen, digging my fingers into their arm.

"We're out here because of some made-up bullshit," West continues. "She lied to us so we wouldn't know what she would do."

"She wasn't like that. Tricking us."

"She made it up to hide what she wanted."

"She didn't want to die."

West pulls away and stares at me with teary eyes. "I've had the mandatory counseling, too."

(When you and I met, you grabbed my forearm and wiped your finger down the long scar that runs from my inner elbow down to my wrist. You glanced up at me with a smirk and said, "Me too.")

(Another time you said it isn't about wanting to die. It's the opposite of wanting. An anti-wanting, a nothingness. Except it hurts. A nothingness of hurt, that's what you called it. And if you stay in bed or lie on the grass under the honeysuckle in your backyard doing nothing and being nothing, the nothingness spreads out in every direction, on and on until it stretches so thin you can stand up again. Then it fits like a skin and you can wear it around instead of suffocating.)

I suck in a slow breath of air that feels like syrup, stuffing me full. It'll come back up as tears. I swallow them, trying to make words come instead. West watches me and blinks. A tear drops from each of their eyes. They reach out for my face and rub their thumbs on my cheeks.

"I'm sorry," West says, pulling me closer. Our foreheads touch.

(You told me about the anti-wanting because you thought that's what my scar was for, too. A way to cut through the nothing-skin. I never told you the truth. I was going to. I was. Maybe at prom.)

Instead of telling West, I say, "I believe her. I know the Prince of Birch is real."

"East."

"The way she talked about her . . ." I drift off, eyes shut. The way you talked about her, she had to be real. A real something.

"It's possible she had a secret girlfriend," West says. "Or this prince was a new therapist, and *that* was the story she was telling."

"Maybe she did run away." I sit up straight again. "With her new therapist girlfriend. But I wish she'd waited until school was out."

I don't believe it. Neither does West. Saying it feels solid, though.

The sun has fallen enough that long shadows reach for us, and there's no more orange gleam on the churning surface of the fairy pool. I sigh. I let my gaze trail the edges of the pool, the shade, the flicker of movement that's probably just birds. Soon the bats will be out. I look past the limestone wall at the Narcissus birches and someone is watching me back.

I squeak and freeze.

"East?" West says, but I can't answer. I can only stare at the eyes, a deep rough black like raw charcoal against a white face. Not white like me, or you, where it's really strawberries and cream or ruddy taupe or pale peach or the dull color of Band-Aids. No: white-white. Bone white, picket-fence white, cold ice white. White like the bark of the birch trees.

"Holy shit," West breathes, so obviously they see her.

Together, hands clutched, we stand up. My legs shake and I think this is what a hot flash must feel like, but we don't look away.

The wind blows and the last rays of the sun flutter between shadows, gilding the birches, and she leans away. She raises an elegant ice-white hand.

Then the sun is gone and the sky is purple and the crickets and frogs are singing up a racket.

And the Prince of Birch is gone, too.

West and I grab our stuff and run home practically screaming. But we don't actually say anything, not even when we're out of the forest and back in our neighborhood. We're jittery and gasping and just wave wide-eyed goodbyes at the corner.

But I text them from bed, huddled under the sheets with all the lights off and my fan oscillating hard enough to drown out the wind through the trees outside.

we have to go back

West answers,

yeah

We wait a few days, partly because of the weather but also it's the last week of school. We act normal, as normal as we can or are expected to, given the eggshells everybody walks on around us. People always stared because you were ethereally beautiful one hundred percent of the time; because West, the best junior on the men's swim team, started wearing dresses to school; because you both treated me, Easter Antonia, like your boyfriend.

Now they stare because you're gone and they don't know what to say.

This time we're prepared, and when we get to the fairy pool, we lay our gifts on a thin slab of slate West pulled up from the creek bottom where it's shallow and slow. Raspberries and apple slices, a teacup of gin, and several flowers from my mom's garden. Taken with permission: Mom helped me pick out the ones she thought you'd like because I let her think we were making our own memorial out here in the woods. Yellow and white daisies, and sprigs of purple hyacinth, mostly.

We kneel beside the altar, directly across from the three birch trees. The sun sinks, and today the breeze is genuinely cooling thanks to the rain blowing in for storms the next few days. While we wait, West unties their strappy sandals and starts painting bright purple polish on their toes. I stare at the quick little strokes of the brush as they work. Their knuckles are knobby but they've always had graceful hands. Their feet are wide and just so masculine I wonder how they can stand it. The shape of them, the slightly jutting balls, the flat big toe, nobody would look at those feet and think anything but *man*. Even with the sparkly purple polish. When they flex and point so the polish glimmers in the sun, the tendons shift and I imagine leaning down to kiss the arch, but really I would bite it, as if I could eat their feet and make them mine.

"East?" They say my name gently and my gaze flies up to theirs; I realize I'm breathing too fast.

I pull my knees up and bury my face in my arms.

West touches my back, palm hot, and their thumb rubs against my shoulder blade. That's where wings would burst free if I could make it happen. My back aches: I bend harder, jutting out my spine as if to press scales or bristles through and West rubs down to the small of my back, then up to the nape of my neck. I shiver. They rest their hand against the strap of my sports bra. It holds me so tightly, too tightly. There will be a mark around my ribs. Good. *Good.* A line for me to cut along, a dotted line, a seam.

I fall against West and they hold me close. They kiss my temple. I turn my face and kiss their lips. Then we're kissing again and again, tight little pecks. My eyes squeeze closed. My whole body is hot, aching. I want so much, I want to mold myself to West I want to switch bodies with them I want to touch them I want to peel my skin away and find scales I want to be flatter harder leaner and I also want you. I want you to jump out of the woods and scare us, to laugh that gleeful high laugh you had when you were genuinely delighted. I want your soft body I want you teasing us you always teased so well I could forget the differences between my body and West's, and I knew we were the same the same the same. It was so good.

You were so good.

West pulls away. Our mouths make a little smack. I blink. West blinks back. Their eyes are delicious hazel with light brown-orange like a sunburst around the pupil and short black curling lashes. I've always been enamored by their eyes.

"Are you crying?" they ask.

I put my hands to my cheeks and smear the tears. I shake my head.

West rolls their pretty eyes.

"Maribel told me you were in love," says the Prince of Birch.

I gasp so hard I'm surprised I don't choke. West spins on their ass. We stare up at the prince.

She's standing in the shade cast by the setting sun, black eyes as big and strange as the other day. There's no nuance to her: She is flat white and harsh charcoal, with a long suit of the same that clings to her spindly elegant body and flows around legs, presumably. Maybe she's got roots instead of feet. I can't see because the bark-edge of her skirts curls against the grass. She leans, head tilted like a bird's. One hand splays on her hip, the other plays with a strand of her sleek black hair. She twists the hair between too-long fingers and there, oh wow, just like you said, is the hooked talon growing from her wrist bone like a dewclaw.

West catches my hand and I pull them up with me as I stand.

"Prince of Birch," I say.

Beside me, West's breathing is harsh. I flick a glance at them, at their blown-wide eyes, parted lips. They stare at her, clearly overwhelmed and terrified that your fairy prince is real.

But I feel better.

Grounded.

This is what makes the most sense to me, about you. About what happened. You didn't—

die—

You rode off with the Prince of Birch.

"Easter," the Prince of Birch says. Their eyes have no color in them, like blackout Halloween contacts, so it's tough to tell which of us they're looking at. Then they say, "Adam."

West jolts and opens their mouth to snarl, but I squeeze their hand hard. They stop. They swallow. Tilt their chin up defiantly.

The Prince of Birch smiles. Wow, her teeth are sharp; you didn't warn us about that. But she's beautiful, you were right. A strange, creeping beauty that pulls at me; I want to know more. It would be easy to step into that pool and drown. Sucked into the caverns below, breathless forever.

West says, "Where's Maribel?" Cutting right to the chase.

I say, "We brought you gifts, if you'll tell us."

The Prince of Birch moves and suddenly she's on the bank right in front of us. The sun is gone; the whole meadow is purple twilight. She glances down at the fruit and gin and flowers. Slowly, she bends, crouching with her knees together. She plucks up the teacup and smells the gin. Her eyes flutter closed.

She smells like honeysuckle—*Taste their kiss*, you said last year when you taught us to pinch the base of the blossom and suck gently. I sway on my feet, thinking of you. This near, not only can I smell her, I can see her sleek hair move strangely, like stop-motion art, ink animated with missing frames. She tips the teacup against white lips. Her wrist is so delicate, the dewclaw surely sharp enough to cut to the bone without pain.

I see it: Her wrist snaps out; I don't feel a sting. Then instead of pain it's warm blood spilling down my throat, soaking the collar of my shirt.

I blink and wait for that pain but the Prince of Birch is drinking gin from a teacup with tiny birds and vines and an elaborate Victorian garden painted onto it. The birds have googly eyes. West made it for you. That's why you loved this cup. From a distance it's fine old floral china; up close it's a joke.

West shifts uncertainly beside me. For a split second their throat is bleeding too, and I open my mouth to panic, but the blood is gone.

It's just me, me, me, my thoughts.

My thoughts except I don't *want* to cut both our throats at all. (It isn't about *wanting*, I remember you said.) I take a deep breath.

The Prince of Birch smiles, white lips whiter than porcelain against the delicate teacup. She smiles and she turns the cup over. A thin trickle of clear gin splashes out onto the ground.

"For the old ones," she says.

"Will you tell us about what happened to Maribel? Is she with you?" I ask.

"These are a gift to give to the pool," the Prince of Birch says. "For those answers, we need a bargain."

"What kind of bargain?" West asks.

"Wait," I say. I tug West's hand. I try to meet the blackout gaze of the Prince of Birch. "Do you know what happened? If we bargain, will we get our answers?"

The Prince of Birch hums. She looks at me, through me, angling her gaze up to my crown, down to my boots.

Nothing so strange has ever happened to me. You loved this feeling, you must have because you wanted her, wanted to be with her, but to me it is like standing inside a dream. I feel the ground under my feet, the breeze on my cheeks, West's hand in my hand, the thick summer twilight. I hear frogs in the trees and evening birds. Everything feels real except there's a fairy standing in front of me, a perfect prince just human enough it could all be fake, all of it a costume, a prank.

It isn't. Those fairy eyes glint deep mossy green like they aren't blackout contacts but a cave, a wide-open mouth leading underhill. (Into the sinkhole.) Her neck is too long, her mouth bloodless, her hair shifting in and out of reality, a shadow.

She is a flaw in the world. In how my brain processes reality.

The Prince of Birch says, "For a bargain you will get a chance to find your answers. In three nights the full moon will rise, and we will ride. If you come, if you give us something in return, you can ride, too, and then you will know who is with us and who is not."

"Ride?" West asks.

I frown. "What sort of gift?"

"Something as fleeting as an answer? As heavy as a question? Something valuable but without value?" she suggests.

A shiver strolls down my spine.

"Will it kill us?" West's voice is loud in the darkening meadow.

I stare at West. Are they right? Is this what happened to you? You bargained with the Prince and it killed you?

But the Prince of Birch laughs. Her laugh is a cold color more than a sound, a dreary rainbow song. She winks at West, and says, “Only if death is your offering.”

The Prince of Birch’s skin hardens, peels in tiny curls like paper bark, and there is only a young birch tree standing in front of us, where no tree was before.

“What?” I whisper. West says, “Holy shit.”

Then we blink again and even the tree is gone.

We’re alone with our slate altar and flowers trembling in the dusk.

West comes home with me.

We wave at my parents and tumble up the stairs to my bedroom, drop our stuff and stand there in the familiar room. Ivy wallpaper with pale green stripes makes the room seem old-fashioned, but I’ve put up framed posters from drama club and every note you’ve ever written me is pinned to a corkboard next to the closet mirror. Some of them are instructions for where to meet after class, others scraps of lyrics that were in your head, and most of the willow cabin soliloquy from *Twelfth Night* because you were feeling dreamy and obnoxious last spring. You passed me one line at a time. I lost the piece with the line *hallow your name to the reverberate hills* and won’t replace it. But I left a space. I stare at it sometimes, and hear you recite the words. I can’t forget your voice. I need to recognize it in three nights when we ride with the Prince of Birch. So I can hear you, if you call to me. If you need to be rescued.

(If you send me away.)

“Was that real?” West asks. I go to the bedside table and pull the tab on the lamp. Warm light floods the room, turning the single window into a dark mirror. For a moment, I see you reflected there, leaning in to check the fall of your curls.

"I think so." I sit on the bed and untie my boots. I kick them off. They thump on the wall next to the desk. West is more careful as they remove theirs. They take off their jeans, too, and crawl under my blankets. It's a good idea. I go with them once I've shimmied free of my own jeans.

We lie face-to-face on my thin pillows. The fresh blankets smell like dryer sheets. The forest and the fairy pool are so far from here.

"Why didn't you let me tell her my name?" West asks.

I glance down. It was a fast instinct. I stare at the loose collar of their T-shirt, at the tan skin glinting warmly in the lamplight. "She could only know those names because Maribel gave them to her. There's only one reason Maribel would say *those*."

West's chest rises sharply, then they reach for me. They put a hand on my cheek and I look up. West nods, mouth pressed in a grim line.

I read up on fairies before we went to meet the Prince of Birch the first time, but there's too much to know. Wear your clothes inside out. Walk backward. Be polite. But don't say thank you. Look through a river-hollowed stone. But don't look directly. They love red—they hate red. Fairies are silly. Fairies are old gods. Fairies are cruel and forgetful. Fairies never forget. Fairies are the spirits of the dead. Never call them fairies: call them good folk, shining ones, good neighbors, friends. Leave offerings. Save yourself with a pinch of salt. Don't lie. They dislike iron. You can defeat them with a bargain, but if you lose you won't remember. They love music and dancing and games of war. They love riddles. There are trooping fairies and solitary fairies. Never throw anything over your shoulder in case you hit an invisible passing fairy. Never eat their food.

Never tell a fairy your real name.

"It's more dangerous for the prince to know our *real* names," I whisper.

You were protecting us. I know that much. I also know my name is slipperier, less adamant than West's. My name isn't what upsets me.

"The Prince of Birch knew Maribel's real name," West says.

I glance at the corkboard. I imagine your voice, listen for you to say *hallow your name to the reverberate hills*.

Did you go with her on your own? Did she make you the same offer to ride with them? I can't remember if it was a full moon the night you vanished.

Did she know your name and know how to make you stay?

"What are we going to do?" West hugs me closer. Our faces are too near on the same pillow to keep our eyes open. I can't focus. I let mine drift shut. In my research I read about riding with fairies. The Wild Hunt. Odin's Hunt. The Devil's Ratchets. The Sluagh. They were stories that linked fairies with the dead more directly than most. With valkyries and ghosts and the unforgiven dead like people murdered and unbaptized babies and people who—

"We'll go," I whisper. I clutch West's T-shirt. "We'll think of something to bargain, and find her."

"Unless she's dead."

We might still find you, even if you're dead. Especially if you're dead and went with them.

I say, "It's worth it."

West kisses me. Their lips are warm and dry and I press in. We've kissed a lot, but not in bed like this. Under sheets with nighttime outside. I breathe in through my mouth and West shifts so their bottom lip is between mine and I lick a little. Taste the kiss.

Then we're kissing harder, messy and jolting. My nose mushes into West's, they knock our mouths together like a knuckle bump. Then

I smile and West smiles so our teeth clash. You told me I can know if a pearl is real if I rub it on the flat of my front teeth. If it's smooth it's fake, if it's gritty it's real—pearls are made from sand and calcite. They're crystal, you said. Concentric crystal formations. You showed me, pearl earring in your fingers, you said, *Smile for me, bunny*. I did, and you dragged the pearl along my tooth. It went straight to my bones.

I think of crystal teeth when I keep kissing West. My teeth are amethyst, glinting purple like the sunset; West's are golden topaz, their birthstone. Yellow and purple are complementary colors, east and west, we belong like this, slotting our not-quite-human teeth together, new colors for in-between boy and girl.

West's tongue is in my mouth and I open up, surprised. I like it. I like the slippery feeling. Slippery like me, like my name. I give back, and West rolls me over, I'm on my back; they touch my waist and I'm still slipping away, liquid between their hands. I hum and kiss and cling to West's shoulders until their one hand brushes my chest, touches the too-soft, too-wrong, not-at-all-crystalline flesh blob and my body goes rigid.

I can't move, calcified, turned into a tree right there in my bed.

West feels me lock up—they pause. I put my hand over their hand and press down as hard as I can. Their palm flattens me, makes the right shape but it's still wrong. Soft. Wrong. I feel a thread of nausea pulling under my skin and squeeze my eyes closed and start to say *I'm sorry* but West kisses me and shakes their head.

They wiggle down, slither both arms around my waist and tuck their head against my shoulder. Somehow it makes them smaller, even with their big feet definitely hanging off the edge of the bed and their soft hair against my jaw. It's comforting to me in a way it shouldn't be. I'm holding them, I'm the boyfriend. I'm the— They hug me close and I can feel their dick. A little into what we were doing. Maybe. I wouldn't know, would I? My body was into it until it really really wasn't.

I sigh aggressively, trying to collect myself. Trying not to ruin this.

West whispers, "If you angle this way I could feel your big dick, too, East."

It startles me into laughing, then we both are. Hugging and laughing. And scared.

Three nights later we arrive at the meadow an hour before sunset. We haul hanging luggage and a tackle box converted into makeup storage.

Our slate altar is still in place, drooping daisies like dead snakes with yellow petal-skin flaking off. I unzip my luggage and the sight of midnight-blue and navy jacquard fills me with tingles. Anticipation, anxiety, both.

We get dressed next to each other, stripped down then slowly built back up with new skin. West says, "This will fit better if you take that sport bra off," and I do with shaking hands. West helps me into the binder-bodice, which they lined with cotton to be softer and better against my skin. They tie me up hard: lacing up the spine, then laced to either side of my ribs for a snug, flattening fit.

I can breathe deeply. The swell of breast tissue isn't even that distracting because it doesn't spill over or catch or choke. Like it isn't even there. I turn and study West's angular face as they finish the ties. "Thank you," I say softly.

They shrug, and smile.

I pull up the wide-legged royal-blue pants I found. They have a double row of buttons at the fly, and belt high around my waist. West ties up my shiny brown Oxfords. Next is my little black jacket. I have a hat, too, but first I help West step into the three layers of skirts. Each one buttons tight and they have ties sewn in that let the top two layers pull up like theater curtains. There's a full tulle skirt under it all, and those strappy sandals West likes so much. The tunic and jacket are very dashing, with an off-center collar that stands up in a spike over one shoulder.

We look fantastic, even before makeup and hair.

We kneel before each other on a blanket, with the tackle box between us, and take turns with glitter and blue and black shadow, matching bloodred lips for us both. I braid tiny fake baby blue flowers into West's hair—not quite long enough for a tiara—and they surprise me with small pale brown branches. "Not quite antlers," West says, but I let them wind my hair into a tangled mess of sticks and mousse.

The sun is gone when we're ready, and we hold hands, facing each other.

"We look great," I say.

"We should have gone to prom," West laments softly. But they're the one who canceled first. We couldn't go without you. Even if you'd left without us.

"Now what?"

West winds our fingers together and we tilt our faces to watch the sky darken. A few early stars gleam, more and more while we stand there with aching necks.

I think we feel it, or you whisper somehow. But we both turn east just as the first white sliver of the full moon tips over the shadowed forest.

When we look back at each other, we're surrounded.

They are ghostly moonlight figures on horses and stags. They're translucent with starlight eyes and hair like icicles. They smile and stare at us, while their ghost stallions paw at the air—they are a foot off the ground, standing on nothing but fog and dreams. I hear the bay of a hound, then another and another, shrieking and cackling more like foxes than dogs.

Crowns glint on their heads, made of nails, scales, flowers, and thorns. Old-fashioned dresses and tattered robes blow in a breeze I cannot feel.

Then I hear the whispers of gossip as the fairies lean toward one another; the tinkle of bells in bridles; the huff of impatient horses. Silver ribbons adorn the antlers of the stag nearest me. Atop its back, perched in an elaborate saddle, is a fairy woman with a bleeding mouth. My heart races as I notice things off about all of them: slit-pupils and seven-fingered hands, fangs and eyes as large as plates. I can see that one's skull through his skin, and this one has a tail. There are wings and clicking teeth.

There, finally, the Prince of Birch nudges her great gray horse forward. She wears a dress like Queen Elizabeth, but those aren't beads and jewels bedecking the bodice and sleeves: They're teeth of every shape. Her hair is wound with bones and the only color I see on her is glinting yellow-gold leaves in her hair, just like you said on the way to the mall, tumbling down from her braids like they grow from her scalp and shake loose in her eagerness to ride.

"You've come," the Prince of Birch says, and suddenly the riders make a cacophony, their stomping and giggles loud as a roar. Drowning out frogs and crickets and my own heartbeat.

"Which one of you will it be?" the Prince asks.

I suck in a stunned breath. West says, "One?"

"One, didn't I mention it? There's only room for one."

"I don't know," I say, and West says, their voice loud, too, "How do we choose?"

The Prince of Birch smiles. "The one who rides must be the one who loved her most."

Peals of laughter ring around us. West and I step nearer each other.

I start to say we loved you the same, but West turns me by my shoulder. Earnestly, they say, "It's you."

"What? How do you know?"

"Easy. I've always loved you more than I loved her."

I nearly melt at the confession and barely catch myself from saying their name at the last second, mouthing it only. It strings silently between us.

But you're waiting.

"I have to go," I say.

"You have to come back," they reply.

My blood is cold in my veins, cold salt water moving in and out under the tide of my heart. "I will."

"Do you know your offering, what is your bargain for us?" the Prince of Birch calls sweetly.

I turn to face her. West puts their hands on my shoulders behind me. "You will tell me if Maribel is with you."

"You will ride with us tonight and find her yourself, if she is with us," the Prince says. "And in return you will give us . . . ?"

"A kiss."

taste the kiss

West sucks in a breath behind me, their hands tightening. They say to the Prince, "And in the morning you bring him back to me. When the sun rises, he comes back alive and well."

The Prince of Birch laughs. "If Easter chooses to, he'll come back to you."

Around us, the horde of ghostly fairies laugh and scream.

"Wait," West says, and drags me down to kneel on the grass. Their skirts billow and pool as they dig into the tackle box and find tiny sewing scissors.

The breath and huff of fairy horses and fairy ghosts feels like wind hitting from all angles, cold and hot and cold. West cuts off a chunk of their hair before I can react. They drop the scissors and say, "Give me your hand."

I do, fingers splayed, and they tie the hair around my ring finger. A promise.

I clench my fist and the twisting black hair pinches my finger, whites out the skin. It cuts against flesh like my sports bra cutting into my ribs, marking me, binding me in my body, making me feel better, forcing my flesh into the shape I need.

I stand. "Be careful," I tell them. *I love you*, I think. I love you and you, both of you.

The Prince of Birch holds out her hand.

I take it.

The Prince of Birch tugs me up into her lap. I hold my breath. I stare down at West, their sunburst eyes fixed on me. I'm fixed on them too.

An arm around my waist like a branch, rough, firm, holds me sideways on the horse's shoulders. I dig fingers into the ghost-horse's silky mane, and grab on to the Prince of Birch's shoulder.

She screams. I jerk, clap my hands to my ears. They all scream. The horse rears, throwing me against her with a soundless scream of my own.

The horse leaps into the sky.

The land falls away below: It is dark, evergreen, rolling beneath us as the hunt rides.

I sit up, lean forward, holding on to the horse. We lead the ride, rush forward, the arrowhead of the gang.

It feels like flying, not galloping, there is only the gentle rocking—it's like rocking against you against West. I close my eyes and the damp wind plasters hair to my face, tearing the stick-antlers free.

Around me they scream.

The body of the Prince of Birch is hard and cold against my side, under my thighs.

I struggle with the sensations, cold, wet wind, rocking, screams bursting the seams of my skull.

Then I look.

The land pours out below us, a rush of black-green and bursts of light from town, the pale horizon. My mouth falls open and I gasp in the night air.

"Give me my kiss," the Prince of Birch says into my ear.

I twist in the circle of her arm and face her. Those charcoal-black eyes are hollow caves, black holes. Her cheeks are scored with tiny lines like bark, cracks too delicate to see from afar, shattered porcelain pieced together. Ready to burst out and reveal what she really is.

I slam my mouth to hers.

If she shatters I want her skin to cut at mine, shred it, pull it away, reveal—

The Prince of Birch kisses me back, one hand cupping my head. She holds me there, her rough lips gentle enough to invite and I let her open me up.

She pulls back with a grin and a laugh. I stare, wide-eyed and tasting leaves. Warm leaves, old tea leaves, thick curling banana leaves, dirt and snow.

"Mirabel?" I whisper.

"Call for her," the Prince of Birch says in a whisper echoed by the wind and rain. "If she is with us, she must answer to her name!"

I turn into the storm and scream your name.

The wind sucks it away. I scream for you again, and again.

It's a rhythm, and the ghostly stallion beneath us runs to its refrain.

Mirabel, they all scream. Some of them roar, some of them shriek, and from some your name is a crack of lightning.

Hands grab at me, and before I can hold tight, I'm dragged off the Prince of Birch's horse into the arms of another one. "Give me *my* kiss," this one says, and claims my mouth with blunt teeth and hot lips, claws digging into my ribs.

I should have been more specific.

Then they toss me off and I fall.

I scream your name again before I'm caught. It knocks my breath away and I cling to a fairy with eyes like two white moons and a mouth like a gash. Before he asks, I kiss him on the cheek—they weren't specific either. The fairy laughs and licks up my jaw with a hot tongue.

I whisper your name.

We ride.

I am passed from horse to horse to stag, kissing and kissing while we fly.

I say your name to all of them, in whispers and cries. I'm not sure if I'm asking or commanding or begging if they know you, if they've seen you, if you came with them went with them.

You aren't here.

The night sky is cold, but we burst through clouds and the full moon turns us into silver. I hold hands, I pull and push, I am kissed on my palms, my cheeks, my mouth, my throat, and because it was my bargain I kiss back: lips, teeth, pebbled scales, downy feathers, hair in my mouth, tasting each kiss, sweet and earthy, chewing pine cones, and I scream. They taste the way I feel inside. I want it all. I want their scales and feathers, their wings. I want my skin to burst.

I fling my arms out and scream as we ride.

My seams are coming apart!

I am kissed and passed and it feels incredible. Free and wild.

Here I am!

The air tugs at my hair, the sharp specks of cloud tear at my face and my hands. I could be stripped of my skin. I see it, I feel it. My skin peeling away and it makes me laugh.

I bare my teeth to feel the cold against them, the kiss of the storm like a gritty pearl against my incisors, grinding at my skin. I lost my jacket; my arms are bare. I reach back to the fairy behind me on this stag, offering my arm. The fairy kisses it, bites down.

Pain blossoms like honeysuckle flowers, and the vine of it pulls down to my inner elbow. Along my scar.

I reach for the antlers before me and hold on, tight tight tight, while my arm bleeds.

The storm rips the blood away and I see it, I see the skin folding back. A seam. A tear.

Under it I am—

I can't see—

I need to rip it wider.

I scream your name, you have to help me. Please, I'll tell you!

(This is what I never told you: I cut my arm back then because my skin was wrong, I was trapped, wrapped, skinned into a body that didn't fit wasn't mine. I saw it again and again, day after day, in my dreams during class in the car eating soup: the cut, the red, the green scales, the flat gray feathers, the sickly tendons and meat beneath, monstrous or human the only way to know was to cut cut cut it away—)

"Stay with us!" the Prince of Birch calls in my ear. "Aren't you one of us? Couldn't you be?"

"Stay with us!" the fairies cry.

Stay with us! cracks the lightning

Stay! Stay! blows the wind and the hounds howl *stay!* and the pounding hooves are thunder beating out a command *stay stay stay*

"Mirabel!" I scream.

I would rip off my skin for you, I would be one of these beings of light and power and raw need. (It's better than being what I am.) If you were here. If you answered.

But my skin won't tear over my ring finger. It's stuck to muscle and tendon and bone.

Tied down with strands of heavy black hair, binding me to my body.

I want to say West's name, but the creatures around me don't know it. They *can't* know it. I can't even say it to the sky. I lean back, head drooped on the Prince of Birch's shoulder, eyes on the wheeling stars. We ride, a calmer pace, a rhythm of dawn dawn dawn and the stars tilt, spin, rush like a river, glimmer like tiny fairy pools under a rising sun.

It is only the Prince of Birch and me, riding the wind back—not to you.

You're gone.

The Prince of Birch pours me into West's arms and promises, "You can try again on the winter solstice. Maybe you can find her then."

"We know where she is now," West says, cradling me in their lap of blue and pink skirts. Tears melt down their cheeks. The glitter unaffected.

We know, at least, where you aren't. I still can't think the answer West knows we know and I hide my face in their chest. I hold on to them tight.

"She's gone," West says.

They mean the Prince of Birch is gone, but you are, too.

"We're here," I say.

Acknowledgments

We are always and forever grateful to thank our agents, Lara Perkins at Andrea Brown Literary Agency, and Suzie Townsend, Sophia Ramos, and Olivia Coleman at New Leaf Literary, who work tirelessly to make our wishes come true. Thank you to the magical team at Feiwel & Friends, especially Jean Feiwel, Foyinsi Adegbonmire, Liz Sabla, and everyone who sprinkled faerie dust on this collection. Last but not least, we are endlessly grateful to the authors of *Faeries Never Lie* who joined us in the faerie forest.

Remember, eat the faerie fruit at your own risk . . .

Contributors

NAFIZA AZAD is a self-identified island girl. She has hurricanes in her blood and dreams of a time she can exist solely on mangoes and pineapple. Born in Lautoka, Fiji, she currently resides in British Columbia, Canada, where she reads too many books, watches too many K-dramas, and writes stories about girls taking over the world. Nafiza is the coeditor of the young adult anthology *Writing in Color* and author of *The Candle and the Flame*, which was nominated for the William C. Morris Award; *The Wild Ones*; and *Road of the Lost.*

Would you eat the faerie fruit? No, because I don't want to be stuck in the fae world.

HOLLY BLACK is the #1 *New York Times*–bestselling and award-winning author of fantasy novels, short stories, and comics. She has been a finalist for an Eisner and a Lodestar Award, and the recipient of the Mythopoeic Award, a Nebula, and a Newbery Medal. She has sold over 26 million books worldwide, and her work has been translated into over thirty languages and adapted for film. She currently lives in New England with her husband and son in a house with a secret library.

Would you eat the faerie fruit? I definitely shouldn't. I definitely would.

DHONIELLE CLAYTON is a *New York Times*–bestselling author of the Conjureverse series, the Belles series, and *Shattered Midnight* and coauthor of *Blackout*, *Whiteout*, *The Rumor Game*, and the Tiny Pretty Things duology, which has been adapted into a Netflix original series. She hails from the Washington, DC, suburbs on the Maryland side. She taught secondary school for several years, and is a former elementary and middle school librarian. She's an avid traveler and is always on the hunt for magic and mischief.

Would you eat the faerie fruit? YES, of course, I would eat the faerie fruit, I'm a monster.

ZORAIDA CÓRDOVA is the acclaimed author and editor of more than two dozen novels and short fiction, including the *USA Today* bestselling novel, *Kiss the Girl*, *The Inheritance of Orquídea Divina*, *Star Wars: The High Republic: Convergence*, and the award-winning Brooklyn Brujas series. She's written for Disney, Marvel Comics, and Lucasfilm Press. She moonlights as romance writer Zoey Castile. Zoraida was born in Guayaquil, Ecuador, and calls New York City home. When she's not working, she's roaming the world in search of magical stories.

Would you eat the faerie fruit? I'd gobble it up. They'll be trying to kick me out of faerie.

CHRISTINE DAY is a citizen of the Upper Skagit Indian Tribe. She wrote *I Can Make This Promise, The Sea in Winter, We Still Belong*, and *She Persisted: Maria Tallchief*, a biography in Chelsea Clinton's book series about inspirational women. She has been an American Indian Youth Literature Award honoree, a Charlotte Huck Award honoree, and a finalist for the Pacific Northwest Book Award. Christine lives with her family in the rainy and resplendent Pacific Northwest.

Would you eat the faerie fruit? I would avoid faerie fruit like the plague.

CHLOE GONG is the #1 *New York Times*–bestselling author of the critically acclaimed Secret Shanghai novels, as well as the Flesh and False Gods trilogy. Her books have been published in over twenty countries and have been featured in the *New York Times*, *People*, *Forbes*, and more. She is a recent graduate of the University of Pennsylvania, where she double-majored in English and International Relations. Born in Shanghai and raised in Auckland, New

Zealand, Chloe is now located in New York City, pretending to be a real adult.

Would you eat the faerie fruit? Yes—I'd eat the whole bucket.

TESSA GRATTON is the *New York Times*–bestselling author of *The Queens of Innis Lear* and *Lady Hotspur*, as well as several YA series and short stories which have been translated into twenty-two languages. Her most recent YA novels are *Strange Grace* and *Moon Dark Smile*, as well as novels of *Star Wars: The High Republic*. Though she has traveled all over the world, she currently lives alongside the Kansas prairie with her wife. Queer, nonbinary, she/he/they.

Would you eat the faerie fruit? I'd prefer to be the one offering fairy fruit to pretty mortals.

RYAN LA SALA writes about surreal things happening to queer people. He is the author behind the luminous and terrifying bestselling horror novel *The Honeys*, which is in development to become a major motion picture with Anonymous Content, and the supernatural thriller *Beholder*. His previous titles include *Reverie* and *Be Dazzled*, both of which made the Kids' Indie Next List. He has been featured in the *New York Times*, *Entertainment Weekly*, and NPR. Ryan is a cohost of the infamous Bad Author Book Club podcast, and a frequent speaker at events/conferences. When not writing, Ryan does arts and crafts, supervised by his cat, Haunted Little Girl.

Would you eat the faerie fruit? No, because no matter how you look at it, me eating that equals cannibalism.

KWAME MBALIA is a husband, father, writer, *New York Times*–bestselling author, and former pharmaceutical metrologist, in that order. His debut middle-grade novel, *Tristan Strong Punches a Hole in the Sky*, was awarded a Coretta Scott King Author Honor, and it—along with the sequels *Tristan Strong Destroys the World* and *Tristan Strong Keeps Punching*—is published by Rick Riordan Presents/ Disney-Hyperion. He is the coauthor of *Last Gate of the Emperor* with Prince Joel Makonnen, from Scholastic Books, and the editor of the #1 *New York Times*–bestselling anthology *Black Boy Joy*, published by Delacorte Press. A Howard University graduate and a Midwesterner now in North Carolina, he survives on dad jokes and Cheez-Its.

Would you eat the faerie fruit? I don't eat fruit from other people's houses . . . why would I eat another realm's fruit?

Named one of the Root's 100 most influential African Americans and *BET*'s 100 entertainers and innovators of the year, **LEATRICE "ELLE" McKINNEY**, writing as L.L. McKinney, is an advocate for equality and inclusion in publishing, and the creator of the hashtags

#PublishingPaidMe and #WhatWoCWritersHear. A lover of comics, anime, video games, sci-fi, and fantasy, she strives to push these mediums toward representation that better reflects the diverse world we live in. Elle lives in Kansas City, spending her free time plagued by her two cats: Sir Chester Fluffmire Boopsnoot Purrington Wigglebottom Flooferson III, esquire, Baron o'Butterscotch and Lord Humphrey Blepernicus Zoomerson Wailingshire Toebeanstein Chirpingston IV, Breaker of Things I Love. Or Chester and Humphrey for short. Her works include the Nightmare-Verse books, *Nubia: Real One* through DC, *Marvel's Black Widow: Bad Blood*, *Power Rangers Unlimited: Heir to Darkness*, and more.

Would you eat the faerie fruit? It would depend on which court. I might try and Persephone it. Have to spend some time here and some time there.

ANNA-MARIE McLEMORE (they/them) is the author of William C. Morris Debut Award finalist *The Weight of Feathers*; *Wild Beauty*; *Blanca & Roja*, one of *Time* Magazine's 100 Best Fantasy Novels of All Time; Indie Next List title *Dark and Deepest Red*; *Lakelore*; and National Book Award longlist selections *When the Moon Was Ours,* which was also a Stonewall Honor Book; *The Mirror Season*; and *Self-Made Boys: A Great Gatsby Remix*. Their latest releases include *Flawless Girls*, and, coauthored with Elliott McLemore, *Venom & Vow,* the world of which is the setting for their *Faeries Never Lie* story.

Would you eat the faerie fruit? Quizás . . .

NATALIE C. PARKER is the author and editor of several books for teens and young readers, including the award-winning Seafire series and Indie Bestselling anthology *Vampires Never Get Old.* Her work has been included on the NPR Books We Love list, the Indie Next List, the TAYSHAS Reading List, and in Junior Library Guild selections. She grew up in a navy family finding home in coastal cities from Virginia to Japan and currently lives with her wife on the Kansas prairie.

Would you eat the faerie fruit? I'm a Sagittarius. No one could stop me.

KAITLYN SAGE PATTERSON grew up with her nose in a book outside the Great Smoky Mountains National Park. After a ten-year stint in West Tennessee, she's once more happily living at the feet of the mountains that raised her. Her debut novel, *The Diminished*, was published by HarlequinTEEN in 2018. Its sequel, *The Exalted*, followed in 2019. Her new middle grade series, Windy Creek Stables, will be published by Feiwel & Friends beginning in 2025.

Would you eat the faerie fruit? While I am altogether too rule-bound and chaos-averse to eat the faerie fruit, most, if not all, of the characters that I write would go absolutely feral on a faerie buffet.

RORY POWER grew up in New England, where she lives and works as a story consultant for TV adaptation. She received a master's in prose fiction from the University of East Anglia, and is the *New York Times*–bestselling author of *Wilder Girls*, *Burn Our Bodies Down*, and *In a Garden Burning Gold*.

Would you eat the faerie fruit? I already have.

Thank you for reading this Feiwel & Friends book.
The friends who made

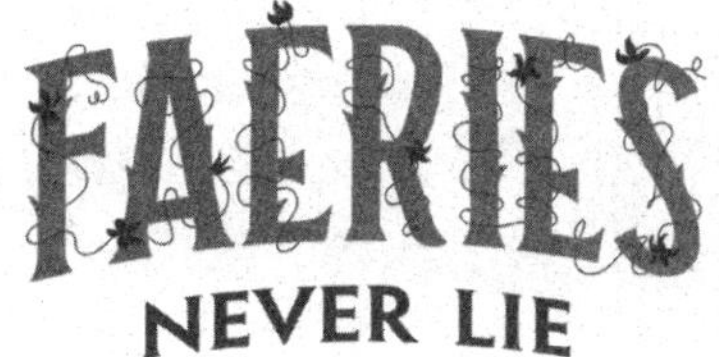

possible are:

Jean Feiwel, Publisher
Liz Szabla, VP, Associate Publisher
Rich Deas, Senior Creative Director
Holly West, Senior Editor
Anna Roberto, Senior Editor
Kat Brzozowski, Senior Editor
Dawn Ryan, Executive Managing Editor
Kim Waymer, Senior Production Manager
Emily Settle, Editor
Rachel Diebel, Associate Editor
Foyinsi Adegbonmire, Associate Editor
Brittany Groves, Assistant Editor
Julia Bianchi, Junior Designer
Ilana Worrell, Senior Production Editor

Follow us on Facebook or visit us online at mackids.com.
Our books are friends for life.